AUTUMN CHAOS

SEASON'S WAR BOOK ONE

OLENA NIKITIN

Content Warning:

Dear Reader, we appreciate that everyone has a different level of sensitivity and may be triggered by different topics. It is up to your discretion whether you can handle the content in our books. The book is intended for a mature audience of particular interests and contains a certain amount of spice and sexual innuendo, as well as scenes of death, physical violence and medical experiments. It is a work of fiction set in a world with different racial, cultural and social norms. Any resemblance to actual persons, living or dead, events or localities is entirely coincidental, and the names, characters and incidents portrayed in it are the work of the author's imagination.

Acknowledgements

This writing journey would be much more bumpy and difficult without the people who helped us create this book. We would like to give our special thanks to

Germancreative – for a beautiful cover that brought Ina and the magic of Autumn to life

Anne-Marie Rutella – for making sure our manuscript is readable, and our ideas sound good on paper and for her enthusiastic support for Ina's adventures

Beta reading team: **andronia001, bawrites, sasha_pj, monicam1001, ra-sanders917.** Your support and feedback helped us to shape this book, plug the plot holes and make Mar a much more pleasant person … although I liked him being an arsehole 😊

Sally Altass for making us feel like "real" writers when we barely published a short story and continuous support and encouragement when we were writing Autumn Chaos.

I would also like to thank my friends and colleagues from **Royal Cornwall Hospital Emergency Department**, especially my best PR woman **Chrissy,** for supporting me when I suddenly decided to become a writer. Yes, I know you bought the books. I still hope it is because you liked it.

FINALLY

WE WOULD LIKE TO DEDICATE THIS BOOK TO OUR
MOTHERS

WANDA AND MAUREEN

FOR THEIR STEADFAST BELIEF WE COULD DO IT

Contents

CHAPTER I

The Black Forest hadn't gained its reputation just from the thickness of the vegetation. While the dense foliage caused deep shadows, it was also full of poisonous plants and animals much larger than you'd expect them to be. The Leshy, the trickster Guardian of the Forest, gave sanctuary to many creatures and spirits rejected by the rapidly expanding world and ensured no members of the civilised races encroached on his domain. However, one person strolled, unconcerned, through the hostile undergrowth, enjoying the sun's rays filtered by dark green leaves. Ina reached up and played with the warm sunlight. Shadows created a pattern on her skin, and adding a bit of magic, she formed the shape of a viper's head rising from her forearm. One of the tree branches reached for her, dark wood stretching out, trying to tangle in her copper hair.

1

"Oh behave," she said, swatting it with a laugh, and the giant oak trembled when Chaos-fed flames consumed the illusory snake. Her carefree manner and random display of magic were out of place here, and Ina often wondered what people saw when they looked at her and whether she even cared anymore.

Exile was difficult for a single woman, but life is life, and one had to eat. For now, she wandered through the forest, picking herbs and some very special mushrooms. The potions she created out of necessity, and for fun, always contained a bit of light entertainment on the side. The wildwood was full of life. A veritable cornucopia for someone who knew what to look for and could find a path in the almost impenetrable foliage. After ten years, she knew every stone here. She peered down into her brimming basket and nodded with appreciation. It hadn't taken her long to gather all she needed today. *Nice and easy, just like I like it,* she thought, heading back to her hut.

With her mind preoccupied with plans for the evening, Ina strolled back to her cottage. The latest batch of cherry liqueur should be ready by now, and she was curious about how her new recipe had come out. Oblivious to the voices that grew louder as she approached the path to her home, Ina came to the clearing, and the view in front of her just took her breath away, but not for long, though.

"What the hell are you doing in my garden?" Ina shouted at the top of her lungs, seeing far too many peasants having what looked like an afternoon party in front of her house. She was a Fury incarnate. The witch was not a hospitable person and, after all these years, the villagers should know this. Her temperamental magic flared up, goaded by her anger, and raw Chaos pooled around her. Golden eyes looked at her from the rim of the roof in silent accusation. *See, see what happens when they are not afraid of you?* Her cat's disdain was palpable.

As Ina looked around, committing each face to memory, she spied a bottle in one of the villagers' hands. Her cherry liqueur— those thieving bastards had found her cooling barrel in the yard. They took her evening reward, and some village idiot was gulping it like moonshine in the tavern.

The sudden change in the air, caused by red mist, swiftly made the common folk very aware of how furious she was. The wisps of primal power sprang forth and firmly attached themselves to the peasants' guts with a rolling curse.

"May you not shit for a week! And when you finally can, you will not make it to the crapper before your arse explodes, you fucking drunkards!"

It was not a very sophisticated spell, but the witch didn't care about finesse. Her visceral curse caused the gathered crowd to run like headless chickens, fleeing her yard as fast as possible. Ina smiled benignly and looked at the cat as if to say. *"See? I can speak their language."*

Deep inside, Ina could feel her curse had anchored itself well. The locals will undoubtedly remember that, while she may not look like it, Ina was still an alumna of the University of Higher Magical Arts. Of course, the "shit you not" curse was not something to brag about to any of her professors. *If I ever got released from this forest, of course*, she thought, feeling a bitter taste in her mouth, then scorned herself. *You will find the way out. After all, you are the incorrigible Ina.* The last words cheered her up, and she chuckled slightly, looking around, only a little surprised that there was still one, or possibly two, people in front of her hut.

Abandoned by his kin and trembling like a leaf, a now abashed headman stood next to a big bundle on the floor that resembled a human shape. She moved closer, observing the heap cluttering up her yard. Ina confirmed it was indeed a human. Massive and almost appetisingly naked, if not for the fact that he was covered in blood and his pale face meant he was knocking on Nawia's doors. The afterlife probably looked pretty damn attractive in his present state.

"So, what is going on here?" she asked. The sweet saccharine of her voice, an attempt to be pleasant and soothing, seemed to cause the headman to go through a speed version of the curse, as he now looked ready to soil his pants.

"Lady, we found him…in the forest, there was blood and others, people that is, but they were dead. This one still breathes, and his armour had gold in it, so we thought…we thought…" the man stuttered.

He looked like his legs would buckle under him, but worse, she didn't like the way this all was heading. The man on the floor looked like a warrior, not a bandit, and he had golden armour? That meant nothing but trouble.

"Headman, where might his armour be?" Ina asked as it suddenly dawned on her that the man at her feet was wearing nothing but bloody breeches.

"We…ehhh…we took it off so he can breathe easier." The headman was getting redder and redder, and Ina thought he would pop a blood vessel in a moment.

"And I'm assuming each of you helpers took a piece for safekeeping, leaving this half-dead body with me. And what do you expect me to do? I'm not a necromancer." Anger raised its head again. These good people complicated her life, and she genuinely hated complications.

"Drag him in," she said, barking a sharp command, and the headman looked at her with a baffled expression.

"But, lady, it took four men to bring him here…"

"Gods give me strength not to strangle this one," Ina said, clenching her fists before casting the feather. The elemental incantation decreased the man's weight to a small fraction of what it should be, but Ina barely noticed. Simple household spells had become her routine and something that allowed her to survive in this godsforsaken place.

"Pick him up now and put him on my bed," she said and opened the doors, leaving the headman, almost as pale as her unexpected guest, to carry the body inside.

As she turned for a moment to put the basket in the kitchen, the frightened villager threw the man on her bed and ran away. Ina looked at her cat, who had decided to strut in.

"Now I have no bed, blood everywhere, and a non-paying job to do, and it is all your fault for letting them in."

Boruta, named after a forest demon, only looked at her, turned around, showed how interested he was in her complaints, and wandered off to sit on the still-warm stove. Left with the body, presumably a dead one by now, Ina approached the bed. Her healing spells were limited but even only quickly examining him, she wondered where she would dig the grave and whether she should spike him with aspen wood now or later. Her musings were rudely disturbed when the pale warrior made a soft, barely audible moan.

"Aren't you a tough cookie?" Ina smirked, but something in the way he was clinging to a life that he should have lost hours ago made her want to give him a chance. "Well, now, let's see what we can do for you."

She got herself ready and placed her hands on his forehead and chest. With her eyes closed, the lifelines of his energy sprang forth in her mind, illuminating the meridians. They were clear and pulsating as a diagram of the human body, with more than a few broken channels and dimmed places. The damage to his body was extensive. Someone didn't want this man alive. Broken ribs, a laceration to the liver, shattered femur, battered flesh, and claw marks everywhere. Still, the most interesting was a single puncture wound to his side. It looked like he was stabbed with a dagger. "Complicated" just became worse, as this looked like attempted murder.

Ina opened her eyes and looked at him with a long, cleansing breath. He was certainly not a spring chicken anymore but still in his prime with only a handful of silver strands in ashen blond hair and a man of the sword, judging by tight rope like muscles.

I wouldn't kick him out of my bed if he were livelier, the errant thought crossed her mind, evoking a brief chuckle. It seemed she hadn't been with a man for far too long if she lusted over this half-dead body. Still, this would take a hell of a lot of energy to fix, so he had best be worth it.

Healing magic had never been her forte. The dedication and compassion it took to alleviate suffering were not in her nature, but leaving someone to die when she could prevent it wasn't either. The fate or Gods had condemned him to die, but Ina always had an issue with authority, disliking those overbearing pricks. Judging by her current circumstances, the feeling was mutual. Except for maybe the Leshy, but the lord of the forest would advise her to feed her patient to the beasts. She almost heard him saying, *they have to eat, too, and the man already looks like a half-open snack.* Ina's attempt to fight her nature failed, "Fate my arse," she grumbled, intending to show all her defiance. Still, under the brass and anger, there was also a deeply hidden, tiny spark of hope that the golden-clad fool could be her passage home. If she dragged him back from Nawia's doors, and that was a big if right now.

Ina profoundly hated this part, but it was the only ace up her sleeve. The ancient spell called "the sacrifice" worked by trading one's life force to sustain another. It was dangerous and frowned upon, not to mention mostly forbidden outside of the family members. Ina rubbed her temples and went to the cupboard for one of her rare concoctions. She needed some reinforcement if she was going to live through this experience, as a spell, once started, couldn't be stopped. Ina opened the door, sending a dubious look at the innocuous bottle covered in dust. Her graduation project would enhance a life force tenfold and speed up any healing. She'd never had the time to improve the formula, so the unfortunate aftertaste would make kissing a ghoul's ass a preferable option.

Ina had concocted the potion when she was young, stupid, and determined to save the world, or at least impress her great-aunt Nerissa. Good times. Now, older and wiser, she didn't look forward to drinking it. *Bottoms up. I've drunk worse in The Drunken Wizard,* she thought, opening the bottle.

Ina quickly downed the oily brown liquid, trying not to gag. It was a truly disgusting crime against her taste buds, and hopefully, it hadn't expired after years on the shelf. She stripped to her underwear and then climbed on the blood-soaked bed. Boruta looked at her with disdain. Her cat was a judgemental arse, but indeed she was about to do something utterly stupid.

Ina shuddered as the sticky linen touched her skin and cast the forbidden spell. The potions and elixirs that could heal or speed recovery wouldn't be strong enough. He needed her magic as well as her strength, and lots of it. Ina whispered a quick prayer to Leshy. There was no turning back, and she needed some help and courage to go through with this.

Cuddled up to the cold, lifeless slab of meat, Ina took his hand and closed her eyes. The heat caused by the elixir spread through her, causing an uncomfortable electrifying sensation but worse was about to come. She gasped when searing suffering almost blinded her and swayed her resolve when her body and mind opened to his pain and injuries. The sacrifice magic connected their meridians, exchanging a life for a life.

Oh fuck, it is worse than in the stories. I don't even know this arsehole, she thought, howling in pain when the ancient spell flowed through her body, breaking her bones and tearing her flesh while it repaired his. Her potion kept her alive, forcing her body to heal when mindless, powerful magic transferred the injuries to achieve perfect balance. They said you would welcome death with gratitude if you went for the sacrifice spell, and Ina agreed.

I'm going to die here with him.

The panicking thought reverberated through her, and the Chaos in her sprang forth, warping the exchange. Raw magic interfered with the balance of the spell and reached for her soul. Tears clouded her vision, and the witch screamed without shame, fighting this self-imposed hell and trying to not lose herself in it. The sun had already set when, after several gruelling hours of painstaking repair of one injury after another, his femur snapped into place with one last effort and the bone started mending itself.

The bed beneath Ina was soaked with his blood and her sweat, all mixed, creating the pungent odour of a battlefield, but exhaustion took the will to care. Echoes of his pain and wisps of magic still coursed through her veins. His body was healed, and so was hers. All that the warrior needed now was some time to recover his energy. He, it seemed, had other ideas, as his life force still tried to pull more from her, more than she could give.

"Not so fast, hero," Ina said quietly, cutting him off. "The rest you will have to fix yourself." Yet despite severing the ties, she still could feel a strong connection between them.

Oblivion beckoned, its irresistible claws dragging her slowly into its depths, still holding tight to the warrior's hand. A sudden spark of white energy in his centre caught her attention, akin to a fragment of the sun with swirling gold hues and flashes of light that felt somewhat alien to the human body. Ina had never seen such a thing before.

"Shiny…" she purred, trying to reach the alluring spark and being blinded by pure agony as soon as her soul brushed against it. Scales and fangs flashed in her mind. The feeling of plunging a hand into molten gold pierced through her, and fuck, but it hurt. Oh, the irony, lying in her knickers next to a handsome man, and all she could do was scream in pain, again, when whatever it was imprinted itself on her. That was her last thought before all went black.

Warm sunlight caressed Ina's face and she stretched like a cat without opening her eyes. She didn't want to wake up just yet, not when it was nice and warm and...fluffy?

Did Boruta jump on the bed when she was asleep? Her hand wandered to the source of the fluffiness against her cheek and started stroking it. It was different, coarser than cat fur, and much more enticing. Ina kept stroking it, trying to get closer to the source of the warmth, with her half-asleep brain musing over the riddle of majestic fur. Suddenly, the pleasant warmth was ripped away, and a deep, grumpy voice boomed straight to her face.

"Who the fuck are you? What am I doing here, and what the hell are you doing to my chest?"

She opened one eye, trying to adjust to the daylight. A sharp masculine face with a clenched jaw was right above her, looking quite hostile. The realisation dawned with memories of yesterday's events.

Ah, my pain-in-the-ass guest is still here. She smiled at her thoughts, appreciating the masculine presence next to her. Unfortunately, the object of her amorous attention was pissed, confused, and demanding an explanation. It looked like the morning brew would have to wait.

You'd think the afterlife would be warmer, Mar thought, as a shiver ran over his body. Awareness crept in, and the lack of pain was the next thing he noticed after the cold. That surely meant he'd passed through the doors of Nawia. The softness underneath him was so welcoming that he must be in Wyraj, the resting place of worthy souls. That couldn't possibly be, though. While not an evil man, far too many acts of violence haunted his dreams for that to happen.

A soft murmur, almost a purr, tickled his ear as a soft stroking hand moved across the expanse of his naked chest.

The pleasure he felt suddenly swept away the last vestiges of what must surely have been a spelt slumber. A homely, if slightly shabby room, came into focus, not to mention the nearly naked woman still happily stroking her hand over his chest.

Mar mumbled a curse when he leapt clumsily from the small bed, sheets the colour of old blood hampering his movements, as unsettling thoughts ran rampant through his mind. He shouted his confusion in the woman's face with uncharacteristic harshness, snapping the questions out in anger.

Ina slowly raised her torso from the tussled linen. She yawned wide, indifferent and unfazed by the sudden outburst of her guest. *Why couldn't you just lie down and take it a little longer?* she thought, trying to focus, still feeling drained after last night, especially after this ungrateful bore woke her from such a pleasant dream.

With nothing better to do, while waiting till he calmed down, Ina assessed his body. There was something incredibly appealing about the way he looked. Lean but well-built, the muscles of his chest and arms rippled with barely restrained violence. He sported a short, slightly ragged beard paired with slightly too long, ashen blond hair. Her gaze slid over his chest. She noticed new and old scars beneath the soft fur covering his torso. Her gaze slid lower with a lazy smile, shamelessly trailing along the hairline adorning his abdomen, stopping at the top of his breeches and her lips parted. *Time to negotiate my release,* she thought, shifting on the bed.

"I'm Ina, and you are coming back to bed," she stated the fact with an alluring purr, patting the tangled linen. "You still need to recover, and I will not drag you back from Nawia twice."

Unfortunately, years of being surrounded by peasants with their trembling fearful voices not only made her feel lonely but must have stripped her of her charm.

The man stared at her in disbelief, and she saw clear judgement in his eyes. She could almost see him thinking. Here he was, a stranger alone in the house with a barely dressed woman. Not only did she not show any signs of fear or embarrassment, but she also openly invited him to her bed. What wasn't to judge? His widened pupils told her it was not without its appeal. Still, most likely, the last thing the warrior remembered was a battle, agonising pain in his side, sharp claws ripping his body, and his desperate attempt to buy more time for his companions to escape. He had reason to be confused, and Ina was almost sorry for him, but her compassion cut off when he spoke.

"I am Marcach of Liath, captain of the King's Guards, and I demand answers. I have no time to spend with the local whore."

Her mouth gaped open at the sheer audacity of this statement, and tension of raw magic filled the air. One look at her face and his tightened lips made it clear he knew he'd made a terrible mistake, but before Mar could speak, Ina raised herself on the bed and shouted, "Oh, go fuck yourself, you ungrateful bore!"

A sudden burst of power came out of nowhere and hit the man in the chest like a horse's kick. The next thing, he was flung backwards, breaking through the door.

"Not a village whore, then." She heard Mar groan out, slowly struggling to his feet and heading back to the hut. The warrior stopped on the threshold and looked back. He appeared unsure whether he should bring the door as a gesture of goodwill, but with a shrug, he left it in the yard.

Ina was livid as she watched him come back. A small voice in her head tried to reason that maybe she had been a little too inviting, but how dare he offend her in her own home? Now she would have to fix the door on the top of all this mess. What was more unsettling was that this stranger so easily coaxed her anger and the magic that comes with it, as if she hadn't spent years trying to suppress her Chaos abilities. Ina watched him, hesitating on the threshold. *Good,* she thought, *at least now you know what you are dealing with, oh mighty Marcach.* Her smirk must have encouraged him because he stepped in.

Mar's posture projected the aura of annoyance likely at her attitude, at himself for sticking his sizable foot in his mouth, and at whoever put him in this situation, not that she cared, but she saw the desire for information that seemed to override whatever hesitancy he had. She smirked when, with a deepening scowl, he moved purposely over the threshold, scanning the surroundings.

Ina finally got out of bed, picked up her trousers and shirt, and deliberately put them on slowly, observing Mar looking around her hut. He appeared somehow bewildered and out of place. Even standing in breeches, the man felt just...so much larger than life. He looked like he would be at home in a barracks, not trying to avoid wooden beams in her tiny abode. Still, she wasn't done with him yet—he'd annoyed her, and her ability to hold a grudge was legendary.

"What are you looking for now?" she jeered. "Your wits, common sense, self-preservation instinct?" She couldn't help herself. This bloody man had hurt her pride, called her names, and his blind rejection was just too close to the memories she thought she had left behind. She saw again a long-forgotten elven face twisted in disdain for the moment.

Boruta felt the change in her mood, and he looked at Mar with his golden eyes before slowly strolling in his direction. Since the darkest days of her exile, this little devil had been with her, comforting and protecting her in his own cat ways. It wasn't clear who owned who anymore, and seeing the stiff tail, the witch picked him up before he fulfilled his revenge, thinking that the last thing she needed was a cat bite to treat as well. After a few calming strokes, Ina put the cat on the windowsill and moved to fire up the stove. Men with full tummies were easier to reason with, and they needed to talk.

Mar's anger reared up as one glance was all it took to see that not only were no answers to be found, but his lack of clothing and costly armour soured his already dark mood. A sneer curled upwards, and words roiled in his gut, silenced instantly as his decidedly voluptuous protagonist stood up from the cot and addressed him in such a taunting manner.

His shock at the coarse insult vied with amusement at her fiery attitude. He pictured her, not in a small hovel cot, begrimed with blood and sweat, but in silk sheets, dishevelled from passionate lovemaking, and not whatever caused this.

That last image compounded his already deep confusion. It had been many years since he'd had such intense and inappropriate thoughts of a woman. *It is not the time or place* he scorned himself. Here, now, he needed to know what was going on.

Carefully, almost respectfully, he tried again. "What happened here? The last thing I remember, I was clothed and fighting some creature with my men. How did I end up here, half-naked, in your bed?"

"So, that's what happened," she said.

Mar noticed she looked at him with something more than desire for the first time. This change, he understood. After all, it was her forest and her village. Whatever attacked him may still be a threat.

With an annoying shrug, she answered, "All I know is that our friendly village folks dropped you at my doorstep, half-dead and more than half-naked. Now, care to explain what you were fighting with?"

She turned her back to him, putting a pan on the stove and cracking a few eggs on the sizzling pan. It seemed like this sudden change in his attitude disturbed her, and she tried to gain a bit of distance. He also heard her muttering about finding him some clothes, as she would not be muddled by those hairy pecs again.

His lips twitched at the last remark, and he instinctively looked down, as that was not a trait his women usually admired.

Thinking about what he'd said, Ina frowned. She knew all the local creatures, the Striga, the few ghouls, and the grave hag from an abandoned cemetery would not wander to the forest, not when the Leshy guarded his domain with his wooden fists. The village had an unofficial agreement with the forest guardian. They didn't mess with the wildwood and the wildwood didn't mess with them.

Except for a few accidents, there never have been any deliberate attacks. Maybe Ina should ask Leshy what happened. With all the thoughts racing through her head, it took more than one pitiful meow to bring her attention back to her surroundings. She stood there licking the spoon like a toddler. Her cheeks heated, as it wasn't her day to make a good impression. Ina attempted to avoid the cat tangling between her legs when she pointed her blunt weapon at Mar and, using a professional tone, asked, "Tell me exactly why you are here and what you remember…please?"

CHAPTER 2

Mar grunted with a frustrating need to shake some information from his tormentor and wondered at his lack of eloquence. *A grunt? Really?* This woman, it seemed, brought out the ogre in him. Taking a deep calming breath and thinking carefully before uttering more nonsense, one thing settled in his mind. She was no simple herb witch, and she must have performed some impressive magic to save him, remembering just how injured he'd been compared to how easily he moved now. There was exhaustion, of course, but despite the generous coating of dry blood, he couldn't feel a single injury. Perhaps, if this woman was the one to heal him, he was lucky to have not been sent back to death's door with his earlier disrespect.

"It seems I have you to thank for my salvation then, my lady." The pause before *my lady* was only slightly longer than decorum should demand. However, equating a powerful magic user to such a small dwelling was still hard. Mar was careful not to mention his mission, and the subsequent battle was doubly important. Suppose this witch or sorceress was as powerful as her healing implied? In that case, the interest she expressed could lead to far too many complications.

He observed her when she rolled her eyes and exhaled. He wondered if she found him infuriating. Mar knew he couldn't offer her a single sensible answer, and she was still in the dark about what had happened. Whoever did it didn't want him alive, that one thing was clear. And, to trade the answers with a stranger that could endanger the court, he would have to trust her, and he could not—not yet at least. Still, she had helped him, and now she added to his debt the plate with well-done scrambled eggs and buttered bread.

"Eat, and I will find some clothes for you. It will spare me curing village fledglings' broken hearts after you parade in front of them flaunting your pert little arse."

It took all of Mar's willpower to not laugh at this snarky yet flattering remark. Instead, he tried to focus on the food. A smaller portion landed in front of the cat, and then she dragged out the ladder to search her attic to see if she had anything that would fit on his frame. *It would be a long morning*, thought Mar, when against his better judgement, he felt attracted to the view. Ina was half diving in the loft when he heard the neighing of horses and the approaching sounds of a crowd.

"Really? What now?" Ina snapped, looking down at him as if to blame him that there wouldn't be a single moment for herself after he'd landed in her bed. The sudden sound of a trumpet almost made her fall off the ladder and disturbed Mar's staring up at such a delicious rump. It was rude and unbefitting of a knight of the court, but despite the rumbling of his demanding stomach, Mar failed to stop himself from revelling in the view.

The noise of approaching horses and a raucous rabble was the only thing to tear his eyes from her, only to be greeted by such disorder that it took a moment to realise that there, amidst the dirty and noisy villagers, were stiff-backed nobles, mounted and pompous.

Experience soon kicked in. If the court were here, he had best fill his stomach before they announced themselves. Food would be a distant memory when those blowhards got into their stride. Plus, it would be interesting to see how his erstwhile saviour handled this mess.

Soon the show started. Even as Mar looked away, the subject of his thoughts leapt from the ladder, more agile than he expected, depriving him of the delightful view. Grumbling under her breath and moving to block her threshold, Ina took an aggressive stance, arms folded under her bosom.

"Inanuan of Thorn, come forth and answer to the king's justice."

Mar sighed in exasperation, pompous idiots confronting a magic user in her domain with accusations. However, something tickled his memory, and it leapt forth with a flash of green and fiery red. The flashback overwhelmed his mind.

He had been standing at rest, waiting on the king's pleasure as he dealt with court matters. A sudden concussive force knocked everyone in the hall to the floor as the throne room doors blasted outwards in a cacophony of splintering wood. A voice strident in its anger roared out of the sudden silence, "You pox-driven idiot of a goat, I will never help you hunt the sacred boar! What were you thinking going behind my back? You can take this position, your hunts, and your limp dick and shove them up your flatulent arse! I'd rather live as a witch in a hut in the woods than help you ever again."

The reminiscence, still vivid in his eyes, distracted him from his observation of Ina as the situation unfolded. Mar still marvelled over the story preserved in his memory. He had been just pulled from the border and placed in the king's service. A novice at politics but a fucking hero, a decorative flower for the king's fur. How he hated it, and yet he'd looked on in awe at that very moment. This woman, glorious in her fury and careless in her actions, strode forth from the king's presence without a single backwards glance, power nipping at her clothes and blazing red hair.

That same red hair was now directly in front of him, those flashes of power dancing in its depths as she laughed in unrestrained delight. It appeared he had missed something crucial during his reminiscence. That force to reckon with somehow ended up living in this hut as a hedge witch.

The day was getting more and more interesting. Ina hadn't heard her full name since…well, an unfortunate incident in court when she lost her temper and ended up in this witch's hut. *I wonder what they are accusing me of now.* The thought of extending her exile was unbearable. Ina stood in the empty door frame and looked at the motley crowd. She noticed a few nobles, guards, and what looked like a judicial mage in front of her. That wasn't a good sign. Those mages did not like to be dragged out of the capital.

Calming her racing heart, Ina dusted off her old court manners. With a formal curtsy and a serious attempt at a benign, innocent smile, she asked, "What can I do for you, my lord? What can be so concerning to bring the king's justice to my doorstep?"

Before the judicial mage could answer, one of the village folk, obviously a bit of an idiot, ran forwards, pointing his finger. "That's her, your lordships. She killed the knight with her magic after we brought him here. We all saw it!" he shouted, and a few other lowlifes she'd helped previously nodded their heads.

"We may not be friends, but this?" she murmured. That was the last straw, she cared no more about this dirty village. Now raising her eyebrow, the witch observed these theatrics born from human greed. They were ready to send her to the gallows for a few golden streaks from the warrior's armour.

"You are accused of causing the death of Marcach of Liath, captain of the King's Guards. What say you in your defence?"

The peasant's words were a trifle, but such an accusation coming from a mage, and this whole entourage coming here to denounce the proverbial evil witch, was unexpected. The whole situation was surreal, and choking on a barely restrained laugh, she shifted her position, showing the interior of her small cottage and pointing out the figure at the table, furiously stuffing his mouth with scrambled eggs.

"You mean...this one?"

With this motion, she couldn't hold it any longer. Ina supported herself on the door frame and bent over with unrestrained laughter, savouring the pleasure of the changing faces of all involved.

When she could finally catch her breath, worry crept in. "Well, what we are going to do now?" she asked, looking at the mage, then averting her gaze to look at the villagers. They stood still, like lambs to the slaughter. She felt no pity for them. She had never been one of them, but she'd always treated them fairly.

Maybe it would be different if this place wasn't a prison, and she hadn't spent the past ten years feeling unjustly punished, but this place was never truly hers. She felt more connection with the forest and its guardian than with any resident of this small-minded community. They only thought of her as the scary Baba Yaga from children's tales. Still, if these nobles found out what the villagers had done, there would not be much of a village left after the court cavalcade's departure.

"It is time for the villagers to bring back Sir Marcach's armour that they have so carefully polished," she said mercifully, looking straight at the headman. Now it was up to them if they took this rope to survive. She looked back at the mage, noticing him looking down at a communication crystal. This affair, it would appear, was more than just a few knights tumbling in the forest.

Mar finally graced them all with his presence. She could feel him behind her, his tall frame filling the doorway, tempting her to lean back just a little and bask in his warmth. Ina's silly thoughts must have been the aftermath of the sacrifice spell, but she felt a little less lonely for the first time in these long years, even if they only bickered and fought.

Mar didn't know what to think. Why did these court members and their entourage come to this witch's home so soon after he encountered the beast? Why did they bring a mage? It didn't look like a simple search party after a hunting accident, and neither was it a sudden court request to check on the good citizens of a Black Forest village. Did someone know about the investigation, someone that wanted to ensure he wouldn't come back from this forest? He looked at Ina, wondering how this stubborn woman got herself into this mess. He noticed her body leaning slightly towards him. And without thinking, he moved closer, still not touching her but close enough to feel the swirls of magic brushing his bare skin. He could feel she was unsettled, never taking her eyes off the mage, waiting for the next revelation.

He barely registered the villagers piling up his belongings, as it seemed her tension was projecting onto him. The feel of her magic confirmed what he'd recalled. This was the powerful woman from his memory, this beautiful creature now pressed against his chest.

The urge to protect Ina was strange and nearly overwhelming, so much so that he felt his arms sliding up her arms and gripping them firmly to add his strength to hers. *Damn it all to Veles. What am I doing?* He felt like the rational Mar was gone. He looked after his people, and since she had healed him, she could be counted as one, but the strength of this feeling was borderline ridiculous. Ina had cowed the king in his palace. She certainly didn't need his support, but as the glimmer of her magic settled onto his skin, the feeling of it soaking into his soul tightened his grip on her shoulders. A deep, primordial growl rolled off his tongue.

Finally, the mage spoke, "Inanuan of Thorn, the Magical Council, has decided to release you from your confinement. You are required to come back to the capital for a hearing on a separate matter." With a single step forwards, the mage pointed the crystal at her chest and muttered something under his breath, making Mar instinctively brace himself for the impact.

Ina gasped as the words she had been waiting for so long came in such an unexpected way. She took a few breaths, finally noticing Mar's hands holding her in position, almost like he cared. With a grimace, the witch took a small step forwards. Was he making sure she wouldn't run away or do something stupid before getting his answers? They weren't friends after all. It was too comforting, and she wouldn't allow herself to show weakness or relief—not in front of all the buffoons now looking at her like an interesting insect in a glass jar.

A burning sensation under her left collarbone brought tears to her eyes. "Bloody hell," she seethed. "I forgot about this crap." Velez, the rune of confinement, burned its way out of her skin. The sensation was even worse than when they had put it in, especially now when she was fully conscious and the anger of betrayal did not cloud her senses. She looked the judicial mage in the eye as he observed her with humiliating curiosity, waiting for her to break and sob like so many others. Scorch marks appeared on her shirt as Ina blinked unwanted tears away, forced a half-sneering smile and addressed the mage.

"And what is your name, my esteemed colleague?" she asked through clenched teeth. He could have done it more mercifully.

Somewhere away from the crowd, somewhere she could cry her pain out instead of using all her strength to keep herself up and not crap her pants in the process, but he had chosen punishment to the very end. *No mercy for the wicked*, she thought when the pain subsided, and she could clear her head and pay attention to her surroundings.

"My name is Jorge, and we have to get moving," he answered. Now that Ina was no longer confined to a hedge witch's hut, she was "one of the brethren." Although she felt he would never consider her "an esteemed colleague."

"I have no horse, and I need to pack," she said. Nothing could have prepared her for such a sudden change in her circumstances. After the peasants scattered to their houses, the witch could see no carriage in the clearing. The only horse without a rider was a massive black warhorse digging his hooves into the dirt. Ina took a moment to admire the animal. He was majestic and looked well trained. This horse was a natural work of art, but she would sooner walk than ride this beast, not to mention that someone would have to throw her on its back.

"Mar, you are alive, you son of a bitch," a noble shouted, directing his horse towards the cottage, "and I can see you had a bit of fun as well."

Ina turned around and noticed Mar still standing there with arms crossed over his massive chest, still only in his breeches. She rolled her eyes. "Would you finally dress? There are no maids here to swoon over you." She pushed past him into the cottage and looked around. There wasn't much to pack, a few books, sundry potions. The only thing that comforted her here was the cat....the cat!!

"How the feck do I pack the bloody cat?" she said, raising her head in exasperation and looking at Boruta, who, unfazed, licked his bottom. She knew she would have to find a way. After all, it was the best and the longest relationship with any male Ina had ever had in her life.

Rolling his eyes seemed to be Mar's new favourite pastime this morning. Nothing that had happened since waking in this beguiling woman's bed had made a single lick of sense or followed any type of order. Chaos must ride her apron strings for this to happen so quickly.

Still, Ina had a point about dressing, especially considering the effect her body pressed against him earlier made. The comment from his comrade-in-arms didn't help. His ire was sky-high as he stepped towards his armour.

"Senad, you pox-encrusted horse's arse. Keep your disgusting comments to yourself. Tell me where the fuck the men are and how I ended up being healed by a thrice-damned witch."

"I should have gelded you when I had a chance." He heard Ina mutter to herself, searching for a suitable basket for the cat. At least, he hoped it was a cat. Boruta was a sizable beast. Mar suspected with his size that the cat's parentage came straight from the forest itself, but other than that, everything pointed towards him being a domesticated pet. And it was clear she would rather die than leave him to perish.

On the other side of the door frame, Mar reached up to Senad and clasped his forearm firmly, nodding to let him know he was glad to see him still alive after the attack. The gesture belying his harsh words showed his deep affection for his subordinate. "Come, tell me everything." A slow look around and a raised eyebrow indicated to his comrade to give him the edited version.

Mar released Senad's arm and began dressing, muttering something about pompous prigs and flowery charlatans. He closed his eyes, sighing with relief to see his gambeson in the pile so at least he'd have some padding underneath all that armour. He shuddered to think about attempting to wear leather on bare skin. A quick look at said armour proved the villagers hadn't removed the runic symbols. Gold they might be, but they were more resilient than they looked.

Ina placed some of her clothes in a herb basket on the top of a soft blanket and hoped this would be enough for Boruta to survive the two-day ride to Osterad. The capital of Cornovii was not far away, but the road there was not a pleasant one. Squeezed between the primordial forest in the east and a mountainous borderland in the west, the country had developed an elongated shape. Osterad was the central trading point between rich agriculture in the south and merchant ports in the north and the cauldron where many races and cultures mixed, creating a unique society. That's where the excitement was, and she longed to be part of it again.

Ina was trying to not pay attention to Mar dressing in an efficient, soldierlike fashion. She just couldn't stop soaking up the strength and agility apparent in his every movement. Previously, the witch thought he was enormous compared to her stature and small bed. Ina looked at him as she stood next to his comrade. The warrior was not just unnaturally tall, he was simply intimidating. She thought about cloudy grey eyes that looked at her in the morning and chuckled at her thoughts. *A veritable mountain of Liath. I wonder who caught his grandma in the fields to create such offspring.*

Putting Boruta in the basket was a daunting task, especially since that cat had a completely different idea about his travel arrangements. Sweaty and on the brink of exploding, Ina finally got him in and waved a cobweb of magical energy around it in a moment of inspiration. She assessed the net, but it looked like this transparent prison would do the job. Angry hissing and spitting were clear signs it would be a tricky ride.

"Will you finally calm down? I'm not staying here, and I'm not leaving without you!" The thrashing basket went still for a moment after her exasperated shout, and with an offended *meow*, Boruta surrendered to his fate.

The rest of the packing took just a few moments, and she could eavesdrop on Mar's conversation. They seemed to keep something hidden, but even a bit of information was good.

⁂

Mar finished tying on his bracers as he listened to the almost unbelievable story from Senad. They had come to the forest after hearing rumours that one of the transformed was seen there. Sophia had issued the order herself. He remembered the brown beast, vaguely resembling a bear with unnaturally long claws and a maw that could bite a human in half, but something wasn't right.

"Where are Ren and Daro?" He cherished all of his men. After all, he trained and led them, but those two were unique. They started working for him when he came from the borderlands and had saved his sanity when past guilt almost crippled him. "Did they survive?"

"Yes," answered Senad. "We lost five men, and when Daro saw you injured by the monster's claws, he charged in. The hothead never knows when to stop, so now he is nursing his broken skull in an inn halfway to the capital."

"And Ren?" Mar felt relief sweep over him. Daro would be okay with that typically thick skull of the steppe orcs. Still, Ren was human. He had come to them after escorting caravans through the forest. He might have been insanely fast with his swords and had an exotic look, but there was no doubt about his humanity. "Where is the Ghost?" Mar asked again.

Senad clasped his shoulder. "Stop worrying like a mother hen. He is at the same inn, with just a scratch or two on that pretty face of his, trying to prevent Daro from drinking himself to death or getting skewered by jealous husbands."

"And the others?" Mar asked quietly, guilt weighing him down again. He had led his men there without fully knowing what they were facing.

"Except those two, just three other soldiers initially survived, but we lost two of them to fever. I thought we'd lost you too when the beast bolted with your leg in its mouth." Senad looked pensive. "I didn't know the forest, so I called the retreat to get reinforcements. Here they are. They arrived just as a sweaty peasant turned up with the news that the witch had killed you."

He noticed the witch stopped her packing and raised her eyebrow as she listened. Mar felt she was hiding something, and he could almost see tiny gears turning in her head. He would get the information from her one way or another. He just had to find the right way. While he pondered his strategy, Ina pushed herself past the two men and winked at Senad.

"How could I kill him? I'm such a merciful, loving soul."

Mar again felt a tingle of amusement. This impossible woman was eavesdropping without shame, and now the swinging of her belongings almost smacked him in the face.

"Are we going or you will stand there like a mushroom?" she asked, and he wondered how she felt this need to goad him every bloody time he wanted to smile at her. Admittedly, she was good at it because Mar would happily spank her arse right now. Two days was plenty of time to make his life hell, and she seemed to set this as her personal goal. Was it because he had rejected her? Hopefully, there were many handsome men to cheer up a starving woman in the city. As soon as this thought flashed in his mind, Mar felt he could not breathe, but the sensation was quickly settled, and a glance at Senad confirmed he didn't notice. Something was wrong with him, but there were enough healers in the capital to find out why he felt searing pain in his core at the mere thought of the witch with other men.

Distracted by his thoughts, he cursed a blue storm as his armour's last clasp bit into his side. A large dollop of guilt over his failure adding to his vehemence, Mar turned and leapt onto the back of the black stallion. An affectionate pat on its neck showed how grateful he was that his faithful companion was still with him.

"Whoa, Woron, good to see you, boy. Now, sorry for this, but I have to ask you to work harder today."

With that said, he leaned down to the side and grabbed Ina by her arm. With an evil grin splitting his face and an exaggerated grunt, he lifted the shocked witch up and onto the back of the stallion, chuckling as he wrapped her arm around his torso. "There you go. We have to make sure you arrive in style for your triumphant return, don't we?"

Ina nearly dropped the cat's basket when she was swept into the air and loaded onto the back of the stallion. Determined not to ride with this man, she looked down, ready to jump off. The earth was far, far away, and the height sent a shiver down her spine. She grabbed Mar's waist and pressed herself to his muscular frame, causing all the men in the entourage to laugh.

"I think your companion likes you a little after all," Senad smirked, bringing his horse closer. "Now, my lady, let me take this hissing burden of yours. We don't want our captain's handsome face to be scratched by another monster."

Ina just cursed under her breath. She would refuse, but it seemed to be the most sensible option. Reluctantly handing the basket to Senad, Mar's proximity befuddled her mind as she breathed in his scent. *It will be a long day,* Ina thought. *Pray we get to the inn quickly.*

She tightened her grip and inhaled the musty scent of leather and the male wearing it again. If only he weren't such an asshole, she could even enjoy it.

CHAPTER 3

The ride to the inn was surprisingly pleasant, though Ina remembered little of it. After the initial displeasure of being thrown over the horse's back like a sack of turnips, she learned to appreciate the smooth gait of Mar's stallion. Contrary to her outward demeanour, Ina took genuine pleasure from Mar's proximity. The only explanation for this had to be the lack of decent human contact. The superstitious peasants avoided her, and no one from her past found the time to visit the now-infamous Ina. She shook her head at such melancholy thoughts, letting the brightly shining sun chase them away.

Ina observed how the forest slowly made space for meadows and hills with only small copses hinting at the earlier wildwoods. She loved nature, but this change of scenery was more than welcome. The witch was grateful it was past harvest time. Lady

Midday was unlikely to attack when there was no grain in the fields. She could be a terrifying wraith to combat if she chose to be difficult. Thankfully, an armed and noisy company would scare anyone, even a wraith. Step by step, Ina drifted asleep, lulled by the warmth of the sun and the soft touch of the autumn wind.

⁂

Mar was still unsure what had happened in the past twenty-four hours. His memories seemed clouded. The more he tried to remember events after Senad's departure, the less he could recall. Deep in his thoughts, it took him a moment to realise Ina was on her way to sliding from the horse's back straight onto the dusty road. It was like watching a tree falling in slow motion as her relaxed, puppet like body bent lower and lower with each step. He caught her at the last moment and whipped her around to the front. His sudden move spooked the horse, and Ina, still drowsy, grabbed his hand.

"What the hell are you doing?" she said, appearing disoriented by the horse's head in front of her.

"Nothing," he answered shortly. "Go back to sleep." To his amusement, this stubborn woman listened for a change.

He shook his head at the situation's absurdity, so at ease with Ina in his arms. How could someone so vexing make him relax his guard so effortlessly? A gruff chuckle slipped out. It must be the relief from her incessant mocking, damn viper-tongued harridan.

A firm punch on his shoulder brought him cursing back to the world. "Swine-fucking ogre shit!"

Mar was already drawing his sword as Senad burst out laughing. "Gods tits, Mar, lost in that witch's bosom, are you? No wonder that beast got the better of you if your wick was doing the fighting."

Mar looked over at his lieutenant, scowl deep and forbidding. "Mind your manners, Senad, that shitstorm was no joke. Now, tell me what happened after you left. There's no way you had time to get to the capital and back, not to mention getting reinforcements so quickly."

Senad looked around at the entourage behind them with a suddenly sober expression.

"As I said at that hovel, I thought you were dead and had to save the men. We got out as fast as the men could travel, and even then, we got only halfway to the inn before this lot came upon us. Pompous twits doesn't even come close to describing them, but they still agreed to help. They took the men in that mage's carriage with a few guards and their healer, but they definitely had an agenda. They went straight to that witch's home, and they didn't even need the villagers to show them the way. It looks like we've dropped into something serious here, and mark me. This matter is related to our work. She was too close to the attack and obviously had connections in the capital. Best to watch your back, as well as your prick, with that one."

The captain slowly nodded, almost to himself, as his thoughts moved in a similar direction. Magic and coincidence just didn't happen in his experience. He focused on the woman in front of him, her body held to his chest possessively. Yes, she was involved in this, but damn it all, he just couldn't see her torturing and killing animals.

Looking back at Senad, he signalled his agreement. "Aye, keep an eye on them. It's too big a coincidence that this is all happening simultaneously. I will make enquiries with this one when we get to the tavern."

Senad burst out laughing and dropped back into formation, joking. "Right, enquiries, that's what they're calling it these days."

The rocking stopped, and Ina slowly woke up in his arms. He looked down, noticing her open eyes, blinking in surprise when she wrinkled her nose buried in his neck. Ina inhaled deeply, and Mar smiled before being taken aback by how comfortable he was with this intimacy.

"Oh…" She sat up straight, provoking his grunt. The witch stretched, visibly stiff from the long ride, but other than that, she looked incredible. And in her annoying manner, she also didn't hesitate to tell him about being hungry, dusty, and desperate to empty her bladder.

"We can solve your problems, as now you woke up and we've arrived at the inn." Mar's body was less than pleased with this experience. He was aching from having to hold one pose. Not to mention, the sleeping Ina seemed to rest her hips on places that shouldn't be touched during a horse ride. The horse's movement didn't help dispel daydreaming of passion when soft feminine curves kept rubbing his groin. Now, tense from unwanted thoughts, he was in a rotten mood. The captain heard Jorge and Senad ordering the innkeeper around and removing local patrons to make space for their group.

"Wonderful, a room, and a decent bed," he said, waiting for Ina to dismount.

"Can you help…please?" He heard her softly spoken question. She was looking at him with a challenge in her eyes, clearly expecting nothing good of him. Ina noticed his curious gaze and huffed. "Well, you put me up here, and now you can get me down."

Simply pushing her off the horse was so tempting, but it would be petty, and for the sake of further enquiries, he didn't want to alienate her further. So instead, Mar grabbed her by the belt and gently lowered her down.

As soon as she was down, Ina sighed with relief—her legs were stiff and her bladder was full. With her luck, jumping from the horse could cause an embarrassing accident. She waved to Senad entering the inn with her cat. "Put him in my room. I will be there in a moment, and please see if they can arrange me a bath," Ina shouted as she rushed to find a woman, any woman that worked here, to be directed to the place of need.

The inn felt spacious and cleaner than expected for a small town, and the food smelled nice, making Ina's stomach rumble. Upon entering, she was welcomed by grim faces and tension in the air. She didn't know what could cause such strain, but it was clear something was wrong. She turned to a random noble. "What happened? Why does everybody seem so on edge?"

Worry was plastered over the man's face. "One of the remaining soldiers died, and another seems to be on the brink of death. The mage and healer are trying to help."

The statement made sense. These people seemed to be a friendly group, so it was no surprise they were all worried now. Still, she decided it was none of her business. She didn't have any genuine talent in healing, and the pain from the sacrifice spell was still vivid in her memory. Besides, it wasn't even a healing spell but rather a desperate measure to keep a loved one alive or die with them. They had a qualified healer now, and her presence would only hinder his efforts. Her place was here with the food, so she nestled next to the fire and pulled on one of the inn wench's sleeves.

"Do you have any fish here?" Much to her family's displeasure and a long-standing joke for her peers, she preferred fish to any other food.

"We have fish stew and fresh bread," the girl answered.

Ina smiled at her, accepting the choice and adding, "Please make sure I have a bath in my room after dinner." She pushed one of her few silver coins into the girl's hand, slipping smoothly into old habits. Now she only needed to earn some money to get back to her comfortable life.

A steaming bowl of stew arrived quickly, with still-warm bread and a generous amount of salty butter. Ina slurped the first spoon, purring with pleasure. It was delicious, not to mention she didn't have to cook or clean, and that instantly made any dish more palatable.

The delightful food reminded her of Velka. Her friend could make soup from a stone, and it would still be worthy of a lord's table. They'd tricked Sophia once, and she devoured it with speed unseen in the king's daughter. Still, best of all, Velka made her laugh. Even when the sky fell, Velka could make it into an exciting experience, and Ina missed her dearly. She relaxed and savoured her dish, observing the nobles and guards flocking into their little herds. *Not much change in the world, it seems,* this thought was quite reassuring. After all these years, she may not have too much trouble returning to civilisation.

"Ina! Upstairs! Now!" Mar's roar shook the inn's walls, surprising her halfway through her food. The crowd in the inn instantly parted, creating a corridor, each of them looking in her direction.

"Looks like no one dares to decline captain's orders," she said, rising from the chair with a smirk. "There is a first time for everything, it seems," she said teasingly, but the guards looked like they would drag her up to avoid facing their captain's wrath. The witch knew how to choose her battles, so she strolled between them with a deep, provocative sway to her hips, purposefully taking her time on the stairs. Ina felt she had to obey, but she could still project her defiance.

"Ina!" Mar yelled again, followed by a shocking, faint desperate psychic cry, "Please," coming from the judicial mage. This thin man with a severe and unforgiving face wouldn't ask if the situation wasn't dire. Specifically, he wouldn't ask her. As fast as she could, Ina ran the last few steps and soon stood at the door frame of the open room. The view that greeted her was grim. The stench of rotten flesh assaulted her senses. A man with strange features lay on the large, comfortable bed, now covered in brown ichor. His face was ghastly and contorted by pain. Deep claw marks across his swollen red cheek exposed his bones. Even from her place in the doorway, she could see he barely held on, muttering something in delirium.

Ashen-faced, Jorge was almost on his knees trying to support the healer in his efforts, but no poultice or murmured spell seemed to help. Mar's frantic face appeared in front of her. He grabbed her shoulder with a painful grip and pushed her into the room.

"Save him," he said with a strenuous voice and placed his forehead on hers in this heartbreaking plea, "please…he is my friend."

"I am no healer. I'm no better than the one you have in here already." She wished she could do something, but that level of healing was beyond her little capacity. Mar didn't listen. He pulled her forwards with a feral snarl.

"You saved me." There was hard, inflexible steel in his voice. "I don't know how, and I don't care. I'll shower you with gold if that's your price. Open the abyss if you must, but you have to help him."

His eyes glowed with inner light and startled her, adding to her distress. Before she had time to dwell on it, he pushed her again, making her stumble on the rug. Landing awkwardly, her face hovered directly over the patient's wounds. The smell caught her unawares. It was so putrid that he must be suffering terribly.

The stench came from the gangrene that had taken hold in the gashes on the soldier's handsome face. This man was unique. The narrow, hooded eyes, now clouded with pain, shaded by straight, thick eyebrows, wide cheekbones, and a shapely but relatively flat nose, were rarely seen in Cornovii. You could glimpse such men when a rare colourful caravan came to trade in the capital. Her curiosity took the better of her, and she couldn't help but silently admire him. Defined muscles and naturally pale skin contrasted well with the thick raven hair. Covered with sweat and burning like hellfire, he still looked interesting. The cuts on his cheek were deep. Ina could see the exposed, shattered bone protruding from them, all of it now oozing a rotten, smelly fluid with torrents of dark magic.

"I can't heal him. Whatever caused the rot is resistant to magic or herbs," she heard the healer's determined voice. "If you have any tricks up your sleeve, now is the time to do them, or he will soon die."

"All I can offer is a quick death," she said with sorrow and was about to push herself off the bed when the patient reached and touched her cheek in a strangely lucid moment.

"Beautiful Phoenix…death I accept," he whispered. There was nothing more. He drifted away, and his breath grew shallow and uneven. She heard Mar's fist pounding on the wall in frustration.

Ina felt the Gods were laughing at her expense when looking back at the man. She realised his peaceful acceptance triggered something deep within her, and she couldn't, in clear conscience, let him die. Her mother's favourite proverb said, *If you have a soft heart, prepare to have an iron ass.* That was never truer than now.

Slowly, she took the stranger's hand and put it over her heart, while her other hand connected with the male's chest. There would be no unique concoctions this time, and it would be one hell of a bumpy ride with Chaos magic she had. She turned to look at Jorge.

"Give me your word. No one will know about this, and please help if you still can."

A stiff nod sealed his agreement, and Ina sat on the edge of the bed. There was no sense in closing her eyes. When Jorge's hands lay on her shoulders, she searched for her patient's life source. His body lit up with the crimson pathways of his life energy, now dull and contaminated. Ina took one deep breath, whispering rite of sacrifice and connected herself to his meridians.

Dirty pollution hit her. She felt dark particles of sorcery that tried to change her, twisting her body and magic until she would become something entirely different. Her cheek burned as claw marks burst open, wringing a pained whimper from her lips. Panic washed over her as her body fought the unnatural sickness. Finally, her magic adjusted, transforming the pollution, and she started to heal her body when the sacrifice spell continued the exchange.

Jorge looked at Ina in disbelief. "The sacrifice?"

Ina knew why he reacted like this. This foolishness was forbidden for a good reason. Every mage could perform if they were ready to face the consequences. Death, pain-induced madness, or a unnatural attachment that could last a lifetime were not uncommon. There were tales that some did it in the direst time for a loved one, but no mage would carelessly do it for a stranger, and she was just about to do it in front of the judicial mage.

Ina hoped now he understood her hesitation and protest. She also knew that the mage would soon realise she had done it before, and Mar, that lucky bastard, did not know and had forced her into this. Still, she hoped for some help, but when she reached for his magic, Jorge howled in pain and broke the connection. He didn't seem ready to sacrifice his life or freedom for this strange man, leaving Ina alone to fight the unnatural sickness. She plunged deep, touching the velvet darkness of the stranger's soul that immersed her like still dark water.

Mar jumped forwards, hearing this bloodcurdling sound. All he could see were the wounds on Ren's face slowly fading away, but something was plainly wrong if a Crown mage screamed and scrambled back from the bed.

He moved to face Ina. The horror that swept through him stopped him instantly. What looked like peaceful healing from behind was something entirely different. What disappeared from Ren's face reappeared on hers.

Mar couldn't stop himself. Whatever was happening to Ina as she healed Ren wasn't worth this. He had been dying, and it looked like that would now happen to her. The instinct inside him made him take hold of Ina's face. He tried to wake her up from this nightmare, to stop her from killing herself. However, instead of stopping, the golden light inside him flared up. It blazed its way into her, fusing them tighter and lighting up her eyes. The overwhelming but strangely familiar sensation cut off almost as quickly as it started, leaving him shaken, unable to look away from the witch in front of him.

Ina's hollow face looked at him with unseeing eyes. Her body jolted, breaking the link, and she curled on the floor, trying to catch her breath. Mar felt that his intervention had given her a much-needed boost at the same time, breaking her focus. She looked like she had almost lost herself in this filth, but Ren's face was healed, and his eyes were clear of fever. Ina, however, was a mess.

Mar wanted to help her, but she stopped him. The pain and betrayal in her gaze felt wrong, and he didn't even know what he had done to deserve it. Time slowed down for him when he watched her fighting an unseen enemy in front of his very eyes. Slowly her breath steadied, and the wounds on her face filled with the red hue of her magic and knit themselves together. She stumbled, trying to get to her feet.

"I want my damn bath." Her voice was hoarse, her face ashen, and even her copper hair seemed to have lost its shine. Mar stepped forwards to carry her, but she stopped him again.

"No, not you," she rasped.

Mar looked at Jorge, who stood there shaken and clearly couldn't believe the turn of events.

"How? How did you do it and live? That's inconceivable," he said, and Mar couldn't agree more. Ina had survived this nightmare and appeared unscathed, albeit drained, but most of all, sane. The men looked at each other, and the warrior noticed the tingles of shame that marred the mage's face. Jorge offered his hand, but Ina rejected it as well

"Maid!" Mar banged on the door. "Get the lady to her room."

The servant arrived and helped Ina, allowing Mar to turn his gaze to Ren. His man looked like nothing had happened. His face was unblemished, and he was already sitting up on the edge of the bed.

"It looks like we are both deeply in debt to her, my friend."

Ren slowly nodded, and Mar's unease grew, seeing a soft smile appearing on his friend's lips. He'd never seen Ren smiling with such tenderness, and it was clear Ina's healing had profoundly affected him. When Ren placed his hand over his heart, Mar recalled his earlier experience and realised that the connection was still vivid in his mind. He could only hope he was wrong, but knowing his friend, he knew the latest event led him to the one conclusion. She had saved his life. Now his life belonged to her.

"Who was that, captain?" His quiet question carried more emotions than Mar had ever heard in his voice.

Suddenly, Mar listened to his own voice with words that shocked him to the core. "She's mine." The men looked at each other. Ren's disbelief and anger flashed across his face.

It faded like a ripple through still water, only disturbing the placid surface for a moment, and Ren lowered his gaze. "If you say so…"

A few moments later, Mar sat hunched over at the table downstairs in the main dining area. He knew from the commotion upstairs that Ina got her bath. It shouldn't affect him, but he could not shake the feeling that he had overstepped, forcing Ina to heal Ren. "It was worth it," the captain convinced himself. "Ren is still alive, and that's all that matters."

His resolve to leave her alone was not that firm, especially when he'd found himself in front of Ina's room, staring at the closed doors, listening to her muffled sobs. Mar tried to go in and explain, but she refused his presence. Now he was sitting here with overly sombre Ren and Daro whose jolly conduct stuck out like a sore thumb.

"I heard you have a miracle healer there," spat out the orc between bites of his pasty. "I wonder if she can cure a hangover, too. Tell me, Ren, how it felt when she caressed you," Daro said and winked. "Rarely do women lay their hands on you, not for free anyway." Daro chuckled, moving swiftly when Ren's dagger hit the table in front of him.

"You will speak of her with respect." Ren's voice was quietly menacing, and the orc raised his hands in a mocking gesture of surrender.

"Calm down or you'll get your bloomers twisted with your bollocks if you're not careful. It seems this illness made you prickly." He looked at their captain, noticing the tension in his posture. "Now, I'm curious," he said to himself.

Ina was relieved when the door finally closed behind her. Everything had seemed to go wrong from the start. Now, tired and weak, she felt very emotional. She shouldn't be angry at Mar. She was the one who made that choice, but she couldn't help herself. He was the one that dragged her into the whole situation, and then he expected her to fix his mess. Ina released Boruta from his basket and cried, pushing her face into his dense fur.

A soft knock followed by a hesitant "Ina?" made her angry. What could he want now? Another corpse to repair?

"Can't you leave me alone at least for a day?" she answered back, annoyed at how pathetic her voice sounded. "Just get out!" she said. The opportunity to bark at him felt nice, and she gathered the remaining energy to have a bath.

Ina scrubbed herself clean, leaving her tangled tresses hanging over the tub's rim. She tried to think about the abnormal particles she'd felt in the soldier's energy. It felt like there was a purpose and maliciousness behind them. She felt slumber sneak up on her as exhaustion set in, and the bed appeared to be so far away now. Warm water provided all the comfort she needed. *Just a quick nap. I will dress myself later,* she thought, closing her eyes.

Chapter 4

Their tankards ran dry when a hissing, black bolt of fur landed on the table in front of Mar, screeching and spitting like a demon incarnate. Daro grabbed the cat by the scruff of its neck, holding it away from his face.

"What the fuck is that thing?" he asked his companions.

"It's a cat," Ren stated. "Most likely one of the tavern's mousers."

"But why he is trying to claw off Mar's face?" continued Daro, baffled by the writhing animal.

"He is Ina's. What else would it do?" Mar barely paid attention to the cat, trying to solve the riddle of Ina's involvement in their situation, and then it hit him.

"It's Ina's cat!" The bloody beast wouldn't leave her side unless something terrible happened. With one abrupt lurch, he pushed the heavy table aside. Patrons scattered like terrified hens as he rushed upstairs with Ren and Daro on his heels. The door was still locked when he hit it, but the deafening silence that followed the heavy impact was more concerning. Ina should already be cursing him to Nawia.

"Daro!" Mar pointed to the door. The young orc didn't need more instruction. One swift kick and the door was now swinging off its hinges. Mar dived inside and scanned the room. In the bathtub, next to the fireplace, was Ina's still body under the water. The few steps needed to cover the short distance felt like an eternity. Mar effortlessly dragged her small limp frame out of the tub and knelt in front of the fire. She wasn't breathing. A sudden flashback from his past blinded him. For the second time in his life, he held a woman's lifeless body in his arms, desperately hoping she was still alive. Natsu, his late wife, was long gone, but he still remembered her last words.

You destroy everything you touch, Marcach.

Desperation clawing at his insides, Mar shook Ina like a rag doll. "Wake up, you thrice-damned witch. I won't let you die like this. Wake up!" Wildly looking around for help, for inspiration, he sees his two men standing on the threshold, gaping like fools as they stare at the naked woman by the fire.

"Boars tits, you idiots, get the healer and that useless turd of a mage. She's not breathing." The stunned men stood still for a moment longer. Ren reacted first, turning and bolting for the healer. Mar knew his friend was filled with guilt. He likely thought it was his fault this beautiful creature was lying there, lifeless.

Daro's departure took seconds longer. His face showed he still couldn't believe his captain, cold and calculating in the direst circumstances, was now freaking out so much because of a woman he barely knew. Not that Mar blamed him, the orc had never seen him this concerned for a stranger. Mar knew that in Daro's mind, his captain was not chaste, but his love life was always short-term. The orc mostly never learned a new flame's name unless he wanted to bed her himself, of course. Not that Mar ever held this against him, he simply didn't care.

"Fuck, I will not allow this to happen again. I. Will. Not. Let. It. Happen." With each word, he shook Ina hard till, at last, he lurched forwards and kissed her roughly, trying to force life back into her body.

Ina was floating in pleasant nothingness, carefree and weightless. It was the most pleasant dream she'd had in years, or at least it was until a violent quaking disturbed the bliss. She wasn't floating anymore. Instead, Ina felt like a bug in a glass jar, shaken by an unruly child. Her consciousness resurfaced, and the awareness of her own body with that. Suddenly her lips were crushed by a desperate, needy kiss, making her gasp, shocked by the sheer audacity of the act. As expected, upon opening her eyes, there he was, the bane of her life, holding her in a painful embrace and shaking her like a rag doll. On top of it, she was naked. Anger gave her strength, and her palm landed on his cheek with a crack, leaving clear red marks on his face.

"Your place in my bed was revoked the moment you called me a whore," she sneered, trying to untangle herself from his arms. "What in the pit were you thinking?"

"What-what the fuck was that for?" Mar snapped back, and she could see his jaw muscles spasming in barely restrained anger. "I was saving your life, you ginger harridan. You were drowning in your filthy bath."

He stood up suddenly, and the act hoisted her onto the floor with a thump. Mar stalked across the room to the bed, ripping off the covers with a final, ground-out curse, flinging them at her naked form. "A thank you would have worked better. Now, try not to die in my absence." Mar's departure from the room echoed through the tavern as he slammed the remains of the door closed behind him. The curses flew high when he pushed past the crowding people that rushed through the corridor towards Ina's room.

Ina looked at the sad remnants of her door and shook her head. "He positively hates doors, it seems," she said, wrapping the covers around her. Ina noticed people crowding into her room and addressed them with the irony that dripped from her voice. "Did someone announce a fayre here?"

Ina was no prude, but four pairs of eyes looking at her with worry, interest, or desire was too much to handle. She wrapped the covers tightly around her.

Ren noticed her discomfort and ushered Daro out. "Go check on the captain. He looked a little disturbed."

Ina smirked at this understatement, but she was grateful for his intervention.

Ren attempted to leave, too, but her small "thank you" stopped him in his tracks. Without a word, he gently swooped her from her feet and carried her to the bed, preserving her modesty. There was reverence and hesitance in his gestures, as if he expected her to scowl under his touch. Instead, she met his help with kindness and appreciation, smiling when their eyes met. Ren gazed into her eyes and held her longer than needed before placing her gently on the bed. She didn't know the captain had tried staking his claim. Still, seeing the strange determination in her new friend's eyes and gentleness in his touch, she was glad there was someone to help her when she needed it.

The healer moved to her side, looking shaken, almost as if he'd encountered Leshy himself. Ina chuckled, seeing his dishevelled beard and messed-up clothes. He examined her briefly, rushing to get out of her room as soon as possible. Then he was gone, leaving only some decoctions on the night table to strengthen her spirit. Jorge's stare pinned her like a dead bug till he eventually nodded and said, "I will send for some food and drinks to help you regain your strength." And with those words, he left as well.

Ina looked at Ren, smiling. "Aren't you going to leave, too?" she asked.

"Not until I'm sure you are safe." Ren positioned himself close but still within a respectable distance. His presence was so unassuming and comfortable that Ina couldn't help herself and reached over to touch his hand.

"Thank you for your kindness," she said, feeling the slight tremble of his fingers in her hand. "I don't think I had the pleasure of learning your name." Her covers slid a little lower, revealing ivory skin and a glimpse of her cleavage. Ren's eyes darkened, pupils taking over already dark irises.

"My name is Sa'Ren Gerel—Ren to those I call friend," he answered, inhaling sharply as he took his hand away.

Ina looked intently into his eyes. "I hope I may be counted as a friend," she said, still remembering the soothing cold that washed over her during the healing and the longing to belong that she had felt in this man. As soon as she finished the sentence, Ina noticed the tension that built up in him, but before she could enquire further, her food's arrival saved the day.

"I will leave you now, my lady."

"Ina, just call me Ina. I'm not exactly a lady here." Ina pointed out the apparent hilarity of the situation.

Ren nodded, and she saw the corner of his mouth lift in a small smile. When he left the room, Ina directed her attention to the food, happy to finally enjoy an undisturbed meal.

The rest of the night passed uneventfully. A full belly and quiet room lulled Ina to sleep. Boruta placed himself on her chest, purring a soft lullaby into her ear. She dreamt about Mar coated in golden light, how she saw him for the first time, and the scent of his skin mixed with the smell of horse and leather. Her hand found its way down, disturbing the cat, but Ina needed her release, even if only in her beautiful dreams.

๑)ᴼᕽᔕᕽᴼᏝ๑

Mar was pacing back and forth in front of the inn with a raging hangover. It was not the best start to the day. Still, after storming out of Ina's room, he had found himself in the bar surrounded by drunken nobles. After he drank the first stein thrust in his face, the drinks seemed to keep coming. Every time that woman's name came up, his temper flared, and another ale passed his lips until oblivion gathered him up into its cloying embrace. Even now, he couldn't stop thinking about her.

With each turn to the east, the blinding sun reminded him of that feeling during the healing, followed swiftly by the pain of the hangover and that damn slap. Everyone around him was avoiding his attention, flinching every time he barked an order to get ready to depart. *Where was that damn woman? Did she think she was in the palace already?*

Dizziness swept over him as he looked around, his gaze catching unsteadily on the three men who were not afraid to look him in the eye. Daro, Ren, and Senad had been making this morning intolerable with their mocking and youthful ability to recover from a night of drinking, the arseholes. A sly grin crept over his face as his stance firmed and focused on the annoying trio.

"Oh, Daro, please be so kind as to find our lady sorceress some suitable attire for our journey. Senad, please talk with the mage and the healer to ensure they have everything they need to be comfortable. Ren, I would appreciate it if you'd supervise Daro in his endeavours and make sure he doesn't lose himself in some serving girl's skirts. Oh, and ensure the lady Ina shifts her pretty little arse along." With a smirk that made him feel much repaired, he turned and strode over to Woron to check his tack for the umpteenth time, using the moment to calm his mind and prepare for the journey.

The morning commotion woke Ina up early. She looked around the messy room at the traces of yesterday's events. The dirty clothes on the floor, a wet stain where Mar held her body, and the bed still smelled of soap. A brief knock disturbed her inspection.

"Enter," she said, pulling the blanket to cover herself. One of the inn's servants timidly entered the room with a pile of clothes.

"His lordship asks you to dress and join them as they are about to leave."

Ina nodded, acknowledging the message, and started rummaging through the clothes. The servant had left a pair of riding trousers with a tunic and waist cincher. It was a good, practical set to pair with her long boots. Dressed, she felt better and more confident, but her life wouldn't be complete without at least one minor problem. Ina tried to brush her unruly hair with her fingers, but unfortunately, it had dried in messy waves and refused to obey her commands. Another knock rattled the door.

"My lady, are you ready?" Ren's clear and calm voice came from behind the doors.

"Ren, I told you to call me Ina. Oh, I don't suppose you have a comb?" She saw her salvation in the shape of this quiet man, and indeed, he didn't disappoint her. A moment later, Ren came back with a comb and handed it to Ina.

She looked at it, and with a mischievous smile, she turned her back to him. "Ren, could you help me, please? I fear I will struggle to detangle it myself."

The silence at her words made Ina bite her lip. She slowly counted under her breath, and just as she was about to turn back, she felt a soft touch on her head. "Thank you," she said and felt her shoulders start to relax under his careful touch. *If only this would allow me to forget the hairy oaf,* she thought, closing her eyes and savouring the pleasure of his smooth long strokes running through her mane.

Mind eased by the morning routine of a thousand journeys, Mar turned around to see two of his three subordinates strolling over without a care in the world, both at least no longer grinning like demons.

Senad was the first to speak, a rarity only in that Daro just never seemed to shut up. He was formal in his address.

"Captain, the mage and the healer are ready and comfortable in the carriage. All the men are armed and armoured, and all is squared away and in position."

Mar raised an eyebrow at Senad's formality and nodded in acknowledgement before turning to Daro, who grinned and bowed with an exaggerated flourish. "Aye, captain, all is good. Your pet sorceress has the finest riding outfit available in these parts, but it may be a little snug in places. Ren himself went to make sure she wants for nothing, though the time it's taking, I'm not sure he's man enough to give her everything she needs." That damn grin came back as Daro spun on his heel and beat a hasty retreat.

The sound of something cracking distracted Mar even as Senad's eyes widened and, with the briefest of bows, followed swiftly on Daro's heels.

Looking down at his hands with a frown, it took a moment to register the crack that now ran along the handle of his axe, an axe that moments ago had still been attached to his saddle. *What in Veles's name is going on with me?* Tossing the remains of the axe to a loitering servant, Mar strode away towards the inn, muttering about "that damn woman" and "where the fuck is Ren?" He arrived on the threshold of Ina's room almost unconsciously, only to stop and stare at the sight in front of him. The beautiful woman he chased through his dreams was sitting there, purring as another man, Ren, stroked his hands through her lustrous hair.

He realised that grinding sound was his teeth trying to crush his anger back. Even as he took a trembling, stiff step forwards, he felt himself rein back the desire to rip his friend apart and barked out a sharp command with a deep, shuddering breath.

"Ren, I do not have time for you to dally with our lady sorceress. Escort her to the carriage now, or it will be you who answers to the Council why their newest pet is late to hand," he said, growling out his frustration. Mar turned and was gone even before Ina turned around.

Ren didn't know what to think as his proverbial invisibility usually extended to women's attention. In this merchant kingdom, he was hardly an object of desire, with no family or money, a stranger in these lands with a face that often brought unwanted attention. Ina not only allowed him to touch her, but she also encouraged it. He slid the comb through her silky strands, wondering what would happen if he buried his face in them. Would she reject him? He shook his head. He still remembered the captain's words the previous day. *She's mine.* It hadn't sounded like an empty claim, and the way he held her, trying to stir her back to life? Ren shook his head. All he could do was daydream and prolong this brief moment of pleasure where he could pretend there was still a chance for him. After Mar's abrupt entrance and ever sharper command, Ren took a step back and bowed deeply. He knew his joy had been short-lived, and now he would pay the price. "My lady, we have to go, please."

Ina ran her hands through the now silky strands with a visible pleasure. "Ren, if I had any money, I would hire you as a lady's maid. You know how to please a woman." She quickly plaited a loose braid and tossed it over her shoulder. "Let's go before this old bore loses all his marbles."

Ren gave her a half smile. He was amazed by her bold words and ability to give Mar a headache. They went downstairs, Ren with the cat basket and Ina following. He noticed she cast a look at Mar, and with a determined expression directed herself to the carriage. Once there, she reached towards him.

"Please, my friend…?" She looked straight at Mar when Ren took her hand and gently guided her inside. He knew she didn't need any help in climbing up, but he didn't that mind she used him to irk the captain. The hint of shame he noticed on her face from pitting them against each other was quickly replaced by a mischievous grin when she saw Mar's scowl darken.

Jorge observed the scene from the window. When the carriage door closed, he turned his serious face to Ina. "I know we are not friends, but let me give you fair warning. You play with fire, be mindful of that one."

Ina looked and laughed. "Oh, I know, and I intend to enjoy every second."

CHAPTER 5

The journey to the capital was relatively uneventful, but Mar's pace made Ina worry about the poor horses. Guilt tickled her conscience. If she hadn't goaded him so much, maybe those poor animals wouldn't draw such laborious gasps now, sides foaming from the effort. Only Woron, Mar's stallion, seemed unbothered by the tempo. She looked at Jorge, worrying he was about to lose his breakfast. His face was an intense shade of green, and he reminded her of a very serious frog with bulging eyes.

"It is all your fault," Jorge gasped, looking at her with accusation.

Meanwhile, the healer seemed unfazed by the situation. Since the beginning of the journey, the old gent had appeared somewhat intoxicated.

Every bump in the road was greeted with a sip from the bottle and his enthusiastic "whoopsie!" She felt like she was travelling with a pipe-smoking, overactive toddler. With one final *whoopsie* from the healer and a deep nauseous gulp from the mage, Ina lost her patience.

"Ren! Ren!" She thrust her head through the window. There was no reason to call for Mar, as he wouldn't even look at her now. Ren, however, tried to keep close to the coach, and she caught him casting glances at the carriage. Ren's horse approached through clouds of road dust.

"Please ask him to slow down," she said. "I feel every bone in my body shaking loose."

Ren shook his head and pointed at something ahead. She squinted her eyes, trying to see. There, through the thick dust, was the city of Osterad. "Fine," she said, tightening her lips. She could suffer a little more.

That "little" extended into two more hours of belching and "whoopsies," and by the end, she was ready to kill someone, something or even ride the monstrosity that was Mar's horse. Suddenly, the carriage bounced to a stop, and the commotion of the bustling city assaulted her ears. Someone opened the door, and she heard a formal voice, "Guards inspection."

"Veles's buttocks!" she shouted when Jorge's torso bent in front of her, barely missing her knees, and the rest of his breakfast landed on the gate guardian's feet.

"Double whoopsie!" exclaimed the old healer, clapping his hands. Ina felt she couldn't take it any longer. Mar's roaring laugh shook the carriage, drowning out the guard's now unfriendly, "Welcome to Osterad."

Their arrival in the capital marked the group's dispersal. Mar gathered his troops and directed them to the barracks. The nobles and their entourage were most likely heading to their own homes and villas in the city. However, the carriage would carry them towards the University of Higher Magical Arts, colloquially called the Cauldron by everyone except its faculty. It was also the seat of the Magical Council. She didn't have fond memories of that part.

Before their departure, Ren drew level with the carriage and bowed to Ina. "My lady, I wish to thank you once more and bid you goodbye."

The smile she sent him was genuine. She had grown to like this man during the short period of their journey. He was an intriguing oxymoron, a warrior, yet his manners and conduct were nothing but caring and gentle. She reached her hand through the window and bowed her head respectfully.

"Sir Ren, I truly hope we will meet again." Ina's voice conveyed sadness, but it was a big city, and their social circles were utterly different. Ren took Ina's hand, but what came next was unexpected. He gently kissed her fingertips and pressed the hand to his forehead in a deep bow. Then he turned his horse and trotted to his waiting party. She could feel Mar's judgemental stare while talking to Ren and remembered there was one last thing she had to sort out. She should tell him about the stab wound. When their eyes met, she waved him in, and although his lips tightened in an impatient line, he obliged. A sharp heel to Woron's side turned the warhorse towards the carriage, and Ina heard him barking commands.

"Senad, organise the troops. I need to go to the chancellor as soon as we can. Just give me a moment to check what that damn woman wants now and why the hell Ren pledged himself to her."

The soldiers formed an orderly line when Mar approached her. She wished there was a better way to tell him, but she doubted ever seeing him again.

"Captain, you helped me yesterday, and I may not have been sufficiently grateful."

Her convoluted apology brought a sarcastic smirk to his face. He didn't make it easy for her, and she did not know how to tell him of the betrayal with the crowd of people around her. Acting on impulse, she grabbed his sleeve and yanked him down. Her mouth hit his cheek with a force that almost broke her nose if not for the cushioning of his beard. While Mar still appeared stunned by her sudden movement, she whispered in his ear, "Someone stabbed you in the forest. It was not only clawing wounds I healed."

She released her grip and let him spring back to an upright position. After her disclosure, the sheer shock painted over his face made her feel better. She had paid her debts, and she even apologised for the slap in the face. That is a good beginning of a new life, and patting his thigh, Ina looked at Mar with a big grin. "We are good now. You can go."

With that done, Ina fell back on the pillow and let the driver take her wherever he saw fit. Her thoughts started formulating plans for the future. First, she would need a place to stay, a cheap one for now, and a workshop. Ten years of keeping herself alive by foraging were not in vain. She could mix a mean potion now and this knowledge could get her a small fortune. Or maybe she should travel. She remembered the salty enchantment of the coastal cities, so perhaps she should move there?

The sudden pressure of a magical barrier told her they had crossed the university's perimeter. Finally, she would find out what they wanted from her. Ina promised herself this time, she would act maturely. After all, she was about to turn forty, still relatively young by magical standards but old enough to know better. Her last tantrum earned her exile to the forest, so now she would present herself as a brand new woman.

Jorge looked with disbelief at "the brand new woman" jumping like a rabbit trying to shake off as much of the road's dust as possible, but Ina didn't care.

"Oh, for… Let's just go," he said, rubbing furiously at his temples.

This journey had been horridly unpleasant, and Ina knew he blamed her. Yes, the prick hadn't forgotten to point this out to her all the way here, but at least Jorge looked pleased that they'd arrived just after midday. Ina hoped she'd get the rest of the day for herself. As soon as they sorted out whatever the Council wanted with her, of course.

They entered the ancient building, passing an enormous set of ornately carved doors. Ina sighed as it appeared this wouldn't be an official hearing. Jorge led her to the chamber where all sensitive issues were swept under the carpet and inconvenient people vanished. The witch's heart thumped so loud she could hear it in her ears. Chaos tendrils reached for her, causing Jorge to shift uncomfortably. *Focus!* she ordered herself. *You have done nothing wrong…this time.* She tried to turn her mind to a different subject, and when it didn't work, she reached for the forest. The pressure eased up under pine-and-resin-scented memories, and she was ready to step into the chamber. As soon as she walked far enough to face the Council, barriers snapped into place.

"Will my esteemed colleagues care to tell me what is happening here?" Ina asked sarcastically. They were locking her in again? Really? Do they think she is so unhinged that she would blow up the Council?

Arun, representing battlemages, spoke first. "It is just a precaution against any accidents, my lady."

Ina knew what he was referring to—the same room ten years ago, where they decided she had caused too big of a scandal at the palace. One smug look around showed that at least she had made it essential to redecorate, and they had omitted any sharp objects this time. This thought was satisfying. If they were afraid of her, maybe there was a slight hope she'd get a chance to turn over a new leaf. The Council didn't like to get rid of powerhouses unless they were batshit crazy.

"Did you or did you not create the monsters?!" the university's rector broke his silence first. He was a small, petty man with a mean streak and overgrown ego. He was still the foremost expert in magical theory, which was probably why he disliked her so much. There was no order or formula to Ina's magic, but it still worked, mostly surprisingly well.

Shocked, Ina looked out at the gathering. They all stared at her with anticipation, and she realised they expected her to answer this ridiculous question.

"I did not create any monsters." Ina's voice was as clear as her conscience, but she didn't feel they believed her. Lashes of magic snapped her thoughts. Fucking Truthseekers—her anger flared up as pressure on her mind intensified. So that is how the Council wants to deal with it. Fine, she will let them, and they'd better be ready for her truth. The questioning started, bombarding her from various angles.

"Did you create a monster?"

"Yes." A collective gasp shook the room.

"When?"

"During my third year of university, alchemy class. This old prick wanted me to transform the frog into an inanimate object, effectively killing it. The creature wanted to live, so instead, I prepared a potion with my magic, the one you called a mutagen. I transformed it, giving the new entity the ability to grow some defences." The disappointment was palpable in the room. Everyone knew about her antics, and the previously mentioned "old prick" had killed her unique creation after it sprayed acid on his hands, maiming him. Her mutagenic formula was immediately confiscated and classified as high transformation magic. Even Ina didn't have clearance for access to it after that.

"Did you create a monster recently?" Arun wouldn't give up the subject.

She looked at the battlemage. What the hell he was digging for now?

"No, I did not!" That was a simple answer. She saw relief on many faces and anger on others. What the hell had they expected her to say?

"Did you use any of your 'special' potions on humans?"

Ahh…there we go. Finally, they approached the subject.

"I use my graduation potion on myself. I needed to speed my regeneration."

"Did it work?" That caught Arun's interest. Regeneration of physical and magical strength was essential for the battlemage. Arun was always willing to catch any potential benefits.

"Yes, it did," she said, not without satisfaction.

"Inanuan healed Captain Marcach from catastrophic injuries," interrupted Jorge.

She had forgotten his quiet presence behind her, and now he stabbed her in the back.

"She performed the sacrifice spell and somehow managed to balance mortal injuries with her own vital force and magic until the exchange was completed." His detailed description of her deeds made Ina curse under her breath.

"You fucking treacherous ass, you gave me your word," she whispered.

Jorge only smiled sarcastically. "I promised not to talk about Ren, and I didn't," he answered, and Ina rolled her eyes. He followed their agreement to the letter but not in its spirit.

"Inanuan Zoria Thornsen! What on earth were you thinking, binding yourself to a stranger?"

On instinct, Ina jumped behind Jorge, hiding behind his back. The Council had brought the legend, the berserker of all battles, and the only reason Ina didn't disappear ten years ago. Her great-aunt Nerissa was here, the chief healer of Cornovii, and she was pissed. Still, the Truthseeker held Ina in a tight grip, and she was compelled to answer.

"I didn't think about much. Mar looked delicious. I was lonely, and this morsel of a man with soft fur on his chest was calling to my senses. I wanted to see him in my bed and maybe help me with my exile. Still, he had to be alive to do both," Ina blurted her answer, causing widespread snickering. The barrier fell, and she felt released from the Truthseeker's grip, so it looked like they heard what they wanted to hear.

Ina's embarrassment was so palpable she didn't even flinch when her great-aunt locked her arm in her vice-like grip.

"Move, girl. I have to examine you. Bloody hell, what got into you to perform the sacrifice? I didn't raise a stupid woman," she said and, with a non-negotiable hold, led Ina out of the chamber.

The meeting with the chancellor went about as well as Mar expected. The old aristocrat always made him feel like a fledgling in the training pit, ungainly and not half as clever as he thought he was. It didn't help when Mar told him he'd lost five men to some unknown monster, and not only did they not kill it, but that it was still loose in the forest did not go down well.

The only glimmer in the dark disappointment radiating off the king's advisor was his mention of Ina, which had surprised them both.

"Well, Sophia will be pleased to see her old friend alive," he said, cutting Mar short.

Mar hadn't known the chancellor was familiar with Ina. Still, mentioning the suspiciously early arrival of the mage that freed her captured his interest instantly.

"Who sent them? And why Jorge? He rarely sticks his nose out of his office, constantly digging in his charts," asked the chancellor, opening a new pit of speculation.

Mar felt like a fool, admitting he hadn't even asked. That damn woman lowered his intelligence below his belt and seemed to have everyone interested in her. His cheek still felt the awkward kiss that carried the words of warning. He was going to have to find out just why this was happening. He needed to have her followed, and Gods be damned, he knew the only person he could give this task to was Ren. The worried looks the chancellor gave him as the meeting ended must have been about the threat and not the thunderous look on Mar's face, even if it felt like he threw him out of the room with muttered promises of more men and equipment.

The walk outside was a blur as plans were formulated, then tossed aside until a workable outline solidified in his thoughts.

After he almost tripped over a rock, Mar focused on his surroundings. He'd unknowingly wandered out to the practice yard. That glance had also revealed the three men he needed to see. Unfortunately for them, they were sitting on their lazy arses. Ina's warning was like a fresh wound in his heart. Each one was there. Each was skilled enough to do it. He was a soldier, and now the most trustworthy person he had around was the bloody witch. Mar felt something clawing its way inside him, and cold anger flashed in his eyes.

"I turn my back for one moment, and you lazy, sow-fucking boneheads forget that you're supposed to be soldiers. Senad, get the company practising shield work. I don't want a repeat of that debacle in the forest. Ren, I've got the perfect job for you. The Ghost gets to follow that blessed thorn in my side and find out why she's neck-deep in this mess. Oh, and before you smile, there's to be no contact unless she's in mortal danger."

His hand dropped to his side as he turned towards Daro, a vicious grin growing with dark intent. "You know what that means, Daro? You get to work on not getting that thick skull split when you're supposed to be in battle formation."

He leapt forth, drawing his dagger and ramming into Daro's midriff, shoulder first. It was like hitting a stone wall. Still, Mar slammed his opponent into the yard's dirt with a twist to the side and a firm grip on Daro's thigh. Tapping him on the forehead with the dagger's hilt, claiming victory in his underhanded trick, Mar rolled to the side and stood dagger blade forwards with a smug look.

"Too many skirts slowing you down, I see. Maybe we should geld you to get you back to soldiering before someone sticks a dagger in your arse, hmm?"

Never one to let anyone threaten his manhood, Daro was up much quicker than his size would suggest. Sweeping his hand through the dust and gravel, he launched it at Mar's face, closing his spade-like paw into a haymaker of a punch, clipping his foe's chin despite a deft move to block.

The sheer force of the punch launched Mar backwards, forcing him to retreat hastily. *Fuck, it always surprises me how quick that damn orc is. Maybe he was the one?* Errant thoughts rushed through his mind.

Daro laughed as his captain staggered back. "Seems to me you left your edge between that witch's thighs. Maybe I should give her a go if she brings the mighty Lord of Liath to his knees. Widowmaker, my sweaty nutsack. Did she fry your brain in this hovel?"

The fury on Mar's face made Daro's eyes widen in bewilderment, obviously wondering what he'd done wrong. During sparring, they constantly bantered, goading one another to put in more effort, and Mar never lost his temper with his men.

Mar saw the orc throwing up his hands, palms forward and scrambling back. Time slowed down as his subordinate tried desperately to yield, but Mar felt he looked into the maw of madness and abhorrent thoughts flashed through his mind.

One of those fuckers wanted to kill him, and now they were mocking the very person who had saved his life. Mar charged like a possessed dervish of fists and kicks.

Daro's teeth rattled as a kick smashed into his chin. Ribs groaned as fists pummelled them. Stars exploded as his nose met a solid forehead. He just couldn't seem to stop a single hit.

Daro's words had ignited something deep within the captain's chest. There was an overwhelming roaring rage, and he launched himself at this snivelling idiot. He knew Daro liked to poach his lovers. He hadn't cared before, not until now. Suddenly, he had only one thought in his mind. No one—not Daro, Ren, or even the Gods themselves—would ever lay a hand on this one. Kicking and punching, Mar attacked, over and over, his dagger lost on the floor as anger burned his sense away. Destroy, rip, and tear. That was all that mattered.

The practice yard was still except for the captain and Daro, slack-jawed men staring in shock at their stoic commander's frenzied attack. Senad and Ren looked at each other in dismay. Seemingly of one mind, they burst into action and sped towards Marcach. The two men smashed into him and tore him away from his adversary, grabbing at his arms and legs and shouting out to the soldiers to help hold him down, all to no avail. Senad couldn't keep hold of his commander, and it was clear to all that nothing would stop this rampage if he let go. The look he shared with Ren seemed to hold a thousand words. Ghost nodded, agreeing that it had to be done. He grabbed a rock from the ground, bringing it down hard on Marcach's head. The measured force knocked him clean out.

Daro was lying on the ground and looking at the evening sky, streaks of blood flowing from his nose to the dirt. He raised his head with a pained grunt, looking at the now limp commander as if he saw him for the first time. His eyes shifted to the companions questioningly, and finally, with sheer disbelief, he spat. "What the fuck just happened?"

CHAPTER 6

The soft knock at the door made Sophia raise her eyes from the stack of papers.

"Yes?" she asked, frowning when she noticed that night had already fallen outside.

"It is time for supper, my lady," said the voice on the other side, making the princess sigh. Another evening with her drunkard father and stupid brother felt unbearable, but she would hear no end to this if she abstained. After all, sad spinsters should be grateful to dine at the master's table.

"Tell them I have a headache, or better say it is this time of the month." The thought of her father's face when he heard about her female ailments during the meal made her laugh. He had half of the court in his bed and yet a mention about monthly time would turn him green in the face.

She turned her attention back to the grain trade and Liath. The damned duke of Liath again asked for supplies. Kobolds are on the rampage again, same old story. One would think Alleron, the current master of the House of Liath, could fix this ongoing problem. Or maybe they should send back his son? After all, he was a damn hero who beat them once. She has no use for him, and he even dared to refuse when she invited him for the night not long after his arrival.

Sophia didn't know why she thought about his words, but she still felt the shame of his pity. "I will never take advantage of a woman in difficult circumstances," he said, making her feel like she was begging for a favour. She looked at the provision letter and pushed the edge into the candle flame. Should Liath ask once more, it will be time to send back their hero.

Another knock on the door was met with a flying inkstone that barely missed chancellor's head.

"What irked you today, my dear?" he asked, sitting down.

Sophia smiled benignly, and this simple gesture transformed her face into breathtaking beauty.

"It's just the time of the month. What brings you here, my friend?" she said, offering the simplest of explanations.

The chancellor shifted on the chair, and she had the impression he was growing unsettled before he finally said, "Inanuan is back."

Sophia felt he was observing her reactions. She stood up and walked around with studied ease, placing a hand on his shoulder.

"Maybe it's for the best. The House of Thorn has pestered us about it for long enough. And you know Nerissa, she is worse than a wolverine. Just make sure Ina doesn't cause any trouble, please."

The chancellor nodded, visibly at ease, and with Sophia's gentle guidance, he left the room. She knew he expected a more dramatic reaction after her and Ina's rough past. Still, the past was best to be left to rot, and she'd decided long ago to focus on the future.

After the sickening journey, Jorge was glad his house was close to the university. He arrived at dinnertime, but his stomach still remembered decorating the city guard's boots. The mage locked himself in his workshop and sighed with pleasure, nestling in his comfortable chair. He felt too old for such adventures, but that had been a request he could not refuse, and now he didn't regret it.

The so-called search party gave him a perfect opportunity to travel to the Black Forest. Still, he returned with more questions than answers. Jorge looked at the diagrams and calculations on his table. His hand moved to the hidden diamond necklace, and he drew forth the energy necessary to cast the spell. Diagrams lit up with one smooth gesture, creating a shimmering board in the air. The lives of those involved shone brightly as variables of the equation. Circumstances, events, and the political situation created the lines that connected them all, and Jorge moved lines and dots as the situation changed. His magic worked up a new connection, highlighting the events and the foreseeable future. That was his talent, pure Order. The highest, most refined enchantment to harness magical energy allowed him to decipher, predict, and alter reality's patterns. The heavy sigh that accompanied the creation of the fiery red dot foreshadowed trouble.

Jorge hesitated about where to put it. So far, Ina seemed to skim the periphery of the web he created with only a few connections to the university and noble houses, so Jorge started just there. The crimson spark lingered only for a moment, but soon Jorge felt the tug of his magic, and connections sprang up, covering almost the whole diagram. It was pure Chaos obliterating any sense or reason, preventing him from seeing even the near future.

Ina surprised him. A pure Chaos mage hadn't been born in generations. Everyone thought of them as crazed idiots, ridiculed in a magical world that tried to eradicate them from the bloodlines of all noble families. And yet here she was, a prodigy, clever and quick with, most important, a strong moral compass. A pity she couldn't control that temper or her viper's tongue.

He thought about the injured soldier and his lips tightened. He would have just let him die. Everybody would, except that silly girl.

Jorge approached the diagram and traced his finger along the line connecting Ina to Ren. It vibrated faintly under his finger. The connection was there but didn't look too strong. Out of curiosity, he touched the line that connected her with Mar, and it coiled, sizzling and protecting the red spark from his touch. Jorge burst out laughing. *Poor boy, he won't know what hit him. Those two are like wind and fire, and it will be interesting to observe where it will lead them.* He playfully traced his finger to the red spark, intending to touch it, and the laugh died on his lips when Mar's variable burst with searing gold, blinding him for a moment.

Jorge ended the spell and let the new diagram settle on the paper. His face was grim when he sat at his desk and wrote a brief message to his patron.

Your request is delivered, but you gambled on things you can't fully comprehend. She has already awakened the ancestry of Liath. Beware, as even I can't see the future events.

Ina was spent after Nerissa subjected her to countless tests and examinations, scolding her mercilessly throughout. Her great-aunt was displeased by Ina's actions, especially those that could have such dire consequences. She saw a fair share of the madness that came with such desperate measures as a healer.

Of course, she was right, but Ina would never admit it, not to the old healer's face. Yes, she should not perform the sacrifice spell with a stranger, but she wouldn't let him die if she could help it. To surrender the battle that hadn't even started was not in Ina's nature. She had chosen the lesser evil or something like that. However, after hours alone with her relative, she wasn't sure what was right anymore. She just wanted it to end.

The exit out of the building was a relief. Ina had made it out alive, physically unbroken, and her cat basket was still there. Boruta was having a tantrum, hissing and spitting at two young witches trying to be friendly. Ina stood behind them, and, seeing their efforts, had to admit they were persistent, but they didn't know her cat. Once he realised his escape and, undoubtedly, murderous plans would fail, this little devil raised his tail and started spraying. Pungent liquid marked the basket, the clothes of his admirers, and would even have reached Ina if she hadn't moved away to safety. Yes, she knew this beast very well. After all, it wasn't the first time he had expressed his disdain for humanity. The curious witches bolted to the sides, squealing like piglets, trying to get rid of the smelliest parts of their outfits. Ina snorted and reached for the reason for all this commotion. It was time to make a move anyway.

A quick sniff of the air around the basket brought to mind her aunt's little gift.

"You look like a beggar," Nerissa said, never one to be gentle with her words. After a litany of Ina's shortcomings, she handed her a heavy purse ordering, "Dress yourself suitably as a highborn lady of our household."

Ina wasn't precisely a lady of the House of Thorn. Her mother was the Lady of Thorn and had married for love far below her status. Ina remembered her as a constantly smiling, cheerful woman who could fix any problem with her cakes and would laugh playfully at her daughter's antics. They lived in the south till her father's death. He was a Nature Mage, not powerful and not the smartest but with enough skills to help farmers in their fields.

He loved her mother dearly, and when the wet, cold summer brought a plague, he used precisely the same method as Ina to help the love of his life. His love healed her mother, but his strength failed him, and he succumbed to the deadly disease. Her mother moved to the capital's outskirts, but she wasn't herself after that, forever connected to the dead spouse. Her noble family took care of them to avoid further embarrassment, as was the custom. Her mother passed away while Ina was in exile. Nerissa informed her that Nessa had lost the will to live after what happened to her father. One day she simply didn't wake up, and the maid found her already dead with a smile on her face.

Deep in her thoughts, Ina didn't notice the person in front of her, and she rammed into the poor victim, crushing her smelly basket between them.

"Ina! It is you! Ina!" Only one person could have been so loud. Before Ina had even registered what was happening, an unstoppable force met an immovable object. Velka grabbed Ina with all her might, locking her in a tight embrace. A northern woman, tall and blonde Valkyrie, the epitome of mother earth, with a braid of thick, luxurious hair, was now pressing Ina to her generous bosom with a strength you would not expect from a human woman. Before Ina could even acknowledge the encounter, she was dragged through the door to a carriage, her feet barely touching the ground.

"You must stay with me!" Velka hadn't changed at all. She'd always had a soft spot for Ina and other misfits. However, despite her barrel organ inability to stop talking even for a moment, she was still Ina's best friend. "Did Morane drag you from the bog? You smell, girl, and your clothes…ugh. We will go shopping tomorrow. We need to find you the perfect dress and burn those rags you're wearing."

"But Velka," Ina unsuccessfully tried to interrupt. Nothing makes you feel more loved than a friend throwing in your face that you are a cat piss-stinking, dirty rat of a woman.

"No, no, no…no discusiones. You are tired. I can see it. You need a hot bath and a cup of mead, and then you will tell me everything, and I mean everything." Velka didn't stop chattering. Then she suddenly looked at Ina, and her voice grew quiet. "They didn't even let me see you. None of us could visit you. It was as if they were trying to make sure everyone would forget you."

"At the time, it felt like everyone did." A burden Ina didn't know she was carrying lifted from her shoulders. More things made sense now. The isolation and the complete lack of contact from family and friends. They hadn't erased her from their lives.

They just couldn't get to her. Tears shone in her eyes. "I'm sure if not for Nerissa, I would have just disappeared, bless the old hag." She shook her head, laughing through the tears. She could start anew, and she was on the way home.

It was a brief ride, and soon Ina stood in front of Velka's townhouse, a prominent villa located between the merchant square and the noble part of the city. The witch wished she could unsee this view. This home was like a virgin bride's dream. The white façade with filigree decoration and an abundance of flowers would haunt Ina's nightmares. She was sure of it. Her hostess opened the door with an inviting gesture.

"Come, come in and get some rest. What do you think about my home?" The Nature Mage was visibly proud of her less than humble abode.

"It is…unique…" said Ina, knowing what she said was true, even if it was far from a complete answer.

Velka beamed and led her to a pleasant interior.

"Can I let Boruta out? You don't have a chicken coop or something?" Not that she expected this in a townhouse, but anything was possible with a Nature Mage. When Velka nodded, Ina removed the mesh from the basket. Boruta darted out without even a glance back. Ina looked at him with a deep scowl, hoping he wouldn't leave a nasty surprise somewhere. She made a note to herself to not leave her shoes on the floor tonight.

Sitting down on a comfortable chair, Ina breathed a sigh of relief. Velka lived a comfortable life. However, there was no hint of a male presence in this house, which was unexpected, as her friend was such a romantic soul. Her hostess came back with a cup of aromatic herbal brew and settled down, facing her friend.

"Come on, talk. What happened to you? We have a little time while the servants prepare your room and a bath."

Ina chuckled. "You know I just spent several hours of interrogation from the council and her maliciousness, Lady Nerissa."

Her friend waved her hand dismissively. "And? You don't have to care about making a good impression this time. Now, speak. The last I saw, you were storming the throne room during a foreign audience, screaming about limp dicks at the top of your lungs. Bards still sing about this story. Of course, not in esteemed establishments," Velka said with a snicker.

Ina rolled her eyes and started her story. "You know I wasn't happy in the court position. If Nerissa hadn't pulled some strings, I wouldn't be there. They kept calling me a protégé as if I had a choice in this matter. My most important task was to cure his royal arsehole's hangover and help with his manly 'duties.' He was chasing every skirt in the palace and even a few breeches as well, but who will say no to the king? Often, he appeared in the morning hissing like a viper's nest because he couldn't stand up to the challenge or because his hangover made the scampering of the mice too loud." It was a long story with a strong pathetic streak, but Ina was determined to continue.

"Some dimwit told him, or maybe it was a rumour he overheard, that using the twizzles of animals with strong magical potential could make you perform like a steppe orc. So, guess what he wanted me to do? During one drunken night, he told me that my kinship with creatures and potion-making skills were the only reasons I was still there. I had to remind him I'm of House Thorn as well as a mage, and initially, everything calmed down.

When he asked me to organise a hunting trip, I was happy to do so. I thought he understood. I should have known better, but I thought this would keep his mind off some mad idea or another slutty arse. Especially as it was supposed to entertain a foreign delegation. Silly me with images of grandeur and my political importance. I thought I'd finally achieved some respect."

Ina took a long sip of herbal tea and stared at her hands. "That day, the priestess of Swarożyc, shaking from rage and fear, came to plead with me, thinking I was behind the hunt for the sacred boar." She looked at Velka, still feeling the shame that came upon her with the realisation of how easily she'd been tricked. "Liander told me the king wanted to use me as bait. I shouldn't listen to this prick, but I did, and when he mocked me that day... everything was just wrong...and I snapped."

She took another pause before resuming the story. "As soon as I walked past the palace gates, a spell hit me and I blacked out. When I woke up, I was tied to the chair in the Council's basement. It was supposed to be a hearing, but I panicked and... well...I wrecked the room, not to mention injured half a dozen battlemages. The next time I woke was in the carriage with the rune of confinement branded on my chest and a note saying I was sentenced to the guardianship of the Black Forest." Ina smiled sadly. "I tried to leave, and I tried to remove the damn rune. I even waited for rescue, even an attempt of one. I finally gave up one day, and if not for Leshy, it would have been the end of me. As for coming back, I would likely still be there if not for Mar and his hairy bloody arse."

Velka, who was sitting there looking at Ina with sadness and compassion, shuffled to the edge of the chair. She was like a pike, sensing blood when it came to Ina's love life, and Ina saw her curiosity was now in full force once her friend mentioned a man's name.

"Mar?" she enquired, smiling cheekily at Ina. "With a hairy arse? How do you know it was hairy?"

"Because he was half-dead and very naked." Ina laughed. "Stop imagining too much. I'm not his type."

"And yet he brought you here," said Velka with a playful wink.

"No, it was stick-up-his-arse Jorge, and as soon as I arrived, they brought me to the same chamber for an interrogation. Can you believe they kept accusing me of making monsters in my crappy hut?"

Velka's sombre face made Ina roll her eyes. "Really? You think I could do it, all because of one incident with an acid-spitting transformation?"

"I know you *could*, I just don't believe that you *would*," answered her friend before a servant in the background caught her eye. "We have had a few incidents here, and everyone is a little on edge, but that is something for later. Now, up you go, your room is ready, and you need to rest. Tomorrow we will go shopping."

Ina was going to protest, but she needed a good wash, preferably not interrupted by drowning. The opportunity to go to town meant she could ask around about a workshop. Besides, going out with Velka sounded like fun. She only needed to be careful not to let her friend pick out her clothes.

CHAPTER 7

The early autumn morning was beautiful, and Ina woke up in a cheerful mood that only got better as the day progressed. She had to admit she needed this. Velka had dragged her to most of the shops in the Merchant District. Ina bought the few things she needed and, contrary to her common sense, a costly dress. Not that she ever had a hope of wearing it, but she couldn't resist. It just spoke to her. In the past ten years, fashion had changed so much, and refined elegance now replaced the earlier frilly and cumbersome skirts. Her dress was made of spider silk, a rich iridescent chestnut bronze with reddish hues, and trimmed with gold embroidery. The cut under the breast enhanced her bosom, simultaneously wrapping itself nicely around Ina's slim waist and generous hips. She was worried that the dress would be too tight, but the fabric was delicate, flowing, and adapted to her frame like a second skin. A translucent golden mesh covered the cleavage and sleeves, and looking at the mirror, Ina felt beautiful. Maybe that was the reason she had paid the hefty price. *I'm going to have it even if I wear it alone in front of the mirror,* she thought.

Ina agreed when Velka decided they would spend the rest of the day strolling around the main square. Many of the old shops were still there, like Philanderus's antiques shop, where Ina loved to pop in to find some new old things or "the artefacts for every purse," which stood there for generations. The witch felt like a little girl excited about the view, and they gossiped about all the changes.

Ina wanted to visit her old haunt, The Drunken Wizard. It was an old tavern on the edge of the merchants' quarter. Close enough to the university to be plagued by pilgrimages of thirsty students and sufficient distance from noble quarters and authorities to be a safe place for many disreputable individuals. It was a place of many fond memories for her.

When they crossed the market square, both women were drawn to a commotion. A sizeable crowd had gathered, and they initially couldn't see what had attracted the fickle mob's attention. Ina was about to move away when a distressed neigh pinned her in place. She grabbed Velka's hand and dived into the crowd. It needed a bit of foot-stomping and elbow work, but she forced her way to the first row by pushing Velka in front of her like a battering ram.

There, some childish idiot was whipping a beautiful grey stallion. Bloody foam marked the animal's sides when it tried to flinch from its tormentor but hit after hit rained down on its back. Ina stepped forwards and grabbed the young man's hand without a second thought. A round, red, sweaty face turned in her direction. She saw streaks of dirt on his clothes and face. It looked like the horse decided not to serve him any longer and sent him tumbling to the ground.

The young fool barked out, "Get lost, wench! This is none of your concern."

Ina only raised her eyebrow and firmly stood in front of the horse. "You should not mistreat your animal, sir. I think it has had enough of a beating today." She tried to reason with him, not because of the goodness of her heart, but rather the number of witnesses here that could testify against her.

"I will do whatever I want with it," shouted the young man, spraying saliva on his coat. "It is my horse, and I haven't finished punishing him."

Ina could no longer suffer this fool, and exhaling slowly, she grabbed the horse's reins. "If you think beating the animal is the right way to proceed, then you don't deserve to have a horse." She attempted to lead the creature away, only slightly concerned this could be perceived as horse theft. Still, she had many witnesses that she was only stopping mistreatment.

"You bloody bitch, I will teach you not to shoot your mouth off!" The lad swung his crop, his strike aimed at her face.

Acting on reflex, Ina flinched, and then with one smooth move, she threw a punch at his face. Of course, she was not strong enough to knock him to the ground, but her aim was good, and he staggered, blood now running freely from a rapidly growing nose.

Ina's patience had finally ended. She looked straight into the teary eyes of her opponent. Wisps of power reverberated in her voice as she compelled him.

"I think you should apologise," she said with a smile, as the sultry timbre of her voice saturated with magic made his eyes cloud over.

"I am sorry, my lady," stated Jessop. He was still there and perfectly aware of what was going on, yet there was no will to resist the persuasion.

"Oh, not to me, young man, to the horse," she replied, beginning to enjoy toying with this imbecile and savouring a long-forgotten feeling of power.

Her puppet turned to the horse and bowed. "I apologise." His face was blank and voice wooden, despite the fear in his eyes, but Ina wasn't done with him. She pointed at horse's rump and licked her lips.

"Now seal it with a kiss."

The crowd anxiously observing the previous exchange roared in delight. They clapped and cheered while Jessop, his feet dragging in the sand, approached the horse's rump, giving it a loud, wet kiss.

The witch turned back to her chastened protagonist and added, "See? Now you two have become the best of friends, and you will never hit him again." Her magic still shimmered in her voice, and the young man nodded eagerly. Well, that was it. She had done her due diligence and helped those in need, feeling very noble and proud of her achievement Ina grabbed Velka's hand and winked. "It's time to go. I'm thirsty." The crowd parted, and they made their escape, escorted by claps and cheers.

Ina aimed for the tavern, utterly oblivious to the dark hooded silhouette following her trail and the emotional turmoil of her past travelling companions observing them from a distance.

Mar and Senad were on their way back to the barracks, both quiet and gloomy. Mar still couldn't understand what got into him to beat Daro to a pulp. He was not grateful for the painful egg on his temple that his loyal comrades had given him, but it could have been worse. Like now, when Senad's irritating silence got on his nerves. He was about to explain events yesterday when a commotion grabbed his attention.

He was grateful for the height of his horse as the crowd grew larger. The citizens of Osterad were always drawn to confrontation, like moths to the flame. Of course, like a bad coin in the centre of all this attention stood his beautiful nightmare. Hard-earned experience brought a wry smile to his lips. Things were about to get interesting. His mood lightened as Ina bickered with Jessop, and when the young man called her names, Mar stood in his stirrups for a better view. They could see a crop flying towards Ina's face, and Senad kicked his horse forwards. Mar knew Senad's honour would not allow him to stand by and watch a woman beaten by a bloody half-wit, but he grabbed his friend's bridle before he could ride forwards.

"Wait," he said, "I still remember flying through the doors of her house for a mere slip of the tongue. This woman can look after herself perfectly well. Besides, Ren will be near, so no harm will come to that delicate little flower. I don't want to bring any attention to us, and it won't harm Jessop to learn some manners as well."

It was a half-truth. Yes, Mar didn't want to draw Ina's attention or grace this hot mess with the presence of the King's Guards, and he still hoped to discover whoever was manipulating her from the shadows. On the other side of the coin, he wanted to see what she could do, and some minor, well-controlled discomfort could help with it, so despite the pull in his chest to run and rescue her, he stayed put.

He could not take his eyes off her, and now seeing her throwing a solid punch in the man's face, Mar gasped and, stifling his laugh, elbowed Senad. Pride and amusement rang in his voice when he said, "I told you she'd be fine, although I didn't expect… that."

As with many things, this woman surprised him again. Life was one hell of a ride with her around. However, Ina's following action was unsettling. The more he looked at Jessop, the more the boy looked like a puppet in its master's hand. When he affectionately kissed the horse's rump, Mar cursed under his breath. What if she'd done that to him? That would explain his erratic behaviour. He knew many mages that could influence behaviour, and every mage was taught how to set up mental barriers, but Ina did it effortlessly.

He looked at Senad, who was now openly entertained by the situation. It looked like his knightly impulses were replaced by amusement, and Mar realised his friend hadn't noticed the compulsion.

Cheers drew his attention back to Ina, whose pretty smile almost blinded him.

"Who are you, fiery lady?" shouted someone from the crowd.

"Oh, I'm just a sweet city rose." Ina mockingly placed her hand over her heart and did a slight curtsy. "Always at your service."

Mar's mood soured again as he questioned his judgement. Since he'd met her, he couldn't trust his own feelings, and he didn't like it.

The same old broken-down door to The Drunken Wizard welcomed them with a loud grating screech. She'd have thought ten years would be enough to fix the bloody thing. The only change was a new bouncer who now threw them hostile stares. "Not for ladies," he grunted when they attempted to come in, clearly mistaking them for some high society damsels looking for entertainment. "We don't want any trouble."

"No trouble here, big man. We're looking for a drink and maybe Gruff if he still works here." Ina's use of the old troll's name worked like magic. The bouncer huffed, letting them into the dark, musty interior. The establishment was, as Ina remembered, a mess of wooden tables scattered around with no rhyme or reason and a large bar on the far side. To her relief, she spotted her favourite place by the fire was still there, more or less intact. She was almost knocked off her feet by a large mutt who shot out from the kitchen door and, barking happily, jumped up, placing his front paws on her shoulders. Ina laughed and roughly stroked its tangled fur. She was happy to see the old mongrel alive. The commotion brought out the owner, who nodded to

Velka and inspected Ina for a long time. Finally, his unkempt face cracked with a broad, rugged smile.

"Look what the cat dragged in, our Striga, still alive and kicking." He covered the floor with a few long steps and locked Ina in his tight embrace. Squeezed between his arms and torso, she tried to wiggle herself to get some air, instantly regretting taking a breath. As expected, the stench was unbearable, especially in such proximity. Rock trolls were not famous for good hygiene. Now, mixed with stale beer and remnants of the last meal on his apron, it was one hell of an assault weapon.

Velka, seeing Ina's face turning a bilious green, pried her out of the troll's embrace. Gruff cackled and nodded towards the bar.

"Same as usual, my lovelies?" he asked, waving towards the honey mead barrel. Velka nodded, and soon two tankards were in front of them. "First one on the house," boomed Gruff, "but you have to tell me what happened. Did you honestly call the king a limp dick?" He cackled again, and Ina sighed with frustration. How many times would she have to repeat the story?

Still, she knew if she wanted to hear about the latest gossip, she would have to give him something in return. Gruff may not look like the sharpest tool in the shed, but behind this low forehead was an astute mind capable of seeing patterns in the Chaos.

Ina summarised her life from that ill-fated encounter in the palace to the day Mar ended up in her hut. The troll looked at her, and she could almost see the gears turning in his head.

"What were the King's Guards looking for in the Black Forest? It is not palace business to inspect this godsforsaken place where dogs barked through their assholes."

Ina shrugged. "You tell me. He was fighting some monster I'd never heard of before. I'm not saying the Black Forrest is a charming grove with fairies and fireflies, but the Leshy is smart and doesn't want any conflict with humans. There wasn't anything special there. Striga, the occasional ghoul, nibbling at a stray wanderer, the usual things, but no monsters requiring trained warriors. Not to mention one that can kick those soldiers' butts."

She must have sold her story well because Gruff scratched his large head and said, "There are rumours. People disappearing, beggars, whores, orphans, the usual kind, sometimes drunk men don't return home, nothing that didn't happen before, just more frequent and no one that would be missed. However, it just feels odd to me."

"How does this have anything to do with a monster in the forest? Is there a killer on the loose? You think the soldiers were sent to catch it?" Ina pondered on what she knew. A human attacker would explain Mar's stab wound, but the claw marks and savagery of the attack? That doesn't seem to be the correct answer.

Gruff shook his head. "There is something else. When you were exiled, they brought a new mage to the palace. Remember that pretty face you cried your eyes out over? The one that pimped you out on a blind date with an ogre for a few gold coins?"

"Liander? They brought him into service?" Ina was astounded. Her former crush was a Mind Mage and a bloody good one. He was also a greedy, two-faced son of a bitch who cared for nothing but money.

Gruff nodded. "Yup, this one. One of the court ladies tried to convince the king that she was forced to take a monster. Of course, no one believed her. She blamed the mage for coercion, but everyone assumed she got pregnant with some scoundrel and was trying to deflect the blame. They found her hanged in her room soon after."

Velka gasped, visibly disturbed as she quietly listened to the story. "That can't be! Why did no one investigate this?"

The troll's voice was full of sarcasm. "Why would they? She was not pretty enough to get to the king's bed, not sufficiently wealthy to interest the chancellor, and her family was from the borderlands. Some minor noble family that no one cares about, she was only a lady-in-waiting, practically a maid for our beautiful Sophia, one that allowed the princess to shine against a plain canvas."

"And Sophia?" Ina asked quietly. "Didn't she insist on an investigation? It was her maid, after all."

"She showed appropriate grief and sent the family condolences with what I suspect was hefty compensation, but that was about it."

Upon hearing this, Ina was disappointed but not surprised. She liked Sophia and had thought of her as her partner in crime for several mad capers and for keeping the king's libido at bay. She had just hoped for a different answer.

Velka, however, didn't look satisfied. "Surely, someone has to do something about it?" *Trust a Nature Mage to get on their white horse and charge an empty field*, thought Ina when Velka, with typical confidence, finished, "We will look into it and the other disappearances as well."

The sun set while they talked, mainly about who had died, married, and was now jumping beds. Ina learned that after her confrontation, "limp dick" was now the official nickname for the monarch. His constant abuse of wine and vitality potions had ruined his handsome face. Some even believed she had cursed the king, a convenient explanation for his ailing condition, much to Ina's bemusement. Only money and privileges could entice anyone to bed him, but the world was full of such people.

Sophia's stepbrother, the king's heir, was no better. She remembered him as a cocky twenty-year-old who wanted to prove to everyone that he was as good as his father. Ina suspected that he could have impregnated the lady-in-waiting. It certainly explained the lack of investigation. She pondered on Velka's declaration and smiled at her thoughts. She had nothing else to do, so sniffing around sounded like it could be fun. Leverage is always good in politics, and if she dug up some dirt? Well, it couldn't hurt her prospects.

A group of loud students settled at the closest table, noisily discussing different theses and experiments and cursing their teachers. As usual, working men of all races began their routine of passing drinks and getting handsy with the agile tavern wenches. It was as if she'd never left. Everything was as raucous and riotous as all those years ago. A young and reasonably handsome man flirted with her, and Ina suspected the main reason was that she and Velka were the cleanest females in the room.

Suddenly, the tavern door slammed against the wall, the screech of its hinges silencing the room. A red-haired giant of a man pushed through, followed by a disorderly group of ruffians. The crowd scattered when he headed straight to the bar, and, pushing himself between Ina and her young suitor, he slammed his massive hands on the counter.

"Gruff! Beer and plenty of it—we come with a trophy today." He placed the head of some creature that Ina had never seen in her life on the counter. This distorted face vaguely resembled a human, but it was also coated with what Ina's nose identified as sewer mud.

"Take this carcass off the counter before I shove it up where the sun doesn't shine," Ina said firmly, holding back waves of nausea.

The redheaded giant's companions murmured, instantly hostile, and he turned around to look at the intruder. He looked lower and lower until his eyes met Ina's. Pale blue irises almost disappeared when his pupils widened. He carelessly threw his head and roared. "Striga! My little kitten, where on Freya's tits have you been?" For the second time today, Ina disappeared in a broad man's arms. She cursed her friend, hearing Velka giggling hysterically.

"Put me down, you oaf, you smell! Did you crawl here through the sewers? Gods, you stink!" Ina, protesting loudly, tried to dig herself out of the fur, bushy beard, and tight embrace. Eventually, she succeeded. Forced to stand next to the laughing giant, she punched him in the stomach. "Janik, you bloody idiot. When will you learn you should wash before hugging a lady?"

Unaware of her guardian's attention, who silently slipped into the tavern, Ina was having the time of her life. Janik was more or less a friend. She knew he would deliver her head on a silver platter if someone stupid paid enough money, but he would also warn her about the upcoming hunt, giving her a fair chance to fight. They had worked a few jobs together in the past, mostly to spite her teachers. Sometimes, he hired her as a distraction or to tame a particularly stubborn beast. Ina didn't mind, especially when Nerissa cut her allowance after a little accident. He paid good money for her services, making her life more exciting and her tavern visits more frequent.

Ina looked at the unfamiliar faces around her and elbowed the mercenary. "New lot, hmm?" Her chin pointed at his troop.

Janik nodded. "Yeah, lifespan is not long in this business, Striga." He chuckled, and his low voice rumbled in his chest. "I thought you would come to join us when you were kicked out of the palace."

"I was not kicked out." Ina's chin rose, and accenting every word, she looked straight at him, saying, "I quit." That demonstration of pride made Janik laugh even louder. She'd forgotten how he liked to goad her.

Suddenly, she heard a youngster addressing Velka. "Why do they call her Striga? Does she have double teeth like the bloodsucking monster?"

Before her friend answered, Ina turned to the man and grinned. "Why? Because of my unquestionable beauty and docile character, of course."

"You'll always be my little kitten." Janik ruffled her hair in a playful gesture, provoking more cursing and a kick to the shin, then turned around and roared, "Beer for everyone, the free company is paying. Drink for a good hunt and a happy reunion."

Ina could not believe her ears. If Janik was paying for drinks, the damned world must be ending. She didn't protest too much when the lively crowd ushered them to the large table by the fire. Ina sat between Janik and some young orc who kept handing her more of the free-flowing alcohol. Velka was being entertained by a mean-looking human. She overheard their conversation about trees and what wood was best for the longbow. The whole situation felt cosy and relaxed.

Or at least it did till Janik turned his face to her and, in a quiet voice, said, "I want to hire you, Ina." She knew it was too good to be true. This northern warrior would never waste money for a joyous reunion.

She sighed and answered, "OK, what is going on? I'm not saying I won't take the job, and I'm still going to drink for free, but I will consider it."

"Listen, you know the city council hired us as glorified rat catchers for the city tunnels?" started the man.

Ina frowned, interrupting, "Yeah, well, it's not the first time something crawled out of there, so why do you need me? A few men can deal with a ghoul or even a basilisk."

It was common practice that now and then, the city council got fed up with constant complaints about missing chickens and lost drunkards and hired some desperado to crawl into sewers and exterminate whatever had bred there. "It is a smelly but not very demanding job. A fool with a stick is enough to deal with the issue most of the time."

Janik frowned. "You don't have to tell me this, but you should believe me when I tell you this time is different. They went through the normal desperate airheads with sticks before they hired us, and for a hefty price." He took a deep breath, and Ina felt he was about to say something monumental as his cheeks flushed bright red. "We are failing, Ina. I lost a lot of men, and this was the first time we caught something. Those things, whatever they are, do not want to bloody die. I want you to check it out for me. We can split the profit if you just let me know how to kill them."

Ina pointed at the smelly bundle, now forgotten next to the bar. "Chopping off the head is proving to be successful."

Janik growled with irritation. "How to kill them fast without losing too many men? I'm getting a poor reputation."

Now she understood his motives. If he lost his reputation as a free company chief, no one would hire him or work for him. It also explained the fresh faces surrounding him. She grinned, and said, "Twenty percent, and I will look into it." She knew he would pay, and she knew she would take this job even for 5 percent and free drinks, but she also had a reputation to maintain.

Janik extended his big hand to her, not even trying to haggle. "Ina, my sweet kitten, you are breaking my heart, but we have a deal."

Life, it seemed, was looking up. A few days in, she had a new job, an address to see for her workshop, a fabulous dress, and a purpose in life. She would have to talk to Mar, of course. She knew he was the first to deal with a problematic monster, but this could wait till tomorrow, or maybe even a few days after all those monsters were old news already. This night was for celebration, and as she felt young orc hands finding their way to her back, she could finally have a bit of fun.

All day today, Ren observed both women strolling through the city. There was nothing suspicious about their actions or anyone else following them. They ran from one shop to another, chatting away as many women do. If not for the fact he could look at Ina, it would be a very tedious job. Even if Mar didn't explicitly tell him to have no contact, he wouldn't dare reveal himself. Ina was a dream and, after Mar's display yesterday, a dream that had no chance of coming true. He had sworn his oath to the captain, and he was a man of his word, but now, looking at Ina touching her body in amazement in a beautiful, rich dress, he wished life could be different for him.

The antics of the idiot beating the horse put him in an uncomfortable position. He slid through the crowd to get close enough to intervene if needed, but Ina handled it remarkably well. And once in the tavern, it was easy to find a quiet corner. Everyone in the bar was engrossed in Ina's reunion with a large party of men. Happy and relaxed, she showed him a side of her personality that was endearing yet still as chaotic as every other side had been. He knew she had a sharp tongue and was prone to angry outbursts, but no one seemed to care, and the picture he had in front of him was a woman happy in her environment.

Quietly, he observed the conversation she had with the tavern owner. It looked like the troll had an extensive information network. He knew about incidents that weren't common knowledge outside of the palace. He decided to discuss the lady-in-waiting case with Mar. Maybe his captain knew something about it. The sudden opening of the door diverted his attention from Ina. The infamous Janik and his mercenaries entered the tavern. He knew the group had been recently hired to deal with an infestation in the sewers. Not that it was a job for a skilled warrior, but one has to eat, and in the time of peace, any job was a good one. Uneasiness crept over him when the mercenary leader approached Ina. Ren tensed, ready to spring to action as the warrior's arms locked around her. The only thing that stopped him in his tracks was seeing how relaxed Velka was in his presence. The exchange between Ina and the men was vulgar and borderline insulting. He usually only heard this language in the barracks. It was a sign of affection between the men that Ren never fully understood. One would have died on the spot in his homeland for such disrespectful words. He slid back into the shadow, as he was here only to make sure no one hurt his woman, not to spoil her fun.

Over the next several hours, wine, beer, and mead flowed freely. Gruff rubbed his hands, looking at the coins rolling into his pockets. Ina was good for business. She always seemed to attract attention. Now a regular patron was spending a fortune to keep her entertained. He noticed Janik's quick nod to a young orc who had plastered himself over Ina, following the unspoken command, showering her with compliments. His hands appeared to be busy finding their way to her skin, the boldness of these attempts growing with each drink the mage poured into herself.

On the other side of the table, the tall blonde was besetting a warrior. His attempts to pull away proved unsuccessful because of her sheer strength and the watchful eye of Janik. The man's boss obviously wanted those two on his side. At some point, the drunken company started roaring out vulgar rhymes. Gruff was more than happy there were no guards around when he heard.

Limp dick, limp dick,
A witch cursed your crusty wick.
Limp dick in a golden crown,
Who will save us from this noble clown?

Ina's mouth gaped open hearing this, but when Janik swung her up, she giggled like a teenager standing on the table. "Velka, they made a song about me." She wobbled, close to falling, and the firm hands of her young companion caught her and placed her on his lap. She released a throaty laugh and wrapped her hands around the orc's neck. Her fingers slowly trailed over his impressive muscles, landing on his collarbone. Her love interest not only didn't mind, but he also appeared to lose all objection, finding Janik's task more and more enticing.

Ina felt dizzy as the world swung around when she pressed her lips to her temporary partner in the attempt at a smouldering kiss. He was not Mar. Hell, he wasn't even Ren, but the young orc would do, and most important, he was not rejecting her. Fighting with the growing dizziness, she pulled her lips away and shook her head. Now she only had to aim at the right pair of lips in front of her. Determined to push past the nearly overwhelming need to sleep, she once again pressed her face to his, feeling his hands holding the back of her head.

Even as drunk as she was, Velka still noticed that Ina's head lolled onto the orc's shoulder. However, he still took liberties with her. It took her a moment to process the facts. After all, she was distracted by a handsome warrior whispering sweet nonsense in her ear. The decision to continue enjoying herself with this unexpected partner was fighting with the need to protect Ina. She was sure nothing would happen. They were in the tavern, surrounded by friends, but she still had an image of a poor lady-in-waiting in her head.

Velka felt an overwhelming need to protect the world. The power built inside her, and she suddenly felt like a heroine from the old books. The stakes were high, and she was ready to face the challenge. No woman would ever suffer unwanted attention, and Velka would ensure this. She pushed her suitor away, and with a wobbly but heroic gait, approached the couple.

"We ging ho," she declared, and the orc looked at her, puzzled. Velka tried again, bracing herself to verbalise her thoughts. She grabbed Ina's limp arm and repeated slowly, carefully pronouncing every word, "We…are…going…home." Ina sagged lower on her companion's lap, muttering something incoherently. She seemed nice and comfortable there, and it looked as if she was going to have a nap. Was Ina trying to tell her to get lost? Velka shook her friend's arm harder, refusing to listen to her drunken mumbling

Still maintaining his position in the corner, Ren sat nursing a beer he had no intention of drinking. It was increasingly difficult to hear the conversations from Ina's table, especially as he couldn't watch the antics of the woman he'd already placed on a pedestal. He wanted to be there in her arms, not some lowlife mercenary that didn't deserve her.

He had a job to do—find out Ina's involvement and keep her safe. He clenched his fists. Ren knew stopping her fun was not allowed, but damn it, this was torture.

Regardless of his feelings, the information he'd gathered would help the captain immensely, especially as it seemed the monsters were here in the city. They could potentially save lives if they discovered what was causing this.

A sudden movement from Ina's table caught his eye, and Ren looked over. Velka seemed to have finished with her paramour and was trying to talk to her friend, making him focus on them. Ina wasn't moving. What had he missed, stewing in his jealousy? Angry at himself and increasingly worried about Ina's condition, he lurched forwards, forgetting the table in front of him and knocking it and the beer flying. Oh, how Daro would laugh at the loss of his famous agility, but that didn't matter, his lady needed him.

The beer seemed aimed by the Gods, smashing on the head of some lout in the middle of his oration. Fists were suddenly flying, and Ren felt his instincts settle into their rhythm as he shouldered the man away into another table. All at once, it was a full-on bar fight. He smiled at having a chance to let off some steam. He allowed himself the pleasure of a few broken noses on his way to Ina, taking in her still-limp form and her companion's wide-eyed stare.

One final barrage of blows, ending with a satisfying punch to the orc's nose, brought Ren into position, and, without a word, he grabbed Ina's arm, flung her over his shoulder and turned. He seized Velka and sheltered her with his body as he pushed through the melee, absorbing several blows to the body to save the women from harm till the door loomed ahead. He kicked it open, forcing them all out into the night air.

Now that everything had calmed down, holding Ina in his arms should have felt like a dream, but her limp body and copious drooling caused him too much worry to celebrate her closeness.

Velka stared at their saviour with wide eyes. One moment, she was trying to get Ina home, the next, she was being dragged through a tavern brawl with tankards flying all around. Her eyes couldn't focus, giving her blurred vision and distorting everything. She could see the stranger gently shifting Ina in his arms, clearly concerned for his burden. Velka felt like a proverbial third wheel. She would like to be rescued by a handsome stranger. Why didn't he carry her out of this roaring anarchy?

She moved closer and put a hand on the man's shoulder. "Who might you be, my lord?" Velka spoke softly, anticipating the play of firm muscles under her fingertips, the danger already forgotten. The stranger didn't take his eyes off Ina for a moment. He seemed to cradle her as if his life depended on it. Velka struggled to get his attention, even when she slid her hand along his back in an enticing manner.

"I'm just a ghost. Please tell me where you live so I can get you home to rest."

Velka felt somehow offended by this complete disregard for her presence. She was spared more embarrassment by a flour cart slowly rolling along the street. A shaggy-looking horse gave her a sad stare as Ren flagged its owner and offered him money to take them home. Velka pouted, wanting to have her own hero.

Ren looked at her while placing Ina gently in the cart. "Are you hurt? Ina will need caring for in this state, and all I can offer is protection," he asked, and Velka staggered to him, placing her hands on his chest.

"Protection? I always wanted someone to protect me." When Ren took her hands away, she shrugged and sat on the cart with sad resignation. "I have servants." Then, feeling utterly pitiful, she sobbed, "No one wants to protect me."

The carter looked at them, but seeing the man just waving to move, he snapped the reins, and the shabby old horse resumed his journey. With Ren following, shrouded in his cloak and Velka's sobs next to Ina's barely breathing body, it all looked like some ridiculous mourning procession, or so thought the servants they woke up to carry their mistress to bed.

CHAPTER 8

On the other side of town, Mar's irritation grew. It was long after sunset, and Ren should be here giving him the day's report. A stray thought niggled at his mind. What if he and Ina… She seemed to like his calmness, and that twit had just pledged himself to her.

She healed them both, and deep inside, Mar sensed Ren would also feel the same connection he felt with Ina. But where Ren, despite his normally icy demeanour, idolised the witch, Mar obsessively needed her. He didn't feel himself lately. His feelings were in turmoil, and every time he thought about Ina's touch and her nearly naked figure, he felt an incredible tension in his body. His hand slid down, and only sheer power of will stopped him from relieving his longing for that delicious spitfire. There was also the thought of what Ren might now be doing to her.

His memories pushed away the visions of Ina disfigured, saving Ren from his poisoned wounds, then dragging her drowning body from the tub, and so soon afterwards, Ren's hands stroking through her long hair. Even through his scattered memories of the day, he could vividly recall the wonder and worship in his friend's eyes as the servant led Ina out of his room. Mar knew he should be happy for Ren. He knew his friend felt lonely, and although he never complained, the tune of his music carried enough longing and sorrow for Mar to recognise it. Even knowing one of the guards stabbed him, he knew it couldn't be Ren. He smiled at the thought. If Ghost wanted him dead, Mar would already be pushing up daisies. There was no deadlier person in Osterad and none more loyal. Maybe that was why it chilled him when Ren made his pledge.

If it were any other woman, Mar would help him serenade her under her window and give them the biggest wedding in the halls of Liath, but it was Ina. Her body was enthralling, but her personality drew him more than anything. She had a smile that could light the room and the sheer defiance that allowed him to cheat death. Mar chuckled at those thoughts. It looked like he was just like Ren, as his memory conveniently omitted the viper's tongue and the ability to make any man's life a pit of nightmares.

Since their arrival, he had taken his time to study the court chronicles and her family tree, and what he found increased his respect for Ina. His fiery witch could be bent but not broken, and the more he read, the less he believed she was behind the monster. The rational part of him was screaming to stop judging by his heart. Mar wanted to give in, but he couldn't. He was a captain of the guards. His duty was to find the truth, even if he was plagued with temporary madness around the bewitching woman. And now she was with Ren, so late in the night. Mar roared, unable to shake off the unwanted image, then covered his face with his hands. *I'm going crazy because of her,* he thought as someone knocked on the door, distracting him.

"Enter!" He looked at the window. Dawn was almost here. He had spent the entire night in his office, stewing in his thoughts.

Ren's tired and sombre figure appeared in the door frame. "I saw the light in your window, so I came with my report, captain."

"About bloody time." Mar pointed to the chair in front of him and tried to hide his impatience. "Speak."

Ren outlined Ina's shopping trip with Velka, the horse incident that Mar already knew about, and the tavern visit. The information Ren had gathered during the tavern visit caught Mar's attention. "So, you say that this tavern owner, Gruff, knows what is happening in the court?" That was unsettling news, but even more disturbing information came next.

"Janik seems to be very interested in Ina. He even delegated his new gallant to entertain her the whole evening. She seemed to appreciate this." Ren's voice stuttered when the pen Mar was toying with during the conversation exploded into splinters.

Ren looked at the captain. Mar knew he was waiting for him to calm down. Ren got straight to the point without talking further about Ina's amorous adventures. "Things got a little out of hand, so I took her home."

"Was there anything else?" A low growl rose in Mar's throat. He had to know what was Ina's choice even if this was going to kill him.

"I took them home," Ren said, correcting himself. "They were too drunk, and this orc took too many liberties for the situation. Ina passed out, and I just took them home."

Mar sat back and inhaled. The air seemed to be easier to breathe now. Ren didn't fail him, but the anger about the stranger touching Ina's body was still there.

"Make this orc disappear." Mar saw Ren's eyebrows rising in disbelief. "Not permanently, just out of town, and you are released from your duty tomorrow—have a rest. I'll get Daro to take over."

Ren nodded without too much of a protest. Mar knew his friend needed a bath and change of clothes, and if Ghost felt anything like him, a time to forget about how much he wanted to slice the orc's throat.

Mar's thoughts drifted in a different direction. His soul would be stained by what he was going to do, but he needed time to sort his thoughts out and, in the meantime, someone to keep an eye on Ina.

"Wake up Daro, send him to me, and close the door behind you."

Mar had the right idea, but he aimed at the wrong target. Velka was the key to Ina's past and her plans. If he wanted to know more, he had to target her friend, and Daro was the perfect choice to charm Velka.

Nerissa woke up early, the rose-tinted rays of the sun barely over the horizon as she stretched and sat up on the bed. She was worried she had driven Ina away after her outburst over her healing of those men, but she felt in her bones that danger was near and her great-niece was in the eye of this storm. Her relative was a rare talent. Chaos magic was always unpredictable and, more often than not, controlled its user instead of the other way round. Yet Ina somehow channelled it to her will. The prank involving that frog would have been just this, if not for the fact that when experimenting with a simple transmutation potion, Ina had created a potent mutagen. It changed the entire structure of a living being as well as its energy pattern. Of course, it was confiscated, and the issue swept under the carpet, but the provost of Battle magic was interested in its potential.

Nerissa had hidden from everyone that Chaos magic was the most crucial catalyst for the mutation. The initial energy settings of the subject had to be disrupted to trigger the mutagen correctly. Of course, the Council was secretly experimenting with it. Still, the final product was unstable, mangled, and short-lived without the proper catalyst. If they only knew that the "perfect solution" was right under their noses, Ina would be locked forever in the Council's basement.

Nerissa was determined to make sure her great-niece knew never to disclose her talent's potential. Bad enough that Jorge had seen what she did to this man in the inn. Thankfully, the healer that was present was convinced it was just "the sacrifice."

Still, after examining Ina, she knew her great-niece had done the impossible. She had warped one of the oldest spells, transferred the broken energy patterns into her own matrix, repaired them, and transferred them back into the patient. The exchange was balanced and hadn't touched her vital force. Still, the sheer pain of such an experience was hard to comprehend. However, it seemed Ina thought she had done nothing special, and Nerissa suspected her great-niece didn't even know her magic had warped the spell.

Nerissa had been worried about the connection such an exchange could create. The obsession, the dark desires, and the inability to live without another were the greatest dangers. Ina's mother had paid the price when that fool of a husband saved her using the spell, eventually withering away after his death. And yet her great-niece was barely touched, maybe more lustful than appropriate, but Nerissa didn't intend to hold it against her. After all, she had been no different at that age. They had avoided a catastrophe, and whatever linked her with those men should fade with time.

Nerissa knew she would have to talk to Ina, but she felt uncertain. They had never been close, not even after Ina's parents' demise. The Thornsen family cast out her mother for a morganatic marriage. Even after they were back, Ina always felt herself not fully part of the grand house. Nerissa made sure Ina received the title of Lady of Thorn. She even put her into court service, hoping the true nature of her magic would never be revealed, and Ina, at some point, would take a fancy to some noble dimwit. That way, she would be safe once and for all.

Ina had destroyed those plans with her court outburst and now almost got herself killed in this new calamity. Now was the time to stop this madness. She was saving half-dead warriors, purging toxic magic, and wielding Chaos as if it wasn't the most destructive magical force. Gods know what else this girl was going to do. Ina walked around like a beautiful catastrophe, and Nerissa knew her luck wouldn't last forever.

The weather was beautiful, yet the man in the guard's uniform appeared nervous. The autumn flowers he held in his hand had lost half of their petals, but he seemed not to notice as he stared at the door finally opening, focusing on the dark silhouette in the hallway's light.

"Have you been waiting long?" The simple question was asked in a soft, melodic voice.

"It doesn't matter. I would wait even longer. After all, it is our anniversary," he said and extended his hand with the sad-looking flowers.

"Oh yes, forgive me, I forgot about it, but I know how to make it better." The woman approached and embraced him, crushing his lips in a long, devouring kiss. She could feel him tremble under her touch, but she slid out of his grasp when he reached for more.

"Tell me about your trip," she asked, avoiding further intimacy. After all, he got his moment of tenderness. Now it was time he gave her something in return.

The man shrugged. "There is not much to talk report. We didn't get the monster, Captain Marcach is still alive, and the witch who saved him was brought with us out of the forest. You'll probably remember her. She was the court mage a long time ago."

Room shadows hid the woman's predatory smile when she spoke, "Oh, that one? Yes, I know her well—the princess's favourite friend, that's what they used to call her. So how is Nerissa's protégé now, and how did she get back to the capital?"

He reached for her again, but with an elegant twist, she avoided his hands, tutting him for evading her questions.

Finally, he sat down and said, "The only judicial mage on this side of the river able to remove the confinement rune was there. After Ina's healing of Mar, he spoke to someone on a communication crystal, and suddenly she was a free woman. I do not know how he came to be there, but in the barracks, the rumours say the chancellor sent the rescue party as soon as he learned about the expedition."

The woman bared her teeth. "Bloody fool, why does he always have to get in my way? Never mind. Have you talked to Liander?"

The man nodded. "The mutagen is unstable, and he doesn't know why, but his control is impeccable, and he's convinced he can stabilise it later."

That was the first good news she heard today, and she sat on his lap, stroking his hair. "Make sure he has everything he needs and keep the captain away from it."

The man sighed under the soft caress. "It won't be too difficult now. He's become obsessed with the witch, and nothing worries him more than her safety. Ren and Daro are running like lapdogs chasing that woman's skirt."

Her excellent mood became even better, and playfully nipping his ear, she whispered, "Make sure he has something to warrant such worry. I don't want him sniffing around, not in the city and not in the palace. Let him play a hero for as long as needed."

The man nodded with enthusiasm, trying to capture her lips, but the woman was already up and heading towards the exit.

"Happy anniversary, my love, and don't forget to tell Liander I need the results, not empty words."

Soon after she departed, he left as well, leaving the sad bouquet on the table.

CHAPTER 9

Ina welcomed the morning through narrowed eyes. The beautiful rays of the sun penetrating through a gap in the curtains were way too bright for her current mood. Birds sang softly in Velka's lush garden while Boruta had found his way to Ina's chest and was now smacking her cheek, asking for food. Slowly raising her head from the soft fluffy pillow, Ina glanced around the room.

"Will you all just shut up?" She moaned, stifling her gag reflex. This hangover was a bitch, the painful cost of such careless drinking. Her cat moved himself to the end of the bed and stared at Ina in patent accusation. Velka's servants knocked softly, and Ina wondered how long they'd stood outside the door listening for signs of life. They entered the room, carrying breakfast and a toiletry set. Their nervous stares when they looked around made her wonder what the hell happened last night. Ina sat on the bed with her head in her hands, trying to shelter her eyes from the daylight. She waved them away, and they spared no effort, leaving the room as quickly as possible. Her memories were scattered, and feeling like a tomb hag, Ina suspected she must look like one, too, especially judging from the servants' behaviour. She felt grateful they hadn't dropped her somewhere in the graveyard to feed the ghouls.

"Why do they all have to be so loud today?" She dragged herself out of bed, moaning and cursing all the way. Even pouring water into the bowl took a heroic effort. After a few initial splashes, she just gave up and dived headfirst into the liquid, but the water was too warm to soothe her headache. When the door slamming again made her wince, she thought, *Oh, just let me die.*

Thunder suddenly assaulted Ina's ears. "Inanuan Zoria Thornsen, what in the Gods' names have you been up to?"

Ina took her head out of the water and raised her bloodshot eyes to her latest torment. Nerissa was standing in the middle of the room, observing her trying to drown herself in the washing basin, and looked ready to spank her like a child. The healer's scowl deepened at seeing Ina's myopic stare.

"We need to talk. Bring me a kettle of hot water," Nerissa said, commanding a hovering maid. Ina noticed Nerissa ignored the sound of the disappearing servant as she focused on her. "I have a suspicion you were behind this brawl in The Drunken Wizard." Her aunt took a deep breath. "Why, Ina? You only just returned to Osterad, and the whole university is full of talk about Janik's free beer, and the healers complain about treating so many victims of a tavern brawl."

Ina tried to shake the fog in her brain and stuttered, "I-I don't remember. Did anyone die?"

"Not that I know of, but your arrival was noticed, and that is why I'm here."

Ina was glad that Nerissa was getting straight to the point of her visit, but she was interrupted by the servant's return. Nerissa reached into her belt purse and retrieved a small vial, pouring its contents into the kettle before pouring the concoction into a cup.

"Drink!" She passed the cup to Ina, who knew she expected her order to be followed immediately.

The witch nodded, took the drink, and started sipping the hot liquid. Pain yielded to blessed relief. Ina knew her great-aunt was one of the best healers, but she was worth her weight in gold for this. "What is it, and where can I get more of it?" Ina purred with delight. Suddenly, the beautiful morning and twittering birds became refreshing and no longer her personal torture.

Nerissa shifted on the chair and frowned. "It's not a cure for your antics. Now listen, we need to talk."

Ina nodded, ready to take her aunt's scolding if the price was this miraculous healing. Still, when her relative started from the frog story, Ina felt a chill running over her spine. Nerissa explained it all. The unexpected mutagen creation, the connection between Ina's Chaos magic and creating new types of creatures and the "healing" ability that wasn't the spell of sacrifice but was some warped version of it fused with her Chaos magic.

During this speech, Ina shifted on the chair several times. Unable to take this any longer, she stated, "I would not create a monster, and I would not twist any living being for what…

power?" She had never sought the family's acceptance, but this time she felt the primal need for Nerissa to believe her.

"I know, child." Nerissa sagged on the chair, and Ina wondered if it was because the burden she'd carried for so long was finally shared. "Many will suspect you, and some will even want to use you that way. There is more to it than your Chaos magic, but for now, please be careful. Don't show off your 'healing,' and don't let anyone know you have what it takes to change the very nature of a living being."

Ina nodded, but her thoughts were already drifting in a different direction. Someone was making monsters using her mutagen. She still didn't know how, but Mar's and Janik's experiences were too much of a coincidence. The witch didn't know who and why, but she felt responsible. Her school prank started this shitstorm.

She would have to talk to Mar but not before she found some more substantial information. Otherwise, he would think she was behind it. They had started poorly, and now she would have to convince this grumpy oaf of a man to cooperate with her. Ina rubbed her temples, feeling the headache creeping back. She needed a plan of action. It all seemed to happen so fast and felt overly complicated. She smiled at Nerissa, and she used a term of endearment for the first time. "I will sort it out, auntie, so please don't worry. I will be careful."

Nerissa appeared hesitant before giving Ina a short, powerful hug. The witch suspected they both felt uncomfortable with this display of emotion, and yet it also felt so right at the moment. "I will be on my way. Let me know if you need me, and please do not heal anyone else. Leave it to the professionals." Her great-aunt left the room, leaving Ina with rushing thoughts and the need to dress.

The door opened again before Ina clad herself, and a green-faced Velka shuffled in, collapsing on the chair. Ina nodded to herself. It must have been a hell of a night if her friend looked worse than a days-old corpse during a heatwave.

"Who was that?" rasped Velka.

Ina pointed to the kettle on the table. "Nerissa paid us a visit, and if there is anything left, then drink it. That is a bloody miracle cure. My headache is completely gone."

Velka guzzled the remaining potion, and Ina swore she even licked it clean. Finally, her friend stopped and sighed. "Well, tell your aunt to visit us more often, especially when she comes with such gifts." Velka started piling food on her plate. "I have to go to the palace today. Sophia's flowers are wilting, and the chief gardener is close to panic. Will you join me?"

Ina shook her head. "No, I arranged a…house viewing with some…dwarves? Velka, how did we get home?"

To her embarrassment, she couldn't recall the latter half of the evening, but Velka only laughed. "Well, you got cosy with an orc, then there was this big brawl, and finally, a handsome saviour carried you away from the carnage."

Ina's heart beat faster when, pretending to be casual, she asked. "A tall man, ashen blond hair, and short beard?"

Velka's eyebrows knitted together, and then she shrugged. "I don't remember, and he was wearing a hood, but he didn't have a beard."

Ina's high hopes nosedived to the ground, so it wasn't Mar. For a moment, she thought maybe he was her knight in shining armour, which would make their next encounter a bit more pleasant. A bitter thought appeared in her head, *Silly girl, swooning over a man at your age.*

So instead, she addressed her friend. "I need to get dressed and see this house and workshop. I can't clutter up your home forever."

Velka nodded. "I will go, then. I have to go to the palace. The messages they sent are more and more ridiculous. You would think the palace plants were riddled with rot." She twisted her mouth in disdain, but Ina knew there was nothing her friend took more seriously than her leaves and petals.

Ina needed a walk to clear her thoughts and start searching for answers, and having a place to live felt like an excellent place to start. She could meet with Mar later to see what he knew about this mess.

The witch strolled through the morning crowd, savouring the old familiar experience. The bustling people rushing to handle their business buffeted Ina. However, she didn't mind as her meeting was still an hour away, so she wandered past stalls that offered a glimpse of all the items essential to city life. Spicy herbs tickled her nostrils, making her belly rumble. Ina bought a stuffed vegetable bun, still hot from the oven, and sighed with pleasure when the first bite melted in her mouth.

Workshop silhouettes loomed at the end of the street when Ina approached the artisans' quarter. Most of the people living and working here were skilled manufacturers of their chosen goods. Here you could find artefact masters, alchemists, even conjurers or simply mages for hire, ready to cast a spell on your purse to prevent its loss. They were also people who knew how to keep to themselves. And Ina cherished this the most. The golden rule of hear no evil, see no evil was strong in this part of town.

Finally, Ina stood in front of a double-story building with a decent townhouse yard. It looked slightly run-down, so she hoped for a reasonable price. Ina decided to worry about cleaning and other trivialities of life later. The dwarven delegation arrived promptly, and as per tradition, both sides haggled to get the best deal for themselves. Still, in the end, Ina paid much less than she expected. She took a stroll around her house, feeling a strange pride and sense of belonging. Yes, the house was shabby, but she could see hints of its old glory, and she had enough money to restore it to a good condition.

Velka guided her horse through the busy streets, her thoughts circling around the events in the palace. Plants were dying for no apparent reason. She had worked with the royal gardener for most of the day, trying to revive some of the most precious vegetation. She hummed happily, pleased with the small successes they'd achieved. She wanted to share it with Ina, and she directed her horse to the market square, remembering her friend was about to buy a house. Ina's new home was easy to find. She just followed the sound of singing and minor curses to a simple townhouse with a pleasing external decor.

Just behind Ina's gates, under a chestnut tree, was the most beautiful man Velka had seen in her life. His walnut-coloured skin and sharp facial features, together with a mane of thick raven hair, distracted her from seeing small fangs marking his lower lip.

His broad chest rose slowly with slow, steady breathing. Velka dismounted and was about to touch his face when Ina spotted her through the open doors. Her friend came to greet her, seemingly as surprised seeing this unexpected addition as she was.

Nature Mages were gentle souls, and Velka intended a tender stroke to the stranger's face to wake him up, but before she even reached out her hand, Ina swung her leg, giving him a swift kick in the side.

"That will wake him up."

Velka gasped at the deep brown of his eyes. However, her appreciation was interrupted by Ina's, "Oi, what are you doing here?"

She noticed Ina scowling as she looked down at him, and Velka worried it was a little suspicious that a man too pretty for his own good had fallen from the proverbial sky to land next to her friend's new home, especially when she remembered Ina was such a magnet for trouble.

Daro followed Ina at a reasonably close distance, still irked by Mar's early wake-up call, and not in the mood to be traipsing after a woman. He felt like he didn't understand his captain anymore. First, he had beaten him to a pulp for some mild teasing, and now he had to guard this one like some overgrown mutt, not to mention the ridiculous request to show attention to her friend.

First thing this morning, Daro observed the friend's townhouse. He observed Velka leaving and admired the majestic woman as she departed. She looked as strong as the steppe orc women, yet soft and cuddly, like she'd be the perfect woman to stay in his bed. He smiled at his thoughts. Seducing her would not be entirely unpleasant, but how he could seduce her when his job was guarding the witch? Of course, the flame-haired trouble walked off in the opposite direction, and now she buried herself in this ruin of a house. To his amusement, Ina was now dancing with a brush, sneezing, and singing ribald sea shanties. Daro found a spot where he could observe her cleaning her new home and settled in for a long wait. The sun was shining brightly, radiating the last warmth of autumn, and, still tired from his early morning, the aching orc fell asleep at his post.

He was comfortable in his slow-flowing dreams when a sudden kick in the ribs brought him back to consciousness. The orc opened his eyes and noticed two female faces now bending over him, one curious, the other somewhat annoyed. It took him a moment to recall what he was doing there and when it finally happened, and with an effort, he stifled his swearing. Mar was going to kill him for this. He wasn't supposed to reveal himself to the witch, and now both of them were looking at him like some stray cat they had just found on the street.

He tried to put the most friendly and alluring smile on his face when he pulled himself up and spoke in a courtly manner, "I'm truly sorry, my ladies. It was a long day, and the shade of this tree was so appealing."

The blonde seemed to melt under his smile. The redhead, however, looked at him as if he just spewed utter nonsense and, with little fuss, she said, "Right, do I look like a stupid tavern wench to you?"

He noticed Ina was preparing to kick him again when Velka pulled her by the elbow. "Ina, please don't. Maybe he is telling the truth."

"Or maybe you are just blinded by a pretty smile," retorted Ina. She appeared to be irritated for no apparent reason. Still, Daro was glad for the lack of recognition in her eyes. She turned to Velka and said, "Whatever, he is a good slab of tight muscles, and I have many heavy things to carry out of the house."

"Ina!" Velka appeared shocked by such a rude statement, but Daro heard enough from the captain to expect this.

"Move. If you have to be here for whatever reason, you will help us." Ina pointed to the house, and Daro could not believe his ears. She wanted to harness him to work like some bloody mule. Normally he would just walk away, but Mar had given him strict orders, and he'd already botched half of his mission. He stood up, observing with pleasure the tall woman's reaction. She might say nothing, but her dilated pupils and dreamy smile revealed she appreciated what she saw. He inhaled deeply because, for some reason, this blonde Valkyrie smelled like roses.

"How may I be of service?" he continued with his "misunderstood knight" pretence, making Ina roll her eyes.

Daro couldn't help but smile when Velka's cheeks blushed a pretty pink, and she introduced herself. "I'm Velka, a Nature Mage, and who might you be?" The orc purred with pleasure.

"I'm Daro," he said, bending and kissing the woman's fingertips. His hand felt the delicate tremble of hers, and he almost chuckled. Seducing a pretty and receptive woman would be an enjoyable task.

Once inside, Velka pointed to a large wooden table. "Could you help me take it outside?"

Ina was furiously sweeping the stubborn dust, and Daro focused all his charm on the delectable mage.

"Of course, it would be my pleasure." He removed his shirt slowly, and flexing his muscles, he grasped it. It soon became apparent carrying the table would be more challenging than he'd first thought. Yet it was too late to stop and ask for help under the beauty's watchful and adoring gaze. He tightened his lips, feeling his back creak under strain, but still determined to be impressive, Daro carried the wooden monstrosity to the yard. As soon as he put it down, a small axe flew through the open door and lodged itself in the wood.

"Now chop it up!" Ina's voice carried from the open doors, and Daro flinched. This damn witch almost cost him his fingers.

The orc took a deep breath to restrain his anger and turned to Velka. "Your friend is a bit…unconventional." His voice lost its courtly manner, but Velka didn't seem to notice.

"Who? Ina? She is always like this." The mage smiled and sat on a wobbly chair she'd carried out of the house. Daro felt accomplished when, while admiring the play of his muscles as he chopped up the table, she told the story of their youth, university times, the pranks they did together, and the frog that Ina had enhanced, giving the Council a mental breakdown. He found out that Velka liked to talk, and he loved to listen. Now he didn't mind all this labour. Thanks to his blunder, his report to Mar would be much better than Ghost's had been.

When Ina emerged from the house, the orc had chopped the wooden table into kindling and was now sitting with Velka under the tree. Her friend was definitely smitten by the handsome orc. Ina sighed at the sight. Velka always was an incurable romantic. Now, basking in the attention, she even made the chestnut tree blossom in the middle of autumn.

Suddenly, she recalled where she had seen this man's face. He was in Mar's group. She remembered catching sight of him on the way to Osterad. So, Mar spied on her. This thought was as exciting as it was annoying, and Ina wasn't sure what to think about it. She resolved to shrug it off for the moment as she had enough issues to deal with without worrying about the nosy captain and his goons. The first thing on her list was buying furniture for her now-clean house. Ina approached the couple.

"Velka, if you don't mind, I will take advantage of your hospitality for a few more days, but I will move here as soon as I have a bed to sleep on. Now, can we go home before you force all the plants to blossom after their season?"

Velka followed Ina's stare, and seeing the beautiful chestnut tree in full bloom, she bit her lip and smiled at the handsome male. "I bid you goodbye, kind sir, and thank you on my friend's behalf."

Daro raised himself from the comfy seat and shook his head. "I will escort you home, ladies."

Ina cursed under her breath, feeling like someone had thrown her in the middle of a love-struck ballad. Still, Daro had already offered Velka his arm, and now all she could do was drag behind them like a sad spinster. It was one more thing to talk about with Mar. Whatever this orc was planning, she couldn't let him hurt Velka.

126

Mar frowned at the most recent reports, pushed them over to Senad, and sighed. "There were more abnormal creatures spotted in the sewers, this time by some merchants." He pointed at one pile, then moved his finger over to the other. "There are more missing people in the capital, as well as the local villages, and we still don't have an answer."

Senad paused for a moment. "Maybe it is about the water? I've heard that a strange rot plagues the royal gardens, and it took a Nature Mage quite some time to get things in order. She blamed polluted water."

"Polluted water doesn't explain why people have disappeared and how this creature in the forest beat us," snapped Mar, visibly irritated by the lack of progress.

A heavy knock rattled the door, and a moment later, Daro came in. "Yes? I hope you managed your assignment." Mar hoped he would get a lead to follow this time.

Daro sat on the spare chair and brushed invisible dust from his vest. "Well, first, you should pay me double for today. I spent the whole day chopping up a goddamn table for Ina."

"You…what?" asked Senad.

"She saw you!" shouted Mar at the same time.

Daro laughed wholeheartedly and nodded. "Yes, she saw me. In fact, this new flame of yours gave me a solid kick in the ribs. Couldn't you find someone more docile? And yes, I chopped wood, all while her friend spilt every secret from their past just to see me flexing my muscles."

Senad leaned forwards, visibly interested now. "And what did you learn?" Mar looked surprised at his second-in-command and his sudden interest in the witch.

Daro started talking, and soon the two leaders learned Ina would move to the artisans' quarter in the upcoming days, that her university nickname was Striga and that she constantly had to fend off suitors. When Mar was about to stop this pointless gossip, Daro added. "Oh, and she made some sort of fascinating potion. Velka said the whole alchemy section gathered to see the spectacular transformation of a common green frog. However, teachers were displeased seeing the results, and no one was allowed to talk about it. The potion itself was confiscated and hasn't been heard of since."

Mar held his breath before asking the most crucial question. "And what was this frog transformed into?"

Daro laughed, slapping his knees. "That is the funniest part. It sounds like your little witch created an actual monster."

This sudden revelation was unwelcome but not unexpected. Mar knew that eventually he would have to confront Ina about it. He still could not believe she was the one behind it all. Both men's reports painted a picture of a woman who just wanted to enjoy her life, maybe in a bit of an unconventional way, but she was no villain. Daro must be wrong, or so Mar hoped, and he hoped his desire did not blind him to her character.

CHAPTER 10

For the next few days, Ina was seen all over town, buying furniture and equipment for her new home. After they returned from their latest shopping trip, Velka's servants informed them that a messenger from Nerissa had arrived with a small chest filled with money, jewellery and a note from her aunt. The letter briefly explained the contents were bequeathed to Ina by her mother, Nessa.

The money made life more manageable, so Ina paid off her old debts and took the time to make her new house into a home, one she could truly relax in. After years in the hut, she was dead set on having the best bathroom money could buy. She was so done with living in poverty or being a guest. Ina hired quality artisans to restore the house and stayed around to oversee the process until everything was to her liking.

Velka, in the meantime, was thriving on male attention. Daro's frequent visits made Ina leave her friend's house even more often. She suspected his motives, but seeing her friend so happy, Ina kept quiet, not wanting to spoil it. Especially since she noticed the change in the orc's behaviour—his initial suave speech and flashy gifts were replaced by laughs, books, and exotic plants he was bringing from the market. One look at Velka's garden, and it was clear she was head over heels in love with Daro, despite the age difference. Flowers were in full bloom, trees covered in fresh spring green leaves in such abundance that it looked more like a fairy glade than a humble town garden. Maybe a younger man was what she needed?

Ina was sure her movements were reported to Mar, or at least she had been sure. Still, lately, Daro didn't seem to notice her at all. She suspected Mar had more reports about the colour of Velka's dress than Ina's quiet investigations. So, the witch used her shopping trips to gather information. It seemed shaking a heavy purse was an effective incentive. Unsurprisingly, she found the king was very unpopular, especially here in the capital. Outside Osterad, ordinary folks didn't care who sat in the great hall as long as their harvests were good and taxes were low. One royal arse on the throne or another, it didn't matter.

Here in the capital, someone was stirring the pot. Her past outburst in the palace was exaggerated to ridiculous proportions. Ina could not believe that she had become a symbol of justice when all she did was have a meltdown when her pride was hurt. Someone hadn't let this matter drop, fuelling the flames of discontent. Of course, it was adorable to hear she was a beautiful, fiery sorceress who took a man's breath away, but Ina would have much preferred for the matter to be forgotten. All this nonsense she discovered from a bard who looked her in the eye as he extolled the virtues and magical prowess of the hero mage, not once realising she was that person.

Someone was portraying the monarch in a poor light, but for what reason? Nobles and merchants liked their kings flawed. Weak kings didn't start wars, stupid kings were easy to lead, and powerless kings let the nobles thrive to rule their lands almost without control, so why did Ina have a feeling it all pointed to rebellion? Roda was not the first drunkard and womaniser on the throne, and, looking at his son, he wouldn't be the last. There wasn't a suitable candidate that could successfully change the ruling class.

Ina couldn't fathom who would benefit from all of this, but one obvious thing was that people were disappearing, and it was all blamed on King Roda. The missing were never people whose absence would trigger an investigation. However, the people on the street still gossiped about monsters, vanishing humans, and the king's depraved life all in one breath.

Ina knew it was about time to investigate the sewers, but despite the bard's tales, she also realised that she was not a hero and needed someone to protect her. She thought about Janik and his company at first, only to find out they'd been contracted to work outside the capital while she was rearranging her house. The only option was Mar, but once again, she found an excuse to put off contacting him.

The day she moved into the new house felt like an adventure. Ina had little to take with her—some clothes, Nessa's jewellery chest, and her cat—but it still felt like a big step. Velka and Daro escorted her to the premises, where her friend, in a strange emotional outburst, wept and buried her face in her paramour's shoulder, stating that Ina would always have a place in her home. It caused a commotion on the quiet street, and several artisans stuck their heads through their workshop doors to see who was in mourning, only to shut their doors furtively.

Daro sent Ina a playful wink and whispered, "I will take care of this," and dragged Velka back to the carriage. For the first time, Ina was genuinely grateful to him. It was about time to take the mage back before she withered all the plants in her grief.

Ina closed the door and looked around the house, her new home. A spacious living area with an intimate fireplace and soft furnishings, a tiny cosy kitchen and, for the most important part, a well-equipped alchemic workshop. There was a bedroom with a small but fancy washroom upstairs, and she was planning to make a small place for a servant or apprentice in the attic.

The cat somehow released himself from the basket. Boruta appeared more curious than annoyed, and Ina was grateful for this. The last thing needed was to chase after a runaway cat. She would have to start the fire and buy some produce to cook later. There wasn't much to unpack, and after Velka had harnessed her serfs, this place was left spotlessly clean. Before she started, Ina sat at the table and wrote a brief note.

To Captain Marcach,

You are cordially invited to call upon me at my home. Please arrive at twilight this evening. I would like to discuss with you the recent disappearances in the city.

Ina

P.S. I'm sure Daro will tell you exactly where I live and many other details.

She unpacked the rest of her luggage and went out to buy some food, passing her note to an errand boy with a small coin. Ina felt uneasy about inviting Mar into her home after their last encounter. She liked how he looked at her, sending shivers down her spine, but the days she would throw herself at him were over. *All I need is to exchange the information and ask for a bit of help*, she thought, planning to be civil, candid, and feed him well. Men with full bellies tended to be more agreeable to any reckless ideas.

With a last look at the table, she nodded, happy that all was ready for Mar's visit. Ina's earlier shopping trip had resulted in a cooking extravaganza. While she was not a skilled cook, she had a few fool proof dishes, so now the aroma of fresh bread and mouth-watering rabbit stew permeated her house. Ina bought some honey cakes for later and sweet honey mead to wash their throats while talking.

She looked at her face in the mirror and shook her head. *Why am I trying to impress him?* Before answering this question, she heard a decisive knock on the door. *Time for the show, and be nice,* Ina reminded herself. Her face resembled her mother's when she walked downstairs, a demure lady welcoming her long-awaited guest.

Mar expected anything but this. Ina opened the door and gestured for him to enter, and he could only stand there looking like a fool. She wore a beautiful, simple grey dress with minimal decor that embraced her body perfectly. Her long copper hair, only slightly braided at the temples, flowed freely down her back. She looked even better than in his dreams, and without thinking, he reached out, wrapping a free strand around his finger and raising it to his nose. She smelled like apples, and he sighed with delight.

"Mar? Mar? Would you like to come in?" Ina asked. She looked somehow unsettled, unable to pull back, and ran a hand through her hair freeing the strand he still held between his fingers.

Mar snapped out of his daydream and stepped forwards, angry at himself for behaving like a love-struck puppy. "No, you just look so different, my lady, and your new home changed. It took me by surprise. You look enchanting."

"The last one was not my home. It was my prison," she said, omitting his clumsy compliment, but her dry reminder contradicted a hint of blush on her cheeks. The awkward moment stretched, and Mar couldn't help but smile. She may look different, but she still had that sharp tongue.

"You wanted to talk?" Talking plainly was the best way in these circumstances. Mar didn't want to rush things just yet. He also had matters to discuss, but maybe he'd gain his answers sooner if he let her talk first.

Ina's cheeks reddened more, and, biting her lip, she gestured towards the dining table. "Would you care to dine with me? I cooked a small supper, and I hope you'll like it."

Mar, unsure of Ina's plans, nodded, and a moment later, he was sitting at the table with a bowl of stew and fresh, generously buttered bread. The stew was rich with a tempting aroma, and his empty stomach growled with anticipation. Ina looked at him, and he saw a hint of a smile playing on her lips. Without further thought, following the unspoken command, Mar raised the spoon to his mouth. His stomach rumbled again, and Ina giggled softly. He gave in to the light mood and smiled. "It is delicious. My unruly stomach and I thank you for the meal."

For a moment, they ate in awkward silence till her cat joined them at the table. "I can't believe you dragged him here." Mar used this opportunity to start the conversation as Ina struggled to convince the animal that dipping a paw in her bowl was not the best idea.

"He was my only friend when no one else cared if I was still breathing," she said with a bitter smile, and Mar realised how scared and lonely she must have felt. Barely thirty years old, exiled to the Black Forest with nothing except a derelict hut, and no experience of how to survive in the wild. When Daro told him Ina was obsessed with her house, he was surprised, but now he understood her more. After finishing his stew, it was time to ask some questions.

"Ina, why did they take you to the Magical Council? Was it because you helped me?"

Ina raised herself and walked to the kitchen, leaving Mar with his thoughts. Soon she came back carrying a platter of honey cakes and a carafe of mead, gesturing him towards the fire. "Please have a seat. It will be a long story, and we should get comfortable."

Mar complied with her request, uneasy at not being in charge of this conversation.

Ina poured a good measure of mead and settled herself on the fur. The heat from the fire seemed to ease her doubts, and the captain hoped it also gave her the courage to share her story. Mar gave her time, admiring her soft features now adorned by dancing flames. There were still questions to ask, but he didn't want to rush her. He shifted on the seat, and the heaviness in his chest grew. He didn't like her tense, and something deep inside wanted to pull her on his lap and stroke her back till she relaxed. Thankfully, she spoke before his imagination produced more vivid thoughts and goaded him to act on them.

"I will not ask you to swear any oaths, and I can only hope I'm trusting the right person with my secret. I know you sent Daro to spy on me, but if you ever felt grateful for having your life saved, please help me, and in exchange, I will tell you all I know about the issue."

Mar felt like she had slapped him in the face. Why did she make this sudden statement? He was welcomed, fed, and now this beautiful creature sat there, freely offering all the information he could think to demand. All she wanted in return was his help, but how she did it highlighted his dishonesty. He felt compelled to say yes, and apologise for his shortcomings. So compelled that the memory of the horse incident sprang to mind. He was not an evil man, and she was still a suspect. The lack of clarity brought anger to his voice. Had she tried to influence him to further her own agenda? "I will do what I have to, so don't try your spells on me. Now answer my questions, and maybe then I can help you."

Ina's head snapped back. Mar saw raw pain flash across her expression before she put on a mask of indifference. Her shoulder slumped for a moment, and he saw her swallow hard before raising her head, sending him a challenging stare. The cosy atmosphere was gone, and now it was time to get down to business. "Ask, and let us be done with this," she said with a grimace.

Mar could swear the temperature dropped a few degrees, and he could only blame his choice of words for making his welcoming hostess so hostile. Somehow, he always went to an extreme in her presence, but she was right, so let this be finished.

"Why you were taken to the Council?"

"They thought I made the monster that attacked you in the forest." She appeared ready to give him his answers, and Mar knew he would have found them anyway. Not all of them, though. He could see his hostility had killed their budding trust. Mar felt something elusive slide between his fingers and knew his accusation was a mistake, but he didn't know how to fix it.

"Did you?" he asked. Simplicity would be best when he no longer trusted himself to be diplomatic.

"No, but I am the creator of the mutagen that someone used for the transformation."

He attempted to soften his tone and regain Ina's trust, even a little. "Why did you make it?" Mar already knew this part but didn't expect she'd admit it so openly.

"I did not intend to make something so dangerous. I was young and had a tantrum during our alchemy class. Instead of making a potion, I created a mutagen. I used it on a frog so it could escape death. It backfired, transforming the poor creature into a completely new species. Our professor confiscated the formula, and I have never made another batch."

"Who could get hold of the formula?" he asked, hoping she might have a clue. As he had thought, she was not the one to make these aberrations, but this may be why all the rescuers came so early, blowing their trumpets.

"How should I know? I have been in exile and isolated for the past ten years." That was a bitter response, and now, observing Ina rising from the fur, he felt like a fool. His earlier outburst seemed to strip her of sympathy, and now she shut him down when he wanted nothing more than to discuss a few theories with her.

When he was thinking about how to mitigate the damage, Ina spoke. "If you're finished questioning me, I would like to ask for your help. Please delegate Ren to escort me to the city tunnels. Janik told me he found some odd creatures there. He asked me to investigate it. I know it may sound foolish to you, but if someone uses my creation, I have to stop it."

Mar leapt to his feet, not expecting this request. He didn't suspect she would ask for Ren. Why Ren, why not Daro, who was around them all the time? Why ask for someone else when he was right there? Jealousy clouded his mind when he growled, "What if I say no?"

Ina stepped back. The hesitance in her pose and nervous clenching of her fists told him she didn't know what to do or say to convince him anymore. He felt like a fool and opened his mouth to reassure her he would take her there when she spoke.

"If you say no, then I will go alone."

As soon as he heard those words, the vision of the forest monster's deformed body slashed through his mind and Mar surged forwards, his arms crushing her body to his chest. She squirmed, attempting to free herself, but he held her tight. He knew she was brave and had powerful magic, but unfocused magic wouldn't save her life when claws and fangs tore at her body. The thought of that scared him more than he wanted to admit, but no matter how safe she'd be with Ren, he couldn't stop thinking of her hurt without him there to help.

He pressed lips against her temple. His breath laboured when he spoke with a quiet intensity born from fear. "You will not go there alone. I forbid it, and I will have Daro drag you back to lock you in this house of yours if you try."

Her breathing quickened against his chest, and he felt her hands slide up when she tried to push him off to see his face. Mar was ready to let go when he heard her soft plea, "Then help me, please, and let Ren go with me. I don't want to go alone."

Hearing Ren's name again, he held her at arm's length, gripping her shoulders tightly. "Ina, why? Why Ren?" he asked, angry she used his name. "Why don't you ask for me?"

"Because he is the only man I can trust right now," she answered, blinking rapidly. Her face contorted with pain when the bruising force of his grip intensified. "Mar, you are hurting me. Please let me go."

A screeching yowl and a sharp pain on Mar's cheek brought him back to reality. Boruta, who reacted to the distress of his mistress, had jumped up and slashed his cheek with his claws. The cut was shallow but sharp enough to draw blood. Mar released Ina and touched his face. He saw the shock in her eyes caused by blood and her cat's attack. She grabbed a cloth to help him, but Mar stopped her, voice subdued, as he looked deep into her eyes.

"No, I deserved it. I will take you there, not Ren, Daro, Janik, or any other goon you think to hire. The only person who will take you there is me. No one else." He turned around and walked out, leaving Ina wide-eyed and cuddling the cat, whose hiss followed his departure.

Mar wandered the streets aimlessly, hoping some stray thief or lowlife would try their luck with him. He would welcome the chance to release some steam. He knew eventually he would have to go back to Ina's. Woron was waiting, tied to the fence, but he needed to clear his mind before returning.

He pounded his chest, feeling the pressure he felt being around her turn into a searing fire. *What in Veles's name is wrong with me? Why do I keep losing my temper around her?* Ina had done nothing but help him, help his friend, and had risked her own life to do it. This maelstrom in his chest seemed to destroy every rational thought except wrapping his arms around her and protecting her from all evil. His need for her was as overwhelming as the fear of losing her. All he could think about was her passionate spirit, beauty, and his own dark, ugly soul marring her light, even as he yearned to embrace it.

He replayed the evening's events in his head, and the one thing that stood out was Ina's reaction. He had insulted her and threatened her in her own home, but he was still in one piece. Not once did she stop him or retaliate with harsh words or the magic he knew could stop him in his tracks. When Mar pressed his lips to her temple and growled those words in her ear, all he received was a scratch, a small price to pay for such churlish behaviour.

Mar felt like a fool. Ina tried to cooperate, and he destroyed her trust with suspicion and jealousy. He turned around, feeling it was time to face the music. He would offer her help in a civilised manner, and if she still chose Ren, he would have to live with it.

As he returned to Ina's home, the battle cry of his horse broke the silence. The sound of wood breaking followed as his Woron freed himself from the stable. Mar didn't stop to think. He started running with only one picture in his head. Ina, alone and in danger, and it was all his fault. The clatter of locking shutters marked his steps. The good inhabitants of this alley once again decided it was not their business. He burst into the yard just in time to see the house doors fly off their hinges and a hideous creature tumbling down into the dust of the yard. Ina's cat was attached to its neck, biting and clawing at thick muscles. Mar froze at the sight of such an appalling aberration.

His eyes widened as he stared at an enormous pale spider, four-limbed as if some cruel child had ripped off the other legs. It pulled itself upwards on its elongated extremities, each one ending in a spear-like claw. The segmented torso was hanging limply, swinging a short stinger on its end. However, the worst was the monster's head, warped humanity, with teeth bared in a vacant parody of a smile and milky white eyes. At this precise moment, Mar realised that the creature in front of him had once been human, now twisted and stripped of everything by corrupted magic.

Ina staggered, appearing in the door frame. The creature's ichor had burned her upper thigh. If not for Boruta, she would most likely be a stinking pile of dissolved tissue on the floor. She'd been so stunned by Mar's departure that the creature's attack had caught her by surprise. The spider must have been hiding in the attic, waiting for its chance. Boruta's sudden hiss meant she glimpsed its move to attack. Still, the only thing she managed was to blast out raw energy as it sprayed her with acid.

She looked at Mar standing there, seemingly immobile, and she felt chills down her spine. "Mar, run! I can handle this. Get help!"

Ina was by no means a battlemage, but she had a few tricks. She could dismantle this monster's energy pattern with her Chaos magic if she had enough time to concentrate. However, it was doubtful the creature would stand there waiting for this to happen. With Boruta and Mar involved, she would have to find another way. Desperately searching, her gaze fell upon a pile of kindling, and a hasty plan formed in her head. Fire spells were easy. A flick of the wrist and a moment later, the kindling erupted into flame, capturing the creature's attention.

"Boruta, get out!" she shouted, hoping he would listen, and, to her relief, for once he did. Cats were attracted by magic, and Ina was now humming with it, fuelled by the slow destruction of the wood.

She saw Mar break from his stillness and draw his sword, rushing at the monster. Even without her magic, time slowed to a crawl as he joined the battle. She could see his attention split between the creature and her. Still, the dreamy smile felt out of place when he looked at her while simultaneously searching for his opponent's weakness.

After starting the fire with a simple spell, she grasped the blaze with her magic tendrils. Carefully controlling and manipulating the searing heat, she intertwined it with her Chaos and created a viper shape. She lashed out at the creature with calm and precise strikes.

Elusive whips of red flame, each ending with a viper's head wrapped around the creature's legs, searing the flesh and slowing it down. Fangs sank into hard chitin, anchoring themselves. Forcefully dragging her arm back, Ina forced the monster to turn, and it crawled in her direction. Another tendril lashed out to pin it down, but the energy from the blaze was almost done, and she was struggling to control it now.

Still, she'd created enough of a distraction, and Mar dived under one of the spider's hind legs. He sliced upwards with his sword, opening the creature's belly. Dark blood drenched the sand as the fire flickered and died in Ina's hands. Mar clambered up, covered in blood. He turned to her, and his eyes widened when she rushed forwards, pushing him away.

The aberration lashed out with the last spasm of its muscles, pinning the mage to the stable's wall like a beautiful butterfly, and Mar's fury erupted as Ina took the blow meant for him. Why did she keep risking her life for him? Mar spun around and lashed out with his sword, cleaving the monster's head in two. His sword clattered to the ground as he grasped the creature's limb supporting Ina's body.

Desperately clawing at his belt, he drew his dagger, using its smaller blade to tear open the joint and cut the leg off. The chitin shell was too hard to cut through, so cutting through the joint was the only way. Mar tried to avoid causing Ina any further damage, but each knife twist made her wince in pain. Finally freeing her, he cradled her in his arms and buried his face in her neck, profoundly relieved she was still alive.

Ina gently tapped his shoulder. He'd seen this pained look too many times on the battlefield, and his heart ached for her while she tried not to show any weakness. "I'm fine. You can put me down."

"No" was Mar's only answer before he gently carried her back to the house. He looked around. There wasn't much destruction, just a puddle of ichor that would take time to clean and the lack of a door. A moment of dark humour slipped out before he could stop it. "Ina, do you have something against the doors in your home?" He asked with a hint of jest in his voice. His body relaxed as he reminded himself that she was safe, and now he needed to look after her.

"What?" she said, stuttering, and when he looked down, he noticed she was confused by his blatant teasing. He'd really messed up if she hadn't expected friendly banter from him, and the gentleness he held her with was puzzling her.

"Well, each time I see you, the doors get blown off their hinges. I thought maybe you just like a fresh breeze in the evening," he said, winking at her when he gently set her down on the armchair.

"It is pure coincidence. We both know I'm too ladylike to cause such destruction," Ina answered. Mar pulled a dubious expression, and she burst into pained laughter. He hoped his attempt at humour helped ease the pain.

Mar chuckled. "But of course, sweet flower, I would never think otherwise. Now, my lady, do you have a healing poultice so we can look after your wounds before I go find Nerissa?"

Ina moaned and covered her eyes. "In the white jar on the shelf. Do anything you want but please, not Nerissa. She will kill me for this."

Mar brought a jar with sticky white ointment and knelt between Ina's legs. "Now, don't tell me the witch who can curse a king is afraid of her little old auntie." He was now openly teasing, observing that Ina enjoyed their banter with pleasure. Surrendering his anger and need for control opened new layers of Ina's personality, and he wished he had realised that earlier.

"She is terrifying, and she keeps scolding me." Ina giggled nervously when he ripped her damaged skirt above her knees, uncovering the damage.

He had to take a deep, calming breath. He would have the rest of the night to think about his failure.

Mar knew placing the poultice would be a painful process, but there was no way to distract his witch from her injury as he worked alone. He widened the rip in her skirt, exposing the wound. Ina stopped talking and now looked at him with a mixture of fear and hope.

"Ina, I'm sorry," he said, and she nodded and gently touched his cheek.

"It is not your fault. You saved my life today. Fancy to be my ardent hero?" she asked, teasing him in return.

His fists tightened. This bloody injured woman was trying to cheer him up, and no, he was not a hero. Otherwise, she wouldn't wince in pain at the mere thought of standing up. Mar felt her soft touch when she lifted his chin up.

"Oi, hero of the night, help me take this dress off. It is a rag now, anyway. We need water to wash the wound, then you place the poultice and hold it in position with the clean bandages that you'll find on the shelf."

Mar looked at her and now exhaled in relief. It couldn't be too bad if his firefly took control so quickly. He snapped out a military salute, saying, "Yes, my liege." Then he retrieved the bandages.

After slicing away the remnants of her garment, Mar could finally assess all the injuries. Both of Ina's wounds looked serious. The burnt skin of her thigh was bubbled and angry, and the monster's barb pierced the shoulder muscle, gladly damaging nothing else. He had no means to pull it out for now, and he didn't want to cause more bleeding, so Mar concentrated his efforts on the burn. He also noticed the bruises his fingers had left on her shoulder, and with a frown, he cursed himself for it. This shouldn't have happened, and his spitfire ought to be safe in bed, not burnt and bleeding in front of him. He heard his voice saying, "I should take you to bed."

"What? Now?" Ina asked.

One look at her face, and he realised she misunderstood him entirely, so he hastily added, "To rest." He wasn't mistaken this time.

The soft twitch of her lips with a quiet, "Oh well," made him a very content man. With a hope he was not making a cardinal mistake, he closed his arms around her and whispered, "I will wait till you are healed to do whatever was in your head. Now please sit and let me tend to your wounds."

Dazed by this bold statement, Ina leaned back in the chair. She liked the captain's new attitude towards her, and she could only hope he wouldn't flip back to being a grumbling arsehole. Maybe it was just a rush caused by the recent battle, and in the cold light of day, he'd not look at her so favourably, but she wouldn't dwell on it now.

Ina had done many silly things in her life, but trusting men was never one of them. She took them as they were and walked away when it was time to move on. As if something deep inside blocked any chance for more meaningful affection. He said he would do what was in her head, and Ina intended to hold him to his word. If he reverted to coldness, there would be no regret and a few fond memories to look back on. Her imagination ran wild, sending her into a pathway of carnal desires, especially now when his fingers slowly trailed up her thigh. The cold water he poured over the burn soothed her pain and shifted her focus to his calloused fingers trailing over her skin.

"Holy shit, cock bollocks, what the fuck are you doing?" Ina screamed, jerking on the chair when sudden blinding pain ripped through her body.

Mar held her firmly in place and continued spreading the ointment over her burn.

"I'm sorry. I am trying to be as gentle as I can," he said through clenched teeth, as his hands trembled on her skin. As he reached for the bandages, Ina subsided to soft whimpers. "I'm so sorry. I wouldn't hurt you unnecessarily," he said, and she nodded. When another jolt of pain shot through her, she placed her hand on his head, grasping a handful of hair.

"I see you like 'em bald." It was Mar's time to hiss when she pulled his mane during one particularly painful touch, and a few strands remained in her grasp.

Soon after the wound was bandaged, Mar found a large blanket. He wrapped it around her, careful of her shoulder, and after a moment of hesitation, he lifted her and lay her on his lap. It felt good, and not one to overthink such a moment, Ina lay her head on Mar's shoulder and ran her fingers through his beard, then down to his Adam's apple. A low rumble made her finger vibrate, and she beamed a beautiful smile up at him. "Thank you…for everything," she said, parted her lips, placed a timid kiss on his cheek, and quickly closed her eyes, not wanting to see if he didn't like it.

Mar didn't dare move till he heard her breathing even out, and he was sure she drifted into a deep sleep. He rested his chin on her head, allowing himself to close his eyes and revisit the battle scene. Ina's magic stunned him, not only by its strength but also its remarkable beauty. He chuckled softly and was startled that it might have woken her up, but thankfully Ina was still sleeping. Fire vipers, what else one could expect from such a spitfire of a woman? He gently stroked her back, careful to not touch the injured shoulder. Not once had he held his late wife like this, or any other woman, for that matter. And he knew he would do whatever it took not to make it the last time. He thought about Ren and his friend's infatuation and rolled his eyes, muttering to himself, "It looks like love at first wound with this one."

CHAPTER II

The candlewick told him it was only an hour since she closed her eyes. Mar slowly stroked Ina's hair while he considered the implications of today's events. He knew Ina would need help soon, but without means to alert anyone, Mar resorted to having a moment to gather his thoughts, and the feeling of holding his little spitfire just seemed right. The sleeping woman in his arms was not responsible for the corrupted creature. However, her invention, the mutagen, had been used to create these monsters. The monster that attacked her went for the kill, not capture, which suggested that Ina was a threat that needed to be removed.

Mar looked at her delicate features. Asleep, she seemed so peaceful and so much younger. It was apparent she had never trained to fight. Yet her flexibility made her a formidable opponent, adapting quickly to the situation. With a mage like Ina in his unit, the battle in the forest would have gone much better. Mar resigned himself to help her investigate the city tunnels and sewers.

He was not looking forwards to crawling in excrement, but she was stubborn enough to go by herself or get one of Janik's goons to help. Mar also knew he wouldn't trust anyone to protect her except himself, or maybe Ren. Thinking of Ren, he realised his men would need to know about these events, not to mention alerting the chancellor and the king, but that could wait till he found a way to get help for Ina.

Mar felt an overwhelming peace sitting by the fire, holding this stubborn woman in his arms despite the previous mayhem. The captain knew he shouldn't, but as her lips parted, he leaned down and kissed them softly, only to pull himself up and look at her face with growing worry. Mar cursed his flight of fancy, realising he had waited too long to get the help she needed. Ina's face was flushed and what he thought was the adorable play of the flickering flames was, in fact, the blush of fever on her cheeks.

He moved to stand up, determined to carry her to the healer's house, when a noise outside caught his attention. "Who is there? We need help!" he shouted, hoping some passers-by would notice. A moment later, a crowd of people rushed into the house, led by…a cat.

"Ina!" shouted Velka, running to her friend and placing a hand on her cheek. Mar saw her frown and realised she completely misread the situation and jumped at him. "Who are you? What have you done to her?" He was sure that if not for the fact he was still holding Ina, this raging Valkyrie would knock the living daylights out of him.

He watched as Daro pulled Velka back, squeezing her shoulders in reassurance. "That is Captain Marcach, my flower. Your friend is safe with him."

However, Velka didn't look convinced. "The hairy oaf Ina told me about?"

Daro sniggered and nodded. "Yes, that one. Now, why don't you help Lady Nerissa while I make sure Ina is safe in bed?"

Velka huffed but went back over to the arch-healer of Cornovii. Mar saw why Ina had worried about calling her aunt. Nerissa's presence towered over the men flanking her. This was the formidable arch-mage, powerful and intimidating, not some kindly old relative. With one look at Ina's burning cheeks and wounded shoulder, Nerissa knew precisely what to do.

Mar felt his courage shrink when she barked her orders, pointing straight at his face. "You get her to bed and finish undressing her. Daro, make sure we have enough water to fill a bathtub, and you Velka, cool it down." It was clear Nerissa expected nothing but complete obedience. Turning, she looked at Senad and Ren. "You two, clear that bloody carcass, best burn it and scrub the floor before it smells and poisons the ground."

If his men had any self-preservation instinct left, they would follow Nerissa's command. He certainly was. Mar nodded lightly in agreement and moved upstairs to Ina's bedroom. He placed her in her bed and started stripping off her undergarments. Guilt burned him more than her flushed skin ignited his fingers.

When Mar unlaced her bodice, Ina's eyes fluttered open for a moment, and she moved to stop his hands. "Mar…I don't think I can…"

"Shh…it's OK, your aunt is here, and she told me to do this to cool you down." Mar was unsure what else to say. It wasn't how he imagined seeing her naked body, but he trusted the healer's judgement.

Ina's reaction was astonishing when, hearing of her aunt's arrival, she tried to scramble out of bed. As soon as she placed weight on her injured arm, giving him a good view of her round buttocks, she yelped in pain and fell back onto the bed. She whimpered when he stopped her. "Show mercy and just kill me. I will never hear the end of this."

"Rightly so," said her great-aunt, entering the room. "Now drink this." She placed a cup in Mar's hand, which suddenly advanced his duty to nurse her. Ina sipped at the bitter fluid, and the redness faded from her cheeks. When she turned her eyes on him, he could see the pain had subsided enough that Ina could think more clearly.

Nerissa looked at Mar. "You know what to do. She should be numb enough." He nodded, and his arms tightened around the witch's torso to immobilise her. He saw her open her mouth to protest when her aunt yanked the remains of the monster's claw out of her shoulder. A scream ripped from her lips, and he knew the potion could not numb that much pain. With Ina on the edge of passing out, Nerissa smeared a thick paste over the wound, muttering under her breath, "There, one problem solved."

He stroked her hair as her breath shuddered in her chest, and soon he heard Velka's voice from the other room. "The bath is ready!"

Nerissa seemed to be pleased. "Good." She looked at Mar, and ordered, "Take her there and make sure she soaks well. Oh, and get that bandage off beforehand."

Mar, grabbing a loose bedsheet to protect her, scooped Ina up and marched to the other room, calling out, "All men downstairs now!" He was adamant no one else would see his woman naked.

Downstairs, Velka warmed some wine for the company as they all gathered around. A loud thud made them all raise their heads. A desperate scream swiftly followed the sound. "What the…! Mar, stop it! I don't want it! Mar, it's bloody freezing, you bastard!"

The sounds of a fight were followed by a large splash and even louder screams. Ren, visibly unsettled, attempted to rush upstairs when Daro held him back. "My friend, we both know it is none of your business."

Velka added with a smirk, "If Ina were distraught, we would have a bathtub and ceiling on our heads by now." The commotion upstairs eventually settled, and after a few minutes, a water-soaked Mar descended from upstairs, visibly beaten, sporting an impressive black eye.

Daro snorted a short laugh at the sight of his bedraggled captain. Mar poured himself some wine and addressed Nerissa, "She is in bed now. Anything else?"

The old healer was visibly amused when she answered, "No, not really. Now give me your hand, boy. It looks like my niece didn't lose her spark."

Reluctantly, Mar reached out, and an odd, numb feeling spread along from where her bony fingers pressed into his skin. Soon the throbbing of his head was left in the past, and the bruise that had blossomed stopped aching so much.

He felt Nerissa inspecting his rejuvenated features. Soon after, she stood up. "My job here is done. You just have to keep her in bed for a day or two, which I'm sure you will enjoy." Mar was petted on the cheek as if she was rewarding a puppy for a job well done, and then she addressed Velka, "Come on, girl, it is time to go home now. You can return here tomorrow."

Daro stood as well, provoking a few surprised looks. "I will escort you back." His hand landed on Velka's waist as he guided her to the exit. Mar nodded in agreement and, turning to the side, said, "Ren, check on Ina." He'd barely finished the sentence before Ren was gone. He was displeased by this choice, but he needed to talk to Senad. It was the perfect occasion with the women leaving and away from prying ears at the barracks.

Mar turned to Senad and asked, "How did you all get here so quickly? Another lucky rescue party?"

Senad smirked. "Not this time. It looks like her cat is more intelligent than you are. The beast appeared at Velka's house, jumped between the lovebirds, and almost bit Daro's nose off when he tried to drag him away. The mage recognised him and raised the alarm, and Daro sent a message to the barracks for reinforcements."

That story and the sight of Boruta attacking the creature earlier showed the cat was far more intelligent than an ordinary pet. "What do you think about all of this?"

"Someone wants her gone." Senad's straightforward answer only reinforced Mar's own belief.

"If you'd seen the look on that creature's face." Mar shuddered. "All these disappearances must be connected with the aberrations. Senad, someone is using Ina's mutagen to make monsters out of people."

"And Ina's role in this is?" Senad was very careful phrasing his words.

Mar waved dismissively. "She is not involved other than being the original creator of the mutagen, and except for whoever got hold of her formula, she's the only one who knows how to make it properly."

Senad tightened his lips, staying silent for a moment. "This makes no sense. What is to gain in making such rabid creatures?"

Mar slammed his hand on the table. "I don't know! This mess is getting out of hand. I'm going to the king tomorrow. He may be an old drunkard, but he and the chancellor must know about this. We'll need the Magical Council's cooperation to investigate this, but they will slam the door in our faces without the king's support."

"What do you want me to do?" Senad appeared unsettled. Mar blamed tiredness. It was past midnight, and even before he came for supper, it had been a long day. Nothing good would come from dwelling on detailed plans today. "Nothing, go home, get some sleep, and be ready in the morning. We are going to the palace." He looked up, thinking it was time to go upstairs and send Ren home to rest. Mar would be staying here tonight.

Ren sat on the bed and looked at the sleeping Ina with awe and sadness. Her face was calm, but he could see the dark circles shadowing her eyes. Her hair fell across her cheek, and he gently brushed it away. Ina stirred in her sleep, frowning at her dreams.

Without thinking, Ren hummed a lullaby, one ancient and native to his land, stopping briefly when Ina, still asleep, reached for his hand. Tenderness spread through his chest as he looked at her. Following his culture's customs, Ren had offered his life for her healing and intended to stay true to his word. But her openness and lack of prejudice meant she stood out amongst her peers, and his feelings were much more than just about fulfilling his oath. He allowed himself to run his fingers through her copper mane and noticed it eased the tension in her body. Whatever came next, allowing Ina to get injured again would not be an option.

Mar entered the room and ground his teeth at the sight in front of him. "Ren," a quiet growl escaped his lips, "why are you on the bed?"

"She had nightmares," his friend said, with no guilt in his voice. "Would you prefer to let her wake up without rest?"

Drawing in a deep, calming breath, Mar closed his eyes for a moment. "Ren, I would rather Ina be alive if there was an attack. Something dangerous is targeting her, and, feelings be damned, she nearly died today when my back was turned. I will not allow that to happen because of your infatuation. Damn it all to Veles. You're the only one that can keep her safe when I'm not around. I need the Ghost, not some mooncalf pining for something he'll never have."

Ren moved, or he must have moved, because suddenly he was in Mar's face, eyes burning with a fury the captain had never seen before. His lips were drawn back in a snarl.

"You think I cannot protect her? Has she been hurt, drowned, or nearly died with me? No, every time it's you that's failed, not I. So, if I want to make Ina comfortable, make her happy, then I will."

The desire to punch Ren's face for his outburst warred with the guilt Mar felt for each of those incidents. Clenched fists and more calming breaths suppressed his feelings, granting him the strength to reply. "Yes, I failed her. I doubted her, her motivation, and her magic. We've been led around by the nose this entire time. We've lost too many to this mess, and she was a convenient suspect. So yes, I failed. I am still failing. We are no closer to finding out who is doing this and how to stop them. Ina needs you, yes, but the kingdom needs you more."

Laying a hand on Ren's shoulder, Mar looked into his eyes. "Ina is a strong woman, capable and far cleverer than either of us. We keep her safe and work together to find out what's happening. I will ask for an audience with the king tomorrow, and I want you to protect her in my absence."

Mar cast a glance over the sleeping Ina, lingering on the dark circles under her eyes, guilt and the stirring of deeper feelings warring inside his chest. "I can't see her hurt again. I know you, of all of them, understand this. Now, rest and come back in the morning to take over the guard. And Ren? Keeping her in bed won't be a simple task, but I trust you will find a way."

He knew his words made sense. Ren nodded, but his grimace showed how torn he was between loyalty and affection. Finally, he said, "I know what you say is right, but I want you to remember she is not yours or mine. You were overbearing and biased, leaving her no choice but to lash out, and I blame you for this, captain. I swore an oath I would not let it carry on." Ren turned and strode off. "I will be back at dawn."

Mar breathed a sigh of relief when the door closed. Another crisis averted, but Ren was right, and he wondered why Ina had helped him at all. He'd been an arsehole, but she also was no saint, and he still remembered her scathing remarks.

He contemplated lying next to her but decided against it. He would wait till he knew he was welcome in her bed. Piling some blankets next to the window, Mar created a makeshift bed, and with his sword unsheathed next to him, he fell into a shallow, troubled sleep.

The cacophony of bells ringing around the capital woke them just before dawn. The discordant sound was deafening. Mar looked at Ina, who sat up, still groggy from her drugged sleep. Her gaze fell on him standing by the window. "What is it?"

"It won't be anything good, not this early. Ren will be here soon, so maybe he can tell us." Mar's body was tense, wanting to take action. This loud wake-up call indicated severe trouble, and he could only hope more monsters were not on the rampage. When the pink hue of full dawn fully brightened the sky, he saw Ren march into Ina's yard with a grim visage, giving Mar even more reason to worry.

"Please stay here," Mar asked, noticing Ina scrambling out of bed.

"This is my house, and I will do what I choose." Ina continued her endeavour.

Mar thought about how to make her listen to or obey his commands. Ren would already be waiting downstairs, and he hated to keep his subordinate waiting. A sudden thought made him smile—"subordinate" was the solution to this problem.

"Ina, I want to hire you as our mage. You'll have to join me underground and investigate the strange magic in the monster we killed, but the crown will pay you well. Maybe you can even buy magically enhanced doors?" he teased, praying to all Gods she fell for this ruse.

Rapidly blinking, she looked at him with an open mouth. "As a mage, and you will pay me?"

"Yes, now do you accept the job?" Mar didn't want to give Ina time to think.

"Hmm, yes, I would do it anyway," Ina stuttered.

Still, Mar was already at the door tapping the handle. "Good, then here is my first order. Stay in bed at least till Ren comes up. I need to talk to him alone first."

"You cheating bastard!" she shouted, throwing a heavy boot at his head. That display of defiance made him smile, but his grin promptly faded when he saw Ren's face.

"The king is dead."

Mar shook his head and tried to focus on Ren's words. He didn't know what to think, but one thing was sure, he needed to speak with the chancellor right away and pray to Gods it was just a coincidence. Mar tried to avoid thinking that the king's death ran parallel with Ina's attack.

He looked at Ren, and steel ran through his voice when he ordered, "Until I'm back, you must not leave her side and trust no one. Ina stays here even if you have to tie her to the bloody bed." Mar grabbed his coat from the chair. "Oh, and I hired her, so tell her it is an order if she is too much trouble. It might even work if you are lucky."

Ren nodded and turned to walk upstairs when Mar's voice reached him. "And if you have the chance, order her some doors, solid, but not too expensive. Those things don't last long around her."

Ren exhaled with relief that the captain was back to his old self. Even better, he was entrusted with Ina's safety. While looking for weak points in the building's defences, he noticed minor details of this house that made it so cosy. Everything was soft, and the earthy autumn colours made one instantly relax. He stopped and knocked on the bedroom door. "Ina, it's Ren. May I come in?"

"Has his horseshit highness left?" The voice on the other side was distinctly angry. Ren didn't wait for permission and opened the door to look inside. If something had happened, he had to know.

"Is everything all right?" His strange accent didn't hide his concern, but he barely restrained his laughter when Ina huffed.

"He tricked me with employment, then ordered me to stay in bed. That is horse bollocks, Ren, and you know it is."

Ina prowled the room like a caged tiger. Finally, she settled down at the dressing table and brushed her hair forcefully. Ren raised his eyebrows, seeing her ripping at the knots. "Ina, let me help you, and I will tell you what happened." He took the brush from her tight grip, and gently caressed her tresses, detangling the long strands. When he felt her body relax, he decided she was ready to hear the news.

"The king is dead. That's why Mar rushed to the palace."

What he didn't expect was Ina's reaction. She laughed. "Well, it took him long enough. Please tell me they found him stiff between the legs of some whore. That would be a suitable ending for a mighty king."

Ren didn't know what to say. Ina was full of surprises, and like a breath of fresh air, she allowed him to speak his thoughts without restraint. His lips twitched in a hint of a smile, and he nodded. "Well, that's not far from the truth. It seems he took one potion too many when preparing for his next lady of the night, or at least that's what the rumour says. I'm sure Mar will know more by the time he gets back."

He felt Ina almost purred under his hand before she turned and winked at him. "I'm counting on you for the best gossip, or maybe we should ask Velka. She will know about these things."

She looked at him sheepishly. "I know you are not a maid, but could you braid my hair, just like you did yours? It looks so comfortable, and my shoulder is still stiff from my wound." She looked good, and he thought this was likely a little white lie, but he was happy to oblige. His life rarely gave him a chance to serve someone he felt truly deserved it.

After Nerissa's healing and a good night's sleep, Ina felt brand new, but why not try to get a little pampering? Ren was so easygoing, and she felt good in his company. Mar had given her the guardian she liked best from his noisy bunch.

Ina reflected on the changes to her life these past days. In less than a few weeks, she'd performed forbidden healing twice, acquired a house, defeated a monster, and was now working for the palace again. Was it such a good idea to busy herself every moment of her life? She thought the passion she felt for Mar was likely the residue of the sacrifice spell. Still, recently he teased her, made her laugh, and looked after her without his brutish venom, or at least with little of it. She could not deny he was the same possessive hairy oaf who thought he had a right to tell her what to do. Annoying as it was, it still felt good to have someone who fought a giant spider in her defence without hesitation. But looking past her lust for a knight in golden armour, their relationship was rough.

The answer to this was simple. She just didn't like being told what to do. Her choices had been taken away for too long, and now she desperately wanted to catch up on lost time. Ina smiled at her thoughts. Maybe this time, she would listen. It was a good idea to have a day off, just for herself, especially now when Mar left her with this kind man who seemed to have a soft spot for her.

Ina feigned weakness a few times just to observe his reaction, and he couldn't be more eager to offer her help. For the rest of the day, she had the time of her life, giving Ren minor tasks he performed without complaint and with clear pleasure. Ina decided she would make not just Mar but also herself happy and stay home, but only this once.

Ren caught on to her quickly, but he played along anyway. Her pretence at being injured was amusing and allowed him to be close to her. The self-control he honed for battle enabled him to play lady's maid without showing his dark desires. He was a cruel man even by the standards of his kin, and, glimpsing the scar on the top of her shoulder, Ren daydreamed of slowly skinning alive the one who had caused it. The burning of the creature's carcass hadn't provided a salve to his burning anger.

Later that day, when the time came to change her dressing, his voice betrayed him. "Does it hurt?" he asked softly, trailing the uneven pink skin on the top of her thigh.

He cursed himself when the tone of his voice made Ina look closer, but he couldn't help it. His jaw was clenched, his eyes narrowed, and Ren didn't want her to see him like this. This visage was the face of a ruthless killer, and he knew the witch needed her gentle friend back. Ina cupped his face with her hand when he struggled for control, forcing his gaze off her wound.

"No, Nerissa did an excellent job of healing me." She dropped her pretence. "It's not hurting anymore. I was just teasing you, and I'm sorry." The worry in her voice shamed him, but Ren savoured her touch, vividly aware that his hands were on her hip and her smiling face was close to his. Awareness fled as vivid images of their lips pressed together and bodies moving in passion took over his mind.

He snapped back to reality as Ina stroked his face and concernedly called his name. "Ren? Ren, what happened? You looked so absent for a moment."

He looked deep into her eyes and gently kissed her fingertips. "It's nothing, my lady. I was just thinking of the one who caused you pain. I promise you I will find them and make sure they never hurt you again." He kept the rest of his thoughts to himself, as he was sure no one except Mar would understand.

"Not if I find them first," she said, touching the tip of his nose in a playful gesture.

Ren was unsure what had happened but it put her in an excellent mood. Later, when Velka and Daro visited, it got even better. Velka, out of concern, cooked a dinner that could feed a small army. The weather was beautiful, so Ina asked the men to carry a table outside. There was no reason they should squash themselves into a small kitchen when they could dine under the blossoming tree.

⁂

Mar was tired and cranky. A restless night, followed by a day in court, didn't improve his mood. The meeting with the chancellor only increased his concern. On the surface, the king's death looked like an accident. A typical older man, trying to recapture his youth, took one elixir too many. There was an empty bottle at the bottom of his bed and no evidence of a struggle. The palace mage who examined the body excluded the influence of magic, and they didn't find any cursed objects. The healer promised the results from an autopsy in the next few days, but he was sure it was nothing untoward.

Everyone in the court seemed content with the explanation that the king's heart simply gave out after years of taking stamina potions. Everyone except Mar and the chancellor. The old official asked Mar what he thought, so he shared his doubts. The captain had talked to the guards on duty, and they'd informed him the king hadn't expected his other mistress to come that night, so why would he take a potion?

Mar asked for permission to examine the king's chamber, this time alone, and what he found was not reassuring. The bed was in disarray, and after a thorough search, he'd discovered a few droplets of blood on the floor. Of course, it could be an accident. The blood was easy to miss, and it could even be a coincidence, but Mar believed the king had been murdered. He shared his thoughts with the chancellor and mentioned the failed monster attack the previous day. The old politician sat heavily on his chair, listening to all of this.

"I wish we had solid evidence, Mar, and a culprit to catch." For the first time since Mar had known him, he looked frail. "There is unrest in the palace and between the high nobles. Our late king was not just or virtuous. He didn't care for a husband's opinion when he bedded his wife. On top of that, the south complains about heavy taxes, while the western lords demand grain and soldiers to repel the bandits and mountain creatures. The north has looked after itself for so long that our sovereignty over them is in word only. The monster attacks and disappearances are likely to be the straw that breaks the kingdom."

Mar nodded. He did not follow politics often, but he knew things were not going in the right direction. "What shall we do now? King Roda's heir should know about these events."

The chancellor snapped, "Prince Rewan? This boy is an idiot and a drunken womaniser, just like his father. He's already announced the coronation ball in three weeks. We will need to be clever about this. I want you to bring this witch of yours, Ina, to the ball. Let's see who will be uncomfortable with her presence."

Mar's blood ran cold. "You want to use Ina as bait? What if she gets attacked again?" he protested. It would be impossible to protect her at the ball. There would be hundreds of people, and any passer-by could simply scratch her with a poisoned blade.

"Marcach, I'm not asking for your permission. I'm giving you an order, and make sure no one knows about the true purpose of her invitation, especially her."

Mar's hands tightened on his sword, but he gave the politician a mockingly low bow. "As you wish, sir. I shall take my leave to begin the preparations." The chancellor waved him away, and Mar stormed out of his office. He didn't notice the startled looks the courtiers sent him as he passed by. He reached the stables and finally stopped, leaning his forehead on Woron's silky coat.

"What should I do, my friend? This plan is a recipe for disaster." The only answer was a soft neigh and nibbling of his coat. He was too tired to think, and it was his turn to guard Ina. Ren must be exhausted trying to keep Ina out of trouble. Mar jumped on his horse and turned him towards Ina's house. A good night's sleep would again have to wait.

CHAPTER 12

Mar, lost in his thoughts, didn't expect the view that welcomed him as he arrived at Ina's home. Reining in Woron, he stopped and stared at the idyllic scene in front of him. There was a table full of food. Ina and Velka were laughing next to the chestnut tree, trying to create a small herbal garden. His men were relaxed, joking around as they tried to fix the door back on its hinges. They were supposed to be on guard, but they hadn't even noticed his arrival.

Mar was fuming. "Ren! Daro! You call this standing guard?" It didn't skip his attention that his men shared a guilty glance. They knew he was right, but it was hard to not give in to those women. Ina appeared to recover first and turned in his direction with an angry grimace that soon dissolved into concern. Mar knew he was not looking good. It had been an awful day for him, and their cheerfulness brought the old arsehole back to the light. Still, he hesitated, seeing her smiling in welcome.

Ina grabbed a tankard of fresh apple juice, whispered what looked like a light cooling spell as the sides of the cup covered in condensation, and held it up to his clenched fist. Quietly, she asked, "They didn't blame you, did they? Come, have a drink and tell me what happened."

He jumped off his horse and attempted to approach his men, but Ina shifted, blocking the way. Didn't she realise she was no obstacle to him? Yet she still stopped him and grabbed his hand. A translucent shimmering net appeared over her property as their fingers touched. "See? Velka helped me to create it. No one intending harm to me or mine can sneak in unnoticed, so now you can relax." Lowering her eyes to the ground, she kicked a small rock. "It would have saved you having to fight the monster if I'd thought about it yesterday. I'm sorry."

Mar relaxed and mumbled his gratitude. Later, he would deal with his men's lack of discipline, but they hadn't been entirely neglectful. He accepted the drink, and as soon as his lips touched the cold rim, his stomach rumbled so loudly that it startled his horse. "Come and eat something, then we will talk." Ina tugged his hand, leading him to the table. Moments later, Mar was sitting down with a plate full of food.

Daro went over and removed Woron's saddle, and then, together with Velka, he groomed the stallion. Woron allowed them to do it with dignified patience, to Mar's surprise. Ren cast him an amused look and went to guard the gate, leaving him at Ina's mercy. Mar's posture relaxed when cool, long fingers began massaging his neck. He'd charged in to scold his men, and in moments, he was disarmed by a bit of food and a woman's touch.

How could he discipline them if their captain behaved in the same irresponsible manner? When his muscles tensed again, Ina moved her hand to his temple. "Let it go, Mar, just this once." She placed her cheek next to his and whispered, "You are safe with me."

Daro's hand slid to cover Velka's, and he gently caressed her. Even if steppe orc love differed from human romance, he knew what his captain was going through. It had taken him only a moment to realise that his mission with Velka had become genuine affection. Under her bubbly façade, the Nature Mage was intelligent and fiercely loyal. She made him feel like the most important person alive, and Daro, for the first time, felt he had met his mate. He had never believed his mother, who kept hammering into his head, that all others would lose their charm once he found his mate. And yet here he stood, happy to spend every second with Velka, praying to the Gods of his tribe that her heart was big enough to forgive his deception. Seeing his captain go through a similar torment was unexpectedly entertaining.

"Velka, my flower, the sun is setting, so perhaps it's time to take you home." Daro turned to his friend. "Ren? Care to join us? Let's leave the captain to apologise for our failure." The laughter in his voice prompted Mar to stand up from the table. Daro noticed his sly smile when he settled back. "That is an excellent idea, Daro, and when you both get to the barracks, make sure you train for at least two hours to remind yourselves you're still soldiers."

After watching the group leave, Mar turned to Ina. "I will stay here for the night, and we'll have that talk."

She raised her eyebrow quiet for a moment, and then she nodded. "I will agree under one condition."

Mar coughed when his food suddenly went the wrong way. He was here to protect her, and she had conditions? What was wrong with her?

"You will bathe, Mar, you reek, and I'm pretty sure I can still smell the creature's blood on you. If you want to stay here for the night, you will wash."

Mar bridled at her words. "Damn it all, you vexatious Striga. The king is dead, monsters are on the loose, and you tell me to bathe?"

Ina's eyes narrowed, and she slammed her hands on the table. "I don't care about that old fart. I've used every drop of my magic to protect my home, and you stink. Don't you dare enter my house unless you're heading straight to the bath!" She stormed off, slamming her recently repaired door, nearly breaking it in her anger. The captain was stunned by her display, but it looked like the only way to have a reasonable conversation with this woman was to clean himself up.

Mar stabled Woron and dragged himself to the house. He knocked on the doors, sighing at his men's shabby work, knowing he would have to sort that out later. "The bath is ready upstairs," he heard Ina shouting from inside. She was seriously testing his patience. He hoped the water was hot after the last time, and so it was. The water was nicely steaming, with a pile of towels and some soap on the side.

Mar stripped himself and entered the bath. The hot water relaxed his muscles, and he realised he needed this, much to his annoyance. It pained him to admit the witch was right, but his smell didn't lie. Half-asleep, he barely registered her gliding into the room. When Mar felt her soft hands on his shoulders, he protested, "What are you doing now, woman? You insisted I bathe. My stink is still as offensive as earlier." His voice was hoarse with tension.

"Mar, you know, you are like a hedgehog with so many spines sticking out." She poured water over his hair and sensually massaged his scalp. Mar was confused. What hedgehog? Ina's ministrations stopped any sensible thought he had. She slowly caressed his scalp and neck, giving such exquisite pleasure then, just as he felt his worries melt away, she asked, "So, how did the king die?"

Ina must have had the idea for this interrogation while she waited for him downstairs, then slipped quietly upstairs and into the bathroom to torture him.

Mar placed his head on the rim of the bath, his body and spirit weary. Closing his eyes, he realised he must share his burden, and Ina felt like his only ally. Thoughts drifting under her gentle touch, he told her about his findings and suspicions.

Ina purred into his ear, "Hmm…but who would want to destabilise the country?" Her hand slid down his body, massaging his chest. Ina rested her chin on his shoulder. Her soft breath quickened, giving him goosebumps.

"We don't know yet, but it doesn't look good. Factions are fighting in the court, some of them trying to prevent the enthronement of Prince Rewan," Mar muttered. His eyes snapped open when Ina stood up and moved to the other side of the bathtub. A mischievous grin blossomed on her face when she started massaging his calves. "Ina, what the hell are you doing?"

He gasped, praying the water was opaque enough to hide his obvious enjoyment. Ina just pulled his leg higher. Wet from the steam, her shirt gave more than a hint of what it was supposed to hide. The smile Ina gave him said she knew exactly where he was looking. "I'm not doing anything bad. You can tell me to stop, but maybe you'd rather tell me who you think would replace Rewan?" Mar, careful to remain covered, tried to pull his foot away, groaning under his breath, but Ina held him tight. "Striga, I don't know! Some say Sophia, but succession law forbids that. It's almost a shame, as she'd make a better ruler. Now, will you let me go?"

It was like taming a wild animal. It left Ina breathing heavily, but, bit by bit, she teased the information out, easing his burden even as she inflamed his passion. Her hands moved higher, threatening to slide up his thighs, and Mar moaned in desperation. Ina's control over him made her dizzy, and with a wet shirt rubbing her tight, erect nipples, she questioned herself. Was she willing to take it further?

"Mar, promise me you will take me underground tomorrow. I've procrastinated long enough."

"I will. Ina, stop unless you want me to…" Mar's voice, roughened by desire, was close to a growl. He hadn't finished his sentence when she dropped his leg and ran from the room, laughing to cover her body's arousal.

"Some other time, Mar. Now finish and join me for a drink."

Bathing Mar left her out of breath, but she knew the best way to get the information was to help him lower his guard. Ina had seen her fair share of men not to shy away from a naked body, and joining Mar had seemed like a good idea. She almost messed it up. She'd intended to wash his hair and maybe massage his shoulders, not nearly climb in with him. His muscled body was alluring and deliciously hairy. It felt like petting an overgrown wolf, and he was so responsive. She enjoyed watching him strain not to drag her in, and the power she'd felt was intoxicating. What troubled her was her strong reaction. She thought the connection they established during the healing would vanish in time, but much to her irritation, the more she knew about him, the stronger she felt it. And she was not one for long-term relationships.

She tried to be rational—now was not the time or place for this. She needed to get ready for their underground exploration, and Mar had to be rested to guard her properly. Nerissa had left some ingredients for a sleeping aid, so Ina started boiling water. She crumbled dry lavender and added a few drops of valerian oil that made Boruta dance between her legs. She smiled at the cat. "Not for you, my love." When the extract was ready, she poured it into a cup and heated honey with water and a hint of milk for herself. She wondered why Mar took longer than she expected. When he came down, he looked suspiciously relaxed, and she could not stop thinking that whatever he had done upstairs wiped away his tension. Ina handed him the sleeping draught and gestured to the bedroom.

"Care to escort me up?" she asked, taking a sip of her drink and hoping Mar would mimic her gesture.

"I just came down. Besides, you should have told me this before you left me alone in the bath," he teased. The hot water and moment of pleasure took the edge away. He wanted to let her know he thoroughly enjoyed her interrogation technique. Mar took a sip of his drink as he followed Ina, enjoying the pleasant but unusual taste. Another sip, and the glass was half-empty. His mother kept telling him tea needed a loving touch to be good. Mar wondered what would his adjutant say if he asked him to make some. Once upstairs, Ina sat on the bed and patted the space next to her. Feeling a little dizzy, he eagerly accepted the invitation. The room started spinning, and a terrible thought occurred to him. "Ina, what have you given me?" His voice sounded distant, and he could barely keep his eyes open.

"Nothing much, just some simple herbs and a little magic. You need a good night's sleep." Her voice echoed in his ears, but he had no strength to object to her. Soon after, oblivion took him.

❧◦⟡◦❧

Ina looked at the sleeping man. He wouldn't be pleased in the morning, but she could not go to The Drunken Wizard with the captain of the King's Guards in tow. Tucking him in, Ina couldn't resist and leaned forwards, gently kissing his lips. Mar's clothes were still in the bathroom, so Ina quickly sorted them, hanging the leather on a rack to air, and throwing all the cloth in the bath to soak. Keeping in mind his warning about the recent attacks, she tried his sword, but it was too heavy, and she would more likely cut herself when using it. However, his dagger fit her hand perfectly, and Ina happily borrowed it. After quickly dressing in male clothes, she walked into the night towards the tavern.

The Drunken Wizard was as busy as ever. Even with the king's death, people wanted to drink. Ina slipped in quietly, almost unnoticed, and found a space at the bar, nodding to Gruff. "Do you have a moment? I need to talk to you."

"Gossip or business?" The troll, as usual, got straight to the point.

"Business, Gruff, I have no time for gossip today," she said, and he ushered her to the backroom.

"What do you need, Striga?" The room was cramped and messy, so Ina sat on an old barrel.

"I know it is short notice, but I need a small energy crystal with a large capacity, and it needs to be fully charged. Do you, by chance, have any or maybe know someone that could sell one for a reasonable price?" After her previous near-death experience, Ina knew she couldn't always count on drawing energy from some convenient kindling. She needed something else, something powerful and easily carried that could be charged daily and would store the power for a time of need. Energy crystals were commonplace, with many mages looking like bejewelled sacrificial lambs wherever they went. She needed something inconspicuous that didn't shout, "I'm a mage, hear me roar," to all and sundry.

Gruff huffed, "Small demands, hmm…" Then he looked at Ina, and she knew his mind looked over every conceivable angle. "Why fully charged? You know it doubles the costs, and you can charge it yourself in a few days. Also, you can buy crystals in any alchemy shop, so why come to me?"

"I need it for tomorrow, and I have no way to charge anything that quickly." Ina knew an honest answer was best with Gruff. He could sniff out a lie like a bloodhound. "I also know if I need something special that won't draw all eyes to me, you are the person to provide it."

The troll smirked. Gruff's deals with the shadier elements of society were well-known but never proven. He looked at Ina with sudden interest. "What happens tomorrow, if you don't mind me asking?"

Ina bit her lip, knowing that he would find out even if she kept quiet. Gruff may help and even lower the price of crystal if he felt it was good for business. "I'm headed into the sewers. Something is brewing down there, and I intend to find out what. Janik and the King's Guards both asked me to investigate."

Gruff went quiet before saying, "Janik got called off and sent out of town to deal with ghouls in a nearby village. If the guards are involved, then the king's death was out of convenience rather than his life habits." He scratched his lumpy skull. "So, you get attacked by a creature. What was it?"

Ina was only a little surprised he already knew. "Of course, you know about it. I have no idea what it was, but I think 'it' was human before it became a monster."

The troll's face darkened in anger, and he walked out, leaving her alone. Ina shifted uncomfortably. Gruff was usually as stoic as a rock, so this behaviour was completely out of character. Unsure what to do, she decided it was best to sit and wait.

Gruff carried the most beautiful peridot Ina had ever seen on his return. The crystal was a vivid green with flashes of yellow light glinting in its depths, mounted on a filigree necklace. Her Chaos magic responded instantly, drawn to the crystal, and when the troll placed it on Ina's hand, it hummed with magic. She could feel its charge exceed even those used by arch-mages. There was no way she could afford such an astonishing artefact.

"How? Gruff, this is priceless. How did you get this?" She was shocked, enraptured, and disappointed all at the same time. The overwhelming desire to keep it fought with common sense. "I can't afford it," she moaned.

She knew the troll observed her reaction with pleasure. "Does it matter where it came from if it delivers all you asked for?" Gruff's face was grim when he continued, "Some of my kin disappeared. Mainly children, as no one could kidnap an adult troll. I gift you this stone in return for a promise. Find whoever did this and make them pay. If you need anything more, just send me a word. I'm not the only one who is concerned about this situation."

Ina nodded. She'd been given more than she'd thought possible with those words.

The Drunken Wizard was the intelligence hub of the city, and Gruff, like a giant spider, held all those threads in his hands. She still felt a bit sceptical. "Is it stolen?"

Her friend wiggled his fingers. "Not from anyone living, and that is all you should know. Now, allow me the honour." He gathered the necklace from her hand. Big rough hands that could easily snap her neck were surprisingly gentle, and soon, the beautiful stone was safely nestled between her breasts. She looked down, seeing her magic slowly seep into the crystal, giving it a warmer golden hue, and yet she could not feel the drain to her energy. This necklace was a royal gift. Acting impulsively, Ina climbed onto the barrel and kissed the troll's cheek. Gruff gasped, and she realised he hadn't expected her emotional outburst, and neither had Ina. After a moment of embarrassing silence, they both burst out laughing.

"You are such an entertaining human, my little friend." Gruff held his ample belly, shaking with laughter. "I would never believe it if someone told me a human would attack a troll with kisses."

Ina felt her face was burning red. Still, she did not know what had gotten into her, but the deed was done, and she could only laugh with him at the situation.

"I'm sorry, Gruff, it was a long day. This necklace is the most precious and beautiful thing I've ever been given. I can't thank you enough."

The troll waved her off. "Do not apologise, Striga. It will be a story for the bards. The human who cheerfully kissed a troll."

Ina chuckled, saying, "And I'm sure the poor troll will have a hard time fending off her fierce advances in this story."

Gruff laughed louder, then wiped tears of joy from his eyes and turned to the shelves, pulling down a small flask of wine. "Take it with you, my little Striga—the sweetest wine I have, for the sweetest girl that ever kissed me. Now go, I have a business to run."

Ina smiled at how successful the evening had been. She had a priceless, unexpected gift, and she'd made one of the most influential people of Osterad's underground smile. Her hand touched the stone, feeling it faintly pulsing in sync with her heartbeat. This peridot was more than just a crystal filled with energy. It was something unique. The stone felt alive, connected with her Chaos magic. With a shake of her head, Ina left the tavern. It was time to get home and prepare some potions for tomorrow. With her luck, she was sure they'd be needed. She felt satisfied with her achievements tonight, and they were even worth facing Mar's wrath in the morning.

A tall man of military bearing frowned as he silently observed Ina walk away. He needed to find out what this nosy witch was doing at the tavern. It wasn't good that she'd recovered from her injuries so quickly. The situation didn't go as planned. She should have been recovering for at least a couple of days, keeping the captain preoccupied with his precious little treasure. Plenty of time to destroy the evidence of their experiments. He was pleased that her bold and reckless nature made her wander the streets alone. She might be the key to stabilising the mutagen, and one more disappearance wouldn't cause too big a problem, no matter whose lover she was.

The sound of a hungry cat loudly complaining welcomed her home. Ina felt the pang of guilt. Boruta was her little hero for bringing Velka after the attack, and she'd forgotten to feed him. She set out some food and water and started making her potions. Ina needed something fast and straightforward. They weren't heading to war after all. It was more likely they'd need them to combat her clumsiness rather than any threat.

She left the concoctions to stew for a while and checked on her sleeping knight. Ina sat down beside him. Sometimes, she envied Velka's faith in everlasting love and finding that perfect match. Ina was more pragmatic in her feelings. A good man should warm the bed and not make too much trouble. Yet here she was, sitting next to one that was nothing but trouble, making sure he had pleasant dreams. Mar stirred in his sleep and grabbed her thigh, pulling her closer. "No escape," he muttered, and Ina raised her eyebrow. Even in his sleep, he tried to catch her. She slowly pried his fingers open and stood up from the bed. "Tempting, but I still have things to do."

Dawn filtered through the curtains when she walked out of the room, picking up some pillows and blankets to nap by the fire. It was clear that he'd be in a foul mood when he woke, and she didn't want to start her day with a screaming match.

She'd worked most of the night before she finished her potions. The last brew still bubbled in the alembic, droplets condensing on the sides. It was so refreshing to have a workshop. Ina smiled when she thought about brewing in her hut, dragging that heavy cauldron back and forth to the firepit. She must have looked like the scariest witch from local folklore. It kept her safe, though, right up to the day the soldiers arrived.

Ina had valued her solitude, and the forest had called to her. Ever since the day she had wandered into the woods, drowning in despair, crying her sorrows, and dribbling her blood on an enormous ancient tree, something inside had changed. Ina no longer felt that anguish, and a feeling of belonging, of home, had seeped into her soul.

It was after that the visits started. An enormous wolf would appear from the shadows, or a strange tree appeared at dusk, vanishing come morning. One night, the Lord of the Forest appeared as a human. He'd helped Ina with her herbs, teaching her more than the university ever had, and she was sure the Leshy also sent Boruta to her. She might not comprehend his inhuman intellect, but he was a good friend and showed her a kindness her teachers never did. Ina deeply regretted that she didn't get to talk to him before she was whisked away to the capital, if only to say goodbye.

Ina rubbed her forehead as tiredness washed over her. Earlier, she had cleaned Mar's clothes and hung them on the chair so he'd have something fresh to wear in the morning. Boruta was purring happily in the makeshift bed. A simple fur and a few pillows on the floor never looked so appealing, and she hoped to catch a few hours' sleep before the sun fully rose. Ina was repeatedly yawning as she stripped herself to a single chemise. The fire's glowing embers warmed her as she pushed the cat aside, muttering, "My turn." Stroking his fur, she burrowed into the warm bed.

Ina reached for the magical net over her home and made one final check. Nothing significant was moving on her property, only an owl and some bats trying to catch their meals. Calmed by her inspection, it didn't take long to fall asleep. Deep in her dreams, she didn't feel Boruta climb onto her chest and fix his unblinking stare on her necklace. An intense purr vibrated through Ina's body as her furry guardian lay there, entranced by the slow, steady pulse of the jewel.

CHAPTER 13

As consciousness slowly returned, Mar wondered at his battle-worn body's lack of pain. Images still moved through his mind, remnants of the vivid dreams he'd had about Ina. Eyes snapping open, Mar looked around. This was her bedroom. Reality crashed down as he realised it wasn't a dream. That mischievous wench bathed, drugged, and got him in bed.

Mar sat up and saw his clean clothes were hung neatly on the chair, but Ina was nowhere to be seen. Had something happened to her? Cold shivers ran down his spine, knowing that bloody witch had made sure he couldn't stop whatever reckless endeavour she'd decided on. He could only hope that she was still alive and well, whatever she'd done.

"Ina!" Mar hastily reached for his clothes. His voice echoed through the house without response. For a moment, he stopped and listened. Normal street noises greeted him, muffled and distant, but no footsteps or voices in the house. Panic crept into him as he ran downstairs.

It took Mar just a few seconds to comprehend the situation. Ina was here, she'd slept downstairs, and she was unharmed. His relief was palpable, quickly followed by anger. A few strides later, she was in his arms. He lifted her like a rag doll, dislodging the blanket she clutched, revealing her barely dressed figure. It surprised him she didn't put up a fight. Mar carried her to a chair and lowered her gently. "Inanuan Thornsen, if you scare me like that again, I will grant you a stay in the palace dungeons. Now, shall we have your explanation for last night?"

It was late autumn, the morning's chill and fresh. Ina barely registered the commotion upstairs as she sat up, stretching and yawning, still wrapped in her bedding. Suddenly she was picked up, shaken, and then placed on a chair like one of those fragile winter flowers.

Ina observed Mar's face as he held her up. She could see a kaleidoscope of worry, relief, and cold, searing anger. Her hopes he would shout himself out and release some steam were in vain. For the first time, she felt uncertain, hoping she hadn't made a critical mistake. "Mar, I needed to go out, and I knew you wouldn't let me go."

"I could have gone with you," he said, and Ina observed him pacing the room, looking like condensed fury.

She shook her head and retorted quickly, "You could have, but the King's Guards aren't welcome at the place I went, especially not their captain." She saw Mar exhale slowly, hiding trembling hands behind his back.

"So you went to The Drunken Wizard, all by yourself. Ina, I know you are bold, but that was fucking dangerous." He looked like he had descended into a pit of madness. "The monster attacked barely two days ago, and if not for your great-aunt, you would still be bedridden with a fever and spike through your shoulder. Why were you so careless? Whoever attacked you could do it again, and you disabled me for the entire night. Why, Ina?"

She could not believe he cared for her, but the raw pain in his voice could not be denied. Ina felt she had to reassurance him. "Mar, I survived living at the edge of the Black Forest for ten years. I'm not that easy to kill. I am not a great mage, and I may not have a talent for complex spells. To have Chaos in one's main domain is difficult, but it also teaches you how to survive."

Mar stopped in his tracks and approached her. She saw him frowning with confusion at her admission. "Why? What do you mean by this?"

"When I'm trying to do the more complex spells, something happens. Sometimes the effect is favourable, but more often than not, it is a complete catastrophe. I've learned to focus on simple actions, like harnessing external force to aid my Chaos magic or working with the elements. Those don't need complex spells, just enough power. The problem comes when you need more energy than you have. At that point, we use complex spells to gather energy without killing everything, or everyone, around us. If I'm lucky, I can use my reserves or nearby elemental power."

Ina tried to explain the basic rules of magic, not only as an explanation for last night's trip but also to make him aware of what she could and couldn't do. "You'll often see mages on the street, rings on every finger and gem-encrusted clothes. It is not purely down to bad taste. Most of those gems store magical power."

She took his hand and placed it on the stone between her breasts. "This was the reason for my trip last night. Feel its power, Mar. For our visit to the sewer, I needed a charged artefact. I can't just be some damsel in distress. I went where you can…get things, and I needed the best." The witch bit her lip and raised her head to look at the captain. He didn't interrupt and appeared intrigued by her words. That warranted a little jest. "You know, looking like a virgin during the solstice fayre would attract attention. I needed a single, powerful, master grade gem. By sheer luck, I got this peridot. Even the arch-mage would covet this stone. Can you feel how it pulses? It is synchronised perfectly with my magic. I can protect us now, and you don't have to worry."

Ina kept his hand on the stone when she reached for his cheek. The soft beard tickled her fingers when she looked at him, searching for signs of forgiveness. Mar held her gaze, and she felt him search for the lie in her eyes, but she knew he would find none.

He pulled her hands down and clasped them together in her lap. "I know you thought it was the best solution, but do it again, and I will drag you to the darkest cell and lock you in it. I won't be toyed with like this again. I have not been the nicest man, and I will take last night as punishment for my transgressions. Still, despite what you may think, I'm only trying to protect you." His voice was grim, but Ina felt they had made progress, and she couldn't resist teasing him a bit.

"Oh, I don't know, you looked so cute when you were asleep." She winked, sliding from the chair.

"Ina!" Mar bellowed, but she was already halfway up the stairs. Shouting back, Ina blew him a kiss. "I need to dress, and you need to start the fire!" She heard Mar curse to himself, "Does that damn woman have an answer for everything?"

After breakfast, Mar sent two messages, one to the barracks informing them he'd be unavailable for the day and another to the chancellor, advising him of today's plans. After grabbing a map from Woron's saddlebag, he returned to the house, stopped, and sighed. As expected, Ina had nothing planned. When he asked her how she would like to proceed with her underground investigation, he got the answer, "We'll go down and see."

Mar placed the map on the table and pointed to the city's outskirts. "Most of the disappearances happened there." Mar circled the area on the map. He pointed to another object. "Here are the Swarożyc temple catacombs. That's the entrance to the tunnel system, unless, of course, you want to start with the sewers?"

Ina traced the tunnels with her finger, and he noticed how fascinated she was by the detailed map. Mar realised she didn't know how complicated the tunnel system was until he laid it clear in front of her.

"We'll start from the temple and check this quarter first." She circled the district. "If we can't find anything there, we can move towards the city centre." Ina smiled at Mar. "I have made something for the occasion."

He raised his eyebrows when she returned, holding a vial with milk like fluid. "Ina, what am I looking at?"

Closing her fingers over the vial, she answered proudly, "Our light source. I will show you in the tunnel." She grinned and packed her various vials into her bag. In the meantime, Mar went to saddle Woron.

The ride through the town was a pleasant experience. Mar enjoyed Ina's embrace, and her voice, commenting on every new shop or exciting event, had a soothing effect. When they arrived at the temple, he left Woron at a nearby stable. Now, they only had to convince a volkhv to let them in.

Ina proved to be a very resourceful woman, and he learned a few exciting secrets from her university times. A few coins exchanged hands, and an old volkhv led them to the tunnel entrance under the pretence of being a pair of thrill-seekers. Mar was initially sceptical when Ina suggested this charade, but she convinced him it was a popular attraction, especially for the junior years. It worked well, and he had to admit she was more skilled at dealing with people than he was.

As soon as the Gods' servant disappeared, Ina pulled out one of her vials. "Now watch this." She uncorked it and threw a small pebble inside. Mar was watching as instructed. Initially, nothing happened, but when he was about to avert his eyes, a sudden blinding light burst out.

"Bloody hell, Ina, you could have warned me!" he sputtered, now completely blind, rubbing his eyes with her gentle chuckle as the only answer. After he could see again, Mar could appreciate her invention fully. The light was now soft and steady, revealing the cause of the musty smell from the tunnel ahead. There were piles of bones everywhere, with only a narrow passage between them. He didn't know many that would be unfazed by the stench of decay and crunch of bugs underfoot, but Ina was focused, the gleam of excitement in her eyes. Mar wondered who else had paid for this dubious pleasure, and this thought amused him greatly. Mar took Ina's hand, directing them to the arch of a doorway, unveiled by her light. "Let's go. We don't want to waste the day."

The labyrinth of tunnels felt endless. Ina wasn't sure how long they'd been under the ground as Mar led them through twists and turns, seemingly without sense or reason. Now and then, she saw stairs leading up or even heard the screeching of carriages and humans. Tiredness and the need for fresh air were overwhelming. She wasn't sure the light she'd made would last long enough. She would shake the bottle to make it shine brighter, but she didn't want to stroll through the sewers performing shamanic dance.

Ina was about to ask for a quick stop to catch her breath and check their supplies when Mar stopped so abruptly that she bumped into his back and had to grab his belt to steady herself.

"There's a large cavern in front of us," he whispered, reaching behind and pressing her harder to his frame. This motion covered the light, and she could only hear his quiet voice for a moment. "Please stay here while I make sure it's safe."

Ina raised an eyebrow, wondering if he honestly thought she would stand there like a damsel in distress? Before she could answer, Mar released her and disappeared around the corner.

"You wish," Ina said through clenched teeth and followed. As soon as she passed the corner, she looked around the empty chamber. The small light she carried couldn't penetrate the darkness, and the air was stale with the faint smell of rotten eggs, making the witch wrinkle her nose. "Mar? What is that stench? It smells like we walked into Veles's arse."

His whisper followed the quiet sound of grinding teeth, "I asked you to wait. Couldn't you follow my instructions for once? Why did I expect rational behaviour from you? What if something attacked you in the dark?"

Ina was having none of his attitudes. "I know you are doing your best, but I'm an equal partner in the investigation, and it was my idea to go underground," she retorted, making Mar growl in reply.

"You wanted me to come here and protect you. I'm simply trying to do my job," he answered. He sounded irritated and seemed to think this would end this quarrel.

"I'm not so defenceless that I can't enter an empty room." When she could see his dark silhouette, she moved to approach him, but an inhuman shriek stopped her in her stride.

"Will you two just shut up?!"

Mar unsheathed his axe and dagger with practised ease, placing himself in front of her. He'd explained to her before he'd prepared for the possibility of fighting in close quarters, but standing here in the empty chamber, she could hear him cursing about not having his long sword and shield. Ina watched him search the darkness for the voice's owner.

She felt tired and frustrated and took offence at being told what to do. So, she yelled back to the disembodied voice, "You want to tell me to shut up?! You sewer scum! Then show yourself and tell this to my face like a man, or whatever you are, you bloody coward." She realised she wasn't sure who or what she was addressing but was too annoyed to care.

"You came here and yelled like a scruffy wench. I'm not coming down. You wake me up, and you mean," came the answer from above.

Mar sniggered, and she saw him relax a bit when the heckler seemed so petulant. She saw him looking at the source of the voice. "Oh, that's precious, Ina. It sounds like our new friend already knows you."

The argument with her protagonist and Mar's remark made her scowl. "I will show you who's a scruffy wench, you misplaced botchling!" She raised her glowing vial, sending a pulse of her magic into it, maybe a little too much, as the dim light shone like the sun, blinding everyone in the chamber, including herself.

"Ina!" Mar staggered, trying to shade his eyes from the light.

"I'm not a botchling, you bloody witch," answered a scrawny imp-like creature on the other side of the room, trying to bury its elongated face behind a crumbling wall.

Ina dimmed the light just enough to see the end of the chamber and asked, "Then who are you?" Judging by its responses, the creature was sentient, even with its small, gnarled form. With the afterimage of her magic dancing in her eyes, she knew she'd overreacted just a little.

"What is it to you? You came here to catch me just like the others did, stupid human!" This statement caught Ina's attention. It looked like this creature had encountered something interesting in the tunnels.

Mar moved to the side and looked like he would attempt its capture, but Ina placed her hand on his shoulder and shook her head. She reached into her bag and pulled out the provisions she had packed for the trip. Sweet honey flans and herbal tea released a delicious smell, filling the chamber with the scent of the autumn harvest. "We will camp here, Mar. Would you like to share my meal, imp? We have plenty of food."

The creature turned pointy ears in her direction. Mar looked at her with bewilderment but took a cake when she offered it. "Erm…yes, we can camp here." He wasn't sure what to say but observed the creature from the corner of his eye, sniffing and licking thin lips with a long, forked tongue. Ina smiled, turned around and extended her hand to it.

"I think we have enough to share. I'm sorry we disturbed your peace, but we are trying to find those others. The ones that tried to catch you. Do you know where they are?" The being came closer, but it hissed and flinched away when Ina moved to pass the cake. She sighed. "I promise we are not here to catch you. We didn't even know you were here."

The creature was fast, and she heard Mar's curse when he saw how quickly it moved, as it evaded her hand. Not menacing in size, but she bet it could be vicious when cornered. Ina appreciated that Mar observed her effort to befriend the imp and kept as still as possible. It looked like the tiny monster took a liking to her baking skills. As soon as the cake was taken, loud chewing and satisfying moans echoed in the chamber. She continued the bizarre interrogation. "Those bad people you mentioned. Do you mean monsters, ones that feel like dirt and tar?"

Ina described the feeling of her encounter. Their unlikely companion moved closer and extended his skinny hand, looking up with expectation. She could see they were dealing with a male imp, so she'd have to be careful how to form the questions. Once she filtered his answers, he could be a valuable source of information.

"No, not the weird ones. Humans, like you…and him," said the imp munching through the second pastry. "The warrior man, he cut me, see?" The imp raised his arm, and they could see a nasty scar on the creature's olive-grey skin.

Ina nodded and tried to appear as sympathetic as possible. "We're not here to hurt anyone that doesn't hurt us first. We want to find those other humans because they injured my friend. I'm Ina, and this is Mar. What is your name?"

The imp shrugged and moved away farther. "I won't tell you. If you know, you will call me and make me do things."

That was the wrong move. Ina had forgotten he was still a demon. "I'm sorry, you are right not to trust us, but perhaps you could tell me—the man who cut you, was he alone?" The little demon reached out for her dwindling supply of cakes.

"No, there was another one, like you, but not. You made the light, but he tried to get here"—the imp pointed to its head—"to make me do things like one of the weird."

Mar and Ina exchanged looks. So, psychic magic was how they controlled the monsters. "Where did they go?" Mar asked impatiently, making the little imp cower.

Seeing this, Ina tried to save the situation. "We don't like people who get into your head. Please, would you help us find him?"

The imp nodded and pointed to the tunnel to the left, his eyes reflecting Ina's light like a cat. "There, but be careful. The weird ones are there, too, and bring more cakes if you come back." He gave her a toothy grin and darted up to the wall, disappearing into the shadows. Ina picked up her bag and turned towards the tunnel, but Mar grabbed her hand.

"You did a great job here. Now please let me do mine. You heard the imp say the weird ones, or whatever he called them, are there. I don't want you to… Just let me do my job, please." Mar's voice was soft, almost pleading. He wasn't ordering her around this time, he was asking, and Ina had to admit he was right, but there was one thing that disturbed her deeply.

"Mar, they have a psychic mage that is strong enough to control such twisted minds. What if he attacks you?"

Ina was amused by his victorious smile when she didn't deny him the lead. "We need to take the risk. The chances we'll be exposed to a physical attack here are far greater than a mental one. Besides, I have you here to deal with it. We just need to find a door you can throw them through." He winked, making her snort a short, involuntary laugh.

Ina punched him in the shoulder. "Will you stop it? It was an accident, and you broke the second one. Onwards, my handsome knight, and let us not perish in the dark."

Now it was Mar's turn to laugh. "Ina, I've been called many names, but *handsome* wasn't one of them." Mar was taken aback when she looked at him with surprise, which progressed into a smile that could light this black hall.

"But, Mar, I think you are stunning. You are my personal mountain of Liath." A sense of closeness spread through his chest. Maybe he'd found the key to her mind. All he had to do was give her a choice and maybe tease her a little.

He looked down, brushing away a few strands that fell on her face. "You will crumble the mountain if you smile like that more often," he said and headed to the tunnel.

The passage felt never-ending but relatively straightforward to follow, with no branches or obstructions. The walls, uneven earlier in the journey, were now man-made, and Mar could even see the occasional decoration. He suspected they were in the central part of town, possibly even under the merchant square. Scraps of fabric and cart remnants gave the impression illegal goods moved through here.

Still, it was not Mar's job to investigate merchants who tried to make some coin on the side. The tax system implemented by the king was harsh enough, and he knew that smuggling was commonplace. He looked behind him to check on his ward, and thankfully Ina was diligently following, but even in the dim light he could see she was tired. She didn't complain, and Mar admired her resilience, but it was about time they took a rest. He decided they'd take the next stairs they found, even if they ended up in some merchant's basement.

Mar whipped around at a sudden crash, and the light disappeared as Ina's muffled cry vanished into the darkness. For a moment, his mind went blank. What had happened? She was right behind him a moment ago. Now there was only silence.

"Ina!" he bellowed, uncaring if anyone was listening. He tried to think. There must be a trapdoor, something she had triggered, but the stones were smooth and unmoving under his touch. "Ina!" he shouted again, but only an echo responded to his call. Mar felt the darkness choking him as he realised he'd failed her again.

CHAPTER 14

Ina stopped to tighten her laces when she noticed a crescent moon on the wall, positioned at a strange angle. She reached over to examine the unusual design, but as she touched it, the floor disappeared beneath her feet, and she fell with a surprised yelp. The drop was short and ended with a wet thud. Something had cushioned her fall, and now she lay there, grateful for the help. Her light vial was gone, smashed as she tried to stop her fall, so Ina summoned a tiny pulsar, congratulating herself for remembering the spell. The peridot wouldn't be depleted quickly by such a minor charm. She sent the ball of light upwards and turned to look around.

Her eyes met unspeakable horror. She lay on a pile of bodies, with agonised human faces staring from every angle. Twisted bodies were partially transformed into travesties of life. Ina didn't know how she'd missed the smell of rotting corpses, gagging as it overwhelmed her. She had to get out of here before she lost her mind to this madness.

Tears stung her eyes when she started crawling over them. She could sense the mutagen with her magic, yet not one body was wholly transformed. Despite warped faces and mangled limbs, their energy signatures still belonged to their race. In the end, Ina scrambled to the floor and backed herself into an empty corner. She swallowed hard. *Think, Ina, keep your head and focus. Get out of here alive and find the bastard who did this.*

She breathed, rocking slowly till her makeshift mantra calmed her enough to look around. Ina added more energy to her light, letting her see the room was almost empty, not counting the pile of bodies. To her right was a solid wooden door. Ina stood up and went there to try it, but of course it was locked. She cursed under her breath, knowing Mar would have the time of his life teasing her over this. The witch braced herself and gripped her gem fiercely, trying to be precise, wanting only to break the lock. When she felt enough kinetic energy condensed in her palm, she pushed it forcefully into the mechanism.

A thunderous boom rocked the underground and destroyed the door and half of the wall. Ina gaped at the large hole as she coughed and wiped the dust away from her eyes. She didn't know what went wrong, but she was definitely free. She'd never had strength like this before, and the only change was the gem. Raising it to her eyes, she muttered, "What the hell are you?" Ina shook her head in wonder, hoping she hadn't depleted the jewel too much with this one burst.

There was no time to think about it now, so she moved to the next room, now devastated by the shock wave, and noticed the remains of a small alchemy stand. Her actions had scattered the vials and tools. Still, Ina recognised most of the ingredients to her mutagen. When she saw an unbroken vial, she placed it in her pocket to test later.

She moved the pulsar around the room with a gentle sweep of her hand. In the far corner sat an examination table, and Ina could see a writhing shape strapped to its surface. Hesitantly, she went closer, wishing Mar was here. She teased him mercilessly, but having the grumpy warrior's support gave her courage she didn't feel at the moment.

The shape at the table jerked its head to the side, looking straight at her. Muscles tensing under the rope, the poor wretch screamed as bones creaked and tore in slow, painful movements from the joints. There were needles still attached to its neck and empty vials on the floor, knocked down by the constant trashing. It was horrid and fascinating at the same time. The tears in her eyes were no longer from the dust as she realised this tortured soul was human, now being transformed into one of the monsters they'd come to find.

Ina was powerless to help. Her magic was useless for stopping the transformation or reversing the effects. All she could do was end the person's suffering. She approached the creature, placed her hand on its head, and sobbed. Whoever did this deserved to die, but all she had was mercy for now.

Magic flowed through her fingers, sensing the unblemished energy of a human soul. No mage had unravelled it to ease the transformation. Instead, they'd forced the change in the most brutal way possible. Ina's Chaos magic slowly unbound the life force under her touch, iridescent pearls of light disappearing into the aether, while the raw Chaos magic that bound his existence seeped into her skin. Memories, joys and sorrows, first love and last friend, faded into nothingness as Ina freed his soul with a last whispered apology.

For the first time in her life, she had killed a sentient being, and although she offered a peaceful passage, she knew this man's death would stay with her forever. Ina supported her head on the cold table. She wept, lamenting the life taken by her hand, the school mistake that had given birth to this tragedy, and her life that would never be innocent again.

Mar was at his wit's end trying to find Ina. His hands bled from frantically trying to pry the rocks from their position in complete darkness. An explosion rocked the corridor, making his heart sink. Only Ina could do something so reckless, and only if she was in trouble. Still, relief poured into him as whatever caused the blast broke open a hidden door, flooding the tunnel with light. *Well done,* he thought. *Blow the doors off for me, every single one of them.*

The passage behind the door was a tight fit but short. After a moment of struggle, Mar pushed himself into a cramped room filled with maps and books. Now that his eyes had adjusted, he saw a small lantern was the only light source. Still he could see the shapes of volumes, rolls of maps, and another open door on the opposite side. Mar didn't have time to look closer. Ina was still lost in here somewhere. After pressing onwards through the next door, he scraped to a stop at the sight of a twisted troll and two hulking mastiffs. The noise caught their attention, and six glowing red eyes suddenly confronted him. Mar ripped the dagger and axe from his belt, eyes widening as the creatures surged forwards.

"Fuck." The curse slipped out as the dogs leapt at his throat. Mar ducked to the side and, stabbing upwards with the dagger, took the brunt of the impact to his shoulder. The pained grunt slipped out as two sets of claws scrabbled for purchase on his chest and arm, and he grinned at the yelp of a hound as he sliced deeply into its flank, even as the weight of the hounds forced him to the ground.

Furiously stabbing over and over at the dogs, they finally freed him from their attack as they rushed to escape the pain. Mar rolled over and lunged to his feet, clumsy with his axe swinging crazily, holding back the animals, even as the impact of a massive fist lifted him bodily into the wall.

"This is it. I'm going to die here," he spat the words out with bloody phlegm at the troll. "Fuck it! You're going with me, big boy," the captain screamed and threw himself at the creature, axe slicing in a vicious arc across his body, tearing into the attacking troll's arm and embedding itself in the thick muscle. The bellow of agony deafened Mar as, once again, he was lifted off his feet and flung back into the other room. The impact left him dazed and confused as the room started glowing. Understanding and fear filtered through his daze as familiar red hair came into focus. "Ina, no! Get out of here!"

Mar lurched onto unsteady feet, determination firming the grip on his weapons as he stepped forwards and let himself go. He had to save Ina, even if it meant his death. A strange calm washed over him, and he smiled as something deep inside awoke, taking control, blue eyes burning gold. Mar's friends would recognise this moment. Their captain became something different, something terrifying when hanging between life and death. Just as now, he leapt forwards, axe and knife a blur, cutting and stabbing at the monsters in front of him.

~ ❦ ~

Ina was drifting deeply in sorrow and self-pity when the sounds of the battle caught her attention. With the flick of her wrist, she rose from her stance and strengthened the pulsar light, fixing it in front of her. The first thing to do was find Mar and get out of this cursed place now that the way seemed clear.

The noise of the fight led to the entrance of another room. Well, the wreck of one, at least. Mar was there, struggling with three opponents who attacked him simultaneously. He was working hard with his axe and dagger. The weapons glided through the air in precise cuts, wounding the monsters. Ina's hand closed on the peridot, and she drew on its power, deeper and deeper. Her sorrow turned to anger at the sight of the troll smashing heavy fists into Mar's chest. Whips of pure fire coiled around her, animated by Chaos magic. Anger and Chaos poured into the stone, and a torrent flooded back, shaping the whips into vipers, beautiful and deadly, as Ina lashed them at the troll. Coils of destruction shot out, slamming into the attacking creature. The beast roared and turned to the source of the pain.

~ ❦ ~

The light glowing in Mar's eyes flared, feasting on Ina, magnificent in her magic. His beautiful distraction gave him the perfect opportunity again. His axe cleaved through the air, crushing one dog's head, killing it instantly. Ina held her ground, her fire vipers lashing at the troll, leaving deep gashes of burnt tissue behind. The beast leapt backwards, trying to avoid the pain, but Mar was there to stop it. This formidable display of Ina's magic terrified the remaining canine to turn tail and run, whimpering into the darkness.

"Ina, stop!" shouted Mar as he ducked to avoid a strike from the vipers, and Ina lowered her hands, letting the energy dissipate in the air. Again, the monstrous troll turned back to her, giving Mar the opening he needed. His axe rose high and cleaved its collarbone so deeply that he could see the heart pulsing through the gap. Then, with a final stab of the dagger, it was stopped dead.

The beast landed on the floor with a heavy thud, and without glancing at it, Mar ran to his woman. In the light of her pulsar, he saw she was crying, her body and hair coated with blood and fluid, his heart aching at her pain.

"Are you wounded?" he asked and felt immense relief when she shook her head. There was something in his spitfire's posture that held him back. "What happened back there?"

"I will tell you at home, but I need to get out of this cursed place to think clearly," she said, and Mar didn't try to make her talk, despite his curiosity.

Mar grabbed her hand and headed to the exit, seizing a few scrolls on the way out to check on later. For now, he was worried about Ina, who was strangely quiet, but despite his best efforts, it took them another hour to emerge from the tunnels.

Thankfully, the sun had already set, and there were only a few witnesses on the street to see their bedraggled state. Mar promised himself he would care for her once they reached home, even if it made her angry. This new silent Ina worried him, and he'd rather face her wrath than her silence.

CHAPTER 15

Ina couldn't stop dwelling on what had happened. The trip to the underground brought her more than expected, possibly more than she could handle. After stepping into the fresh air, the witch noticed her stench. The gore from the rotting corpses was drying on her body, and while its stench was less offensive now, she still felt dirty inside and out.

Mar held her hand as they trudged along, and she noticed him looking at her with concern in his eyes. Thankfully, her house was not too far away. They stopped briefly as Mar caught some errand boy. She heard him ordering someone to bring his horse here, and he'd asked for Ren to come as well. After he issued the orders, he sent the boy to the barracks. However, her mind was so preoccupied with flashbacks that she ignored most of his actions. Upon their arrival home, Boruta greeted her at the doors, only to hiss and dart inside at the first whiff of Ina's pungent smell.

"I need to wash," she said.

He nodded, dropping their belongings in a pile next to the door. "Ina, I need to go to the chancellor as soon as we talk, but I don't want to leave you." He approached her, and despite the repulsive smell, he locked her in his arms. "I don't know what happened there, but I want you to know you were formidable. You saved my sorry arse from the troll with your magic vipers," he said and then attempted to jest, "I would kiss you for it, but you smell worse than the troll."

She knew he was trying to make her feel better, but the burden she carried stopped her from appreciating it. Ina detangled herself from his arms and headed upstairs, leaving Mar to his own devices.

❧

Mar slowly mixed some warm milk with a few spoons of honey. The mixture may not be as good as hers, but it would help as a harmless distraction. He walked upstairs, cup in hand, only to find Ina was not in her room. He heard the splash of water and moved to the bathroom door, hesitating. It wouldn't be the first time Mar had seen her naked, but this time it felt wrong. With a growing ache in his chest, knowing Ina was in pain, he let himself inside with downcast eyes.

The mage looked lost in thought as she left the bath and slipped into a long nightshirt. Mar put the cup on a shelf and approached her as she sat in front of the mirror. "Ina?"

His arrival shook her out of her stupor. "Oh yes, I will be done in a minute." Drying her hair, she smiled at him with eyes still sad and distant.

"Let me help you." He took the towel and gently squeezed the water out. Ina didn't protest, allowing him to slide the shirt off her shoulders when his hands moved to the nape of her neck, each action delicate and careful.

"I'm not made of glass, Mar." Her lips twitched slightly as she handed him a brush, and it was the first animated reaction he had seen since they left the tunnels. "Let's see if you are better than Ren."

Mar welcomed this minor act of defiance, deciding to act on it. "I'm always better than Ren." The playfulness in his voice brought another half smile to her face. He felt like a hero until his fingers tangled in her mane.

Their eyes met in the mirror, and she noticed his utterly lost expression. Her lips twitched once more, and when he uttered an exasperated sigh, she started laughing. "I think we just found something Ren is better at than you." Mar only grumbled, happily giving his friend this minor victory if it made her smile.

He raised a hand in surrender. "I will bow to his superior brushing skills if I must. Now, I'm sorry, but I have to ask—what happened when you disappeared?"

Ina took a deep breath and reached for the cup. "I don't think this story can be avoided." She told Mar about the rock that got her attention and the surprising slide that ended on the pile of corpses.

"I think I found the alchemy workshop where they made the mutagen." That reminded her of the vial she'd taken. "Mar, I found a potion. If we can get it to the university tomorrow, my friend may help me identify the ingredients, but I'm already sure it is based on my work."

"Was that all that you discovered there?" Mar asked, as he didn't think a pile of corpses would shake her this much.

Ina was quiet for a moment, then looked at him in a way that made him uncomfortable. Her eyes lost focus, recalling the situation. "I killed someone there," she stated.

Mar realised she was expecting his judgement but to his dismay, he found out that he didn't know what to say. Her eyes were pleading for absolution, and he knew she was asking the wrong person.

"Ina, you aren't someone that would kill without good reason. There's not an evil bone in your body," he started seeing the glimpse of hope on her face. "Tell me exactly what happened."

When she did, he lifted her from the chair and placed her on his lap, despite her initial protests. He touched her chin and gently turned her to face him. "I know this feeling. Every soldier knows it. The faces of those who die by my hand haunt my dreams, but what you did was different. You ended his suffering. You freed his soul from torment and let him go to Nawia to be reborn. Don't punish yourself for this. Those who captured and tortured him are to blame. You did all you could and set him free." His lips touched her with the gentlest of kisses when he tried to reassure her. "You showed mercy, and I know he would thank you for it," he said, and Ina wrapped her arms around him. Mar had distant memories of his despair and how he wished someone had told him he was not to blame when his sword bled for the first time. He was glad he could do this for her.

The creak of the doors and footsteps downstairs caught the captain's attention. He released Ina from his embrace and gently stroked her cheek. "I will go see who is here."

Ina nodded and reached for a simple house dress. A few minutes later, she stood on the top of the stairs as Ren looked at her with growing concern while Mar issued short, quiet orders.

"You will not stay?" she asked when he started picking up his weapons. He sensed her disappointment when he shook his head.

"I need to talk to the chancellor about what happened today. We will need reinforcements to search the tunnels and access to the university archive. But you won't be alone. Ren will stay with you." He saw the sadness creep into her eyes, and Mar felt lost—she needed him, but he had duties to fulfil. Besides, she needed someone who would understand, not a brutish captain who would pat her shoulder as if she was a young soldier and tell her to carry on.

"Perhaps you should let him brush your hair, if you want him to keep besting me in this task, or he can play for you. Ren is good in many things."

Mar felt he was talking gibberish and rushed to leave before her jade eyes made him change his mind. Ren's eyes darkened, and he sent him a questioning look that Mar tried to shrug off.

"I will be back later or tomorrow, so Ren will keep you company, but I'd ask you not to do anything dangerous tonight. Just have a rest until I'm back. Please."

Ina observed them for a moment from her position. "Mar, as much as I like Ren's company, I don't need a guardian. Please let him go back and get some rest."

Mar knew she was right. She could look after herself. This constant stream of imposed guardians must be tiresome, but he didn't want her to be alone, not after what had happened.

Ren moved his gaze from Ina to Mar, his posture tense as if he was unsure of what was happening.

The warrior bowed deeply when he addressed Ina. "My lady, I won't disturb your rest. I will take my stance outside the house, but my orders are to ensure your safety, and I intend to carry them out."

Ina rubbed her forehead. She must have been tired, irritated, and judging by her gesture, she had a headache. She pointed to the chair. "No, you will not! It's almost winter. Stay here by the fire if you must."

Ren bowed even lower. "There is no need for it. I'm used to harsh winter weather."

The pressure in the air grew oppressive as Ina's magic swirled around her hands. His spitfire, already at her wit's end, didn't like to be denied in her own home. "Ren, you will do as you are told. You are a guest in my house now, and I will show you hospitality even if I have to fry your brain to do it. Now, sit on the bloody chair," Ina said slowly. Her voice was edged with steel, enunciating every single word.

Mar reacted first, guiding Ren towards the chair. "Go, and do your best to help her calm down, whatever it takes." With a courtly bow, the captain said, "I will bid you good night, my lady. Oh, and Ina? I offer my gratitude for your assistance in the tunnels." The wink he gave her as he left offset the formal words.

Mar told her he needed to speak with the chancellor, so why did his departure feel so painful? Despite his hairy bear hugs and obvious concern, he'd found the right words to relieve her worry, almost causing an embarrassing meltdown.

The witch noticed Ren's confusion and cursed her lack of control. He wasn't to blame for the situation or her awful mood, yet she'd taken it out on him. Ina moved and sat on the opposite chair. "I'm sorry, Ren. It has been a long day, one of the worst I've ever had."

"No need to apologise, my lady. The captain told me you were attacked in the tunnels."

Ina raised her eyebrow at that summary. "Is that what he told you? Then let me tell you what actually happened. I only landed head first on the pile of corpses. It was Mar they attacked in the tunnels, and he fought them off like a bloody wyvern, with this yellow glow in his eyes that still gives me a chill," she said and amused by her comparison, she added, "maybe he really is a wyvern—he keeps guarding me like a pot of gold."

Ren nodded. "I've seen it before in battle. The captain is ferocious when he is defending those he cares about," Ren said and pondered for a moment. "He said you held off some monstrosity of a troll?"

Ina shrugged. "What else could I do? Mar was attempting to die there, and I kind of got used to him being around."

Ren snorted a short laugh. "That was not the summary I expected, but between you two, it sounds like an accurate account of the events." He rose from his chair and approached Ina. "You need to sleep, my lady. I know that night is still young, but you look exhausted." Ren sent her a small, playful smile. "Please don't make me beg you."

His plea amused her, but she was afraid to close her eyes, still seeing the dead man's face. "I don't think I can sleep tonight, and I don't want to cloud my thoughts with potions and herbs."

Ren reached his hand to her. "Let me help you, and if you're still not asleep in an hour, I won't insist."

Ina was curious, and she let him lead her to the bedroom. When he tucked her in, she chuckled. "Ren, I don't think it will work. What you're doing is sweet, but I'm wide—" Soft lips touched her forehead in a chaste kiss.

"He is not the only one who cares for you, so please don't make me worry. I can be worse than Mar. Close your eyes, Ina. Close them for me, please?" He addressed her directly, and Ina's eyes fluttered at this strange combination of plea, order, and threat, but she decided to humour him. From half-closed eyelids, she noticed he positioned himself on the windowsill. His silhouette framed in the moonlight was so unreal that he truly deserved the nickname Ghost. Soon she heard the soft tones of a bamboo flute. Love and longing mixed with sorrow and heartbreak danced in the shadows as he played for her and her alone. The captivating melody soothed her soul until she finally fell asleep.

After a protracted meeting with the chancellor, Mar was exhausted. His superior wanted to know every detail of the expedition. Mar could see how disturbed the old politician was hearing about the pile of bodies and alchemy workshop. With reluctance, Mar mentioned his stab wound and disclosed there might be a traitor in the guards. He didn't want to blame his friends and hinted at it being a poor soul who died during the attack. He had already started a discreet search in the barracks. Outside forces would only cause distrust between the soldiers, which was the last thing he needed. Only one good thing came from this. They now knew it wasn't some natural catastrophe or monstrous horde overrunning the city, causing the disappearances. That there was some malicious will behind everything was less frightening than some God's wrath. The paperwork that had needed to be done didn't help either, and when the words started dancing on the page, he gave up and left.

Mar swayed, half-asleep, as he rode Woron, trusting his steed to take him home. His awareness returned when the slow, soothing gait stopped right in the middle of Ina's yard. "Oh well, you like it here, do you?" said Mar, patting Woron's neck. "Good boy." He slowly looked around. The house was still standing, and the door was there. It looked like Ren had tamed the raging fire. The weary soldier stabled Woron, giving him a thorough rubdown in thanks, then made his way to the house.

"Something told me you would be back sooner than later," Ren's voice greeted him as soon as he opened the door. "How did it go?"

In the light of the slow blaze of the dying fire, Mar noticed his friend sitting in one of Ina's soft chairs, his short sword naked on his lap. Mar sat heavily on the opposite chair, his weariness apparent. "As well as expected. The chancellor decided we needed to clean the sewers. Instead of Janik's company, our guard will crawl in the shit and mud." He removed his leather armour and sighed with pleasure. His body demanded rest, and he had no will to ride back to the barracks. "How is Ina?"

"Asleep. Now care to tell me what exactly happened there? My lady came back a changed woman." Ren's concern was evident, and Mar knew he would have to give him an explanation.

"She had to kill someone, and not in the heat of battle. We both know how it feels, and it didn't sit well with her nature. That Striga is stronger than you'd think, and if you'd seen her…" Mar closed his eyes for a second, picturing Ina's face, frozen in a fury, as her magic whipped through the air. "She was magnificent,

Ren. If my fate is to die on the battlefield, I want death to have her face when she comes for me."

Ren's hands closed on the blade so hard that blood trickled from under his fingers. His soft voice was full of suppressed anger. "Mar, this is wrong. You're using her as an asset, but what about her? Have you thought of her?"

Mar watched his friend thoughtfully. Ren rarely gave a glimpse of his emotions. His calm, almost otherworldly attitude was legendary, but the man in front of him barely resembled the Ghost he knew.

"What exactly are you asking, Ren?" But the way his friend looked at him, Mar had a feeling he would not like the answer to his question.

"Leave her out of this problem and out of your life. She is getting hurt, broken, and I…I can take care of her. I know you are fascinated by her and attracted to her magic, but you will push her aside like the other women in your life when this fades. I saw how she looked at you, and I swore to protect her."

"And you, what you will give her?" Mar asked calmly, despite the fury thrashing inside him.

"The love and peaceful life she craves so much. If she is nothing else to you but a key to a riddle, then leave. She will hurt for a while, but she will understand."

Mar felt like the weight of the world was bearing down on his shoulders, and looked at his knight, his comrade. "You don't know her at all, do you, my friend? Neither do I, really, but I know one thing. In anger or love, Ina will never be happy with the quiet life you offer. That Striga survived the exile meant to kill her. She befriended Leshy and gave her everything to save

214

two worthless soldiers. My brother, that is who she is, and I am lost to all of her."

Mar's eyes glowed like embers in the fireplace. He wanted to go upstairs and make her choose who she would welcome in her life, but he forced himself to sit still. "Does she love you, Ren?" His question sounded hollow to his ears.

Ren shook his head. "No, but you already know this. She likes my company, and maybe with time, she would learn to love me, but if not, being by her side is good enough for me."

Mar locked his eyes on Ren. "Then you have no right to ask me to leave. She is not just a key to the riddle…not anymore."

"So be it. I won't stand against you if she chooses you, but I will be there for her, and you can't take that away from me." Ren relaxed on the chair and broke into a short, hollow laugh. "We are doomed, my friend. Fate pitted us against each other, and only time will tell which one of us was right."

CHAPTER 16

The noise of the conversation broke through her dreams. Ina sat up on the bed and looked around, seeing bodies and monsters superimposed over the room until slowly they faded into the moonlight. The quiet hum of male voices raised her curiosity, and she wrapped herself in a blanket to walk to the top of the stairs in time to hear them describing her so vividly. She didn't expect Mar to think about her so highly, but here he was, a man of many hidden depths.

"Ren? Mar?" Her quiet voice filtered down, making both men stop and lift their heads towards her.

"Ina, I'm sorry we woke you up." Ren was first on his feet. "Would you like me to play for you again?"

Ina descended to the living room, shaking her head. "Mar, what are you doing here?" she asked, yawning slightly. "Besides, you both should be asleep now."

Mar grimaced, trying to remove his jacket. "My horse seems to like your stables, but unfortunately, the three of us won't fit in your bed, not that I would share you with another man." Ina was taken aback by his bold statement right after the flowery speech she heard.

Before reason could close her mouth, she said, "Well, that is a shame. I was going to tell you both to sleep there as you look so cosy together."

Mar threw his jacket into the corner and grabbed Ina by her wrist, pulling her onto his lap. "Ina, it was a challenging day. I need something to distract me from my troubles, so please close your eyes before I kiss you."

When Ina gave him a questioning look, he eased her head to his shoulder. "Could you help me fall asleep?" he whispered when she tried to protest.

Ina's body stilled. She realised, being so focused on herself, she'd missed Mar's struggle, and while she at least had a bath and a nap, he hadn't even fully undressed yet.

Relaxing on his chest, she whispered back, "Just this once—don't get used to it."

She snuggled her head into his neck and added a little louder, "Ren, would you play that beautiful melody again, my friend?"

The sound of Ren's flute filled the room, entwined with the fading light of the moon. His music hinted at the anger and regret he felt when he looked at Ina nestled against his friend. It should be him embracing her as she slept. His finger missed a note, but he quickly corrected himself and slowly changed the tune to the song of his homeland. Ren thought how different it would be if he'd taken the dragon throne. He didn't blame his brother. The new emperor was a good man, showing him mercy with exile. Would he have been happy sitting there in jade and silk? Would he have a woman like Ina, a woman he didn't have to share? His past filled his memories and dulled the anger. Ren finally relaxed.

Ina woke up feeling refreshed, breathing in Mar's scent, while his arms embraced her tightly. Yesterday's events seemed to be a distant nightmare that quickly faded in the morning light. A movement to the side and a quiet voice caught her attention.

"Ina, are you awake?" Ren's smiling face appeared in front of her. When she smiled back, he added, "I've made some tea." That sounded like a lovely idea, especially at the start of a busy day, but there was one problem. The giant whose lap she occupied held her close, and he was still deeply asleep.

She pointed out the apparent problem and winked at Ren. "If I only could, I would gladly accept your invitation."

Ren put his sword away with an exasperated sigh and then approached Mar with a wooden spoon and a malicious smile. "Get yourself ready," he said right before placing the spoon handle to his captain's throat, growling, "Give me your money, you noble scum."

Ren was flipped on his back in a blink of an eye, and Mar hovered above him, one hand on his throat, the other sheltering Ina. The conspirators were now roaring with laughter at the captain's confusion. He released them and ground his teeth. "Are you fucking out of your mind, Ghost? I could have killed you." His chagrin only caused an even greater burst of merriment.

Ina was now practically hanging off Ren, patting her friend's back. "Ren, you are the best. You just made my day, and Mar, don't be angry over a simple joke. Come, Ren made breakfast for us all."

After the meal, Ina announced she was going to the university, and no escort was needed. Mar's smug face told her he was planning something. "Velka will be disappointed since I already sent a message that you will visit your school grounds. Now, I will have to tell Daro to stay away from her, as I'm sure she would like to join you."

Ina was speechless. This sneaky bastard had already arranged her day, saddling her with Velka and her newest love interest. She slammed her hand in front of him. "That was a low blow, and you know it."

Mar took her hand and kissed the soft skin on her wrist. "I will stop at nothing to keep you safe, and I'm not ashamed of it." Ina looked at Ren, trying to find an ally, but he only nodded in agreement. *Bloody men, manipulative sons of bitches.* Now they stood in brotherhood against her. She was about to kick them out of her house when, after a brief knock, Velka's head appeared at the entrance, followed by the massive frame of the young orc. Ina rolled her eyes, knowing it was too late to protest.

Mar took Daro aside while Velka showered Ina with a relentless stream of questions. She watched while, together with Ren, he caught the orc up on the latest news. Daro kept nodding, his face turning grimmer and grimmer. Ina wished she could hear at least a word or two, but before she knew it, she was packed into a carriage and sent on her way.

The carriage moved slowly, manoeuvring through the busy streets. Velka spent the time commenting on the recent events in the court. It appeared the new king differed little from the old one, mostly because he was more focused on professional women to fill his bed during the long autumn nights. However, to Ina's surprise, he cut food taxes and decreased the influence of wealthy merchants and noble families. It felt like a foolish attempt to cause a coup, but Ina suspected there was an ulterior motive. Why didn't he bed the countless daughters of nobles that filled court halls? It would be the cheaper option. Her political analysis was stopped short when they arrived at the university gates.

While she walked through the halls, Ina was unaware of the impression their small cavalcade left behind. She wore practical trousers and a long, belted tunic slit on both sides to allow freedom of movement. After recent events, she'd chosen black to hide the inevitable stains if she got in trouble. Her long hair was braided into a high dragon knot. She looked powerful with the royal Nature Mage and massive orc warrior in tow.

Before reaching the alchemy department, her path crossed with the provost of battlemages. "Lady Inanuan, I would like a word, please." Seeing her companions coming closer, he added, "Just you, I must insist."

Ina nodded to her friends and followed the provost. Once the door closed, he turned to her. His gaze pinned her to the wall like some fascinating insect.

Finally, he spoke, "I heard you missed your calling, my lady. A potion master fending off a warped troll? You should have studied as a battlemage."

Ina felt tendrils of his magic sliding through her consciousness and instinctively snapped her barrier shut.

"Don't be rude," she said, addressing him casually, which helped her remain composed. She was not his student, and as powerful as he was, he couldn't do anything with witnesses waiting outside.

The mage looked at her and shrugged. "You can't blame me for trying, but let me be blunt since we're heading in this direction. Do you know who is controlling them?"

"Don't tell me you still suspect me?" Ina answered, sarcasm dripping in her voice.

The mage nodded. "After you showed off with fire magic in your yard, which should not be so easy for you, I don't know what I should believe anymore."

"Is defending my life showing off?" Ina became annoyed by his behaviour. "I should ask you how the mutagen that was confiscated from me as soon as I mixed it ended up in the sewers of Osterad?" she said, anger heating her words. Her temper flaring up was not a good thing, but Ina was past the point of caring. "I clearly remember the renowned council taking it away, not just the potion, but also my formula, all my notes, and everything that even touched on it. Yet here it is, causing so much death and suffering." The surrounding air shimmered from the heatwave she unintentionally created.

Arun backed away, casting a shield and barking a short laugh. "My little Ina, how you've changed and yet not at all—so easy to anger, goaded by simple words, but the level of your magic? How could I have not recruited such a talent?"

"What the hell are you talking about?" Ina almost shouted. This arrogant man brought out the worst in her, but when she looked around, she saw wood seared by the intensity of her magic.

Arun smiled and said, "You did this without even trying. How could I not believe you'd be able to control the monster if you can do…this?"

Ina looked him in the eye. "Well, then I think you'll just have to believe your truth spell. If you are that concerned about monsters, find out who had access to the Council vault and could steal or copy the formula."

She turned to leave the office, but one thing stopped her. She looked at Arun once again. "How did you know what I've done so quickly?"

The mage smiled. "I assume you didn't know your lover is the chancellor's lapdog, and the Council has its ways to know what goes on in the chancellor's office."

Ina's peaceful face didn't reflect her emotions. "What else would you expect from the captain of the King's Guards? Now I'll have to inform him they have a spy owned by this honourable Council."

Arun bared his teeth. "You wouldn't dare."

This time, Ina had the last laugh. "Try me, Arun, test my famous insanity, but I may keep quiet if you give me the names of all psychics powerful enough to control the monsters."

She left his office depleted, gaining yet another enemy, but now she had a list of potential puppet masters. She'd need to cross them off one by one. If that wasn't bad enough, there on the list was Liander, and she doubted her ex was less of an arsehole than the last time she saw him.

Velka was pacing back and forth in the hallway. Seeing Ina, she ran over. "What did he want? Why did it take so long?"

Ina gently patted her friend's shoulder. "It's fine. We just talked. Arun was curious about what exactly happened in the tunnels. Mar has his authority to answer to, and we have ours." She looked at Daro, who, upon hearing her words, looked at the wall paintings with extra attention. Ina hid her smirk. She'd deal with them later. "Oh, and you know what, Velka? I will have the chance to meet with Liander again. It will be good to see his handsome face." The witch was sure that Daro would repeat it to Mar, and she was happy for her small revenge for snitching on her to the chancellor. *Let's see who will have the last laugh today.*

Unfortunately, Velka spoiled it all as, baffled by Ina's statement, she exclaimed, "But you told me you never wanted to see this arsehole ever again."

Daro's laugh echoed in the hall. His little flower and her honesty were so refreshing. He looked at Ina. Did she even realise her play on Mar's feelings could cost someone their head? His captain was so fixated on this one that Daro didn't dare tease him, at least not much, and it was worse now that Ghost lost his head for her. This morning's lecture on how he should guard her, with instruction to pay attention to anything unusual in the university, was bizarre enough. He was also tasked with searching the barracks and gathering all guards' rota for the past few months. Still, it was better than Senad's orders, who had to crawl around the sewers.

He looked at Velka and smiled. He hadn't considered an older woman until she had entered his life. He didn't even know she was older until one night in the bed when she teased him about his youthful stamina. Mar might like his women overly complicated, but Daro wanted Velka, a brilliant and strong woman, but also soft and sweet, just like steppe wine. Last night, lying under the canopy of flowers that blossomed under the mage's touch, he thought he wanted to spend his life with her. He understood now why his captain fretted so much over the bath accident. Daro wouldn't hesitate to trade his life for Velka's. He found it easier than to tell her the truth about his initial motives.

Their visit to the alchemy workshop didn't bring any fresh revelations. The alchemist confirmed what Ina had already suspected. Except for a few modifications, it was her mutagen. Unfortunately, neither the vials nor the contents showed who was responsible. That was disappointing, so Ina decided walking home would help with considering her next step, much to the displeasure of Daro, who thought a carriage would be safer. Before long, he had to admit it was a good idea. Velka's cheerful nature and the vibrant city life lifted Ina's mood, and soon both women were darting from stall to stall, buying a mountain of unnecessary things for Daro to carry.

"I need a servant and a horse," Ina stated suddenly, much to Velka's enjoyment.

Daro moaned painfully, "I barely can see the road behind these boxes, and you want to go to the livestock market? You need a bloody mule, not a guardian."

The women ignored his grumbling and jauntily marched towards the horse ring, only to be stopped by a grimy street urchin.

"Are you Lady Ina?" he asked, looking at Velka. "I have a letter for Lady Ina."

Ina pushed herself forwards and stretched her hand to him. "I'm Lady Ina."

The child looked at her in disbelief. "But you don't look like a lady."

Ina chuckled. "Well, you should not judge a lady by her skirt. Now give me the letter, please."

Opening the envelope, she recognised the brief sentence was in Nerissa's neat handwriting. *Come to my house now.*

With a deep sigh, Ina turned to Velka. "Nerissa has summoned me, so if you'd be kind enough to take my things to your home, I will pick them up later. Now I need to find a carriage." Daro tried to protest, but he failed to stop her. He could only watch as she stopped a passing conveyance and disappeared into the crowd.

⁂

Mar was sitting at his desk with a deep frown on his face. Senad and several guards had searched the tunnels, but they found nothing except for several bodies, including the troll he'd killed. Worse, someone had dropped a lamp in the dark, and now the office contents were destroyed. Senad was injured trying to put the fire out, and now his friend was sitting at the healers' with burnt hands. Nothing had gone well today. Daro's entrance surprised him, as he could swear Ren was still in the barracks. "Did Ren release you from your duty already?" he asked, looking in disbelief at the orc shaking his head.

"No, Ina got a letter from her family and headed off to see them. I escorted Velka home and came here to tell you what happened today—"

Mar didn't let him finish. "Have you seen the letter? What if this is a trap?" he asked the stunned orc, who finally lost his temper.

"For fuck's sake, Mar, you told me she fought off a troll. She doesn't need an escort to visit her old aunt. And I haven't seen the letter. Anyway, she should be back home by now."

Mar paced the room. Daro's explanation was logical, but deep inside, he felt unsettled, and she was there all alone. "Fine, now show me the reports on the guard schedules."

Daro rolled his eyes. "Reports, hmm? Is that my punishment for leaving her?" His response was not well received, and Mar's fist squeezed on the chair rest.

"No, it is your job, as it is mine. It is time to focus on it. Your punishment is to find some fancy treats for her bloody cat and have it ready for tomorrow."

Daro's mouth gaped open before he walked towards the captain and placed a hand on his shoulder. "Mar, are you well? What on Veles's arse do you mean? A cat? Maybe buy her jewellery or a dress?"

Mar shrugged. He had a plan to win Ina's heart, and now he was preparing for the campaign before Ren, and his enchanted music, beat him to it. "Don't let me remind you how you ran back and forth to Velka with those cut flowers till she told you she doesn't like dead plants. I don't know what Ina likes, but she loves her cat, and I'll make this bloody beast love me. Now, reports. The sooner we finish, the sooner I can make sure she is home and unharmed."

CHAPTER 17

Ina didn't know what to expect from Nerissa or why she'd requested a meeting in such a manner. She arrived at her great-aunt's house and greeted by a servant who stood outside visibly relieved to see her. The maid escorted Ina straight to the drawing room, where her great-aunt waited. Nerissa stood up from the chair with surprising energy.

"Ina! What took you so long? We have so much to plan."

Ina was stunned seeing her relative so animated. Did she miss something important?

After a quick peck on her aunt's cheek the witch got straight to business. "You wanted to see me. Dare I ask what this is all about?"

Nerissa gave her a sly smile. "Have you heard about the coronation ball?"

"Yes, but why should I care? Do you genuinely think I'd ever be able to show my face at the palace after how my court career ended? Even to visit Sophia?" said Ina, unsure where this conversation was heading. Her great-aunt walked to the desk, picked up a small gold-trimmed piece of vellum, and passed it to her niece.

As she read the first line, Ina's blood ran cold.

Grand Duchess Nerissa Thornsen and Lady Inanuan Thornsen are cordially invited...

Ina looked at the gaudy missive, but it made little sense. "What the hell is this? Why am I getting an invitation?" She looked at Nerissa, perplexed. "It's because of me his father got nicknamed 'limp dick.' Why would they want me there? It must be a joke, or someone plans to make a spectacle out of me."

Nerissa shook her head. "You are the flavour of the season—the untamed witch that came back from exile, fought an overgrown troll, and romanced half of the King's Guards." She looked at Ina with amusement, seeing her niece pale and supporting herself in the chair. "We will use your dubious fame to get you back into court."

Ina looked like a scared deer facing a pack of wolves. "I'm not romancing anyone, and I'm not going. I don't want to give them the pleasure of mocking me behind my back. Whatever your plans are for me, I do not want a court position, and I will never work for them again."

Her great-aunt stood up, towering over Ina, who involuntarily shuddered. "It doesn't matter who you have in your bed. There is a stream of men passing back and forth through your door, and that is enough for the gossip. The grand ball is in two weeks and you are going. That is an order from the king, his chancellor, the Magical Council, and your family. You had better get yourself ready. You will have our family's money at your disposal."

Ina rose, shocked that Nerissa would try to intimidate her. The look on her face was one of pure disdain. "No choice, then, huh? And I thought you, out of all the Thornsen clan, were the one that understood me." Her great-aunt tried to say something as Ina turned to leave, but the witch didn't care. She walked out to the street, slamming the door in her fury, her cloak forgotten in her aunt's house.

Oblivious to the evening chill, Ina walked ahead, trying to gather her thoughts. She had two weeks to prepare and didn't even know what was coming. Did they want to make an example of her or ridicule her? She didn't trust the new king's good intentions. The only positive that came from this was that she'd be able to talk to Sophia, and maybe with the princess's support, she could somehow survive this event.

The young princess had been her friend when Ina lived in the palace. Ina hoped she still remembered her. If she sent a letter and asked for help or to be taken off the guest list entirely, would Sophia help her? Probably not. People's attitudes changed towards those who appear inconvenient.

Then there was Liander. Knowing that prig he'd rub the change in their social status in her face. They had parted ways after Ina was given the court position straight out of university. He thought himself superior to everyone else, so Ina's posting as the king's advisor was not well received. The pompous arse never failed to tell her he could do a better job. His constant taunts finally wore her out, and she told him to get out of her life.

At that point, she learned Liander only cared about her family's status and had slept his way through half the court.

The streets were dark, and Ina shivered. Looking up, she was surprised at how far she'd walked. Her pale skin looked grey, and her teeth chattering reminded her it was time she headed home.

Mar was pacing in Ina's house, feeling like a caged animal. She wasn't here when he'd arrived, but he had hoped she would appear any minute. He waited at her door like some lost puppy till the worry took the better of him. After all, his witch had unhealthy tendencies to heal strangers, drown in the bath or be burned by spider venom. He searched the house, deciding to wait a little longer, just in case Ina had another boozy night with Velka.

When Nerissa's servant appeared with Ina's cloak and disclosed she'd left her great-aunt's house angry and in a hurry, Mar cursed. He sent his men out to search the city. Ren, Daro, and Senad were questioning her acquaintances, and he was here waiting like a fool. It was past midnight, but he hadn't wanted to start a fire. With his mood, the darkness felt more appropriate. Boruta trotted to his chair and looked at him with his golden eyes.

"You would know if she was in trouble, wouldn't you? You always knew it before." asked Mar, trying to find a glimmer of hope in his worries. He found it strangely reassuring when this black devil huffed on his words and raised his leg to lick his backside. Mar sighed and shook his head, feeling as if he'd lost his mind. Now he was even talking to the cat.

Ina entered her home with a magical pulsar above her shoulder to light her way, and Mar's face flashed before her, and his body pressed her to the now-closed doors. Withdrawing a half-formed curse, she asked, "What the hell are you doing here?"

Mar held Ina tight, eyes scanning over her face even as he felt the chill of the night seeping through to his skin. "For fuck's sake, woman, do you not care for yourself at all? No cloak, no weapon, and I bet no idea how long you've been outside on this cursed evening."

Again, she had to face someone who wanted to command her, and she jerked away, trying to slip out of his grip. "Why do you care? Why do all of you try to tell me what to do? The king, Nerissa, and now you. Why can't I just live my life as I see fit without explaining my every step or attending some bloody ball to give idiots cheap entertainment?"

She was cold and angry, and he hadn't even started the fire. Ina didn't know what irritated her more. The fact he was telling her off, letting himself in or that it looked like he was waiting for her arrival to host him, and she lashed out. "Oh, and since you entered my house without permission, shift your arse, and start the fire! If I'm chilled to the bone, it will be challenging to cultivate the so-called romance the entire city is gossiping about."

She observed how he slowly shook his head and whispered, lowering his lips to her ear, "You think after our adventure in the tunnels I would tell you what to do, my wee spitfire? But I worry, especially when you come home so late. Accidents happen more often than not when you are around." He grinned widely as he leaned back and released her. "I'm glad to hear the entire city knows you're mine. It spares me the trouble of spreading the gossip myself." The captain sent her a playful wink and turned to the fireplace, hands retrieving his flint. "Are you sure a fire is what you want to warm the chill in your bones?"

His teasing baffled her. How could he take it all so lightly? She wouldn't care much about her reputation if it hadn't got her noticed by the court again. The other day, Ina would have welcomed his interest. But today, she was cold and angry that life had forced her hand again, and he was there when she needed something, someone, to help unload her anger. Ina looked over at the captain, busy with the kindling, and answered with false glee, "Oh, Mar, but that means we will have to invite Ren and Daro. The gossip says you all are rolling in my bed every night. If Nerissa knows this, it must be true!" She approached him, trailing her hand on his back. "Or maybe I'll only invite Ren and Daro. After all, you had your chance once, and you so brutally rejected my advances."

Mar's hands stilled at Ina's words. He knew she was goading him, but the image of her being touched by anyone else ignited that part of him he could never control in her presence. A flash of fire, and Ina was in his arms, his focus boring deep into her soul. "No, my spitfire, you burn for me alone." Lost in her eyes, Mar didn't even feel the heat of the impossibly high flame roaring behind him. Not with this sassy woman pressed against his chest and the need to possess her body, heart, and soul.

Ina looked at Mar in surprise. Did he just claim her for himself? Even as she felt the outrage rising, her body desired a better channel for her emotions. An overwhelming hunger for this savage man awakened inside her, answering his need to possess her. *He had it coming for a long time, and he will only have himself to blame if this hurts*, she thought as her hand softly traced upwards till her fingers tangled with his hair. Ina pulled Mar's head down and pressed their lips together, tongue gently tasting them as she whispered, "You can have me tonight, but you can't hold me forever as I'm not yours to take. Now, give me the beast I crave."

Mar felt bewitched and followed her command, crushing Ina's lips fervently, with his golden eyes slowly closing as he lost himself in the kiss. Fiery passion swept through him as he clawed at her clothes, the fabric tearing easily. Mar turned, lowering Ina to the furs, as his lips descended to the sweet hollow of her throat, tongue striking out to taste her.

She revelled in his hunger, yet the need for control, to mould him to her desire, was even more intense. It took one smooth motion to flip him on his back, and she was sitting on his hips, mounting him like a stallion. Mar did not resist, only gave her a questioning glance. Ina smiled at his eyes, burning bright like the fire behind him. Her lips parted as she said, "You are mine tonight, and I tame all who are trying to rule me." Wisps of magic flowed from her hands, wrapping themselves around his wrists and pinning him to the ground.

Mar gasped, a low growl rose in his throat when he trashed his hips under her. "Ina!" His voice was husky with desire.

The witch licked her lips, dragging the remains of her clothes down. The bright green gem of her necklace rested between her breasts, casting an eerie glow onto her milky skin. Her hand played with it, acutely aware of his watchful state and hard cock pressing on her thigh.

"Tell me," she purred. "Tell me you want this to end, and I will release you this instant. We will part as friends and never talk about it again." Her nails scraped his chest. "Tell me you don't want me, Mar, or else grasp the fire and burn with me."

Never had Mar been restrained like this. His need for Ina raged inside as her magic shackled his body to the floor. Nothing had prepared him for this, and no woman had ever tried to dominate him. He felt her touch like a sweet agony. The pain in his wrists was nothing compared to his craving to touch this beautiful enchantress.

Ina's passion removed his last concerns, offering the freedom he didn't feel with other women. She wanted the beast, and he was close to becoming it. The madness that stripped his reason on the battlefield was beneath the surface—this time focused only on her.

Even if he had to wreck the world to have her, Ina would be his, and she would yield to him tonight. "Toy with me as much as you want, but I will have you, witch, and you will love it." His voice rasped as he struggled to stay in control of his body.

"Gods, you are strong." The pride in her voice was unmistakable when she struggled to keep on top of him when he bucked beneath her like a wild horse. He didn't refuse her, but he fought for control with a passion that scorched her skin. He dared to challenge her? Let's see how much he can take. He promised her once to make her dreams come true, and people should stay true to their promise. She bent and kissed him again. Bare breasts rubbed his hairy chest, sending shivers of pleasure down her body. "Mar, you are delightful, now lay there and take it like a man," she quipped breathlessly as her arousal made her reckless.

His skin was hot, and beads of sweat gathered on his scarred chest. Slowly sliding down to kiss it, Ina trailed her lips over the old wounds, grazing his nipples with her teeth, wresting a tortured moan from his throat.

Opening his trousers, she released his manhood and licked her lips, trailing her hand along its length. Now she knew everything about this man was immense. She toyed with it while observing his reaction. Mar was so receptive, and the hunger she saw in his eyes set her on fire.

Directing his glans between her folds, Ina gently rocked her hips, stroking the most sensitive place but denying him entrance. "Do you like it? I certainly do." She moaned, raising her moist fingers to his lips, letting him taste her. Finally, she lowered herself and wrapped her mouth around his shaft, tongue trailing around the tip as she savoured his flavour.

Mar, previously restless, was frenzied now. His growls increased as the contour of his body seemed to blur in front of her eyes. Her magic danced, holding him bound, a mighty warrior entirely at her mercy. He was exactly what she needed, and Ina felt, in this very moment, her fractured world was complete. Suddenly, her spell broke, and the magic resonance made her eyes snap open in shock. That shouldn't be possible.

Tremors shook Mar to the soul as the dew of Ina's passion touched his lips. His tongue flicked out, gathering the sweet nectar. Wildfire engulfed his reason as the taste stripped the last of his control. He tore at his restraints as a monstrous power erupted, shattering her hold on his body.

The beast she craved broke free, teeth exposed in an evil grin. Mar's hands circled her waist, eyes hunting out those of his prey. "You are mine now, pretty minx." His burning gaze captured hers as she looked up with disbelief and desire mingled at the shock of him breaking loose. A low bass chuckle rumbled from his chest as his hand snapped out, capturing her nape and dragging Ina's lips to his.

All restraint was gone as Mar crushed her lips in unbridled passion before twisting to the side and pressing her to the floor.

Ina gasped, her body suddenly vulnerable beneath him.

Mar paused, licking lips moist with the mix of their desire. "Mine." The word reverberated deep inside as, with smooth, slow movements, he took hold of her wrists and pressed them above her head. Intoxicated by her scent as he leaned in and kissed along her throat, Mar grazed sharp teeth over the pulsing vein.

Enthralled as he lingered there, he revelled in her rapid heartbeat. The woman beneath him was pure magic, and tasting Ina's skin, he felt connected to the source of life itself. Mar moaned and moved to her breasts with ardent intent, teasing the delightful flesh, before drawing the hardened nipples into his mouth. Her stuttered breath made him bite down, looking up to study Ina's reaction. His tongue darted around her areola as her lips parted in ecstasy.

Her strength was no match for his, and she couldn't free her hands to touch him despite struggling desperately. Mar looked at her with amusement. "Not liking the taste of your own medicine?" His mouth captured her nipple and he sucked hard again.

"Fucking hell!" She gasped, arching in pleasure.

He adjusted his grip, freeing one hand and, to her damnation, slowly slid it down between her legs, stroking her folds with expertise.

"Tell me you don't want this, and I will release you right now," he purred, mocking her tone.

Ina's temper flared, and the whirlwind of her magic hit him like a hammer, loosening his hold for a moment. She pulled one hand free and surrendered to her primal instincts, reaching for his cock and guiding it inside. Her legs wrapped around his hips, giving him explicit instruction, and Mar lost it. He entered her body and his breath shuddered when tight walls embraced him. A small voice in his head insisted on giving her time to adjust, but he couldn't think clearly. The pleasure of her body wrapped around him was exquisite.

His desire seared her senses. Ina didn't need his stillness and rolled her hips to slide onto his shaft. It felt so good that a small moan escaped her lips. Mar looked at her, enchanted. She knew what she wanted and, even pinned down, was taking it from him. "Care to join me?" she rasped, breaking the spell.

He slid into her body like a well-oiled piston, leaning down to taste her lips in a bruising kiss. Lost in passion, they ravished each other, lips and nails clawing and biting, feral and fierce.

Ina's nails tore into his skin, driving him to the edge. His breath quickened close to release as he desperately held on to the shreds of control. But when she arched under him, gasping his name, her body pulsing around his cock, he was lost. Mar's roar shook the walls when he filled her with his seed before collapsing, spent and satiated. He knew he would never let her go now. All he had to do now was convince Ina. Mar pulled her close to his chest, arms curled around her with tenderness when he stroked her back, feeling this one night sealed his fate.

Ina's thoughts, muddled by the aftermath of passion, refused to gather into any semblance of order. She should not have given in to her desire, but once again, she had made a rash decision and now was the time to deal with the consequences. His word *mine* still reverberated in her mind. Would Mar understand she didn't want a commitment? Or not the commitment he might have wanted. Yes, she wanted him, but she recently learned to see him as a friend, an awkward one who never agreed with her, who was nonetheless someone she could rely on, and she liked it. And now they'd made it complicated. She was a bloody idiot for letting her lust take the reins.

The upcoming gala worried Ina, and she couldn't drag Mar into her personal drama. That's not what you did to a friend. After all, he was a lord of Liath. He had his career, his family obligations, and risking it all to bed a disgraced witch was foolish. No matter what he thought about it now, this hairy oaf could not become a target because of her.

She stroked his chest, the majestic fluff that had started all of this, finding more excuses for why she should not even think about being with him. She tried to live her life without being a coward, yet she had to admit she was avoiding the biggest issue. She felt attached to him, which terrified her. Every evening, his company provided comfort, especially lately. She almost expected to find him here each time she returned home. But she didn't want to become the lady of Liath or guard the home fires bearing children when the men went to war. He was intelligent, ruthless, and fiercely loyal, not to mention he had a body to die for, which she almost had. Still, he was also possessive and overprotective and, worst of all, the scion of Liath with the obligation to his family. She needed time to think it through.

"Mar, I think you should go now." Her voice rang with confidence she didn't feel.

Unaware of her thoughts, Mar, half-asleep, was taken by surprise. "Why? Have I done something wrong? Did I hurt you?" He wasn't gentle with her, but she seemed to enjoy it. Hell, he was sure they had both enjoyed it. She had matched him in passion, or so he thought. Now he wasn't sure, and this uncertainty was weighing on him.

The witch shook her head, giving him a soft smile, confusing him even more.

"Then why, Ina?"

She gently stroked his cheek. "It was a wonderful moment, but our lives are complicated, so it isn't a good time for us to continue. I don't know what I feel, and I need time to sort things out. I'm sorry if I gave you hope or confused you with my actions. The fault is all mine, but I think it is best if you go. I promise to stay home for the rest of the night."

Mar stood up, grabbing his trousers, confused and uncertain. *Fault? What was complicated? What on earth did she mean?* There must be something she wasn't telling him, but he knew if they were ever to have a future, he had to respect her wishes. "Ina, I will go now, but before I go, I want you to know that I know what I feel. Tonight was not an impulse for me. I fell for you when you broke your door with my back. I was just too stupid to realise it." His lips covered hers in a long, longing kiss, testing her resolve, and when she responded, he sighed with relief. "Take your time, my spitfire. I will wait as long as you wish, but I'm a soldier. I know how to besiege the fortress. Your passion tells me I already have one ally. I just have to crumble these walls you've built around your heart one stone at a time."

Mar gathered his belongings and walked into the cold of the night. His thoughts were too chaotic and disturbed to say anything else. His confidence in speaking about his feelings crashed after he closed her doors. *Will I be able to overcome her defences?* He wanted to go back and argue his case, explain himself, just do something in the hope she would give him a fighting chance. Still, he knew her enough to realise arguing would only harden those defences. Besides, arguing with Ina was like kissing a dragon's arse—no pleasure in the deed and sizable danger you will get your head ripped off. And he wasn't ready for this tonight.

⋆⊱────⊰⋆

Ina sat by the fire, feeling the claws of uncertainty closing around her heart. She'd done what she thought was best, but now she wanted him back. Boruta approached her and looked into her eyes, and the witch could swear she felt the cat's disapproval. Ina stroked his lush fur for a moment. "Sometimes I think it was better in the forest, my friend, with just you, me, and the Leshy, where there was no heartache, monsters on the loose or worry that I'll disgrace my family again. I don't want to be remembered as the crazy mage, creator of monsters."

While she was dwelling in self-pity, Boruta went to the fur and sniffed the place where they had made love. Suddenly, he started rubbing himself all over the bedding with a loud, satisfied purr. Ina tried to grab him, but he protested loudly, behaving as if possessed.

"It's not a catmint, you idiot," she said when she finally picked him up. After putting him aside, Ina looked at her hands, and to her surprise, they were covered in metallic grey-and-gold dust. She rolled her eyes at her cat. It seems like she wasn't the only one busy this evening.

CHAPTER 18

Mar returned a guard's salute as he arrived at the quiet palace barracks. Each time he passed the main gate, it irked him how indefensible it was. The palace sat at the kingdom's major rivers' confluence. In the past, the rivers had been the main line of defence and the principal transport routes for the original merchant town. The walls that divided the palace from the rest of the city reflected Cornovii's style. More decorative than defensive, it was a nightmare to guard, even for battle-hardened people like Mar.

The captain's office was above the gates, with large windows facing the spacious courtyard. Despite the time, he headed straight there. There were too many reports piling up on his desk. Ina was partly right—their lives were complicated, and he had pushed his responsibilities aside over the past few weeks, letting

Senad deal with them. So, knowing he wouldn't be able to sleep, he sat at the desk and started working.

Most of the reports were nothing special. There were provisions, armoury expenses, and purchase orders for new winter uniforms. Those he put aside, as Senad and the quartermasters could deal with them later. He paid more attention to the reports from the court itself. There wasn't much overly concerning, except for the recent increase in the palace's servant turnover. He'd expected this to a certain degree. The new king would want staff he could trust, so he had replaced several servants after the old monarch's death. The only question was, why had Princess Sophia exchanged half of her servants?

Mar would have to ask Senad about it. His second-in-command found pleasure in being in the palace, especially at Sophia's side, and she often asked for his escort. Not the first one who fell for the lure of politics and likely not the last. Senad seemed to love the atmosphere of the court and was so well-known that many thought he was the captain. Shuffling through today's reports, one document caught his attention. Upon reading it, he felt his hackles rise. It was the king's autopsy from the court physician. Mar's eyes spotted one line amongst the many findings related to his lifestyle and age that hit him like a hammer.

At the base of the skull above the hairline, a faint bruise with associated minimal puncture wound was apparent.

An assassin's needle. Mar had been right from the start, instantly recognising this type of injury. Someone had murdered the king and disguised it as substance abuse, and he, the captain of the King's Guards, had almost missed it. If not for a few drops of blood, he wouldn't have insisted on an autopsy, especially when the heir to the throne and his sister had opposed it. He cursed under his breath and leaned back in the chair. He would have to inform the chancellor. They both knew the king's death wasn't an accident, but now they had proof.

This new information raised several questions about security in the palace and any potential enemies within it. King Rewan's position on the throne was already precarious, and news like this could weaken it further, overshadowing the beginning of his reign. Without humour, he thought that Ina would have her time alone, as now he needed to inspect the guards, check their schedule, and see if he could find any issues with it.

"Guard!" The head of a young soldier appeared at the door. Mar handled him a letter. "Deliver this to Lieutenant Senad in the morning and tell him to meet me in the court." When the guard disappeared, Mar turned towards the fire and sighed. It wasn't the first time he would have to sleep in his office, if he could sleep at all, of course.

Ina was determined to make progress as the date of the ball approached. The day after her unforgettable evening with Mar, she went to see Jorge. Not that she trusted the judicial mage after he'd happily tattled on her to the Magical Council, but he had the skills she needed. Unsurprisingly, he was not impressed by her visit, but he listened to her with attention and picked out the obvious holes in her reasoning.

Next came the list Arun had given her. After a quick skimming over, Jorge crossed several mages off as out of the capital when the disappearances started. After a moment of debate, a few others considered too weak were also removed. That left them with ten potential names—four of them the king's drinking cronies. The remaining six would be nothing but trouble, especially since Liander was one of them.

"How will you find out if they're connected with the current problem?" Jorge's down-to-earth question was unsettling simply because she didn't have an answer.

"I don't know yet. I was trained to make potions, not to solve crimes. Any advice for a novice?" Ina winced as she received a disgusted look from her fellow mage.

"Start with establishing who, where, and what. Check each mage's location during the events and see if they had any motive or a sudden influx of income, then trace the connections. You know how to draw a simple divination diagram?" Jorge's patience was short when he relayed the basics. The instructions were so abrupt. "You also mentioned the imp said that armed men accompanied the mage. Ask your mercenaries if any of them had an unusual escort job."

Ina was surprised she hadn't thought of that herself. "What if they won't tell me?"

Jorge gave her a long-suffering gaze. "Ina, for some reason, those boneheads like you, so use it. I'm sure your captain won't mind."

"Jorge, how does everyone in this damned city know what is happening in my bed?" Ina asked as she was losing her patience with her private life being everyone's business.

While observing her struggle, his rigid face flashed her a brief smile. "Ina, it is my job to know, and since a little bird came back to the city, many people's lives have become more interesting," he said and, in a rare display of goodwill, added, "They believe you are neck-deep in it, Ina, and you are under surveillance."

"Why are you telling me this, Jorge?" It was a simple question she hoped he'd answer truthfully.

"Because although I believe you are neck-deep in it, I know you are trying to solve this problem. That is the main reason I'm helping you. Come back to me when you have some answers. I will dig into the university and Council records. We will find out who is behind this, my little friend, and we will stop it." With his last words, he stepped in front of her. Long cold fingers tapped on the desk when he inspected her with his analytic stare. "I need an apprentice, and you have potential, and more, you have magic that balances mine. I will write to the Council, and from tomorrow, you will officially work for me."

Ina pulled back in a defensive gesture. "I have enough jobs already. That is not a good idea."

"But you won't say no," he answered. "I've observed you since your theatrics in the court. You have the sense of justice I need, and you won't take a bullshit answer just because it came from high above. That is the path you chose ten years ago. Think it over and give me your answer tomorrow."

Ina stood there in silence. Judicial mages were traditionally associated with Order. They were mages that could see patterns and sense in seemingly unrelated events. She was Chaos incarnate, rarely seeing a log even if she tripped over it, yet Jorge seemed convinced of her skills. Something in this tidy office made it difficult to breathe. "I will think about it and let you know later." Offering a curt nod, she turned around, slowing her steps, so it didn't look too much of an escape. Jorge followed her departure, then sat back at his desk and wrote the apprentice drafting form.

⁘⊶⊷⁘

Despite it being the end of autumn, it was a beautiful day. Ina stood on the street, basking in the warm light of the midday sun. Jorge had given her some much-needed direction and a scary opportunity for the future. She strolled along the streets, letting the noise of the crowd work as the background to her thoughts.

When she joined the university, she was actively discouraged from pursuing a career as a judicial mage. Graduating as a potion master seemed to be the only reasonable choice. Still, Ina could not deny she felt the thrill of excitement when she investigated the tunnels. And after she stopped brooding over an unfortunate man, she had to admit she felt good about her fighting skills. They weren't good enough to fight the monsters alone, but she could ask Mar or Ren to give her some sword lessons. Her imagination ran wild, picturing her fighting alongside those two against some nameless enemy. What better opportunity for this than investigating injustice?

There was another aspect of Jorge's proposal. She would be practically untouchable but that would require a blood oath. Such safeguards guaranteed the judge's impartiality and prevented abuses of power, but other than that, Ina would be free to act as she saw appropriate. It made the assignment very tempting.

She stopped by a beautiful fountain in the city square and contemplated the cascades of water falling from the hands of exquisitely carved nymphs and statues of water horses leaping from the pool. Rainbows shimmered in the air as the spray danced playfully in the sun. Ina closed her eyes and rolled a coin in her fingers. She called on her name patron, Goddess Zoria, "My Lady of the Dawn, I've never asked before, but this time I'm lost. Help me choose the right path." Whispering to the coin, she flicked it into the glistening fountain.

"Ina! I finally found you. I have a message for you." A low, pleasant baritone rumbled behind her.

"Daro!" she exclaimed, trying to calm the fast beat of her heart from his startling appearance. "Where is Velka?" She didn't expect to see him here alone, but her friend was nowhere to be seen.

"In the palace gardens—some idiot dug up the flower beds or something. She's as angry as a bag of badgers, and the gardeners are running around, frantically trying to sort it out. It's best to stay away." Daro placed his hands on the fountain rim. "It always charms me to see this little display of human art." He trailed his hands through the water, and Ina could not help but smile, looking at his dreamy expression.

"So, what was the message you supposed to tell me?"

Daro turned in her direction. "Well, this is strange. The captain asked me to tell you he will respect your wishes and told me to give you this. Then he rushed off to court, and from what I heard, several guards almost soiled their pants when he carried out a shock inspection."

Ina looked at the bag the orc handed her and opened it carefully.

"What is it?" she asked when the pungent smell of dry meat strips assaulted her nostrils.

"Cat treats straight from the palace. I'm sure Sophia's cats won't miss a few."

Ina shook her head in disbelief. "Why cat treats?"

"How do I know? I don't play your games. I suggested a necklace or something a woman would like, but he insisted on cat treats. Whatever happened between you and Mar is beyond my comprehension. I don't want to nurse broken ribs again, so please talk to him."

"And I have enough people trying to tell me what to do. Maybe I should talk to Velka and accidentally tell her about the origin of her beautiful romance?" Ina's temper got the better of her.

The orc's features paled, his massive hands closed on his axe. "I know we met under false pretences, but my love for Velka is real, and I will ask her forgiveness when I tell her. I'm just trying to help, Ina, so please don't see me as your enemy. I had to fight the maids for these treats because Mar claimed this would make you happy." Daro's fingers drummed on the shaft of his axe. "I never saw him investing any time or interest in a woman. And trust me, I know because I slept with most of them as their consolation prize. He is not an evil man, so why don't you want to give him a chance?"

"I did, and that's probably why the guards are soiling their pants now." Ina couldn't help but smile. Cat treats, his way of showing appreciation after a night of passion, was indeed unique. But she should stop thinking *what if?* and focus on her task. "Daro, please tell him Boruta is grateful and that I took the position of judicial mage apprentice." When she turned back, her face was calm. Her decision was made—she now had to focus on what was ahead of her.

"I'm not an errand boy," Daro tried to object, but Ina only patted his cheek.

"Oh, you will be for me, and in exchange, I will show you the pastry shop that sells Velka's favourite sweets."

He raised his fists to the sky with a mocking gesture. "Women!" A few passers-by sniggered.

Since her fate was now tied to the city, Ina decided it was about time she got a horse and a maid. Her chance to become a respectable professional depended on being able to conduct herself properly, and the Lady of Thorn needed a maid who would feed her cat his treats. Ina shook the bag and laughed. That was a smart move, oh mighty Marcach. She would be faithful to her words and reject flowers if he sent some, but meat strips—she couldn't do this to her cat. Maybe she would even send him a letter later.

Daro left her as soon as she pointed him to the pastry shop. Ina headed off to the trading halls to look for a servant. She could always ask Nerissa, but after their last encounter, Ina didn't want to rely on her aunt any more than what was essential. It was a necessary evil to come here. She'd always found this place depressing. Respectable staff was not found here—just those too old to work or too young to know what they were doing, and of course, criminals or those so poor they'd been sold to pay their debts.

Debt bondage, although frowned upon, was not forbidden in Cornovii. Ina had intended to pass by the bondage hall when an unexpected commotion grabbed her attention. A feline humanoid stared directly at her. The intelligence in the creature's eyes was unmistakable, as was her hatred. A guard pulled on a leash, and with a growl, the were-cat followed him onto the stage.

The humiliation of a sentient being disturbed Ina, and she knew she'd hate to lose her freedom. Bidding started as she stared. The witch learned the female had been caught stealing and condemned to pay her due or be sold for a three-year contract. Ina listened with repugnance to the explicit comments and plans of the men. Finally, the mage lost her temper and raised her voice to outbid them.

"A hundred gold pieces from Inanuan Zoria Thornsen of the House of Thorn."

Murmurs swept through the crowd. Outbidding one of the most powerful noble houses in the country was never a good idea. Merchants and minor nobles suddenly lost their taste in the prize. Ina knew that her family was an excellent source of income for most in the city. Few would stand against her when she was flaunting the family name.

Acting more regal than she felt, Ina approached the trader, a pouch of gold in one hand, reaching for the leash.

"Any problems? Or I should tell my uncle he will miss out on such an extraordinary servant?" The lie came easily to her lips, intimidating the slaver into handing her the leash and a small gem.

Answering Ina's raised eyebrow, he explained, "That is for controlling the dangerous beast." And to demonstrate, he rubbed the rock between his fingers. Magic snapped from it, striking the collar. Soon the were-cat was twitching on the ground in agony, much to the audience's amusement.

A deep need to punch the guard in the face almost overwhelmed her, but Ina played her role with an inscrutable expression to the end. "Yes, this will do." She pulled the leash with studied boredom, and the creature followed her without resistance. She only needed to get home without making too much of a scene.

The palace was quiet at this time of the day. The morning court session had finished, and the ministers and courtiers returned to their offices to continue their work until the evening entertainment later. Few people would notice a commonly dressed woman heading towards the river. They would assume she was rushing to meet her lover even if they did. She stopped in the boathouse's shade and tapped her foot on the wood. Soon, a tall, handsome man in a guard uniform appeared and rushed to meet her.

"Did she buy it?" The woman's voice was tense, but to her delight, the man nodded.

"Yes, our people followed her, and when she headed to the market, they set the were-girl out. Liander observed the auction. He even paid the guard to demonstrate the function of his collar, the damned fool. It appears you know her well, and you should have seen the show she made. I could almost believe she was a high-born lady if I hadn't seen her in that hovel." Confidently he stepped close to embrace the woman, but his attempts were rebuffed.

"And the collar? Did Liander guarantee it will work?"

The warrior kicked a stone, visibly irritated by her tone of voice. "I don't know. I will check it later, but he assured me the curse will hit her hard if she tries to break the spell."

The woman raised her head to the sun and sighed with delight. "Oh, she will break it for sure. Ina always rescued stray cats and dogs. If only she hadn't rushed so much to save the sacred boar, we could have avoided all these problems. Being the queen of the Southern Kingdom was the life I deserved." Satisfied, she pulled his head closer, demanding a kiss. It looked like he'd pleased her again.

"I feel sorry for Mar, picking the witch for his attentions, but plenty of women will console his broken heart after Ina is gone. Once we've achieved our goals, we should buy him off and make his loss work for us," the man said, gazing at her with adoration.

She knew he liked tall blonde women, and it pleased her he couldn't resist and came to the palace on her every call. But this devotion to his captain was annoying. Still, it was not the time to bring it up, so she changed the subject.

The lady's arms surrounded his waist. Her gentle massage took his breath away. "Are the tunnels ready for the coronation ball, my love?"

"No, Liander can't control all of them, not yet. But he told me he is building something—a piece of jewellery of sorts that will give the wearer the ability to direct their movements. He likely will be ready for Forefather's Eve." He had trouble forming coherent answers with her hands distracting him.

Sharp nails digging into his skin made him contort in pain. "Gentle, my love, you don't want to geld me." His voice was pleading, trying to reason with her.

"I told you I wanted it ready for the coronation ball. Everyone will be there. We can't miss this occasion." Her beautiful features were now twisted in fury, and he realised he was walking on thin ice.

"They will be here after the coronation ball, too, but the witch and the captain destroyed the workshop. We have to start anew, and soldiers are all over the tunnels like a rash. It is just a tiny delay, my love, and it will be easier to do it under the guise of death's day."

The woman pushed him out of her embrace. "I don't want to wait that long. Make sure there are no more delays." She spoke harshly, leaving him standing when she marched back to the palace. There were books to check and orders to sign, and this idiot lowered taxes without talking to her. The missed chance ten years ago was still burning like a fresh wound, and she knew who to blame.

CHAPTER 19

Their exit from the building was more like a parade than a stroll, with gawking traders and customers staring at their passing. Her new serf followed her without protest, but someone of the were-cat race was rarely seen outside the Grey Mountains, especially in their animal form. Ina had to chase away street urchins and endure curious, often hostile, stares.

As she closed the door to her house, Ina looked at the creature, uncertain what she should do now. She wanted a servant and now had one. Just not the one expected or needed, as the girl didn't look like a lady's maid.

Ina congratulated herself over the depths of her stupidity, thinking she was turning into a bloody white knight before asking the girl, "What should I do with you now? Are you hungry?"

The were-cat looked at her dubiously, clearly surprised that Ina had addressed her directly.

"You can take this collar off for a start," she said, and Ina stared at her, open-mouthed.

"You can talk in this form?" Feline features didn't convey it well, but Ina could swear she saw pure sarcasm in her guest's eyes. The witch searched for the clasp, only to find it magically sealed with a very inferior spell and coated in grease.

"Stay still. This spell is an appalling mess, and we wouldn't want me to blow us both up dismantling it. What imbecile made this awful thing?" Oil from the lock coated her fingers as Ina's magic flowed into the collar, searching for a weakness.

In the end, the clasp snapped free, and the were-cat collapsed on the floor, her body shuddering. Ina looked at her, worried she messed up something while disarming the spell. A powerful transformation started that Ina, fascinated, watched avidly. Bones cracked and moved, fur retracted, and after a few agonising moments, a young woman was lying on her floor. The witch crouched next to her. "Well, that was an unexpected turn of events."

"You don't say," her guest answered, irritable and defensive. Ina wondered whether she was testing her patience or maybe just the charm of her character but ignored it as she fetched a blanket.

"What is your name?" she asked, handing over the coverlet.

"Marika," the woman answered and looked around, raising herself off the floor.

Ina knew that her house, cosy as it was, didn't look overly impressive. The living room was spacious, with easy access to the kitchen. Still, the neutral decor with plants on every surface was far from the abundance you usually saw in noble houses. "So, what do you want me to do…mistress?"

Sarcasm again, the undertones of this question made the witch grind her teeth. It looked like she had met her match, but instead of answering the question, Ina went upstairs and retrieved her old clothes. She placed them in front of the girl. "Nothing, get dressed, and get out. Consider your debt cleared."

The now-free woman pushed the clothes at Ina. "I don't need your charity."

The witch stepped aside, moving to the chair. "And yet you need it, or you will have to walk around naked." Gently touching her temples, she tried to shake off a burgeoning headache.

"Where would I go?" Her guest finally had a more polite tone to her words, but Ina was too focused on the increasing pain to care.

"I don't know and I don't care. You are free now and with that comes making your own decisions. You obviously don't want to be here, and I don't blame you. I was going to offer you the position of my housekeeper. Still, I won't live under the same roof with a person who hates me, whatever her reasons."

The soft rustling of cloth told Ina that Marika had accepted her gift. Now, she only had to wait for the door to slam shut, and she'd be able to close her eyes for a moment. A shadow appeared before her, making Ina raise her head to the now-dressed guest pensively standing there.

"So, I'm not in a bondage contract anymore?"

"No." The headache intensified, and Ina squinted her eyes to stay focused

"And I can leave anytime?"

"Yes, how about you leave now?" Yet, despite her hostile tone, the girl was still standing there.

"No, I will stay, and I will be your housekeeper. I will pay my debt to the very last coin."

"But I don't want you." Releasing slow, shallow breaths, Ina fought nausea roiling in her stomach.

"I don't care, and I am staying." Marika marched to the kitchen. The clattering of dishes and the sound of a crackling fire told Ina that food was being prepared. The witch knew she should have protested, but a wave of dizziness overcame her. Last night must have worn her out more than she expected, so she curled up in the chair and closed her eyes.

Ina knew something was wrong but couldn't control it. She walked through her dreams, watching a kaleidoscope of blurred images from her past slide away, just out of reach. She couldn't stop them, no matter how hard she tried. Everything felt unnatural, memories seen from another's perspective, not her own. The witch tried to focus on the core of her existence and untangle the stream of consciousness imposed on her. The fear at the realisation that it was a mind curse was overwhelming. How did a psychic mage delve into her mind and release her sorrows and regrets? She could feel someone shaking her arm and shouting her name, but she couldn't seem to control her body enough to answer.

Ren had wanted to check on Ina for some time, but an unrelenting Mar kept giving him task after task, keeping him at the court. By the time he finally freed himself from guarding the young king, it was already evening. Ren made his way to Ina's home. He had a few pieces of information that could help her with her investigation, and he wouldn't mind a homely dinner. It was nice not to see Woron in Ina's yard when he arrived. His rivalry with Mar was calmer recently, as though something had changed for the captain, but Ren didn't ask. It was better not to know. When he tied his horse and approached the house, the sound of a commotion made him hurry to the door.

"Get out of here, you demon!"

Ren didn't recognise the voice, but the unmistakable hiss belonged to Ina's cat. He rushed inside and noticed Ina's sleepy frame curled up on her favourite chair. Some strange young woman was trying to pull the ferocious cat off the witch's lap.

"Who the fuck are you?" Ren instantly got close to Ina and grabbed the stranger by the neck.

Her face was full of fear and anger as she practically spat in his face, "I'm the new housekeeper. Something's wrong with my mistress, and I can't wake her up."

Ren pushed the girl into the corner and knelt in front of the witch. "Ina, please wake up." He shook her shoulder, but her unnaturally still expression didn't alter. His mind searched for a solution, and in a split second, he turned to the girl and barked a sharp command, "Go to the noble quarters and get Lady Nerissa. Her niece needs her." He noticed the girl open her mouth to protest. "Now!"

Boruta used the commotion to jump back on Ina's chest. He placed his paws on her shoulders and touched his head to her chin. Ren didn't attempt to pull him away. After all, this weird feline had saved her more than once.

"If you know something I don't and can help her, do it." He couldn't see any physical injuries, and Ren's only explanation was magic. Not knowing what else to do, he pulled out his flute. A melody, crisp as the first snow, filled the air as the warrior bared his soul in the faint hope she would hear it.

⁂

It was more and more difficult for Ina to focus. Her mind was assaulted by an overwhelming stream of memories. A haunting melody and the echo of a voice centred her thoughts, slowing the flow, as the whirlwind of images finally came to a halt at the majestic oak in the heart of the Black Forest. As Ina admired the sparkling snow under her feet, she didn't notice him at first, but when a sleek black shape stood in front of her, she whispered, "Boruta? What are you doing in this madness?" The cat's body stretched out, transforming until the Guardian of the Forest stood before her. He placed his hand over her heart, the gesture centring her, and she exhaled with relief.

"Time to go home, my dear."

"Leshy? But how?"

"Listen to the melody and let it guide you home." His fingers stroked her cheek in a fatherly gesture. "You are the child of my heart, little witch. Harbingers of Chaos live in the centre of the storm, but you are not alone, and you have work to do. Get rid of the taint that pollutes these lands. Go now, follow the music." His voice faded, and Ina listened to his command. She slowly woke up from her vision and flinched as her door slammed into the wall, and Nerissa's voice shouted out.

"What the hell happened this time?! One day without being called to save your hapless rear. One day, Ina! Do I ask too much?"

Ina wanted to crawl back into the vision, but her mind had already resurfaced, and she felt Ren scoop her into his embrace.

Why did this keep happening to her? She just wanted to be alone, and she could only hope she could send everyone away before they drove her insane.

"I'm fine. I was just tired. Ren, put me down." Downplaying the situation seemed like the best idea.

Nerissa hit her with a spell so suddenly that Ina bent in half. The oily residue from the collar burned the skin of her hand and then dripped slowly to the floor. Her aunt stood before her with a thoughtful expression. "Nasty curse." Her eyes moved to her niece, studying Ina's face. "How did you break it?"

"The Leshy helped." The confidence Ina said it with made Nerissa back away, almost tripping over a chair.

"The Leshy is here?"

Ina saw an almost primitive fear in her aunt's eyes and started her explanation. So, Nerissa was afraid of something, after all. This thought amused her more than it should have.

"I don't know, here or in my head, but he helped me. He is good to me. He always has been. I don't care what you think—he is a good spirit, and the stories people tell are not always right."

Nerissa laughed anxiously, leaving Ina uncomfortable seeing such a strong woman close to hysterics. After a few moments, she calmed herself, speaking between gasps of breath, "Only my niece could call the Forest God a good spirit. Child, I don't know if you are cursed or blessed, but you are unique. I will go home now. Burn the physical remains of the curse and tell Jorge you are accepting his proposal. The poor man thinks he lost his knack for magic."

Nerissa left, still laughing nervously under her breath, and Ina focused on the remaining two.

"How did she get here?" After the last conversation with her aunt, she didn't want to be more indebted to her relative.

Marika shamelessly pointed to Ren. "He told me to get her."

Ina looked at her. "And what you are doing here? I told you to leave."

The girl shrugged and marched to the kitchen. "I'm working here now."

Confused, Ren's gaze followed her till she disappeared. "Is she working here?" He asked Ina, still unsure what had just occurred.

"I suppose so." What else was to say? She needed a housekeeper, and the girl didn't fret at Ina's "special," near-death experience.

"Ren? How are things in the barracks?" she asked, noticing Ren's lips twitching.

"If you're asking about Mar, he is busy. There are some security issues he's concerned about, but if you'd like, I will let him know what happened here."

Ina shook her head. "No, it's better if he doesn't know. He will charge in here, cavalry and all, even though nothing happened."

Ren chuckled slightly and pulled her into his embrace. "Cavalry and all, that is a very accurate description. If you don't want cavalry, let me offer you a deadly swordsman." This light banter was so comforting that Ina wished she could divide her heart in two.

"I know this will sound strange, but hear me out. This curse could be the key. I think I might be able to extract the energy signature of the mage who cast it. If it's the same as the one from the mutagen sample, we will have our culprit."

"Ina, you still won't know who did it." Ren pointed out the obvious. "Maybe you should ask the girl instead of playing with the curse?" He pointed towards the kitchen.

"I don't know. I was in a cell, and the next thing I remember, I was on the market with a collar on my neck," shouted Marika from the kitchen, clearly eavesdropping on their conversation.

"See, she doesn't know, and I have a list of those who could do this. I just need to make a solid connection." Ina allowed herself a slight chuckle.

A plan took shape in her mind. She would go to Jorge and accept his apprenticeship, then visit all the psychic mages from her list. It wouldn't be easy, but she was sure, with enough time, she could examine their signatures till she had a match. All she needed was some sort of recognition spell.

Her friend listened in silence as she shared her plan. "Are you sure about this?" he finally asked. "An apprenticeship with Jorge won't be easy or safe. I thought you wanted to settle down away from the court and just live your life?"

"I tried, but a peaceful life didn't want me." Ina sat on the edge of the chair. She supported herself on Ren's shoulder. "Look what is going on around me. The Council exiled me, my mutagen was misused, and I've been attacked twice for no apparent reason. So, I may as well embrace it and be the incarnation of Chaos. That way, I get to keep some control over my life."

It made sense, but Ren's face told her he didn't like the tone of her voice or her plans. She shrugged. He was no different from Mar in this matter, only that her hairy oaf never hesitated to tell her about it. She would prove them both wrong, and with this thought, Ina jumped off the chair, almost knocking Ren over.

"Ren! The recognition spell!"

Her sudden exclamation made him stutter, "The recognition spell?" but Ina was already a whirlwind of activity.

"Marika, get me a vial," she shouted, kneeling next to the puddle that had been the medium for the curse.

"A what?" her maid answered from the kitchen as she tried to cook dinner.

"A vial, a jar, something made of glass, oh, and a knife."

The confused girl appeared with utensils and looked at Ren, who only shrugged. Lucky for them, they didn't try to stop her. Once she set her mind on something, there was no way back. The witch carefully scraped the remains from the floor, cursing herself for losing so much time talking while her sample decomposed in the room's heat. Still, she had enough to complete her spell.

"I'm going to the workshop. Do not disturb me," she commanded, noticing Ren was trying to stand. "No, I need time alone to focus."

Her excitement made him worried. "Are you sure? It doesn't sound like it's safe or straightforward."

Ina beamed a beautiful smile. "Ren, I'm a Chaos mage and a potion master. If there's one thing I know, it's how to extract energy and transmute it into a recognition spell. Go home and have a rest. I will be busy tonight." She turned around and almost danced to her workshop.

❧

Ren took Marika to the side. "If anything happens, send a message to the barracks, to myself or Captain Marcach."

"I'm not your servant," retorted the girl, but Ren looked at her in such a way her that courage shrank instantly.

"I don't know you or why she hired you, but somehow you earned her trust." He stopped, and his voice was now cold and threatening. "Do not fail her. I will not take it kindly." A silver blade flickered over his fingers, reinforcing his words.

The now-pale Marika pulled back and nodded.

Ren left Ina's house knowing he needed Mar, and maybe even Jorge, on board with this madness before Ina's enthusiasm got them all in trouble.

As he arrived at the barracks, Ren talked to the sentry. "The captain?" he asked, simply hoping to meet with Mar as soon as possible. The palace was his first guess, as Mar had become obsessed with security. Ren was not sure what to think. Maybe it was the coronation ball, but something in Mar's behaviour seemed odd.

"Upstairs in his office," answered the young soldier, saluting him. Ren breathed a sigh of relief. At least he wouldn't have to brave the hallways to the court.

Ren climbed up the stairs and knocked on the doors. He didn't expect them to snap open, revealing Mar standing in front of him with a frown on his face.

"Ren, good, it's you. I need to talk to... This is just insane."

Ren entered the room. Scraps of paper, records of court appointments, and guard rotas were everywhere. Mar's bloodshot eyes told him the captain had gotten little to no sleep. "What happened?" he asked and blinked when Mar pushed a pile of notes in his direction.

"Look at this and tell me what you think."

"Well, those are guards' rota for the past six months, mostly related to the Council, high nobles, and royal family. Why?"

Mar pulled them out of his hand and handed him another. "Now read this."

His erratic behaviour worried Ren as he unfolded the paper and scanned it. "Assassin's needle...but how?"

"You tell me, Ren!" Mar slammed his hands on the desk. "You tell me how we could allow an assassin to get into the king's quarters in a palace full of guards."

"Maybe it was one of his ladies?" started Ren, but the captain's laugh stopped him in his tracks.

"You're not suggesting one of those noble coquettes not only knew but could perform an elite skill known only by a few people. Most of whom were trained by you."

Ren's lips tighten into a thin line. "Captain, you don't think it was..."

Mar approached him and clasped his shoulder. "Did you forget that both you and I were with Ina? It was the day she was attacked. I thought she was the target, but now I think maybe she was the distraction. But it was one of us, Ren. When we came to Osterad, Ina told me someone had stabbed me in the forest. I pushed it down, thinking maybe one of the dead soldiers did it. I truly hoped for this, but now? I don't know what to think, but I know you are the only person who I don't suspect. But if it was the same person, that leaves us with two choices—Senad or Daro."

Ren slowly exhaled. When he understood Mar's dilemma, his behaviour made more sense. "Tell me how I can help you. But before we start, I need you to know that Ina was attacked again..."

Mar staggered, and Ren grabbed his arm to stabilise him. "If you are here, does it mean she is uninjured?" he asked.

Ren smiled a little. "Are you telling me you trust my judgement? Ina said not to mention it or you would run there, cavalry and all."

Mar tried to jerk his arm free. "I want this so much that it burns in my chest, but if we catch the culprits, the attacks will stop, and isn't that the best way to help her?"

Ren nodded. It was both comforting and unsettling to see Mar back in control and not a slave to his anger. He reached for the papers when Mar's voice stopped him.

"I was with Ina last night. I know you love her, and I wish I could spare you this, but I can't."

Ren's hands trembled, but he was not entirely surprised. He'd seen it coming since their conversation in Ina's house, but it still hurt. With a bitter expression, he turned his eyes on the captain. "Where I come from, there is no shame in unrequited love. Your revelation doesn't change my feelings. It just adds another layer. Can you accept this?"

He saw Mar's nod and felt an overwhelming sadness. The Gods must be laughing now, making them love the same woman. When he was calm enough, Ren gave Mar the shortened version of Ina's trip to the trade market, the strange new servant, and the curse that kept her mind locked up.

"She is trying to create a spell to find the mage who did this, believing it is connected with your findings in the tunnel."

Mar's anger was palpable, and the gold flecks in his eyes grew brighter when he turned to Ren. "Are you sure she is not going out tonight?"

"Yes, and I made sure Marika knows that this information must be delivered directly to you or me if she leaves."

"Good, then we will stay here, and you can help me with the rota. We need to find the pattern that ties the attacks in town to the king's death. I need to make sure we eliminate them before the ball." Mar passed him the folder of notes. "Those are crime reports from the city hall." He pointed to another. "This one I got from Jorge, magical manifestation and monster-related attacks from the past six months. See if there is any pattern in it and note the dates. I will compare the movements of the guards and nobles through the palace gate, including the river patrols."

Ren found himself a comfortable seat. It looked like a long night was coming with not much sleep for either of them.

CHAPTER 20

"It was easier said than done," muttered Ina, still struggling to extract the core signature of the spell from the remains of the curse. Nerissa's magic appeared to be very successful in burning the energy links. Still, after several attempts, the witch had enough material to work on its energy signature. She had chosen a peridot crystal as a matrix for the spell and woven the delicate lines of the curse infused with light magic. She looked at the result with pride as she put the stone into a simple bracelet. Not only did she prepare the identifying spell, but she also made it match her necklace.

The idea behind it was simple. If the bearer of the magical signature came close to the crystal, she would see sparks of light dancing across its surface. Or at least, so she hoped. Now she needed to do the legwork and visit the mages from her list. Hopefully, one of them would activate her spell.

It was late morning when Ina left the workshop, and she looked around her home. Marika seemed to have settled in quickly, even without permission. The house was clean and a stew was bubbling on the stove. A rumbling in her stomach made Ina realise she hadn't eaten for several hours, and, with the plans she had for today, it was better to have her fill before going out.

"Marika!" she shouted, and when the tussled head of her new maid appeared in the attic doors, she added, "Come here."

The girl sauntered over, dragging her feet, eventually standing in front of her.

"Why did you stay? I gave you back your freedom."

Marika stood there in silent defiance. "Where would I go? I have no money. If I steal, they will hunt me again. Here, I have a roof over my head, and you need someone to look after the house. I may be a were, but we pay our debts."

"Really? You'd better think it over. It is still my house, and I need a housekeeper, not a were-cat throwing a tantrum every minute. That is my job." Curled up on the chair with a bowl of stew, Ina relaxed a little.

Marika raised her head and looked at Ina with a challenge. "I can work, and I can fight."

Hearing this, Ina laughed. "I need a lady's maid and housekeeper, not a berserker."

The girl gave her a mocking curtsy. "Yes, my lady, but I dare to disagree."

When her new servant disappeared back to the kitchen, Ina realised this woman would give her a headache, but at least her cooking was good.

Ina spent the rest of the morning discussing her contract with Jorge. He wasn't surprised by her early arrival and already had a draft written. Still, Ina insisted on a few concessions that would give her more freedom in picking up cases. Jorge was fascinated by her recognition spell. Its simplicity was the most appealing part. Unfortunately, extracting the signature pattern, the most crucial thing for the entire process, required her particular type of magic.

He approved Ina's plan and even gave her a convenient excuse. It gave the witch more work, but saved her from having to make up some ridiculous lies to see the mages on her list. As his apprentice, she had to visit all those practising psychic magic to make them aware that no spells were allowed during the coronation ball.

She roamed the streets like a stray cat and knocked at one door after another over the next few days. Her path led her farther into the direction of the noble district. Now standing in the middle of the street, Ina heard the screeching of a carriage wheel behind her. The crack of a whip split the air, followed by a female voice. "Why did we stop?"

The tone of voice was familiar, and Ina approached the carriage, beaming a big smile. "Sophia?"

A dainty hand pushed the curtain aside, and the princess's face appeared in the window. "And who might you be?"

Ina didn't blame Sophia for not recognising her. She was dressed simply, with road dust all over her, barely resembling a court mage. "Sophia, I'm Ina. It's so good to see you, my friend. I would visit, but—"

Ina was so surprised at meeting her friend that she missed Sophia's eyes darken and her jaw clench briefly in disdain. "Ina, how good to see you! You must forgive me, but I'm in a rush. I will see you at the ball."

Ina nodded, stepping aside. The encounter was so impersonal that it felt odd, but the witch knew ten years could make even good friends grow apart.

A day before the ball, she was almost sure her recognition spell hadn't worked. It had reacted to none of the mages despite Ina dangling her bracelet in front of them and even trying to rub it in one mage's face. While sitting next to the fireplace, she turned the small spell stone in her fingers, slowly losing hope, when a sudden knock on the door disturbed her thoughts.

In an attempt to settle into her new role, Marika opened the door and shouted, "Ina…I mean, my lady, some street urchin is here to see you!"

Ina walked to the door; a small, dirty errand boy waited there. At the sight of her, he bowed with respect. "Mr. Gruff said he wants to meet you at the tavern tonight."

Ina passed him a small coin. "Tell him I will come." She was deeply indebted to the troll for giving her the peridot, and refusal was not an option.

The boy disappeared, happy for the reward, leaving Ina to dress for the evening's visit.

"I will come back later," she told Marika, leaving the house. Not knowing that soon after her departure, the maid slipped out to deliver the information to the strange man who so deeply scared her.

⁂

The Drunken Wizard welcomed her with its usual noise, but Gruff was nowhere to be seen. Ina sat at the bar and waved to the dwarf working as a bartender today. "Gruff sent for me. Could you tell me where he is?" she asked quietly, trying not to draw too much attention   He pointed to the back door, leaving Ina alone with her question and no other choice but to follow his direction. The storeroom welcomed her with a musky smell, dimmed lights, and three pairs of eyes turned in her direction.

Gruff was sitting on a barrel, seemingly unfazed by the missing part of his forearm. Ina gasped and pushed forwards. "You're injured?" He couldn't have called her here to heal him, not with the small healing ability she had without resorting to energy exchange.

Gruff pointed to the seat next to him. "I was wondering when you'd come. We have a problem."

She nodded. "Yes, I can see that, and I will try to fix it as best as I can."

Her statement was met with silence. "Oh, you mean my arm? No, that is not the problem, but the fact that we can't use the tunnels is. That affects our business."

"What do I have to do with it?"

"Tell me what you encountered and why the guards now comb the underground?"

Eyebrow raised quizzically, Ina looked at the two others in the room.

Gruff chuckled slightly. "Where are my manners? Let me introduce you. The gentleman on your left is none other than the head of the assassin's guild, and on your right, you have the king of thieves. Of course, we will skip the names. I hope you understand, my dear. As all of us are affected by this unexpected attention, I thought it best to hold this meeting."

Initially, Ina tried to make out the faces behind the shadows. Now she made a conscious attempt not to look at them. How bad must it be for Gruff to drag her here and place her among these wolves? With no way to politely leave, she gave them a curt nod and told a censored account of the situation.

Gruff's face turned grim when she mentioned an encounter with a warped troll, but he commented little. "I'm glad he is at peace," were his only words, and the slight rasp in his voice made Ina believe it could be the kin he asked her to find.

When she finished, the silence was deafening.

"You are a reasonable person, and I believe we all benefit from cooperation. The information I'm about to share comes for free, but if you ever disclose the sources, you will be as dead as our dearly departed, limp-dicked king," said Gruff.

Ina was grateful for the lack of light, as she felt suffocated by the air of menace. Part of her mind felt detached, looking on with amazement at the confident person standing up to the crime overlords of Osterad. "As you said, I'm a reasonable person. Disclosing my sources would overshadow the quality of information and my reputation as Lady of Thorn. Making threats will not change or influence my decision. Will you kindly share what you brought me here for, or we will continue to bolster your bollocks?"

Her audience erupted in laughter, and Ina thought she had overdone it for a moment. Alone in the basement with three men—all of whom could kill her easily—so she decided not pick at their egos any more.

Gruff stopped first. "My dear Striga, you never cease to amaze me. Now, back to business. First, our friend here wants you to know that no one in his guild was involved in the old king's death. If you could kindly direct your captain elsewhere, he would be grateful."

"And why I should believe this? Maybe a rogue one took a job without informing him?" Ina asked, without letting them know it was the first time she'd heard Mar suspected the assassin's guild.

The man stepped from the shadow, observing her shocked expression with amused interest. "Because, my Lady of Thorn, I'm giving you my word and the information your captain is after. There are some additional names to the ones he knows that are skilled enough to manage it. All of them were in the court that night, but none belonged to the guild. We could also eliminate them if this is his wish."

Ina still struggled to collect her jaw from the floor and almost missed the parchment he held for her. Kaian, scion of the House of the Water Horse, looked at her with amusement. "Now, if you'll excuse me, I have other business to attend to this evening. I will introduce myself properly some other time, my lady. Till then, I hope your investigation goes well." He bowed politely, leaving through the back door.

Ina folded the paper without looking at it; she moved her gaze to the troll. "Is this all?"

"We've barely started," answered Gruff, and the thief master pushed a map in her direction at this remark.

His voice was high-pitched and grating. Ina was almost thankful he stayed in the shadows, just in case his face matched. "This is a map of the tunnels and sewers. The ones marked in red are new, and the ones marked in blue have recently collapsed, likely on purpose. My people keep disappearing, and those who survived reported monsters digging new passages. If you see more beggars on the streets, it's because no one wants to go back in there. They are not welcome on the surface, and if you ask me, it will soon cause a riot. Sort it out or there will soon be blood on the streets."

The man clasped hands with Gruff and left. Ina looked at the troll, who suddenly lost his rigid posture and gasped slightly, moving his injured arm to a better position.

Without a second thought, she was next to him. "You are a bloody fool, You're injured, and instead of letting me help you, you sit here like some beggar king ruling his realm. Also, why me? I have no power. All I did was a stroll through the sewers and fuck the captain, not exactly stellar achievements to be rewarded with such a lofty position."

Troll barked a short laugh. "Well, you have to do what you have to do to maintain your reputation. The weak get replaced." His laughter was short-lived, and Gruff turned his sombre face towards her. "The thief master was correct about the city heading towards a riot. Every guild is unsettled, and almost every mouth blames the ruling family for it. Sophia's name is the only one not criticised, and we both know she is simply more discreet with her antics. I'm sorry to use you like this, but I need time to find out who is pulling the strings before it bursts into flames. For now, my little Striga, you are the mediator between the high and the low."

"Oh, go fuck yourself!" Ina's very unladylike response made him laugh again. Despite her harsh words, she tended to his wound. "You could have chosen Jorge or any of your other friends. That was a shitty move, and you know it."

She was irritated by this sudden grace, but the troll understood it. "My dear girl, you are both the Lady of Thorn and the incorrigible Ina. You stood up to the king and lived to tell the tale." His big hand landed on her shoulder. "That troll you killed was likely my brother. He did not deserve to be a puppet. Thank you for freeing him." The sadness in his voice and his hunched posture told her all she needed to know. Before she could express her condolences, he added, "Also, Janik sent a message. There is unusual activity on a farm outside the city, and it's likely related to the current investigation. He will look into it in a few days, and he would like you to join him."

This message made little sense, but she nodded, adding it to the pile of issues that waited on her time. "I need to go now. This bloody ball is tomorrow, and I need to make sure I look at least half-decent."

The troll pushed the door open for her, and as she was walked past, he said, "Be careful. Many people there will be unhappy with your return, even some you thought would welcome you with open arms."

A loud pounding on the door awoke Ina, and she sat on the bed, trying to orient herself to the intrusive noise. Her visit to The Drunken Wizard had ended quite late but with an interesting outcome. She should tell Mar about her findings. An invitation for dinner would do, and Marika's presence should help restrain her from pinning him down to the floor and ripping off his clothes again. Ina stretched on the bed, feeling heat pooling inside at that reminiscence. Life would be so much easier for them if he were not the scion of Liath or if she ever saw herself as a prim and proper lady of a high house.

"Marika, open those bloody doors before they fall off their hinges."

Ina reached for a dress. Whoever was outside clearly wasn't going away. She was barely ready when she heard Nerissa's voice.

"What do you mean I can't come inside? I will see my niece whenever I please, not only when she is at death's door."

Ina knew Marika was fighting a losing battle, but it was impressive that she held her ground as long as she had.

Quietly chuckling, Ina finally shouted, "Just let her in before my aunt hexes you."

She was almost ready when the door to her bedroom bounced off the wall, and her great-aunt, looking like a grey wrinkled Fury, barged in. "We need to talk now! And keep that insolent child away from me."

Ina nodded despite tears pooling in her eyes, laughing would only worsen the situation. Instead, she led her aunt to a chair and helped her sit. "What can I do for you?" She pointed to her dress in the corner. "As you can see, I'm going to the ball as you wish. Is that what you wanted to talk about?"

Nerissa looked unsettled, and for the first time, Ina noticed how old and fragile her great-aunt was. Her words were met with silence, and finally, Ina snapped, "What is it, then? You didn't come here just to sit in my chair."

That seemed to work as her aunt raised her head. "We need to talk about your magic."

Now that was an interesting choice of topic. As far as Ina remembered, her magic was a subject of ridicule. A Chaos mage, the bottom feeder of the magical hierarchy in the family that gave the world more than a few arch-mages, was considered an enormous scandal. Ina was made acutely aware of it throughout her childhood. "My magic is nothing special, and we both know it, so why now, Nerissa? I promise I will do my best not to shame my family in the court…again."

"Well, my child, that's simply not true. Your magic is exceptional. It's just that very few bearers of Chaos were sane enough to give it a good name."

Nerissa sat there smiling sadly, and when Ina looked at her with confusion, her aunt explained, "You must have read about wars of the past and the battlemages leaving the land bare and people dead or destitute in their wake?"

Ina nodded. "Yes, but what does it have to do with me? I'm not a battlemage. I can defend myself with some fire whips, but it is nowhere near a deadly weapon."

Nerissa rubbed her temples, making Ina's anxiety grow. "That is what you were taught to believe. The Council decided long ago that every Chaos mage would be trained without knowing their power's true nature. All magic comes from the same source. The difference is how the mage gathers and utilises it. The Council promotes Order. It allows them to tame the magic in predictable patterns with predictable outcomes, harnessing the magic with sigils, words or gestures and turning it into elaborate spells stored within their minds or artefacts. Order is easily controlled but can't be fed by raw energy. You can't bend the lightning into an elaborate pattern. Instead, its energy has to be filtered and tamed by the magic bearer with enough time. The opposite side of the scale is Chaos. Those like you who bring change. They harness raw, chaotic energy with the strength of their will or need to cumulate it because the world, with its endless circle of destruction and rebirth, is full of Chaos."

Ina looked at her with a slight shrug. "I still don't understand what this has to do with me."

Nerissa released a long sigh. "Don't be obtuse, my child. I'm telling you all this because nothing is more chaotic than war. In the past, a Chaos mage on the battlefield meant carnage. The destruction of life fuelled their magic. Because, my child, what we call life is raw Chaos magic that animates us all, so they didn't need any other sources to give them power, just death and destruction. Once started, it was a cycle of self-renewing energy. Where battlemages and necromancers would fall into magical exhaustion, Chaos mages could carry on until nothing was left but scorched earth."

Nerissa rose and stood in front of the window. "There is nothing more alluring than limitless power. The Council decided they would suppress knowledge of Chaos. Mages with this ability were discouraged from taking a partner or even put under the geas to let the lineage die out. Children with this trait were taught to practise another form of magic, and knowledge of the nature of Chaos was kept to members of the Council, the king, and his heir."

"Why are you telling me this now?" Ina asked, her voice trembling. For almost forty years, she had lived feeling something was wrong with her, and her family knew the answer all along.

Her aunt looked guilty when she turned around. "Jorge came to me last night. He analysed his diagrams and told me I must tell you the truth about your magic. Otherwise, I would never choose to let you carry this burden."

Ina was sitting in silence as many things suddenly made sense. There was relief and resignation in her voice when she finally spoke. "It is not a burden but the essence of who I am. I can't believe my family would keep it from me and let me believe I'm a failed result of my mother's tryst." Nerissa flinched as Ina's words lashed like a whip.

"Many of your family genuinely believe that, my child. As for the Council, they are still afraid you are a threat that can snap and lose control of your power, as happened to the mages in the past." Nerissa stopped for a moment. "Today at the ball, I believe there will be those that will try to prove you are still an unruly, short-tempered witch, and some members of the Council will hope for your failure. Now you know why, and I can only ask you to be careful."

Ina's icy demeanour told her aunt it was time to leave. "I will see you at the palace, my dear, and send a carriage for you." When Ina protested, her relative placed a hand on her shoulder. "Just humour me this once. Oh, and I will send you a small gift, your grandmother's circlet. She also liked green gemstones."

Nerissa was long gone, but Ina could not stop thinking about what she'd revealed. Even a hot bath and the sweet fragrance of the signature apple oil she poured into the tub didn't dispel her bad mood. How many warnings had Ina received that the ball could go badly for her? The first step was to look her best to avoid comments on her appearance. A noble lady's armour, that's what her mother called it.

Marika entered without warning, carrying the stack of towels, a small box, and a letter. "If you soak more, you will look like a prune. Oh, someone brought this to the house saying it's from your aunt, and the letter was slipped under the door."

Unwillingly, Ina got out of the bath, and with Marika's help, she quickly dried her body. While torturing herself by brushing her long mane in front of the fire, she looked at the dress.

Whether fate or luck made her buy this ridiculously expensive piece of fabric, it would be perfect for this evening's ordeal.

When her hair fell in soft copper waves on her back, Ina asked for Marika's help to create an elaborate up-do. The dress fitted as well as she remembered, and the person who looked at her in the mirror was anything but ordinary. Soft curves enhanced by the dress gave Ina a sultry look. The necklace drew the eye to her cleavage, and the braided chignon displayed the line of her slender neck. Ina intended to ignore her aunt's gift, but her curiosity got the better of her. There lay a beautiful circlet with a teardrop gemstone on a velvet pad perfectly matched in colour the peridot between her breasts. Marika nagged until she included it in her outfit.

Her eyes were drawn to the letter. There was no name on it, and Ina hesitated, worrying it was from Gruff. She didn't want to hear any more news from the underworld, but what if it was something important? She opened it, and a small object landed on her hand. It was a small charm that noble ladies pinned to their dresses or bracelets. The tiny black cat with piercing green eyes was adorable, prompting her to look at the letter itself.

Knock 'em dead like those bloody doors. M.

When the carriage came to a halt in front of her gates, Ina was still laughing, but she pinned the tiny cat to her spell-tracking bracelet. She had never felt so beautiful and yet so vulnerable. "I hope Mar will like it," she said, and the real Boruta's eyes looked at her with a question, and Ina felt compelled to answer. "I haven't made up my mind, so don't look at me like that. Just because he fattened you up doesn't mean we will have him." She was ready to face the wolf's den now.

CHAPTER 21

Mar yawned, feeling his age as a young officer assisted him in dressing for the ball. He'd spent the last night making sure Ina was safe. As soon as her insolent new servant informed him that her mistress had taken a solo trip to The Drunken Wizard, he finished his duties and headed there. Ina was nowhere to be seen in the tavern. He knew Gruff wouldn't let anything happen to her, and their strange relationship constantly baffled him. When she emerged from the backroom, the frown on her face almost broke his resolve to remain unseen.

Even at her house, she seemed troubled, and Mar wondered if she was worried about the ball. After all, it was her first visit to the palace since her return to the capital. He observed her cuddling the cat till the light went out, which gave him an idea, one he hoped she would like.

Today, Mar's valet surprised him, ordering the barber to come to his quarters. Scrubbed clean, the face that looked at him in the mirror appeared much younger than he expected. Turning from the image, he nodded his thanks to the old barber and left for the palace, as he had to be there before the guests arrived. His ceremonial uniform, although rarely used, still fit him well, and he noticed the impressed looks of the servants when he walked down to the already saddled Woron.

Luminous lamps, lavish decor, and lush plants and fountains greeted Mar's arrival at the royal residence. Fountains and exotic plants testified to the wealth of Osterad. Once the stunned guests passed the courtyard, they would enter the main palace. A grand entrance hall decorated with many objects d'art, interspersed with small meeting rooms, led to the large gold-encrusted doors of the throne room. The hall opened out into two corridors. The corridor to the left led to the ballroom while the right went to the living quarters. The rear of the residence was Velka's pride and joy, where the king's garden nestled between the two rivers. Overall, the palace gave the impression of a people that valued comfort and beauty but cared little for their security. And now, thanks to the efforts of Velka and the army of gardeners, all the plants were in full bloom, despite the upcoming winter.

"Ren?" Mar asked the gate guard, giving him Woron's reins.

"Already arrived," saluted the man as he answered, letting his captain pass to the open courtyard. A few nobles were already there, and Mar felt uneasy under the speculative stares of the women. Each one assessing the potential value of the scion of Liath, despite years of him showing a lack of interest in the court's romantic affairs.

Ren was in the throne room, positioning himself behind the throne as they previously agreed. In the event of an attack, he would secure the back while Mar held the front. Mar nodded to him and smirked, seeing his friend look as uncomfortable in parade uniform as he felt.

"Has Ina arrived yet?" Mar didn't hide his interest from Ren as he already knew of his feelings.

"No, not yet, but hopefully soon. The king is almost ready to enter, and the rest of the nobles are gathered outside for the presentation and oath ceremony," answered Ren grimacing. Mar couldn't agree more. Providing security today would be a nightmare, especially in such circumstances. He would prefer Ina was secure before some assassin needle found its way to her neck.

The king's entrance stopped all conversation. Rewan was young, in his thirties, but the law appointed him as the heir to the throne despite having a capable, older half-sister. Much like his father, he preferred the company of women and strong liquor rather than ruling the country, leaving the latter in the hands of his sibling. The chancellor hoped that marriage would help stabilise the situation, but Rewan resisted all forms of matchmaking.

Behind the king, his sister, Princess Sophia, couldn't be more different to her brother. He had inherited his southern mother's dark hair and complexion, while Sophia's fair skin and bright blue eyes were typical of northern heritage. Poets compared her beauty to Lada and praised her kindness and compassion, but Mar knew from experience she was anything but kind. When her brother was disinterested in any responsibilities, Sophia actively participated in Magical Council meetings, often enforcing harsh decrees. He suspected part of the recent unrest was related to her treatment of smallholders. Everybody except the closest advisors blamed the king, who seemed oblivious to his lack of popularity.

King Rewan returned Mar's respectful bow with a brief nod. As he straightened, Mar felt Sophia's hostile stare on his back, his rejection of her advances never forgotten or forgiven. Their mutual dislike was the main reason he never advanced beyond the position of captain.

The procession of noble families streamed in continuously, and soon not only the king but also Mar had to stifle his yawns, listening to the monotonous pledges of loyalty. Two hours later, when the spacious throne room was bursting at the seams and bored families engaged in casual conversations, the herald announced, "Arch-healer of Cornovii, Grand Duchess Nerissa and Lady Inanuan of Thorn."

The silence that followed his words was deafening. Nerissa glided forwards slowly. Her deliberate, leisurely pace made it clear she was not happy to wait till the end of the ceremony. The scowls from the more senior nobles meant this insult to their status would not be forgotten. The king was making them a spectacle, but both women strolled through the room, the epitome of elegance.

Mar could not take his eyes from the witch. Sophia was the inspiration for poets in her pale blue silks and crown on golden hair, but Ina was the woman they saw in their most fevered dreams. The vibrant colours she had chosen for her attire stood out from the pale pastels now prevalent in the court. Spider silk reflected the light of the candles, enhancing Ina's curves and leaving very little to the imagination. The peridot resting in her cleavage, barely covered by translucent golden mesh, drew every man's eyes to her bust. Her copper hair was braided and tied up behind an intricate circlet, exposing her long neck.

Gasps and the murmur of voices broke through the crowd, and gossip about her past deeds spread like wildfire. Mar felt movement behind his back. For the first time since the ceremony started, the king rose from his throne. Standing in front of Ina, the monarch reached for her hand, helping her up from her curtsy. Mar frowned when Rewan lifted her hand to his lips in true gallant style.

"My lady, your beauty has been too long hidden. Dare I ask what castle hid your exquisite face?" One look at Ina and Mar knew it took her a lot of effort not to wince at hearing such nonsense.

Instead, she gave him a smile that could send a thousand ships to war and answered, "I was a guest of a hovel in the Black Forest thanks to your father's kindness."

She heard murmurs sweeping through the crowd following her words, but Ina noticed the king's lips twitch as he suppressed a laugh. For a moment, she saw sharp intelligence hidden behind his simpleton façade.

"Indeed, my father was a man of many faults. I'm glad to have you back in the court. Hopefully, we will have time later for a closer encounter."

Behind the king, Mar's eyes flashed to pure gold. Ina looked at his rigid posture, and against her better judgement, she tilted her head and said, "In that case, I will request a dance later."

The voices growing louder behind her with each passing minute told her she had stepped too far, but Rewan just laughed and nodded. "That is a pleasant reminder that it is time to start the ball." He attempted to take Ina's hand, but Sophia was quicker, grasping her brother's arm and leading him from the throne room.

Ina tried to disappear into the ballroom crowd. Still, no matter what corner she stood in, she was soon encircled by men with lingering eyes and overly grabby hands, trying to gain an invitation to her bedroom with sweet words and nonsensical promises. She was close to screaming when a servant found her.

"My lady, the king requests your presence at his table."

Her suitors parted, and Ina again had to parade in front of all the courtiers.

Sophia greeted her with a pleasant smile. "Ina, how good to see you! I thought we'd lost you for good when you were exiled." The royal embrace felt odd, and there was no mention of their carriage encounter. The witch followed the custom and placed a brief peck on the princess's cheek.

"We have both changed so much," Ina answered, observing her former friend, now a regal lady, examining her with a disdainful smirk.

The king pointed to the seat next to him, but Sophia interjected, "But, brother, you promised us dancing."

Rewan nodded and turned to Ina. "Indeed, shall we dance, then? I remember I promised a certain lady at least one dance." He pushed his chair to stand up, but Sophia placed a hand on his shoulder.

"It is your coronation ball. Your promised dance can wait, but I wish to see something special."

Ina wished she could quietly sneak out during the siblings' squabble. What was she doing here, and what kind of game was being played?

Rewan smiled. "I'm afraid our marshal prepared nothing special for the ball, so we may as well let everyone entertain themselves. Starting the ball with Lady Ina will be special enough."

Sophia's smirk deepened when she turned her eyes on Ina. The cold and calculated eyes didn't match the beautiful face, and Ina realised she was looking at the enemy. Why, from all of them, must it be Sophia? The witch expected an attack but not a betrayal by a friend.

"Oh, but Lady Ina is a lovely dancer. Perhaps she could dance for you as a gift. The dagger and sash dance is well-known, and I haven't seen it for ages, especially since you resist marriage. I'm sure we would all enjoy watching it."

Ina was close to panicking. The dance Sophia mentioned was an ancient tradition performed at weddings where the newly married pretended to fight while being connected by a long red ribbon. Of course, the steps were structured to avoid any incident, but the weapons were sharp, and the fight was meant to look natural. The legend said if they were destined to be, the sash wouldn't be cut.

Ina bowed slightly. "I must politely refuse. Two lovers perform this dance, and a solo dancer would look ridiculous trying to swing a dagger around."

Sophia's smile grew bigger. "Oh, in that case, it is good we have Captain Marcach here to assist you. I believe you both know each other rather well."

Ina's head snapped around when a snigger sounded behind her. Sophia made sure those standing nearby clearly heard her insinuations.

Ina gave Mar an apologetic look but to her surprise, he smiled. "I will be more than happy to assist."

Anger slashed across the king's face when servants brought two matching daggers and a red sash, clearly stored nearby for this occasion. This spectacle was not only humiliating for her and Mar, but it also portrayed the king as a weakling in front of the nobles. Now it was clear his sister was holding the reins.

Mar came closer and whispered, "Do you know the steps?" Ina nodded, but the uncertainty on her face made him smile. "Then trust me, it will be fine."

The music started, and they moved into the opening stance. Ina observed the captain's movement and countered it with her own. Despite their lack of practice, Ina mirrored Mar's movements naturally. Even a slight hesitation at the start felt planned, a feint to build tension. As the tempo picked up, she smiled. Attack and parry, twisting under and around the red silk fast and precise without a single cut to the sash.

Claps and cheers sounded after each complicated sequence, working against Sophia's intent. Suddenly, a golden button came out of nowhere, rolling under her feet. She lost her footing, and the crowd gasped in horror when the dagger slipped from her hand, flying towards Mar's chest. He dodged it, but a sudden swipe of his blade cut the red silk. Ina panted, lying on the floor and looking at what tripped her. The button, engraved with the royal crest and Sophia's triumphant smile, told her everything she needed to know. Mar had almost been killed to have this little drama, and blinding rage erupted in her. If this bitch wanted a show, let it be a show to remember.

Slowly rising, she drew energy from the countless candles scattered around the ballroom. Not that she needed it with her stone, but dimming the lights increased the dramatic effect. The crowd's anxiety was palpable, especially considering they knew she was the source of the magic. Ina looked at Mar.

"Trust me," she muttered quietly. When he nodded, she exclaimed, "Lord Marcach, I don't believe we finished our dance." A flick of the wrist and a fire serpent coiled around her arm. Ina whipped it towards Mar, who let it wrap around his arm without hesitation. The link between them flickered to her heartbeat, and his eyes lit up, answering her call. The music started again on the king's command, and they resumed the dance.

His Majesty stood up, looking pleased. "I want to see this, my sister. I have to thank you for such a surprise. It has made this a coronation ball worth remembering."

Without even realising it, Mar and Ina changed the moves. The dance moves intensified, changing from a stylised fight to a lovers' ballet as they circled each other, exchanging attacks under the stream of fire. She could see Mar breathe deeply as her movements fuelled his desire. Still, he was not alone in being affected by this erotic display. When they finally stopped, and Ina lowered herself in a deep curtsy, an intricate apple blossom pattern appeared on the floor. And the crowd gasped, seeing the magically engraved royal flower of Cornovii honouring the ruling house. The candlelight flared up again when she slowly rose.

"The House of Thorn and House of Liath pledge the oath of loyalty to Rewan of Cornovii. May your rule be fruitful."

The disaster turned into a political statement, changing the balance of power, and the room erupted with cheers, "Long live King Rewan!" a popular refrain.

The king approached them, clapping slowly. "I have to retract my promise, Lady Ina. I don't believe anyone could do better than this." Then, to her surprise, he added quietly. "Thank you."

The king, turning to their audience of wide-eyed nobles, jested, "Now I have to release our captain for the rest of the night. Hopefully, he will invite us to the actual wedding soon."

Muffled laughs followed his words, and Ina breathed a small sigh of relief when the monarch turned around and returned to his seat.

Nobles and merchants parted before her as she dropped Mar's hand and headed back to the corner. It was time to become invisible. Ina had "enjoyed" enough entertainment for the night, and avoiding conversation also sounded like a good idea. She rushed, glancing back, not noticing she was heading straight for Liander.

The half-elf looked at her with a pleasant smile. "Ina, you haven't changed a bit, alluring as always, and such exhibitionism." When he saw Mar behind her, the mage added, "It reminds me of those delicious times we had together, but I see that some of your skills have improved with age. You even charmed His Majesty. I heard they are looking to marry him off."

"And I see you finally found a place for yourself in the court." She was determined to not react to the obvious goading and be civil to the arsehole who toyed with her in the past.

"Well, you vacated this position so suddenly, and my skills are always useful. Please, tell me, how was life in your hovel? At least you have washed the forest dirt off, and if gossip is true, I'm not the only man that noticed this improvement."

Before she replied, Mar placed his hands on her shoulders. Ina ground her teeth, concerned about Mar's reaction. Liander knew how to hurt her, and he'd obviously heard the conversation she'd had with the king.

"Be careful how you address my betrothed, or I may take offence." Mar's voice was calm and pleasant, but the half-breed's face changed. Mar was so calm that Ina involuntarily looked back. Yes, it was still Mar, but why did the damn man insist on fuelling this gossip? The captain leaned down and kissed her exposed neck. "I see you liked my gift, also, the stone in your bracelet is glowing," the barely audible whisper reached her ears.

It was hard to not look directly at her wrist. Ina extended her hand to Liander. "Please don't mind my… Mar can be a little jealous. My belated congratulations on your position, my friend."

The mage took her hand, and Ina's bracelet glowed eerily. Ina chuckled melodically to cover her fury. "Forgive me, it reacts to powerful magic. You must have honed your skills as well during my absence."

Liander puffed his chest. "I see you haven't lost your touch, Ina. You can still recognise true talent. I'm practically indispensable now. Even our snow queen Sophia is impressed by it."

Ina effortlessly slid from Mar's embrace and smiled at Liander. "You've advanced so much, if I had only known this all those years ago."

The admiration in her voice pumped his already inflated ego. "But of course, my dear, things could be so different if you'd only listened to me."

Mar stood there like a pillar of condensed fury. He hoped she was doing this for a reason, but why did she shower this fop with attention? He yearned to rip him apart when a servant appeared, carrying an order from Sophia.

Liander glided away full of his own importance, and Ina grabbed Mar's hand and pulled him towards the open doors. "I need to go to the garden. Now."

He didn't protest, curious about what she was planning. The manicured shrubbery gave them plenty of opportunities to hide, but Ina dragged him farther from the illuminated ballroom. Seemingly satisfied with the distance, she pushed her face into his chest and shouted. "Motherfucking bastard, dim-witted gold-digging scum. How the fuck dare he? I will kill him slowly, revive him, and then kill him again."

The stream of obscenities kept rolling out, and Mar smiled, embraced her closer, and stroked her back. He was right. She had done it for a reason. When Ina finally stopped, he lifted her chin to the moonlight. "Now, care to tell me what was this all about, and in a free moment, can you teach me your colourful language? The men in the barracks will be thrilled," he said.

"He was the one who put the curse on me. The bracelet contains a detection spell in the gem, and he lit it up like a Yanwo firework." Mar already knew about the curse, but knowing the author was so close and walked free triggered the part of him he thought he had lain to rest.

Ina grabbed him by the sleeve when he stepped away. "Where are you going?"

"To arrest this bastard. He will pay for this, and when I finish, I will let Ren have a go." Mar's face, distorted in a predatory snarl, looked terrifying.

Ina firmed her grip. "No, you will not. First, it is the king's ball, and second, I don't think it was his idea. Liander may be a great mage, but all he cares about is money and prestige. The attack would make little sense unless he'd been bribed." Mar tried to pull free, but she only held him closer. "Please, we need to talk. I have some news for you, and we have a firm lead. We can't spoil it now."

Her quiet pledge seeped through his rage, and he shook his head to dispel the thoughts of tasting this buffoon's blood. He literally wanted to taste it. Mar breathed heavily, as Ina's hands reached his cheek and cupped his face.

"Thank you for trusting me in the dance." Ina's soft voice and gentle touch relaxed his tense muscles.

He reached for her and leaned down, capturing her lips. The long possessive kiss tamed the beast inside him.

He missed her these past few days, but now his witch was here, soft and inviting, melting under his touch as if she'd never kicked him out in the cold of the night. "In all but the vows, you are my wife." His own words stunned him, but not the certainty he felt about this statement.

Ina chuckled slightly, taking it as a tease. "Well, you definitely left the court thinking that after your behaviour a few moments ago. Really, Mar? Calling me your betrothed in front of that gossip Liander? The entire city will know about it by tomorrow." Ina's carefree laugh stabbed him straight in the heart. She didn't even consider this a possibility.

"Would it be so bad to be a lady of Liath?" he asked quietly, but some voices disturbed their seclusion before the confused witch could answer.

Mar placed his hand on Ina's mouth, preventing her from speaking, observing a man and a woman entering a small clearing.

The shadows hid their faces, but their clothing suggested nobles from the ball.

"What the hell were you thinking, provoking her today? We lost the advantage. She pledged two houses to Rewan, not just her own, but the whole military power of Liath, and her magic display...?" a male voice exclaimed, clearly berating the woman.

"I did what I wanted, and you forget your place. Did you think I would stand meekly in the background when this dirty witch turned everyone's heads? After all she has done, my brother was an idiot to invite her." The female's tone was bitter, and her words lashed out at the man who dared to rebuke her.

"Sophia, my love, all eyes were on you. You were the most beautiful and intelligent woman in the room. Why do you think such a hellion as Ina would turn any heads? She is just a cheap one-night sensation, that's all."

Ina bit into Mar's hand, trying to break free. "I will show you a cheap sensation," she muttered.

Mar, unfazed by her bite, only bent lower and whispered into her ear, "Hold your horses. It's the princess. I want to know what is going on here." Her struggle intensified until he finally snapped, "Don't be difficult. I didn't run after Liander, so now it's your turn to be patient."

Sophia was still pouting when the man cupped her cheeks and slowly kissed her. "Don't forget our goals and plans, and don't lose your head over one scruffy witch."

His hands roamed more freely over the princess's body. One slap on the wrist and his eager attempts were rebuffed. "No, I told you we will have time for this after our plan comes to fruition."

Her partner lowered his hands and sighed. "We are almost ready."

"Good, we will have to bring it forwards. I was not too fond of the way Ina talked to Liander. Now, let's go back before anyone notices my absence."

"I knew someone would make a move on me, but I didn't think it would be her," said Ina after Sophia disappeared from the garden.

Mar's face was grim when he answered, "I think we now know who is behind all this. I suspect who the guard might be, but I need proof, and we need to find out when they will do it."

"Mar, about this—I have something to show you. Could you perhaps visit me tomorrow, just to talk, of course?" Ina desperately tried to make sure he understood her, especially after his silly declarations this evening.

"Of course, I will." His smile was genuine. "Let's leave worrying for tomorrow. For now, let's enjoy the ball, Ina. Whatever they plan, it won't happen tonight, and I want to spend just one evening simply savouring your company."

His request was so sincere that, standing in the moonlight, Ina could not resist the magic of the moment. Early fog and stray will-o'-the-wisps were slowly coming from the riverbank. She stood there looking over the water as they gathered around her. The little spirits followed the movement of her hands as she slowly glided through the grass to the echoing sounds of music from the palace. Mar smiled as he watched, waiting for her answer.

He came to her, placing his hand on her cheek. Ina looked at the ethereal lights. "Why not? What else can we do?" She pointed to the little spirits. "Beautiful, aren't they? Sad, the more you want them to be real, the weaker they become, just like love."

Mar sighed and kissed her softly. "You, my love, have the strangest ideas about relationships."

Ina's eyes widened before slowly closing as she savoured the sensation. "Why? Because I don't want a commitment that will fade with time? I'm not Velka. For me, love is like those lights, beautiful while it lasts, but not real and rarely wins when it clashes with life."

Mar shook his head, hearing her strange statement. Life had given him a complicated woman, but he had a lifetime to make her change her mind and enough patience to do it.

CHAPTER 22

Ina woke up with memories of the previous night crowding her thoughts. Mar had been attentive and gentle till the moment she lost her patience and grasped him by the beard, pulling him down into a passionate kiss.

With barely a moment's hesitation, Mar deepened the kiss. His hands freely roamed over the silk of her dress, stroking the now-fevered flesh beneath it, the growl of his voice as he once more claimed her as his betrothed speaking to something deep inside her.

As soon as he mentioned the oath again, she bit his lip, pulling back and, with a shuddering breath, tried to explain it was just for tonight, and she didn't want to tie herself to one man forever. Mar raised an eyebrow, and she saw mischief in his eyes before he descended to her collarbone. When his lips touched her bosom, she lost the will to care if he listened.

The rest of the evening passed in a blur of desire, and when Mar gallantly escorted her home, she could not help but invite him inside. However, her rugged warrior had other ideas and, after one more blistering kiss, stood in front of her, smirking. "Till tomorrow, my lady." With that, he leapt on his horse and rode away.

She had to admit she was disappointed by his decision. He was an excellent lover and her body missed his touch. Even when his dominant nature took control, he focused on her needs, and she definitely wanted his body and his intelligence. Even his awkward possessiveness had stopped bothering her that much. But the whole package? Becoming a lady of Liath with all its duties was not on the menu. Ina moaned and covered her face with a pillow. Why did it have to be so complicated?

Mar arrived at noon, as promised, and Ina invited him straight to her workshop. He looked around the cluttered space and asked in an overly formal manner, "My lady, what did you want to discuss?"

Ina gestured him closer and unravelled the scroll she'd received at the tavern. "My... Erm, a source gave me this map. All the red lines you can see are new tunnels, and the ones in blue have recently collapsed. I feel the solution in the back of my mind, but I can't fully grasp it. Does it mean anything to you?"

Mar studied the map for a moment until he finally picked up the one they'd used for their trip to the underground. He put them together and held them to the window. They noticed the red dots from Mar's map aligned with the entrances of the tunnels in Ina's. She took a quill and, making sure to follow the open pathways, drew a walkable line from one end to the other. He noticed her frown when she looked at them. "It's like someone tried to herd cattle underground."

"Ina, do you have a map of the town?"

She nodded, and when they placed her made-up line on the map, the witch gasped. The entry point was somewhere on the outskirts, but the exit was directly in front of the palace gates.

Impatiently tapping her fingers on the table, she asked, "Mar, correct me if I'm wrong, but the palace doesn't have a strong defence, does it?"

Her companion only shrugged. "None of the monarchs saw the need for it. Most nations prefer to trade with Cornovii rather than attack it, especially with such well-defended borders. The King's Guards may protect the palace, but, more often than not, we're tasked to investigate any problems not covered by the city magistrate. The Liath clan controls the military, the royal family controls the money, and everybody is happy with these arrangements. We only maintain a decor guard, mostly manned by youngsters."

That made her burst out laughing. "So, a nobles meat market. How did you end up in this, then? I saw you fighting. You can't tell me you are one of those decorous fools?"

"They needed a heroic wolf to lead the lambs, and I needed to get out of the borderlands," Mar said, simply cutting her off.

Ina sighed and came back to the map. "So, we have a defenceless palace and large corridor that goes straight to the gates." She went silent, clearly thinking of something. "Mar, if someone pushed a horde of monsters that way…and it is easy for a strong psychic—"

"The palace would be overrun in a matter of hours, but why, Ina? All the nobles are happy with a weak monarch. Could Sophia want the throne? If you planned it, why would you do it?"

"Sophia may be a bitch to me, but this? There are only two reasons I can see. To kill the king and those willing to stand by him, or maybe play the hero saving him in front of the court. I don't know, Mar, it sounds too insane even to consider it." Ina leaned in, looking at the maps. "I forgot to tell you. I have a list of people who could have killed the old king. They are provided by…erm, a reliable source." Stuttering, she passed him the assassin's list.

This time, it was Mar's turn to laugh. "Ina, I know you are collaborating with Gruff and his contacts. I don't mind you covering for your 'sources.' I trust you. Also, I have my suspicions, especially after what we heard last night, but let me see."

Mar cursed silently, looking at the parchment, and Ina asked, "Do you recognise anyone?"

He nodded. "It is Senad."

"Mar, I'm not defending him, but except the name on the paper, what proof do you have?"

With resignation in his voice, Mar started explaining, "The only four people that survived the forest attack and knew the assassin needle technique were me, Ren, Daro, and Senad. Ren was with you when the king was assassinated, and yesterday I sent Daro to the city barracks to search the higher officers' quarters. Besides, I wouldn't mistake his tall, bulky arse for the person in the garden. That leaves Senad and me."

He missed when she approached him and placed her hand on the small of his back. "Not that I'm bragging, but you would not have survived the forest if not for me, and it is his name that is on the list."

"I know, Ina. I knew it yesterday, but I just wanted us to be happy before reality could smack me in the face. Senad has been infatuated with Sophia since the day he saw her in the palace gardens. I tried to keep him from anything that concerned her, but I didn't expect he would leave me to die. I'm sorry, Ina."

"For what?" she asked, and Mar turned her around and buried his face in her hair. The scent of apples still lingered from last night, comforting him.

Inhaling her perfume, he answered, "For not keeping you safe from the mess I involved you in."

"There's no need to apologise for someone else's actions. Anyway, I was going to tell you, tomorrow I'm heading out of town. Janik sent a message that there was a strange activity on a farm outside the city. I have to make sure it is not connected to our investigations."

"No," said Mar, holding her at arm's length. "You are a target now, and I can't escort you while I have to sort through this mess. I can't even spare Ren. I know you can look after yourself but going alone into a potential trap is foolish."

Ina stepped back. "Janik is more or less a friend. We went through a lot during my student years. He won't hurt me if he wants to show his face in Gruff's tavern again."

They quarrelled, but he didn't sway, and she seemed to lose the will to discuss it further. Instead, Ina changed the subject to plans for the palace defences.

She suggested asking the dwarven mining guild for help in collapsing part of the tunnels near the palace, but Mar disagreed, explaining it would expose the city to attack, and his palace garrison at least had weapons. He agreed to the second suggestion, though. Ina wrote a letter to Jorge asking him for help by delegating a few battlemages to reinforce the palace walls in the upcoming days.

Finally, when the conspiracy plot discussion ran dry, she turned to him and said, "We need to talk."

Mar suspected what was coming. Last night had been a bit of a revelation for them both, and Ina felt the need to dissect the subject further.

"Can we just be friends? I like you. I just don't want all this sentimental nonsense in my life. So, can we be friends with some fun on the side?"

Mar approached her, placed his hands on her shoulders, and stroked them gently.

"I will consider this if you tell me—what is it about being with me you are so afraid of?"

He saw her raise the proverbial hackles, but he kept looking at her till she shrugged and said, "I'm not afraid. I just don't like oaths, the responsibility that comes with them, and being with someone when love fades, just because you were sure you weren't making a mistake long ago."

Mar kissed the top of her head. "And we can work on that, my spitfire."

With these words, he kissed her goodbye and returned to the barracks. Behind the gates, Mar pressed his head to Woron's neck. The way she set her boundaries was discouraging, but at least now he knew why. Ina didn't trust love and didn't want to get tied up to another proverbial "hut in the forest." He must convince her he was here to stay and that he didn't intend to put her in any role she didn't want to take. The turmoil of the current events didn't make it easy. He felt like a plaything in the hands of forces far more powerful than himself, but he was determined to persevere.

After writing a brief letter and leaving it with Marika in the morning, Ina prepared for the journey. She let Mar believe he'd won the argument, but he was right about the backup plan. Marika didn't look happy when she told her, "If I don't come back this evening, send this to Sa'Ren Gerel at the barracks. He is the exotic man that visited here."

The servant nodded slightly, trying to not look at Ina. Still, her employer was too preoccupied with her thoughts to notice. The note she'd sent to Gruff last night gained her a horse that was now waiting, tied to the post in her yard. Nothing too flashy, as she had asked. Ina hoped this journey was not a terrible mistake as she climbed into the saddle. Still, the stakes were too high, and she must find whether the conspirators had created a second base on the farm.

Velka was unsettled. She knew Ina had been busy the past couple of days, as was Daro. She hadn't had a chance to properly think about it because of constant problems with the gardens. Today, the Nature Mage felt it was about time to talk to Ina and raise her issues with the soil and collapsed riverbank. It was still early when she arrived at Ina's yard, and the witch's new housekeeper answered her knocking.

"Ehh…is Ina home?" asked the mage hesitantly.

"No, she just rode off somewhere, leaving me with a letter to deliver if something happened to her."

Velka cursed under her breath. "Alone?" When the servant nodded, she commanded, "Give it to me."

Marika stepped back. "No, I have to deliver it to someone called Sa'Ren Gerel in the barracks."

With a short, impatient gesture, Velka grabbed the servant's hand. "Then we are going to the barracks. Now." Dragging the much smaller girl to the carriage wasn't difficult, and the mage didn't have time for pleasantries when her friend may already be neck-deep in trouble. She yelled at the coachman, and they raced through the streets to find Sa'Ren.

❧◦◦◦❧

A messenger's arrival halted Mar's pacing. When Daro came to talk to him in the morning, one look at the orc's grim face and Mar knew things did not look good for Senad. Although his quarters in the barracks were pristine, Daro found a note about a flower delivery to an address he did not recognise, so he followed the lead. The building was in a quiet, run-down part of the city, but they found dried-out flowers and several notes exchanged between Senad and Sophia. Mar was not even angry at reading how Senad provided information about their movements and investigations to his lover. He had the proof now, and he just needed the chancellor to put an end to this.

Mar rushed to the palace only to wait the whole morning to hear from the chancellor. The old politician kept him waiting, with the Council and the king claiming his time. When Mar was finally let into his office, he didn't know where to start.

"Tell me you brought some good news," said the old noble, rubbing his bloodshot eyes.

Mar felt sorry for him when he placed the results of his investigation on the desk.

"Unfortunately not. There is a threat of an imminent attack on the palace." The captain unrolled the map and pointed to the open passage. "The disappearances and monster attacks you told me to investigate are closely connected with a variant of Lady Inanuan's mutagen. Somehow the result of her experiment was removed from the Magical Council's vault, and now a group is transforming the missing citizens into aberrations. If enough of those reported missing have been changed, there could already be a small army in the tunnels."

"You and she gave quite a show at the ball." The chancellor gave him a tired smile, ignoring the part about the attack.

"Ina is someone special…to me, and not a part of the plot." The captain did not expect this diversion, but one look at the chancellor told him to stop.

"Stop fussing. I already spoke with Jorge. He confirmed she was not the maker or ringleader of this plot." The old man cut him short. "The group of people you mention, do you have a lead?"

Mar felt it was a time to reveal the most uncomfortable part.

"Princess Sophia, court mage Liander, Senad, and I suspect, a few other guards and nobles. Mostly second sons hoping for advancement under a new ruler."

"What proof do you have? Mar, are you talking about a palace coup? That's not an accusation to be thrown around lightly."

They were simple questions, yet Mar found it hard to answer, and he knew his answers would bring the old noble to his knees. Sophia was his pupil, and he treated her almost like his own daughter.

He pointed to the rota schedule, where he'd marked the names. "Senad was the only one who had access to King Roda when he was murdered, and he was also the only person present versed in the technique that was used."

"That proves only he was there. He could have simply failed to notice the attacker," retorted the chancellor.

Holding up an order bearing Sophia's seal, the captain snapped, "Yes, but it does not explain why a troop of guards was sent to the Black Forest on the personal order of Sophia. How I, amongst all the wounded, was the only man stabbed with a dagger and the only one left to die." The grief of betrayal roughened his voice. "Not only this, but Senad's and two other guards' names occur in every place where the disappearances happened." Mar closed his eyes and sighed. "I also overheard his conversation with Sophia during the ball, and they were undeniably plotting together."

"All right, all right." The chancellor raised his hands in surrender. "And how is Liander involved?"

"Not so long ago, Ina bought a bondage contract—a were-cat woman with an unusual mind-controlling collar. The mage was hit by a spell or curse embedded inside the collar as she broke the enchantment. After she recovered, Ina tracked the source of the curse to Liander." Mar's anger reverberated in his words.

"That only proves that the mage is involved in trade and pocketing some money from his magical skills."

The captain hoped the politician was playing devil's advocate and not defending the culprits.

He answered, "It also implies that if a sentient were-cat can be turned into an obedient slave with nothing more than a piece of leather and a small gem on the lock, how difficult could it be to control a horde of monsters?"

The chancellor took a moment to clean his glasses. Mar had often observed this gesture and learned the noble used it to buy himself time to think. "And Sophia?" he finally spoke.

Mar knew it was difficult for him, but he could not cover up the truth and placed a stack of handwritten notes and purchase orders with Sophia's personal seal in front of him. "Sophia is Senad's lover, and we overheard their conversation during the ball. After hearing about their plans, I ordered a search of Senad's quarters and, following the lead, Daro found those notes. That should be enough to prove them guilty, but we have to act now."

"And what were you and Ina were doing in the garden?" The chancellor again cut him off.

Mar's temper flared. "I was trying to warm her up to the idea of being my wife! Stop changing the subject. I know Sophia is like a daughter to you. Still, you can't be blind to her deeds. For the past ten years, she's been grabbing power piece by piece, and you averted your eyes, giving her permission, but this is going too far. She must be stopped."

Alarmed by raised voices, guards entered the room and looked anxiously at the captain, but Mar waved them off. Turning to the old lord slumped in his chair, he asked, "What is your decision? Or should I go straight to the king?"

"Do what you must and prepare the defence. Remember, you are going after someone with royal blood. There will be no winners in this battle, whatever you do." The chancellor hid his pale face in his hands.

Mar could see a broken old man, but he was right. There were no winners in political wars.

CHAPTER 23

As he marched into the gate garrison, Mar barked out his orders. This place was a nightmare. Young guards, mainly second sons of noble families, who'd never even smelled an actual battle, were now looking at him like deer at the hunter. Mar left Ren busy fortifying the gates as he turned to his sergeant.

"Daro, find someone, not from the guards, but someone we can trust. I need to know their every step till the chancellor secures a detention order from the king. Also, get this letter to the Magical Council. We need Jorge's help to deal with Liander."

Daro looked at him with concern and resignation. "We're going that far?"

The captain noticed the orc looked like he had aged several years in the past two days. While Mar felt closer to Ren, Daro and Senad often trained together, and he suspected the young orc saw the lieutenant more as a member of his tribe than a fellow soldier. Senad's betrayal seemed to have shaken Daro's world deeply. Mar knew there was nothing he could do to help him and turned to leave as Ren burst into the room.

"Sir, we have a problem." Handing Ina's letter to him, his newly nominated second-in-command looked on the verge of leaving as he waited for him to read the letter.

"Fuck! Why can't she listen, just this once?" Mar's roar shook the walls. "Ren, go after her. Daro, do what I've ordered. And who the fuck brought this letter?"

"Velka and Ina's new servant, Marika." Ren turned around and bolted out, eager to get to Ina as soon as he could.

Mar turned to Daro. "Take those two and put them somewhere safe."

Daro only nodded, his new sombre attitude only adding to the grim start of the day.

❧❦

Ina wasn't sure she was heading in the right direction. The map showed the farm right in front of her. Still, instead of fields and buildings, she saw an unending mess of brambles. Ever since she'd left the main road, the pathway in front of her had narrowed down to nothing. Soon she would have to leave the horse behind and walk. Stopping to unhook the tree branch that caught her coat, Ina finally heard the faint murmur of voices. After several painstakingly slow minutes, she walked into a clearing, seeing Janik's team lounging around a small fire.

She emerged from the greenery, and the mercenary leader greeted her. "Ina, I was losing hope that you'd come." He

314

embraced her in a quick hug. The witch's world disappeared into his tight embrace for a moment, blocking her view of the two stealthily departing men.

"The road here is not exactly fast or well-marked," she answered.

Janik laughed heartily. "Well, I didn't choose where the suspicious activity occurred." He pointed past the fire. "Come with me. The farm is over here. It was abandoned by the tenants earlier this year, so no one should be around. We need you to check for magical traps and help if we run into trouble."

Ina looked at him with doubt in her eyes. "You realise I'm not a battlemage?"

Janik nodded. "Yes, but you are also the only witch I know who will leave the city to come here and will still leave me some money after I pay her."

"Well then, let's go. And make sure you guard my arse." Ina pursed her lips. Bloody mercenaries, not much sense but plenty of greed.

Ina followed her guide and walked along the small path that soon widened enough to show the half-derelict buildings as they approached. The farm must have been an excellent source of income in the past. The crumbling buildings still bore marks of wealth. Janik gestured her to silence and pointed towards the house. She noticed some movement in the window and nodded, letting him go first. After a moment, he emerged and gestured for her to come in. Making her best impression of sneaking, the witch approached the house. After a moment of hesitation, she entered the dark hallway.

"Janik?" she whispered, trying to orient herself.

"Here."

His voice came from the end of the hall, and Ina walked farther into the house. She was shuffling her feet slowly when a sudden noise made her turn around, but she was not fast enough to evade the fist that struck her temple with a loud thud. Janik caught Ina's unconscious body and carried her down to the basement.

⁊᠊᠊᠊᠊᠊

Liander was pacing in the small room when he saw the mercenary enter. "What took you so long? Tie her up."

Janik shrugged and tied Ina's body to the only chair. The side of her face was already changing colour, and the swelling had spread to her jaw. Ina drifted in and out of consciousness. Her mind was groggy and pulsating pain prevented her from gathering her thoughts. A splash of water forced her to open her eyes. The world spun around crazily, and Ina vomited the contents of her breakfast on the feet of someone standing in front of her.

"You bloody bitch!" the man howled, and she braced herself for another strike that somehow didn't come.

"Go clean yourself up while I guard her." The voice was Janik's. She raised her head, and, looking at the mercenary, Ina tried to understand what was happening here.

"Janik, why? Release me, please." She tried to reason with him, but he only shook his head.

"I'm sorry, Striga, it's nothing personal. The princess paid us in gold, and lots of it, to get you here." He approached her with a bowl of water and wiped her face. "Besides, you wouldn't want to be in the city right now with how nasty it's going to get there," he added.

Ina realised he was talking about the attack she had discussed with Mar yesterday.

She jerked in her restraints. "Janik, I will pay you double. My family will pay you double, just let me go. We have to stop it."

He put the cool cloth on her bruise with a guilty expression and shook his head. "I can't, Ina. Besides, it is too late to stop anything. As soon as we finish this deal, we'll be leaving Cornovii. It won't be a safe place to live, with Sophia using monsters to keep the throne."

The cool water helped her gather her thoughts. It made Ina angry how Janik was trying to be nice to her after betraying her, but at least he was giving her some information, so she needed to play along.

"And how did you get into all this?" she asked.

Janik went quiet for a moment. "Remember how I was paid to clear the tunnels and sewers? Well, it didn't go as planned, and as we were all about to be killed by some mutant troll, this one guard made us an offer I couldn't refuse. Everybody wants to live."

Ina jerked once again. "Janik, I will explain it all to Mar just… For fuck's sake, release me so I can stop Liander."

The sound of the footsteps on the stairs stopped their conversation. "Way too late for that, Ina, but maybe this will help you." He held up her enchanted necklace and placed it back on her neck, tucking it out of sight.

Liander entered the room, giving Janik an arrogant glance. "You've been paid, mercenary. Now leave. This bitch is mine."

Janik left, and Liander came closer. Ina jerked on the chair, and, seeing this, his smile grew bigger. He reached for her, his hand slowly trailing along her leg, making her shudder. Was that the reason she was here? That was just ridiculous. He'd never seemed interested in sex. Even when he'd cheated, it had always been about gaining power, and yet, he was here with a sleazy smile, examining her thigh.

"Why am I here? Surely not just to be held in the basement?" The witch spat, trying to shake off his touch, which only encouraged him.

"You looked so alluring during the ball. It's a pity I didn't have the chance to make you scream for me that night." His other hand painfully squeezed her breast, but Ina kept a straight face. "Oh, you are so quiet now. Before we start, Sophia wanted me to ask you if you will work with her, but…please, say no. I want to see what is in this little head of yours."

His face was so close when he inspected her body that, against her better judgement, she head-butted him. The crunch of a broken nose and the blood pouring from it were worth the slap he gave her. Ina's head bounced off the chair, and she desperately tried to stay conscious, watching as Liander staggered back for revenge.

"I told her you would say no. It looks like it's time for me to have my fun." The mage stood behind her and grasped her swollen face. Ina, fighting panic, snapped her mental defences in place moments before his dirty consciousness slammed into her mind like a sledgehammer. Beads of sweat appeared on her forehead as she tried to defend her psyche, but each time she fixed a weak spot in her barrier, he found another. Ina's thoughts raced in this silent torment, but giving in meant losing herself and all that she was. Pressure built in her head. She was no match for a psychic mage, no matter how hard she resisted. Desperate to stay conscious, she called upon the forest.

In the centre of the city, Boruta woke from a restless sleep and stared, transfixed, at the fire, and when Ina lost all hope, the horned God answered her plea. "Why do you fight him?" his voice, full of humour, confused the witch.

"I cannot lose myself. I can't let him take the power of Chaos."

His presence flickered in front of her when he answered with amusement. "Let him. There is so much inside you for him to feel. Let him see all that you've become." The advice made no sense, but Leshy was the only one who had never failed her.

Gathering all her courage, Ina let go. Her barriers crumbled, flooding Liander with her memories. The near-death experience when she healed Mar, purging the mutagen's poison from Ren, unravelling the life of that nameless man. She gave him everything, and her magic flowed through it all, burning through the link and flooding his mind with Chaos.

Raw pain ripped through him, fracturing his attack, and seizing his body. The tension in her head subsided, but the connection stood open, and Ina took her chance, attacking his mind.

What she did to him was wrong. Memory after memory, she erased the man he was, taking what she needed as his mind emptied into nothingness. She lacked the finesse of a psychic mage, and Liander's body convulsed in agony. Ina had no mercy, avenging his victims and herself, and feeling justified in how she administered the punishment. When she finished, he was curled up, babbling incoherently to himself on the wet floor. Ina looked at this act of destruction and felt nothing. Why didn't she feel guilty about erasing a person's mind?

Boruta circled three times and curled up by the fire, purring with satisfaction. He had chosen his champion well, and time would tell how far the witch progressed.

Surprised that no one came with all the screaming, Ina tried to break free from her restraints. The rope was sturdy and protected from magic, but the chair underneath creaked ominously. She jumped up and down with little thought, trying to break it, but it was sturdier than she expected. She felt utterly stupid jumping like a frog around the room and was about to give up when one leg fell into a crack of the uneven floor, and finally, the chair broke.

The witch gathered herself from the floor, looking at Liander and reassuring herself he was no longer a threat. Now was the time to face the real enemy. She didn't expect Janik to let her go, but he was not an entirely wicked man despite his betrayal, and she did not want to hurt him, at least not much. The sounds of battle solved her dilemma.

At first, when she walked out of the cottage, she couldn't see through the whirlwind of dust in front of her, but as Ina moved forwards, bodies appeared from the storm. It was Ren, surrounded by mercenaries, his sword and dagger a blur as he glided through Janik's men, cutting them down like wheat at harvest.

Still, there were too many of them for a single warrior, and after a few seconds of being entranced by the beauty of his dance, she shouted, "Stop!" When her order fell on deaf ears, her vipers sparked to life. Lashing searing whips between the fighters, she roared, "I said stop, you idiots!"

The fighting stuttered to an end. Men stood gawking at her as if she were a demon. Ina walked between them and stood next to Ren.

"I see my reinforcements have arrived. As per our conversation, Janik, if you'd be so kind, fuck off from Cornovii and never show your ginger arse here again."

The battered mercenaries laughed nervously, but Janik approached her with a serious look on his face. "Liander?"

"Curled up on the floor in his own shit and piss. You can pick him up if you want." Ina's vicious smile made the massive mercenary step back. "I'm afraid there isn't much left of his mind after I finished with him, but maybe he will recover or even become a better man one day."

Janik stared at her in silence before he shouted his orders, "Get the wounded and saddle the horses." Turning around to Ina, he added, "It was just business, Striga. My people need to eat."

Ina shook her head. "No, Janik, your friendship was not just business to me. It's the only reason you all walked out of here alive. Remember this kindness if I ever meet you again."

She sagged, observing as the group disappeared into the distance, supporting herself on Ren. Her head was spinning like crazy, and she welcomed his presence.

She swallowed to hold back the bile in her throat and pressed her forehead to his shoulder. "Thank you for coming. I walked into this trap like a fool, and Liander almost destroyed me."

Ren held her tight, trying to calm the erratic beating of his heart. He felt unhinged from the fight. Ina's hair still smelled of perfume, and her body leaning against him released the chains of his passion. When he'd learned she'd been with Mar, he had buried his hopes and settled with just being close to her. Now, the unrestrained desire was back. Ren bent down and captured her lips. The kiss was harsh, and he knew he was stealing something that was not truly his, but he savoured the kiss while it lasted. Surprised, Ina didn't resist at first, but she pulled back and laughed after a moment.

"I heard that battle can make a man crave another's touch, but I never thought I would experience it." She gave him a brief peck on the cheek and added, "We need to find you a woman. You could make a rock melt with a kiss like that."

Ren looked down at Ina, hiding his thoughts and longing behind a melancholy smile, when the distant toll of the city bells vibrated through the air.

"The attack has started," he said, running to his horse and reaching his hand to Ina. "Come, my lady, we have little time."

The ride back to the capital was a blur. Ina took a horse from a dead mercenary, feeling guilty for her mount as Ren set a blistering pace, exhausting the poor animals in their need to return to the palace. Her companion cursed, seeing the city gates were open and unguarded. There were few patrols on the street, and the citizens had locked themselves in their houses. With only their horses' hooves striking the cobblestones, it felt like they galloped through a ghost town.

They approached the main road to the palace, and Ina caught sight of heavy black smoke lingering above the gates. Ren held in the horses, hearing the sounds of battle, and gestured her to stay. With his attention focused on their surroundings, he directed his horse towards the commotion, and Ina followed him, ignoring his instructions.

The closer she came, the more her Chaos magic stirred within her chest, swirling and gathering in strength until a tornado of power ignited her body. Strength and energy flowed through her veins. Gone were the headache, the bruises, and every pain from her ordeal. Every part of her felt young and invincible. Now she finally understood Nerissa's words. This magic was overwhelming and addictive, and all she needed to do was surrender control.

Ren looked around, feeling the annoyance at Ina defying his order replaced by concern. The witch looked younger, and fiery vipers writhed beneath her skin as she rode behind him with a euphoric smile. The gem on her chest was glowing like a beacon, and the air seemed to shimmer like a desert mirage. Ina seemed utterly unaware of the carnage surrounding them.

The battlefield at the gates was worse than Ren had imagined, but Mar had somehow successfully defended them. It looked like whoever directed the monsters aimed strictly for the palace, as none of the aberrations rampaged through the city.

There were gaping holes in the ground, torn open by inhuman hands and claws. The palace walls were battered and crumbling, strewn with bodies, human and monster, but the gates still stood. There were men in the towers, some in uniform with crossbows, others in garish robes tossing fire from their hands at the rapacious creatures climbing towards them.

Ren stopped his horse, dismounted, and drew his sword. Ina copied his movements, only half-aware of losing her horse as it bolted, terrified by the cacophony of war.

Careful steps became a gliding dance as Ren moved into the battle, a tear escaping his eye as he ended the torment of the men begging for death, remembering his suffering from the monster's poison. Bit by bit, they approached the main gates where the final stage of the battle unfolded.

.⊙⅁⌒⅁⊙.

Mar was fighting beneath the gate tower. His full battle armour, resplendent with a golden dragon, the crest of the House of Liath, clearly marked him as the leader and made him a primary target for the attacks. He and a squad of veterans had stormed from the gates once they'd broken the creatures' assault. The captain knew they couldn't be allowed to rampage through the city and had ordered the mages to drive them back with fire if any of the monsters strayed back. Ina's earlier remark about cattle had given him the idea of herding the monsters and letting his men attack as a pack.

Now they fought face-to-face. The savagery of the monsters summoned the bestial brutality from deep inside him, and his swords danced effortlessly, slicing apart the mutants.

A flash of flaming red hair caught his eye. He recognised Ina, then Ren, the lethal dancer gliding before her, protecting her with a whirling shield of death.

The fear and relief of seeing them both broke Mar's focus and a jagged claw sliced across his arm. With a ferocious roar, Mar leapt forwards. The only thought left in his mind was he must protect her as a golden light burst from his eyes and he tore into his assailant.

.⊙⅁⌒⅁⊙.

Death and destruction called to her. The strange hum of magic in the air and sparks of Chaos caressing her skin all conspired to overwhelm Ina's senses. The pressure to welcome them in and release the power, creating a cycle of destruction, was almost unbearable and strangely sensual.

An enormous hound leapt in front of her in slow motion, surrounded by swirling colourful energy. With a flick of her wrist, Ina captured the Chaos magic that fuelled his life, freezing the creature in place. Another flick scattered the power into a beautiful rainbow, tearing the hound apart.

Bloody particles sprayed everywhere, and the rush that came with it made her moan. Suddenly, a large hand grabbed her wrist and turned her around. Mar's lips found hers in a primitive, brutal kiss that took her breath away, and before reality snapped back into place, she felt complete, standing next to her equal.

"For fuck's sake, Ina, couldn't you humour me just this once and sit on your arse when asked?" Mar's scowl made her raise her eyebrow.

"Couldn't you wait for me before starting a war?" she said.

Mar looked at her, then burst out laughing. "You are fucking impossible. Did you at least find what you wanted?"

Ina purred, "Liander is no longer a threat. Can I get my reward?" She felt so intoxicated. The magic and adrenaline coursing through her body from fighting for survival made her so reckless she could bed him right now.

"Shouldn't we find the king?" Ren said, clearly irritated at the kiss.

Mar nodded, releasing the witch.

"You are right. We need to find His Majesty." Even through her magic-induced haze, Ina saw Ren wished things were different, but loving the same woman could bring discord even between brothers. Ren's fate was hard enough without Mar displaying his desire right in his friend's face. Mar clasped his hand with Ren, and when their foreheads touched, Ina was taken aback by this simple gesture of respect and trust, even with her standing between them like a sore thumb.

While she walked past the gates, Ina noticed the damage done to this beautiful building. The courtyard garden behind it appeared intact, but she could see echoes of the battle even here. Servants were nowhere to be seen, most likely hiding to keep safe.

The gates to the grand hall stood intact. Elaborate metal patterns meant to give the impression of grandeur shone in the light of sunset. Still, as they expected, the gate itself was bolted shut. No matter how hard men tried to pry it open, the door stood closed as if someone had put a curse on it.

The captain looked at Ina and pointed to the door with a teasing gesture. "Care to try your charm on those?"

But before she could do it, a small figure shot towards them from out of the shadows. A young boy coated in dirt and debris stood there, trying to catch his breath under their suspicious stares. "… orc said… second attack…in the garden." The panting child was maybe six or eight years old and now, having delivered the message, broke off crying.

Mar gripped his swords, shocked as the realisation hit him. While he had deployed his veterans and mages at the gates, Sophia and Senad had used the diversion to send another force to the unprotected gardens.

The protection of the rivers he counted on so much had failed. He just didn't know how. The rivers near the palace were fast-flowing, full of dangerous rapids and whirlpools, and able to drown the most capable swimmers.

Without enough men to defend everywhere, he'd concentrated his forces where he expected the monsters to attack. Now he had to face the truth. He'd failed, and now the attackers had a clear path to the ballroom, grand hallway, and even the king's quarters. He crashed into the door again, but the reinforced wood held, leaving him cursing and frustrated, but he couldn't waste any more time.

"We have to go around." Mar looked at the boy. "Show me the way you came in. Ren, call in every remaining guard. Ina, guard the doors, but mostly stay the fuck out of it, for once." Barking out orders, Mar turned around, leaving her to her own devices.

CHAPTER 24

Ina eyed the doors. She was confident she could break them. It was the fastest way to get to the gardens, so blasting them down sounded like a good idea if only Mar had enough patience to wait for her to try. The witch smiled at her thoughts. She will show this hairy oaf that she won't stay put like a good little woman.

Chaos was all around her, and now, feeling justified in her actions, Ina reached out, pulling the power into her hand. Placing her palm in the centre of the door, the witch released her magic. The brutal force of it threw her backwards, and Ina landed on her arse like a sack of turnips. "Inanuan Thornsen, all-powerful warrior mage, falls on her arse facing the mighty door monster," she muttered, scrambling to her feet and massaging her aching backside. "One day," she snapped, "I will master breaking doors with ladylike elegance. All I have to do is practice."

A creature poked its head from the rubble of the doorway, a corrupted steppe orc, wearing only a leather collar with a small gem embedded in the lock. For a moment, they eyed each other in mutual surprise, and Ina thought there was intelligence behind the eyes of the monster. This impression was short-lived as the beast shook his head and roared, running in her direction. The witch panicked, utterly unprepared. Her limited experience was at blasting the enemy from a safe distance while Mar did the dirty work.

"Fuck!" she screamed, throwing her hands forwards and releasing an uncontrollable blast of power. Ina heard a mindless roar, the snapping of broken bones, then deafening silence. Looking at the lifeless heap of flesh on the other side of the hall, an amazed witch gazed at her hands, nodding with appreciation.

"I could get used to having power like this." Armed with newly gained confidence, Ina ran towards the ballroom.

With exhaustion weighing her down, Velka's vision narrowed until Daro's face was all she could see. She never thought the beautiful gardens she created could become a slaughterhouse filled with suffering and death.

After she'd dragged Marika to see the exotic soldier that was none other than Ren, they'd been bundled into a glorified cell. Velka was about to lose her temper when Daro stole a kiss and whispered in her ear. The shock at hearing that Princess Sophia was planning a coup left her speechless. She knew her friend had become more ruthless and jaded these past few years, but this?

Velka had taken Marika's hand and, saying nothing, led her to the palace garden, the one place she felt safe and comfortable. Showing the maid around the exotic plants and trees had slowly relaxed her, even as she observed the guards and nobles organising the defence of the throne room. Daro came out for a moment, kissing her passionately and explaining they wanted all the nobles to gather in the throne room for their safety, joking that it was worse than herding cats.

The apprehension of the moment felt so distant, with Daro striding forth, issuing orders, and commanding respect. Velka believed they would be safe under his protection, right up to the moment the earth convulsed, collapsing in on itself, and monsters streamed forth, followed by Princess Sophia and the officer Senad.

Unsure what to do, she sent Marika to tell Daro and dug her hands into the ground. Her magic responded, and the garden opened for her like a book. Every root or leaf was now under her control and ready to answer her command. Velka's green magic had little value in combat, but she could buy them some time till reinforcements arrived.

Vines and climbing roses submitted to her demands and formed a high thorny wall between the palace and riverbank. Abnormally long thorns protruded like spikes to block the way. Still, she had a small hope of stopping the attackers. When the first wave of monsters crashed into it, tearing a large hole, Velka pushed harder, stripping the soil of nutrients to feed the plants springing up to seal it.

"Hold on, my love," she heard behind her.

Daro rushed forwards, leading the few remaining guards and a small group of armed nobles to the rapidly expanding gap. Velka withdrew from it, directing her magic's green force towards the trees. Daro worked hard with his axe, chopping through upcoming monsters like a lumberjack, but it didn't stop the abnormal army, only decreased their speed.

Desperate times created desperate measures, and with no other way, Velka poured her consciousness into the trees, accelerating their growth and impaling the attackers on the branches. She bought them more time, but soon more guardians fell, injured or dying, mauled by claws and teeth. Velka, to her despair, saw Daro thrown in the air. His body met the ground with a vicious thud, and she sprinted towards him. Roots and branches sprang to life following her command. Tears streamed from her eyes when she finally covered his body with hers, and a wooden shelter arose to shield them from the battle.

"Don't cry, my love," his whisper was rasping and weak.

Velka was happy he was still alive. She pressed her hand to the gaping wound in his stomach and noticed his arm twisted at a strange angle, limp and lifeless. The orc's face was ashen, and the woman realised that her chances of saving him were very slim. She needed a healer. He was not a broken twig that she could repair herself. His hand touched her face, and the rasping sounds coming from his chest made her cry again.

"I have to tell you something." Daro was determined to come clean in these last moments of his life. He felt death's door opening wider for him with every breath, and he was desperate to make sure his death wouldn't leave her crying for a love that wasn't worth her tears.

"Please don't cry for me, love. I'm not a good man. I was with many women, sometimes only to spite the captain. You were supposed to be one of them. You were my order to fulfil." Daro was determined to face her anger instead of her tears. "I knew it was wrong, but I still did it. It was all to get access to Ina and her secrets."

Velka sobbed even louder now. "You bloody moron, you thought I didn't know? You thought Ina didn't know? Men! You think you are so fucking smart! Just live for me so I can kill you later, but you must live."

Daro didn't know what to say to her. Velka already knew, and yet she let him stay beside her. His breathing grew shallow as death drew closer. No one from his clan was afraid of it, but his lady forbade him, and for once, he wanted to follow her order. Tired, he closed his eyes and cuddled into Velka's lap.

"The hell you are dying on me now." A slap in the face broke his slumber, but he was too weak to speak. The face he loved so much looked at him with new resolve. Velka didn't have Ina's versatile magic, but she had just as much determination.

She used his dagger to cut a sigil into her palm and placed it on the orc's chest. Her blood, mixed with magic, soaked into his skin. The pain of the sacrifice spell tore through her body, but the mage knew better than to scream. Instead, she bit down on a branch, hardly believing such torment was possible to survive. How on earth had Ina performed it twice?

Velka sobbed. The healing had depleted her so much that she nearly passed out, but as she looked down at Daro, the bleeding slowed, and colour returned to his skin. It wasn't perfect, but hopefully, now he'd live till a healer could take care of him. Pale and trembling, Velka lay next to him, listening with relief to his breathing even out.

Surrounded by the sound of marching feet, she grabbed Daro's hand. "If you dare to die now, I will resurrect you and kill you again. And I will repeat it over and over until you understand the message," she muttered, eyelids heavy from exhaustion.

※

Sophia pursed her lips, looking at the Nature Mage's pathetic attempt to stop her attack. The mind-control necklace Liander finally gave her worked perfectly, despite the idiot's absence, and the horde of monsters moved as one, controlled by her thoughts. Her unfortunate lover looked unsettled when his friend joined the fight, but otherwise, he hardly protested, even when the orc was thrown to the ground like a rag.

Sophia had long since learned that love could make you a fool. First, her mother wasted away in her room when that pig of a father took one woman after another to his bed. Then, when she thought she'd found the love of her life, that self-righteous Ina destroyed everything with her outburst and for what? For a bloody boar. The southern kingdoms wanted nothing to do with "Limp Dick's" daughter. However, she was grateful for this lesson. Instead of acting like her mother, sitting in the room or bearing children, she practically ruled the kingdom. This coup would be the last step to make Sophia queen. The inconvenience of sleeping with lesser nobles was a small price to pay, and they all thought they would be the one she would marry.

As the orc writhed in pain and the blonde Valkyrie rushed to protect him, she saw Senad flinch. "Don't kill them, please," he pleaded. "Once you take the palace, I promise they will swear an oath to you, same as the others."

Sophia shrugged off his hand, but she let them live. After all, she liked her flowers, so killing such a talented mage and her lover would slow the restoration of her gardens. Her plan was simple: the city, with its economy, would be preserved, and she could rebuild the palace more to her liking. The princess diverted the monsters' attention from the makeshift shelter and directed them to the main building. She left most of her army outside, picking a few of the most intimidating to enter the ballroom. There was no more resistance. The defenders' bodies were now watering the grass with their blood.

Glass doors burst open under a troll's fist, causing the gathered crowd to scream in panic. Many of the nobles from all over the country were still there after the coronation ball, and she'd counted on that. It was good they hadn't left for home. It made everything much more convenient for her plans.

Walking in after the troll, Sophia addressed the assembled aristocrats, "What a pleasure to see you all here. Please don't mind my pets. They won't do anything I don't want them to do. Now, where is my dear baby brother? Hopefully not hiding in some woman's skirt?"

The glee in her voice was unmistakable. More creatures entered the room at her voiceless order and encircled the nobles, who now flocked together like scared poultry.

Rewan stepped forwards and gently inclined his head. "What brought you to the palace, sister, and with such an entourage?" He had a distinct tremble in his voice, but before he came closer, he exchanged a slight nod with a white-haired noble. One could have thought he was in control of the situation.

"Your crown, throne, and life, not necessarily in that order," Sophia answered with a smirk. "The men in our family have proven they cannot rule. If you abdicate, I may let you live. You can even choose your future career. Being a pimp in some brothel would be your dream come true. Wasn't that what you always wanted?"

"And if I don't?" Rewan asked quietly

"Then you will die, and it won't be pretty. My pets have to eat, and I need to make an example of someone." She wasn't settled on this course of action and turned to Senad, pointing to the king and ordered, "Take him to the throne room and let him sit on it one last time."

She nodded to one of her creatures and the beast grabbed Rewan's shoulder. He flinched as Sophia approached closer.

"When I come to you, my brother, be ready to renounce the crown and kneel before me…or die."

She looked after the departing monarch for a moment, then turned around and sat on the king's chair. "Now, lords and ladies, it is your turn. I'm sure you remember how from the coronation ball. I want an oath of loyalty and servitude."

Despite his wife's attempt to stop him, a single noble stepped forwards. Sophia did not recognise the man and assumed he came from the borderlands. The princess, expecting the man to bend his knee, was surprised when he spoke with disdain, showing her nothing but defiance.

"You have no right to the throne, not by law, and not by virtue, even if your brother is a womaniser. At least he didn't barge in here, threatening his subjects with a horde of monsters."

"Oh…" She bit her lip, her gaze falling on the woman holding a small boy and looking at the man with fear and concern. Sophia's smile returned. "I don't think I made myself clear."

A lizard-like creature slid into the crowd and snatched up the child. His mother resisted, but she was knocked to the ground with one swing of the monster's tail, and blood began pooling around her head.

The nameless lord lost his resolve. "Please, no!" he screamed, running towards the child only to witness the snap of the jaws that ended the little boy's life. Howling like a cursed spirit, he drew a dagger and turned on Sophia, only to be crushed to the floor by a massive troll's hand.

Screams and sobs echoed in the room, but when Sophia stood up, they fell to their knees one by one.

A sudden commotion outside drew the princess's eyes from this act of submission. Mar, his remaining guards, and the battlemages charged into the garden in the last glow of sunset. The roar of battle reached the ballroom as Sophia directed her monsters against the new threat.

Mar felt like he was coming home, confronted by an army almost as large as the one at the gates. He was relieved to see Sophia standing alone, so maybe Senad still had some honour and had refused to take part in this madness. The monsters moved in unison, not mindlessly as before, so someone must be coordinating their attack. A smile slowly grew on his face as he drew his swords. Ina was safely back in the courtyard. All he had to do now was fight.

Mar drove forwards with a rallying cry, breathing in the garden's scent as his senses distilled into a focus that encompassed the whole battlefield. A massive lizard leapt towards him, and with a twist of his body and twin cuts across its belly, Mar disembowelled it, kicking the bellowing creature to the side.

He ducked down, and thrusting up, he avoided a striga's bite, skewering her through the neck. Mar pushed up, using her body to deflect the claws of some nameless horror.

Buffeted by the force of the blow, time slowed, and Mar beheld the surrounding carnage. He saw Ren gliding through the battle like his namesake, leaving a trail of severed limbs and heads behind him. The martial dance that made Ghost so terrifying was controlled and focused. Every single cut was so fast and precise, making the air around him blur with the flash of steel and a blood-red mist.

Fire spells blasted through the air, burning the flesh of every creature they touched. If he lived, Mar would thank Ina for this idea. Damn it, and if he lived through this, he would make sure every larger unit would have a battlemage and a healer. Still, surviving this onslaught didn't seem likely. There were too many monsters, and the scales of the battle were tipped heavily against them.

⋘～⋙

Ina crept through the main hallway, mostly undisturbed. Occasionally, she saw the disappearing faces of the palace staff, but nothing to break her stride. Incoherent screams startled her, but their source was unmistakable. Abandoning all secrecy, Ina ran towards the ballroom. After coming around the corner, she had barely stopped before running into the king. Behind him, holding his shoulders in a steel grip, was a massive beast and Senad, who now looked at her like he saw a spectre.

"What the…" Ina said, throwing herself backwards as the beast attacked her. Armed from previous experience, she drew power from her necklace and pushed it into the creature. Raw Chaos slammed into it without directed intent, and the monster disintegrated, splattering the corridor in viscera. Stunned, Ina looked at bubbling goo on the floor.

The distraction she created was enough for the young king to take action, and Rewan slammed his fist into Senad's temple. Still shocked by Ina's sudden arrival, the guard reacted too late. His hands were too low, and now he was heading towards the floor with a grace of a falling log. Rewan used a curtain cord to bind Senad's wrists and looked at Ina. "Go, help them. Kaian will come to your aid if needed."

She followed the command, leaving him to deal with Senad. Part of Ina's mind marvelled at the king's close connection with the master assassin when she burst through the ballroom door. The front wall was non-existent. Only one window survived, and through the massive gap, Ina saw the gruesome fighting outside. Civilians huddled in the far corner of the hall, and three bodies lay in the centre.

The noise of the monsters' roaring and the smell of fresh blood assaulted her senses when she stepped forwards. Screams of the dying and a maelstrom of Chaos hit her simultaneously. Her head spun and cramps contorted her body as she fought for control. Sophia turned in her direction, baring her teeth, and the beautiful face lauded by poets was now twisted with rage.

"Why can't you just die?!" the princess spat, and the nearest monster moved into Ina's path.

Nerissa's words rang inside her head. Only blood and the scorched ground were left after the Chaos mage walked through the battlefield. Her vision was blurry from the tension, but all it took was a wave of her hand to toss the creature aside. Ina, overloaded with magic, stood tall, shielded by the shimmering air as she forced her body to obey. Her copper hair floated in the unseen wind as she turned her eyes towards Sophia.

"Let these people go. You have lost. The deaths of women and children will bring you no glory." Her eyes looked behind the princess, where Mar and Ren were fighting for their lives, overwhelmed by monsters. The magic that connected them tugged her heart, causing a painful contraction in her chest, but there was more to it. Mar's honesty and Ren's kindness had grown on her. They belonged to her, and now those pitiful creations would take them away. Air tightened with a red hue as she absorbed more and more Chaos from this destruction.

Sophia looked at the witch. Her nemesis stood motionless, barely touching the ground. Her eyes were as red as jasper, full of spinning magic. The chance of failure occurred to the princess, and it stung like a wasp.

She was too close to winning for all to be lost. In a fit of anger, she reached for the mind-control stone and crushed it on the floor.

"Let them go? Here, have them all and see what happens. If I can't have the throne, then no one will."

๑๖๐๛๛๕๛๑

The roar of unleashed monsters shook the palace walls. Uncontrolled, the aberrations began their bloody harvest, ripping and tearing through the defenceless people. Ina gasped, struck by the terror of this human abattoir. Her eyes glimpsed Ren disappearing under an abomination, and something deep inside her snapped.

The floodgates inside her broke, and Chaos rushed through her, directed by a single thought, *Set them all free.*

Crimson lightning hit the nearest monsters and spread, hitting creature after creature. Their twisted bodies contorted, suddenly stripped of their unnatural shapes, revealing mutilated flesh. Tormented souls flared, breaking free of their prisons, finally finding peace. Ina pushed further, reaching behind the palace walls, stopping the fighting as she ended the monsters' suffering.

Their cries and moans stopped as a thunderous roar shook the remaining window loose, smashing it to dust. As Ina looked out, the sight of a massive grey dragon shocked her to her core.

Mar fought with a light heart. He always knew his last moment would come with a sword in his hand and a trusted friend by his side. Now facing inevitable defeat, all he could do was take as many of his enemies to the grave as possible. Swirls of the red light inside the palace caught his attention, and he pushed forwards, cutting down the creatures in his way with renewed strength. The last rays of sunset turned the sky red, and eerie lights floated in the air.

Mar felt Ina's energy radiating through their connection. Then red streaks of Chaos struck the monsters surrounding him, killing them. The relief at surviving was short-lived as a stream of Chaos caught him in the chest, and, gripping his midriff, Mar fell to his knees. Ina's magic swamped him, and a long-dormant spark, the genetic remains of his ancestry, answered the call breaking free from human constraints.

Mar felt his body tearing apart piece by piece, re-forming and changing into something new. Panting, he attempted to stand up, but he fell back, unbalanced, into the wall. One of his men ran towards him, sword raised, and Mar raised his hand to stop him. A huge grey-scaled hand appeared before him, knocking the guard backwards several metres. Shocked, the captain cast around, looking for the source of the monstrous limb. The flash of a reflection caught his eye, and Mar stopped, focusing on it. A grey dragon's head looked back at him, moving in sync with his panicked actions. He couldn't be, that wasn't…him? Was he a dragon? The remaining guards turned their weapons on him, the last remaining monster on the battlefield.

"Ina!" he shouted, but it sounded like a battle roar even to his ears. Confused and angry, he tried to understand what had happened and why he had suddenly changed into a dragon. How could he stop his men from attacking and avoid further bloodshed?

Mar's tortured call snapped her back into reality. Ina gazed at the dragon, who suddenly collapsed into the rubble. She almost attacked him with her magic, but something stopped her. The dragon looked at the glass reflection, and she could swear that his muzzle was a mask of shock.

The creature was beautiful. Steel-blue scales mottled with golden streaks reflected the light. It moved gracefully for such an enormous beast, and despite the scales covering his body, he moved like a cat. Unexpectedly, she wanted to touch him. The urge was so strong that Ina walked outside, disregarding her own safety and Sophia's presence.

She could see a bright spark pulsating in the centre of his chest, and it called to her in a way that felt oddly familiar. The dragon was not attacking, just staring at her with his golden eyes. Suddenly, it hit her. This dragon was Mar, and something had changed her warrior into this magnificent beast. Eyes wide, Ina realised it was her. The magic she'd unleashed had "freed" this dragon.

So close, Ina looked at him, towering above her, and he was beautiful. His slender head traced her movements and bent down when she reached up with her hand, and then all hell unleashed.

Mar tried to rein in his sudden panic when he saw Ina approaching. He didn't expect his lady to look at him with such a dreamy expression. When she came and reached for him, he slowly bent his long neck, craving her acceptance. Moving back was not an option. He couldn't control this form well and didn't want to hurt the surrounding people. Ina would know what to do, or Nerissa, he just had to stay still.

A sudden blast seared his side. Acting instinctively, Mar turned around with an earth-shattering roar. More shots followed, and suddenly his men were attacking him from all sides. His tail swiped, scattering them on the bloodied grass. Mar felt the choice taken from him and spread his wings, surging into the sky with a few powerful strokes. Killing his men to save his skin was not an option, and he couldn't even blame them. Only Ina could look at such a monstrosity with stars in her eyes, but his witch deserved better, and he had to flee to find the solution to his present state.

⋅෧෨෬෮⋅

Ina could not believe what was happening. Why did they attack him? And Mar, running away like a coward. She screamed, "You bloody morons, stop. It's Mar! I can fix him!" She raised her fist to the sky and shouted, following a rapidly disappearing point, "Come back, you fat-ass, pox-ridden, overgrown lizard! Come back, or I will find you and make your life hell!"

Ren, battered and limping, approached her and attempted to stop her mad screaming. "Calm down, Ina, please. Mar made the right decision to go. It would have broken him, hurting those he cared about."

When Ina turned on him, her anger as she shouted in his face forced him back several paces. "Calm down? I am not done here. He might fly away, but I will find him, and I will kick his scaly arse back to Cornovii or die trying."

Ren nodded quickly. "We will do it, but now we must focus on the situation at hand. We need to find the king and end this plot once and for all."

CHAPTER 25

Finally, free from the terror of the monsters' rampage, the remaining nobles organised themselves quickly. Kaian, whose distinctive white hair was living proof of the House of the Water Horse bloodline, held Sophia with a dagger to her throat. She stood there with no signs of remorse as King Rewan entered the demolished ballroom in the company of several servants. All were carrying makeshift weapons, but thankfully, nothing was left to fight.

Sobs and moans filled the air as almost every family had someone either hurt or dead from the slaughter. Several heads turned around, looking for someone to lead them. This was the young king's time to prove himself. The burden of power was now on him, but Rewan seemed unfazed as he took control.

He nodded to the master assassin, and Kaian returned the gesture with a grim smile. The king turned to the remaining guards and began issuing orders. "Escort the uninjured ladies and their children to the living quarters. Make sure they are comfortable and looked after." His gaze fell on the remaining battlemages attempting to heal the injured. "Send someone to the university and bring all the healers they can spare."

When he noticed Ina and Ren, Rewan's frown eased slightly. "My lady, gather those who can walk in the throne room..." He frowned and paused, looking around, "...is Captain Marcach...?"

Ina swiftly answered the question that hung in the air. "No, but he was called away to deal with another crisis. I will explain later."

It was a strange answer, but Rewan nodded and turned to Ren. "That makes you in charge of my guards for the moment. Make sure that the wounded are taken care of, and the bodies of the dead are looked after appropriately." His mouth twitched when he pointed to his sister. "Take this...person and her lover and lock them up somewhere secure."

Ren saluted and marched off, leaving Ina alone with the king and the remaining lords. Visibly distressed, the surviving cream of Cornovii's nobility exchanged dubious looks until Ina pointed towards the doors, unsure what else to do. "Shoo..." She waved her hands, and those closest to her stumbled back.

"We are not a flock of chickens to be chased away," said an affronted noble, crossing his arms on his chest, but Kaian burst out laughing and pushed him towards the throne room.

"Let's go, you old rooster. Otherwise, this sorceress will turn us all into dragons or worse."

Ina sent him a grateful nod. The master assassin was clearly on their side, and since Rewan told her to look for his aid, he must be working with the king. She turned around and, seeing the question in Rewan's look, shrugged sheepishly. "Long story. I will tell you later, I promise."

As the king led them all to the throne room, she felt the explosion of her magic had done more than kill a few monsters and change Mar during the battle. She could still feel the Chaos magic around her so clearly, as though she'd established a permanent connection to the source of her power. Was that how they felt, the Chaos mages from the past? The temptation to keep gathering the energy was strong, but Ina was not a novice. A long time ago, she learned brutally that all actions come with consequences. She already felt she was the sole reason for Mar's misfortune. If that wasn't good enough to stop her from reaching for power, nothing would be.

The throne room was intact, and looking around, it felt like nothing had happened except that the remaining Council members were so few. Both sides of the conflict had suffered from Sophia's last act, most dying defending their families. The throne room now echoed with the voices of the remaining handful.

Ina wondered about the purpose of gathering the nobles here, especially since it was clear how many had perished during the attack. Rewan waited for a short while, doubtless expecting more arrivals, and those gathered started murmuring angrily. Soon the doors opened, and Jorge, Arun, Nerissa, and Gruff walked in, causing several shocked gasps.

On this signal, Rewan finally started, "I could talk about how difficult this day has been for us all and how grateful I am to be still alive, but the time for speeches and condolences is not now. Today I want to clarify what happened and discuss the changes I would like to make in Cornovii. You are welcome to speak freely." The king looked around as a few raised eyebrows and surprised coughs followed his announcement.

"What happened here has no precedence, and the future of our kingdom will depend on those gathered in this room." Uncomfortable murmurs followed his words. Rewan gave it a moment to settle before he continued, "My sister thinks she would be a better monarch, and many of you knelt to her under duress, but now I am giving you a choice. You saw the deeds of Sophia. If your will is to have such queen, I won't stand against her."

Ina blinked in surprise and looked around. What sort of game was he playing? She noticed Jorge smirk as he gave the king an appreciative nod. Shouts of disbelief and protest filled the air. Did he think anyone would support the princess after this slaughter? He couldn't find the worst moment if he wanted to give up power. The grieving people wouldn't have her, even if she were the last member of the royal bloodline. Nerissa and Arun, however, exchanged uncertain looks.

She looked at Gruff, who exchanged quiet words with the judicial mage, and Ina realised that both the troll and Jorge knew something she didn't, and then she heard her voice asking, "Where is the chancellor?"

The king lowered his head, and although Ina didn't know him well enough, she noticed the satisfied gleam in his eyes that didn't match the humble posture. But his voice sounded sad when he answered, "I'm afraid my trusted advisor was so heartbroken by my sister's betrayal that he took his own life. Kaian found him in his room right before we came here. I hope he knew that even though he was like a father to her, I do not blame him for her actions."

A chorus of voices welcomed this revelation, but Ina looked at him with disbelief. Did he just let her know he had orchestrated the old chancellor's suicide?

Before she could ask further questions, Rewan stood up from his chair and exclaimed, "Time for your decision. What say you? Who will be your monarch?"

"Rewan, all hail the king!" Shouts started slowly, but soon the entire room called out in unison. Ina could only look wide-eyed at how the remaining nobles gave their vote to the king, no questions asked. It was a master move. With Sophia's disgrace, the old chancellor's demise, and the apparent support from two of the four ducal houses of Cornovii, Rewan was in an unassailable position, and the king's face radiated success as he bathed in the fickle nobles' adoration.

The remaining gentry didn't represent any real power, but they were excellent witnesses to his honourable deeds. Yesterday, the people who called him dimwit and womaniser now shouted his name as if he had single-handedly saved the day. The king looked at Ina, and she saw the same sharp intelligence that she'd sensed during the ball. She noticed Rewan looked at Jorge, and the mage performed a slow handclap.

The king bowed slightly to his allies, and he continued more calmly, "Today's events stripped us of many whose absence will be deeply felt. The chancellor and court mage positions are empty, and I would like to ensure we have suitable replacements. Please propose your suggestions for the chancellor's post. However, I would like to propose the person who saved us all from this dreadful ordeal for court mage. Lady Inanuan Thornsen, would you do me the honour?"

"Hell, no!" Ina was on her feet before he finished talking. "I've been there before, and it was catastrophic. You need someone reliable, a mage who sees solutions to the problems, like Jorge. I'm sure he will continue to advise you properly." She couldn't help it. But her sarcastic remark didn't faze the king.

Instead, Rewan seemed pleased by her outburst, but one of the aristocrats couldn't stay quiet and snapped, "Address your king properly!"

Ina raised her eyebrow, and a thin wisp of Chaos shot from her hand right to the leg of his chair, snapping it and tipping the insolent man on the floor.

"Is he not our king?" Ina smirked at the noble as he spluttered over his mistake. "I think I have earned the right to speak as I please."

The more she realised Rewan had his own plot inside this coup, the angrier she felt about it. Steel rang in her voice. How quickly they forgot their fear and those that fought to save their lives.

Turning back to the king, Ina gestured to the broken chair. "Do you really want me? Do you honestly want to see what I would do with your politics? Choose Jorge or Arun. Anyone is more suitable than me for this position. There's a dragon that needs me more than this court." It was challenging to rein in her anger, but the last sentence was almost a plea. "Rewan, please don't make it more difficult than it needs to be."

The king looked at her with amusement dancing in his eyes. "If you don't want to be my court mage, maybe you would like to be my queen?"

"Are you fucking mad? Why? There is nothing between us." Ina's visceral response evoked displeased grunts.

Taking a deep breath while his lips twitched in restrained joy, the king nodded. "There is the nature of your magic. No one would threaten Cornovii with a queen that could obliterate an army in a blink of an eye."

This was true kings' logic, and it was sound, but Ina was never the most logical person. "Obliterate? Do you think I'm Morena, Winter's Death? No, Rewan, I saw enough today. I can be your asset or pain in your royal arse. Force me to kill, and I will knock down every fucking door you try to lock me behind."

Now the king was openly laughing. "I won't hold you here, but I hope I can hold your loyalty. Your straightforward way of dealing with issues is so refreshing."

"I think I've proven it enough," Ina said. He had played her, and he knew she now knew it. It was time to change the subject. "What do you want to do with Sophia and Senad? People will need justice, and they won't be happy with sweeping everything under the rug."

This simple question brought a frown to his face. "I don't know. The crimes are indisputable, but Sophia is still my sister."

That didn't go well with the new Council. Its members shouted one across another as rage, mixed with grief, made it clear they wouldn't let her escape justice.

Gruff, silent up to this point, suddenly spoke, "The city will demand a public execution. Many families lost their loved ones through Sophia's actions, not just nobles."

Rewan hung his head. "Well, if that is the citizens' wish, the execution will happen tomorrow in the main square." He gestured to the servant. "Tell Captain Ren to bring the prisoners back. I want to know what my sister was thinking."

When the servant disappeared, he once again addressed the gathering, "I spoke about changes. Please welcome Master Gruff. He will represent the ordinary citizens of Cornovii and the non-human races. It's about time they have a voice in this court."

Ina wasn't sure about the king's goals. He already seemed to have what he wanted, and his cunning ways made her want to laugh. Rewan was more intelligent than she'd realised, and this was another master manipulation. While Sophia toyed with monsters, he secured the true power behind the city's prosperity. The guilds and the master spy will now sit in his Council pretending to be a dumb old troll.

Deep in her thoughts, Ina missed the prisoners' arrival. Their demeanour couldn't be more different. Senad's pose was that of a broken man who had just lost his reason for living. Sophia struggled and hissed like a feral cat, her vicious glare directed towards Ina and the king. The guards held their charges tightly, uncomfortable in their duty.

Rewan looked at them both and seemed to deflate. Sadness filled his voice as he spoke, "Why Sophia? You were the precious jewel of Cornovii. Why?"

Ina cringed at his overacting, but Sophia caught the hook and spat it out. "Because I deserve to be queen. You are nothing but a womaniser and a drunk, just like our father. Do you think you will keep this kingdom? Look at what is happening on the streets and the borders. You will lose it all. Not even your bloody witch will prevent it."

"I'm no one's tool, Sophia. What you did was wrong. I don't care about politics. I was just trying to fix the mess—" Ina was cut short by Sophia's laugh.

"Oh yes, unblemished Ina. You tried to fix things? Who started them by creating the mutagen? Do you think I don't know you fucked both the captain and the quiet freak that trails behind him? Or that you were dealing with the troll and his underground network? Don't play the innocent here." Sophia kept lashing out. Suddenly, Rewan's voice boomed in the air.

"Princess Sophia, you are sentenced to death for your heinous crimes. Your execution will be carried out tomorrow at noon. Senad, you were supposed to be her guardian. Instead you joined her in this madness. Therefore, you will join Sophia in her punishment."

The guard bowed deeply. "Thank you, Your Majesty."

These quiet words made Ina stop and look at him. He hadn't struck her as a renegade when they first met, and she always saw respect in how he treated Mar. Consumed with curiosity, she asked, "Would you tell me why, Senad? You did not appear to be a person who would happily betray his captain."

His half smile was sorrowful, but he wasn't asking for compassion. "Love, Ina. I'm sure you know this feeling. What else could it be?"

Sophia turned to him and sneered, "I never wanted your love, you fool. It should have been Mar in my bed. With him, I would have won. Your ineptitude caused my death."

Ina observed how Senad shrank under her lashing words, and raw anger heated her blood. Rewan's plotting was to save his sorry arse when Sophia reached for the power. As much as she disliked it, she understood his motives, but Sophia's actions had no excuse, and while Senad deserved to die, he didn't deserve this.

On her way to Sophia, Ina gathered up her magic. "I don't like your words, princess. You and I have history, and maybe I deserve your cruelty, but this is wrong. You are ugly inside, and maybe this wouldn't have happened if not for your beautiful face. Now it is time to show everyone the hatred you carry. You sent Liander after my magic, so let me give you a taste of what you wanted."

Ina dragged her in front of a polished silver mirror. She stood behind the princess and cupped Sophia's face, forcing her to look when she let her magic flow. Red lines cut across the woman's cheek as Ina unravelled the bonds of her essence. The skin under the witch's hands melted and flowed, destroying and re-forming the beautiful features. Sophia's screams filled the room, but Ina showed no mercy, wanting to destroy the pride that had started all this. Soon, dry greenish skin spread over the collapsed bones, and boils covered the woman's face. Only the eyes she left untouched, as beautiful as they always had been.

Sophia jerked and howled, but Ina held her tight, forcing the woman to see the ultimate result. Loud gagging sounds behind her revealed someone's stomach failed, and soon, more retching sounds followed.

"Now your face matches your soul, princess. That is my judgement. You will die tomorrow, but everyone will see how ugly you are inside before you die. No bard will sing about your beauty or the tragedy of your actions. All they will remember is the true face of your evil."

Her display of power made an alarming impact. Men who dismissed her or thought her a weak woman moments ago now looked at her with fearful eyes. Even the king appeared disturbed by her wrath. Only one man remained calm.

With a slight half smile ghosting over his lips, Ren approached her, fascinated by Sophia's new look. "That is interesting work, but don't let your magic get the better of you, my lady."

Ina nodded and stepped to the side, letting the guards take the prisoners away.

Tired by the day's events and looking at mostly unfriendly faces, she asked, "Are we done here? Can I go home now?"

Not waiting for the king's answer, Ina moved between the nobles, who hastily got out of her way. She didn't care—all she wanted now was a hot bath and a lot of wine to help her sleep through the night. Nerissa's cough stopped her, reminding Ina it was time for diplomacy. Therefore, with a deep curtsy in front of the king, she said, "I hope you are pleased with how your justice was served, sire."

The king nodded lightly, accepting her olive branch graciously.

On her way out, she noticed Jorge approach the king and place a hand on his shoulder. The young monarch turned towards him, and although she couldn't hear his words, she could hear Jorge's response clearly.

"Yes, my lord, you gambled well."

Velka drifted between darkness and brief moments of confused consciousness. She didn't know how much time passed as she lay there and held Daro's hand, drained from her magic and exhausted by the energy share. His chest's slight rise and fall were encouraging, but she knew if help didn't arrive quickly, all her efforts would be in vain. As she regained consciousness once more, she noticed the lack of noise from their surroundings. Had the battle finished? Were they victorious, or would she need to escape with her injured lover?

Ina walked down the hall when she felt something was amiss. She turned around only to find Ren walking towards her with a grim expression, calling out, "Daro is missing, and so is Velka."

Ina stopped, shocked by the news. "Velka? Why is she missing?" Then she remembered the small boy from the battle. "And Daro was fighting in the garden. Oh, Morena, no, she'd better not be dead, or I'll bring her back and kill her myself."

Grabbing Ren's arm, she broke into a run towards the gardens. "Get some servants, guards or somebody. We need to find them."

"Velka!"

Hearing Ina's panicking voice shouting her name, the mage started crying.

"Where the hell are you?"

She heard Ina trying to untangle the vines and branches of their shelter. Velka attempted to help, but she had no magic left, and the dead foliage could not hear her commands.

"Here!" Her voice was small, but she had to try. "Here! Ina! Here!"

The increased sound of snapping branches and the loud thud of a falling axe told her help had arrived. The hole widened, and covering her face in her sleeve as debris rained down, Velka sobbed, finally allowing herself a moment of weakness.

Ina pushed her face through the gap and inspected her friend. "Are you hurt?"

Velka shook her head but didn't answer. Concerned by her sobs, the witch had a dreadful thought. "Is he alive?" The second subject of her enquiry was pale and motionless on the ground.

"Yes, but he is badly injured." Velka's sobs intensified, and Ina withdrew from the hole, letting the gardeners finish their job.

"Ren, we need Nerissa, stretchers, and some room for Daro."

A few moments later, efficient as always, Ren brought Nerissa and servants with makeshift stretchers. Her aunt was not pleased, but she quickly took control of the situation. Ina and Ren ran back and forth, fulfilling her orders and taking Daro to an unused room nearby. Finally, her great-aunt locked herself in the room, removing anyone else from her presence, and Ina couldn't do much more than stay with Velka while Nerissa fought for the young warrior's life.

"I love him, Ina. He can't just die now, not after all we have been through." Velka sobbed into the witch's shoulder.

Ina attempted to cheer her up. "He is with Nerissa. Do you think my aunt will let him die? He will live just to suffer moving into this fairy glade extravaganza of yours."

Her jest brought the desired effect, and Velka looked at her with a pout. "You said you liked my house."

"I was practically homeless then. Of course, I loved having a comfy bed to sleep in." This distraction worked well, and Velka stopped sobbing, but now she asked uncomfortable questions.

The Nature Mage gave Ina a crushing hug as she asked, "Where is Mar? Is he…?"

"No, he is alive, but it's become complicated, and once things are more or less sorted here, I will have to leave Osterad."

The mage looked at her with wide eyes. "How complicated is your 'complicated?'"

Ina didn't know herself, so she chose the most straightforward answer. "I think my magic turned him into a dragon, just don't ask me how. I don't know that myself." She leaned against her friend, locking Velka in a tight hug. "I have to find him and see if I can turn him back. I don't even know where to start." Saying it loud brought all the complexity of the situation right in front of her.

Velka pondered over it for a moment. That Ina had turned someone into a dragon was not the most bizarre thing to happen around her friend, and the mage focused on potential solutions, finally saying, "Mar is from Liath, yes? The last battle against the dragons was at Liath in the Grey Mountains."

Ina beamed her friend a beautiful smile, and her arms wrapped around the mage even tighter. Her non-judgemental Velka always knew the right thing to say.

"Ina, have you thought about what you will do if you can't turn him back?"

That was a question Ina had asked herself too. Now she had an answer. "I will stay with him. After all, it is my fault he changed. Besides, our recent encounters gave me some idea what we can do with his new forked tongue." She winked at her friend while demonstrating with an obscene gesture, trying to trivialise the severity of the situation. "Also, I always wanted to ride a dragon." This statement was genuine, and Ina gave herself a moment of daydreaming. If Mar didn't hate her, maybe he would let her do it.

Their bantering was interrupted by a young healer. "The Lady Nerissa requests your presence."

CHAPTER 26

Pale but conscious, Daro looked at the two women entering the room. "So, we won, then?"

Velka ran to him and threw herself on the bed. "I thought I'd lost you. Why did you have to be the hero?" Her eyes gleamed with tears, and she hit Daro repeatedly on the shoulder without warning.

Ina stepped away, letting the lovers sort themselves out, and Nerissa answered her silent question. "Oh, he will live, now excuse me. This"—she gestured to the unfolding pillow scene—"is unbearable."

Ina walked behind her, chuckling. Nerissa was right. They should both leave and give the couple a little privacy before witnessing things that couldn't be unseen.

Ren found her later. Ina was halfway to her home when he stopped her. "They found Marika. She is badly injured, but the healers said she would make it."

Surprise and guilt overcame her. She hadn't even asked about her servant and hadn't even known that the woman was in the palace. "Tell them to bring her to my home. I will make sure she is cared for."

A hand on her shoulder stopped her, and Ren said, "What are you going to do now?"

Ina shrugged. "Nothing much. I will go home, have a good rest, and make sure all my affairs are in order. Then I am going after Mar to rip him a new arsehole for flying away like the bloody idiot he is."

Ren's tense posture told her he had something to say. Indeed, after a moment of silence, her friend spoke, "Give me a day or two, and I will go with you. Not that I have doubts you can do what you say, but I want to be there to watch."

Ina laughed softly, feeling the weight of the day's events catching up with her. As much as she didn't wish to admit it, travelling alone was a daunting prospect. "I will meet you in two days at the barracks. Please don't tell Daro. He will tell Velka, and before we know, it will be a full entourage, cat in tow." She sighed deeply, biting her lip, but he needed to know. "If I cannot bring him back, I will stay with him. He can't face this alone, especially since it is all my fault."

Ren took her hand and raised it to his lips. "You do what you have to, and I will be there to help. Ina, please don't go alone. I know you well enough that if you thought it best, you'd do it. It is easier to travel with you than chase you around all of Cornovii, so please don't go without me."

Ina chuckled faintly. After her drugging Mar to visit Gruff, it was not an unreasonable suspicion.

Thinking deeply as she walked, her plan was in place by the time she got home. Her simple life meant there was little to arrange, but Ina had to make sure her household and friends were safe. She needed to speak to Jorge and Nerissa, especially her relative, who'd done so much to make Ina's stay in the Osterad bearable.

It was late at night when she pondered over the day's events lying in the bath. Since Nerissa told her about the properties of Chaos magic, Ina had high hopes she would be recognised the same as her great-aunt. The battle was a revelation, and she'd never felt such a rush of power. She'd been intoxicated by the endless stream of magic that filled every cell in her body and wanted more. It was a step away from making horrible decisions. Ina hadn't cared about the dying soldiers or the surrounding destruction. All she had wanted was more magic, almost as if some strange will had possessed her, stripping her conscience away. That was a terrifying thought, and while Ina knew she would always fight to control that desire, there would always be those that couldn't or chose not to. The Magical Council was right in trying to eradicate this ability. If Sophia had it, would anyone in Cornovii be safe?

When a Chaos mage fights, only blood and scorched earth remain. Ina couldn't shake the dread she felt inside each time she heard those words in her head. She could be the one walking like Morena through death and destruction, laughing from pure joy. If not for her friends… She blessed those few that kept her grounded, not letting Chaos take over. Touching the stone on her chest, Ina decided. She had her potions, elemental magic, and a stone that provided her with the power needed for most spells. Let the Chaos rest to stop her from becoming a puppet of the force she could barely control.

Ina dunked her head below the water level and blew a few bubbles. The decision, once made, lifted an unseen weight off her shoulders. That was the end of it, and she could finally laugh that she'd almost made a room of aristocrats crap their pants. All hail the mighty witch! A hearty laugh made her choke on the water, and when she sat up coughing, Ina heard a persistent knocking. The witch rolled her eyes, getting her wrinkled body out of the tub. *Let's see what the cat dragged in this time.*

A court messenger stood at her door, looking surprised at the half-naked, sodden woman peeking through a slit in the doors. He stuttered but valiantly delivered the message that Ina was summoned and expected to attend His Majesty immediately.

"In his dreams," she said, closing the door in his face. Half an hour later, she heard another rattling of the doors. This time, guards and a carriage had arrived to take her to the palace. Ina politely explained she was drying her hair, and if His Majesty so needs to see her, he can shift his arse here. It didn't go well, and she had to throw a few fireballs to convince the commander of the strength of her convictions.

Just past midnight, King Rewan strolled in.

"Ina, for fuck's sake, *you're* supposed to be *my* subject!" he grumbled from the threshold.

"Aha," said his subject, nestled in her favourite chair and pointing to the seat opposite. "Just sit, and explain to me why the hell you dragged Mar and me into all of this. And just so you know, you might have fooled them, but I saw you in the throne room. You knew about Sophia's coup, and you killed the chancellor."

Rewan looked at her, calm and unfazed. "I'm sorry. What choice did I have? My father gave Sophia all the power, but she still wanted more. Everybody wants to live, and I had to resort to unusual means. Why didn't you say anything in the throne room?"

"What would it change? The country needs a king, and Sophia went too far. You both did. You allowed this to happen, but she was the one who orchestrated all those deaths." Ina tapped her fingers on the chair, pondering, "But why the chancellor?"

"The old fool treated her like a daughter. She plotted against me from the day I was born, and he helped her." Rewan raised his hand when Ina wanted to ask more questions. "Let me talk now. As you said, the matter is settled, and I have the throne, but Cornovii is weaker than she has ever been. I proposed marriage not out of love but out of necessity."

Ina looked at him, raising her eyebrow. "Not this again."

Rewan chuckled. "Oh, I do like you. The woman who made the king shift his arse is worthy of being queen." His merriment quickly died out. "I know you are going after Marcach. His friend Ren has already resigned from his post. If your path takes you to the mountains, something is going on there. Villages were attacked, with no witnesses left alive, and the borderland garrisons are no longer the military power they used to be. I don't have the resources to send an army there, but maybe you can find out what is causing such unrest. Ina, I'm asking for your help. Please."

The witch sat in silence. Rewan was ruthless and intelligent, but it looked like he could be a reasonable ruler. Still, her priority was Mar, not another plot to untangle. Ina shifted in her chair and was ready to refuse when the king spoke.

"I know Jorge enlisted you as an apprentice. I will give you the documents to make you a full judicial mage and the royal envoy. All the doors will open for you. Ina, all I'm asking is for you to look around and see if there is something that can stop the attacks."

"Fine," she said after a long pause. "But don't get used to this."

"You can always marry me." The king winked, ducking when she threw a shoe. He burst out laughing as he walked towards the exit. "You are my one and only royal witch. Bring me my dragon back. He has not been dismissed from service." As a second shoe hit the door, he hastily ducked as he left. Even through the closed windows, she could still hear him laughing.

The following days were a blur of activity. In short, Ina visited Jorge and told him what she thought of his manipulations in remarkably obscene words. His response was far from expected. The mage grabbed her hand and placed it on a diagram. Symbols and foreseeable futures flashed in her mind. She learned that day that Sophia's rule would have been worse, so much worse—unrest, racial cleansing, the army of monsters with no consciousness but with fangs and claws to keep the queen's order. When sickened to the core, Ina ripped her hand from his grip, and he looked at her with serious eyes. "Now you know why I did it."

"But why me, Jorge?"

"Because you are the harbinger of Chaos and the only variable I knew that could change the future. But don't get me wrong,

I hesitated. But Rewan, in his own words, said this kingdom needed to be frightened out of its apathy."

They spent some time discussing the boundaries of each other's magic. It was refreshing to meet someone on the opposite end of the magical spectrum that could give her some perspective.

She purposefully avoided the execution square, but Ina heard that Sophia's and Senad's executions were spectacular. The crowd was pleased by the bloodshed and seeing the faces of the culprits behind their grief calmed those with rebellious intent. With Gruff's people doing the rest, people now praised the king for sacrificing his own sister in the name of justice. Someone started a rumour about the Gods' punishment for the disfigurement of Sophia's face, which the local bards lapped up. Ina could only snigger hearing the newest satires. After all, it wasn't every day someone mistook her for a deity.

Nerissa, as expected, told her off, calling her preparations insanity. Once again, the old healer had aspirations for her, especially after the king's unfortunate announcement. Ina dispelled them quickly, and their loud discussion scared the servants, but in the end, she got an awkward hug and a few gems loaded with healing spells. Her aunt also promised to assign someone to look after Marika until the woman got back on her feet and could take care of the household. It was the best display of affection Ina could expect.

Velka visited to tell her about their preparations for a winter solstice wedding. The pair's adventure in the gardens had solidified the mage's resolve, and Daro was more than happy to tie the knot. Velka changed as well, and her new radiance and confidence told Ina she wouldn't have taken no for an answer, even if he'd protested. There were, of course, obstacles. Velka's family was not too keen to accept the union between mage and orc, but the king made it loud and clear he was giving his blessing and even offered the ballroom to hold the wedding. If they managed to repair it on time.

Since Ren had given up his post in the King's Guards, preparing to go with Ina, Daro had become the only reasonable choice for the position of captain. Rewan, true to his words, was more than happy to have an orc in the top rank. The sudden and utterly unwelcome advance exasperated Daro. However, he still wished them well on their journey, muttering something about dragons getting what they deserved.

The most interesting meeting happened in The Drunken Wizard. She visited Gruff to thank him for his support, which made him visibly happy. Once again, she ended up in the backroom, where a sizable pouch exchanged hands, a payment for "solving the problem," he called it. Ina tried to protest, but the troll didn't let her.

"I knew what was going on, and I let you walk into it unprepared. I wish I could say I did everything to protect you, but I can't. I didn't know about Janik, and my ignorance almost cost you your life. I'm sorry, Ina."

She rarely saw him so upset, so when Gruff hauled her into a crushing hug, she patted his back and joked that free drinks would solve this issue. The troll said she would always be welcome in his tavern, despite her fame. It was not a statement the taciturn troll would usually make. He led her to the door when she asked him why he needed to say it. A tavern bard, dressed like a peacock and twice as loud, sang a discordant ballad of the battle for the palace.

The crimson witch upon you
with Chaos in her eyes
Her magic will transform you
Severing all the ties…

Ina could only roll her eyes as she listened to yet another poem about her exploits. Each time she got involved in palace affairs, she became the target of satire that provided food and beer for the local bard population.

The morning of her departure welcomed her with fog and a chill that soaked into her bones. As she had already packed her bags, Ina exchanged a quick goodbye with Marika and a much longer one with Boruta, then walked out of the house. She'd left buying a horse till the last moment, hoping Ren could help with it. For now, she simply walked to the barracks with her carefully packed belongings, demanding to see Sa'Ren Gerel. The sentries let her in and allowed her to wait near the paddock. While observing the horses playing around on the frosted grass, she noticed Woron.

The majestic black horse slowly trotted in her direction. She reached her hand to stroke him but stopped short when one of the stable boys shouted, "You should not touch this one, my lady. He is a beast only our captain could groom. He may bite your hand off."

Ina looked at the horse. "You wouldn't do this to me, my beauty." Her voice was soft and filled with affection. Woron snorted, steam coming from his nostrils before leaning into Ina's hand and touching it with his muzzle.

Ren looked at this exchange from the top of his grey horse. "I see you made another friend, Ina."

That gave her an idea. She gestured to the stable boy. "Bring me his tack and saddle. I will take this horse with me."

The young man tried to protest, "But this is the captain's horse, I can't—"

Ren's glare stopped his mumbling. "The lady said to get the stallion ready. We will be taking him to the captain ourselves."

Hopefully, dragon Mar won't treat him as a snack, Ina thought, while stroking Woron's head. Only the determination to find her dragon gave Ina the courage to climb onto the stallion's back. The warhorse appeared amused by her clumsy efforts, and when once again she hopped up without success, he bent his front legs, allowing her to mount him.

Ren reached for her hand when they were passing through the city gates. "Are you ready?"

"Ready as I'll ever be. Now, let's find this arsehole." A snowflake landed on her face when she looked up, hoping a dragon silhouette would cut through the sky. Winter had finally come to Cornovii.

Afterword

Dear Reader,

We hope you enjoyed our book and would love to hear about your experience. We would kindly ask you to leave a review on your chosen website. If you are interested in following Ina's adventures second book in the series called WINTER DRAGON will be released at the end of December, and pre-orders will soon be available on Amazon

For more details, please check our website: www.olenanikitin. uk

Looking forward to reading your review.

Olga&Mark (aka Olena Nikitin)

Glossary

Baba Yaga – (Slavic mythology) in Slavic folklore, the wild old woman, the witch; mistress of magic and a mythical creature.

Botchling – a lesser monster, a small creature resembling a highly deformed foetus - created from the improper burial of unwanted, stillborn infants - preys on pregnant women.

Boruta – (Slavic mythology), a forest demon, often considered an avatar of Leshy.

Cornovii – Merchant kingdom between the Black Forest and Grey Mountains. Because of the geographical position it is a multiracial centre of trading.

Daro – "dark power" steppe orc, the rebellious son of a tribe thane drafted into the King's Guards, known womaniser.

Gruff – "the rock" rock troll, owner of The Drunken Wizard and spymaster of Osterad.

Hela – also referred to as the "two-faced terror," is a Goddess of the dead, especially those who drown in the sea.

Imp – a lesser demon. Imps are often shown as small and not very attractive creatures. Their behaviour is described as being wild and uncontrollable. Imps are fond of pranks and misleading people.

Inanuan – "beautiful destruction." Also known as Ina or Inanuan Zoria Thornsen. High-born lady of the principal ducal house of Cornovii, and the first pure Chaos mage born in a generation.

Jarylo/Jaryło – God of vegetation, fertility, and springtime.

Jorge – "supreme knowledge." Arch-mage of pure Order. He can foresee the future by applying his Order magic to the reality patterns.

Kaian – "strong warrior." Scion of the primal ducal house of Cornovii, the House of the Water Horse. Also head of the assassin guild.

King's Guards – also called the second sons' company. Unit designed strictly to guard the palace and investigate issues related to high-born nobles or state affairs.

Kobold – member of the kobold race. Cruel and proficient warriors and metalworkers living in the mines and tunnels in the Grey Mountains. Shorter than humans, often seen in bulky black metal armour. Their race has zealous adherence to oaths, pacts or customs.

Lada/Łada – a Goddess of love and Nature's rebirth in the spring, patron of weddings and matriarchy, and protector of families and ancestors who passed away.

Lady Midday/Południca – a mid-class demon who makes herself evident in the middle of hot summer days, takes the form of whirling dust clouds, and carries a scythe, sickle or shears. She may appear as an old hag, a beautiful woman, or a twelve-year-old girl. It is dangerous at midday when she can attack workers, cut their heads off or send sudden illness.

Leshy – (Slavic mythology) a God of wild animals and forests. He protects the animals and birds in the forest and tells them when to migrate. He is a shape-shifter who can appear in many forms and sizes but is usually a tree, wolf, cat or a very hairy man.

His fickle nature causes him to help one he deemed worthy and punish those who mean wrong to the forest.

Liander – "flower of pride." Half-elf, the strongest psychic mage of his time. Also, the court mage after Ina's departure.

Liath – dukedom of Cornovii associated with House of Liath. It is a mountain region on the west defending the Grey Mountains and known for its military power.

Litha or Kupala night – a midsummer solstice celebration dedicated to love, fertility, and water. Young people jump over the flames of bonfires in a ritual test of bravery and faith. The failure of a couple in love to complete the jump while holding hands signifies their destined separation.

Marcach – "wind rider." Also known as Mar or the scion of Liath. The oldest son of the principal dukedom house of Cornovii. A war veteran and current captain of the King's Guards.

Marika – "kitten." Were-cat from a Grey Mountain clan and Inanuan's housekeeper.

Morena/Morane/Marzanna – She is a personification of the repetitive cycles regulating life on Earth, the changing seasons, and a master of both life and death. Morena symbolises death on the battlefield.

Morganatic marriage – a marriage where a high-born woman marries a commoner, losing her status.

Meridian – The meridian system is a concept in traditional Chinese medicine adapted for this series. Meridians are paths through which the life energy is known as "qi" or Chaos flows.

In the book, meridians are energetic highways that distribute life energy/raw Chaos along the body.

Nawia – (Slavic mythology) is also used as a name for an underworld over which Veles exercises custody.

Nerissa – grand duchess of House of Thorn. Arch-healer of Cornovii and Inanuan's great-aunt.

Osterad – The capital of Cornovii. Started as a simple river port but with time grew in riches and became the centre of human magic on the continent.

Phoenix – (Greek mythology) Immortal bird that dies in flame to rise from the ashes, a good omen.

Rewan – "the cunning one." Heir apparent, and later ruler of Cornovii.

Roda – "the nest." Womaniser and drunkard. King of Cornovii, also known under the moniker of "Limp Dick" after Ina's outburst.

Sa'Ren Gerel – "son of a moonlight." The native name of Ren, one of the King's Guards, also known as the Ghost.

Senad – the bastard child of a high house, lesser noble. Second in command of the King's Guards and Marcach's friend.

Sophia – "the white gem." Princess of Cornovii, sister of King Rewan, renown for her beauty.

Striga/Strzyga (Slavic mythology) – a female creature who feeds on human blood. Their origins are connected to the belief in the duality of souls. A common explanation was that a human born with two souls could become a *strzyga* after death. Such people were easy to recognise, born with two rows of teeth, two hearts or other similar anomalies. They could die only partially – one of the souls leaves to the outer world, but the second one gets trapped inside the dead body, losing many aspects of humanity. *Strzyga*'s appearance can resemble an average person with a mean character. The longer they live as a *strzyga*, the more they change. They are often presented with birdlike features: claws, eyes, and feathers growing off the back.

Swaróg/Swarożyc- God of fire, blacksmithing, and creation, pictured as an old but powerful man with white hair and a hammer. Often believed to be the creator of the world.

Truthseeker – a branch of mind magic associated with Order. A psychic mage that can connect with another person's brain to trace patterns of lies and, if needed, dissect memories looking for the truth.

Tomb hag/Grave hags – territorial creatures. Their lairs resemble caricatures of human homes and are built near burial sites. They venture out at night to hunt, stalking straggling travellers or mourners too lost in their grief to notice the sun's setting.

University of Higher Magical Arts/The Magical Council – School and the highest authority for practising mages, witches, and warlocks that have supreme jurisdiction over the magic of Cornovii.

Volkhv – high-ranking priest of Slavic religion.

Veles – (Slavic mythology) a major Slavic God of earth, waters, livestock, and the underworld. A shepherd and the judge of the dead that rules Nawia. Associated with swamps, oxen, and magic.

Velka – lesser noble. Gifted Nature Mage with a strong association with trees and flowers. Also, Ina's best friend.

Vyvern – a large winged lizard, distantly related to the dragon, with a poisonous stinging tail and sharp teeth.

Were tribes – shape-shifters with the ability to change into three forms, human, animal, and were-form that contains both aspects of their soul.

Wyraj – (Slavic mythology) part of Nawia, an equivalent of heaven.

Yanwo – far east land, ruled by the Jade emperor and trading silks, spices, and gems with Cornovii.

Zhrets – low rank priest in Slavic religion. A man who performs the sacrifices.

About the Author

Olena Nikitin is our pseudonym. We are life partners and an enthusiastic couple of writers fascinated by fantasy/paranormal romance. We love humour with a down-to-earth approach to life, and all of this hit a bit of steam and spice you can find in our books.

Hidden behind the pen name:

Olga is Polish, armed with a wicked and often inappropriate sense of humour and typical Slavic pessimism. She has written stories since childhood, initially mostly about her work. As an emergency physician, she always has a story to tell and often not much time to write. Also known as The Crazy Cat Lady and proud to be one.

Mark is a typical English gentleman whose charm, refined taste and undeniable sex appeal tempted Olga to fly across the sea. Don't tease him too much; this man has an impressive sword collection and knows how to use it. He also can fix everything, including Polish syntax in English writing. He got shot in the Gulf War, and if you give him good whiskey, he will tell you this story.

For more, check: https://www.olenanikitin.uk

For updates and Newsletter, sign in: http://eepurl.com/hZhWcT

Also By:

A LITTLE ACCIDENT, Season's War Prequel

"PRIDE AND CHAOS SHOULDN'T BE MIXED IN ONE CAULDRON."

Nerissa the Arch Healer of Cornovii

Life is complicated enough when you are the scorn Chaos mage and the lady of the noble house. However, Ina took the art of misfortune to new heights, the day she decided to save the life of the common frog.

There is a reason the common folk say "no good deeds go unpunished," and Ina's moment of weakness can bring catastrophic consequences.

Available on Amazon: https://www.amazon.co.uk/dp/B09XLM1CWG

CPSIA information can be obtained
at www.ICGtesting.com
Printed in the USA
LVHW110721120822
725756LV00004B/25